THE EXTREMELY INCONVENIENT ADVENTURES of Bronte Mettlestone

·JACLYN MORIARTY·

Illustrations by Karl James Mountford

GUPPY BOOKS

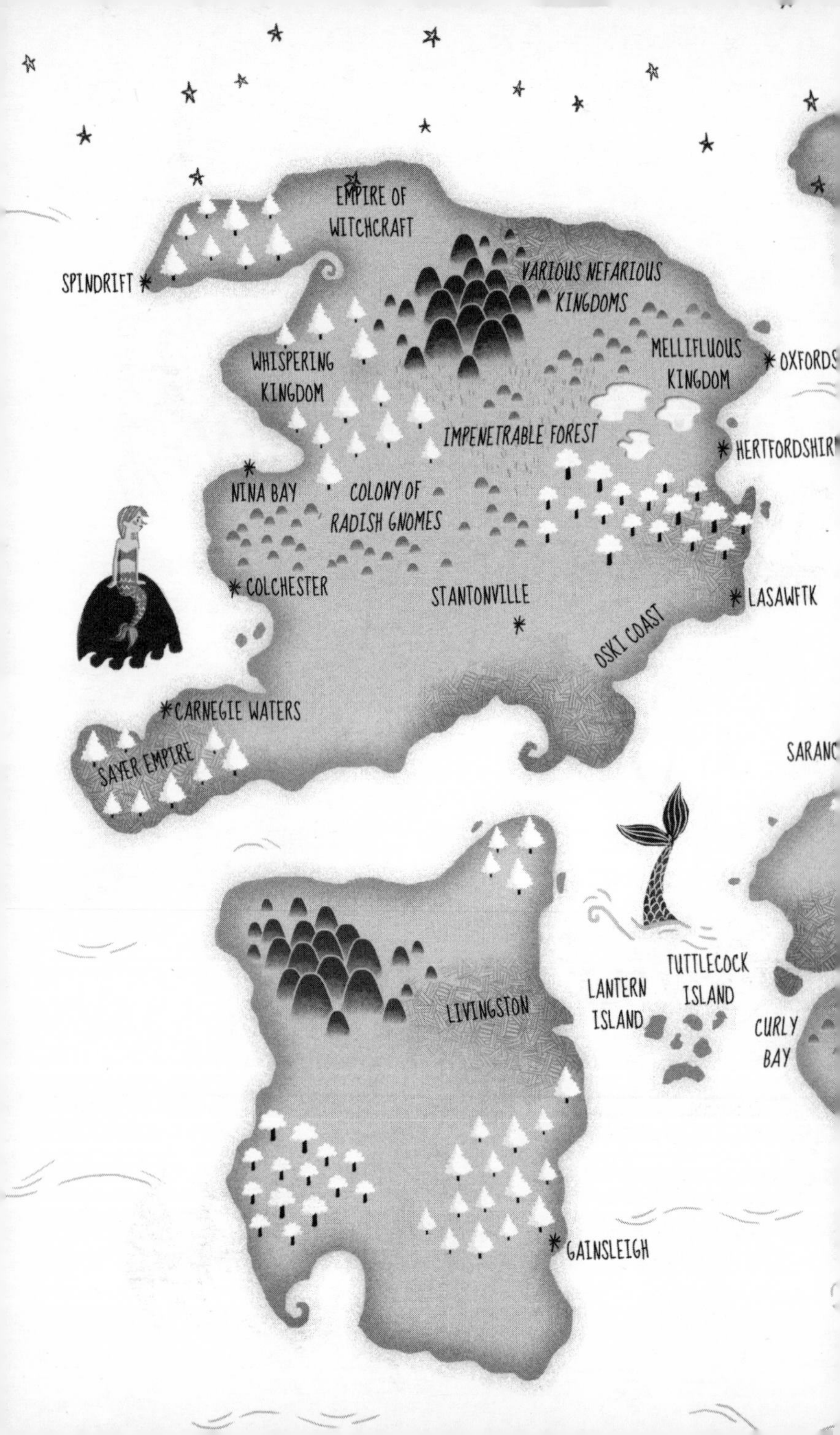
EMPIRE OF WITCHCRAFT
SPINDRIFT
VARIOUS NEFARIOUS KINGDOMS
WHISPERING KINGDOM
MELLIFLUOUS KINGDOM
OXFORDS
IMPENETRABLE FOREST
HERTFORDSHIR
NINA BAY
COLONY OF RADISH GNOMES
COLCHESTER
STANTONVILLE
LASAWFTK
OSKI COAST
CARNEGIE WATERS
SAYER EMPIRE
SARANC
LIVINGSTON
LANTERN ISLAND
TUTTLECOCK ISLAND
CURLY BAY
GAINSLEIGH

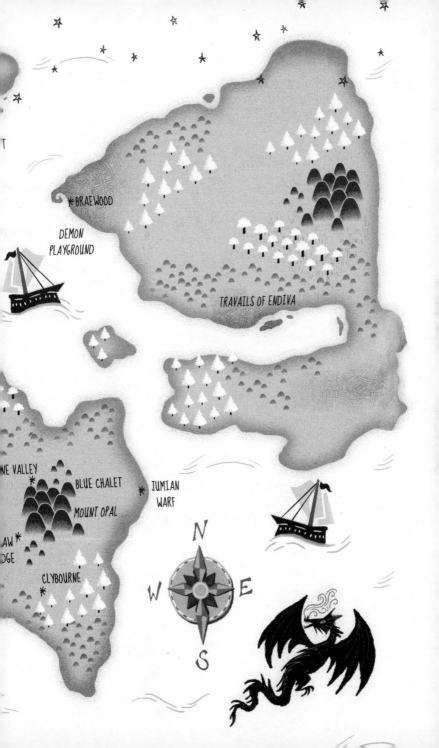

To my boys, Nigel and Charlie, with my love

Aunt Isabelle

I

I was ten years old when my parents were killed by pirates.

This did not bother me as much as you might think — I hardly knew my parents.

They were a whirling pair of dancers in a photograph my aunt kept on her mantelpiece. There was a jazz band in the corner of that photo, and I'd always been more taken by the man playing the trumpet than my mother's gauzy scarf or my father's goofy grin. That trumpeter! His face like a puffer fish, his wild swing of hair, the light springing sideways from his trumpet rim!

But Aunt Isabelle was in a state about the news. She was my father's eldest sister and had taken me in when my parents set off on their adventures. She hadn't had much choice in the matter: she'd found me in the lobby of her apartment building, rugged up in my pram one frosty morning.

There had been a note, my aunt said, but that had been lost when her housekeeper did a spring clean. There'd also been a bottle filled with milk (for me) and a canister of cloudberry tea (for my aunt).

It was the cloudberry tea that she wept about most noisily when news of the pirates was brought to us. The Butler presented the news on a small white card in the centre of a silver tray. This was unfortunate. White cards on silver trays generally said things like, WE REQUEST THE PLEASURE OF YOUR COMPANY AT OUR FANCY DRESS BALL, or WHAT A SPLENDID TIME WE HAD AT YOUR GAMES NIGHT! WE SHALL RETURN THE FAVOUR SOONISH!

So my aunt and I smiled at one another over our afternoon tea when we saw the silver tray floating towards us. Then we read the card.

WE REGRET TO INFORM YOU THAT PATRICK AND LIDA METTLE-STONE HAVE BEEN TAKEN OUT BY CANNON FIRE FROM THE DECKS OF THE PIRATE SHIP *THISTLESKULL* (208 TON, 103 FT LONG, 24 FT AT THE BEAM).

At first, my aunt was simply incensed by the choice of diction. *"Taken out!"* she exclaimed. *"Taken out!"*

Whereas I was confused. I had been taken out myself, on occasion, by one of the other aunts when they were in town, and also by my governess. If Cannon Fire, whoever that was, wanted to invite my parents out – to the Arlington Tea Room for lemonade and cakes, I presumed – what did it matter?

But then my aunt turned to the Butler and said, "Did you *read* this?" and the Butler stepped forward, affronted: "Of course not!"

2

He leaned over my aunt to read it now.

"Oh my!" he said, and shook his head slowly, with a "tch, tch," as if he disapproved. He looked down at my aunt, and his face became rueful.

"Taken out!" my aunt said to him. "Can you believe it? Could they not have chosen a less *flippant* turn of phrase?"

"In the circumstances," agreed the Butler.

"They should have said 'murdered'!" exclaimed my aunt. "Murdered by pirates!"

So then I understood that my parents were dead. I widened my eyes.

The Butler assumed a thoughtful expression. "Perhaps," he said, "it was an accident? Perhaps Patrick and Lida were simply in the *line* of cannon fire at the wrong time? In which case, it would not be murder so much, would it?"

"Manslaughter?" my aunt wondered moodily. *"We regret to inform you, they've been manslaughtered.* Sounds wrong, doesn't it?"

The Butler was still studying the card. "Odd," he said. "The level of detail about the ship. Perhaps there are a number of pirate ships called *Thistleskull,* and they needed to distinguish this one somehow?"

"It's scandalous!" said my aunt.

"It's rather as if they think you might want to run up an outfit for the ship on your sewing machine and require its measurements."

3

"Ha!" said my aunt. She and the Butler smiled. Their smiles settled down.

There was a long silence. I took a sip from my chocolate and the sun poured through the French windows. It sparked against the silverware and lit up the white linen tablecloth.

"Oh!" cried my aunt suddenly, making both the Butler and me jump. "Ohhh! They gave me cloudberry tea and now they're gone!"

She began to weep noisily.

She had been moved, you see, by the gift of cloudberry tea that my parents had left in my pram (along with me). It was her favourite tea, and they must have remembered this. "It is touches like that," she often told me, "the little thoughtful touches. *Those* are what distinguish the *gracious* from the rest."

She used to tell me I should aim to be just as gracious as my parents. So, for a while, I carried about a little notebook and took down the favourite hot and cold beverages, fruits, sweets, and ice-cream flavours of everybody I encountered. That way, when I myself grew up and abandoned my only child in the lobby of somebody's building, I would be sure to add a sample of their preferred treat to the pram.

At other times, my aunt told me that my parents' approach to life was "as chaotic as a barnyard fire".

Now, however, we sat at the table in the afternoon sun and listened to Aunt Isabelle sobbing about the deaths of her brother and sister-in-law, and especially about the cloudberry tea.

2

The next day, my aunt telephoned the family's lawyers, and they invited us to their office for the reading of the will.

A will is what people leave behind when they die. It's also the name of my dog (only with a capital *W*), and it's what Aunt Isabelle always told me that I had.

Only mine, she would say, was very strong. "You've a strong will there, haven't you, Bronte?" she frequently observed, sometimes irritably, and sometimes with a smile that seemed proud.

"Yes," I always replied, trying to be agreeable. "I have."

Aunt Isabelle was surprised that my parents had a will. "Don't you think," she said to the Butler, "that they were too *chaotic* for a will?"

The Butler agreed. "I'd have thought they'd be more likely," he said, "to have a *won't*!"

Aunt Isabelle and I laughed at that, and the Butler looked pleased and laughed too. Then my aunt's laughter stopped suddenly and she stared out the window at nothing. So the Butler and I stopped laughing and stared at the same spot.

I wore my white dress with the blue sash to the lawyers' offices, and I felt very excited because my aunt had said that afterwards we would stop for an ice-cream soda.

There were two lawyers, both men with skin as white and damp as the flesh of an apple.

"You will find the lawyers rather old," Aunt Isabelle had informed me earlier that morning. "Even though they are not."

I thought about that, but it made no sense.

"They're old for their age is what I mean," she explained. "It's because they're lawyers. Now, if they'd chosen different careers – circus performers, say, swinging from the trapeze—"

"Or zookeepers," the Butler suggested, "frolicking with the friendlier of the lions?"

"Exactly. If they'd done that, they might be quite youngish for their ages. Do you see what I mean, Bronte?"

"No," I had replied.

But now I stared at the two men. They hunched in their chairs and in their double-breasted suits, peering through their spectacles and chewing on nothing, and I saw what Aunt Isabelle meant.

Their chairs were huge and soft, the kind that swivel and make squelching noises whenever you shift your behind. Aunt Isabelle and I had regular, hard-backed chairs. So at first, I didn't concentrate on what the lawyers were saying because I felt too angry about this. Why didn't *we* have the soft, fun, swivelling chairs?

Then I realized that the one on the right – Mr Crozer – was speaking to me.

"Bronte, isn't it?" he said. "If I know anything about little girls like you, you'd rather we got this over with fast as a flash, so you

6

could be out of here and off to your afternoon tea! What do you say? Am I right?"

I said nothing. I looked down at my feet and tried to see if they could reach the floor if I pointed my toes. I *was* keen to get out of there to my ice-cream soda, it was true, but I was not going to delight Mr Crozer by agreeing with him.

"Bronte," said the other one – Mr Ridgeway – fixing his spectacles on me, "the testators have stipulated that you must carry out a number of preconditions, after which your inheritance will crystallize."

I stared at him.

There are certain adults who speak baby-talk to children, making their voices rise up at the end of sentences. Your job as a child is either to giggle or nod your head and smile. Mr Crozer, the first lawyer, was one of those. Then there are adults like Mr Ridgeway, who address children as if they are mini-adults. They do it with a proud smirk, and with a glint of their spectacles. I'm not sure what the child's job is. I suppose I was meant to gaze back in wonder, or to burst into tears and say, *"I don't understand!"*

I crinkled my nose at him.

"Good heavens!" said Aunt Isabelle. "What *are* the pair of you on about?"

The leather chairs squeaked as Mr Crozer and Mr Ridgeway leaned back.

"It's like this." Mr Crozer addressed Aunt Isabelle now.

"They've left instructions for Bronte. A treasure chest has been placed in the vault at the bank. It's filled with gifts. Bronte is to *deliver* these gifts to various people. She must start the journey in exactly three days. Oh, and she's to do it alone."

"Alone! She's ten years old!"

"Perhaps her parents didn't expect to die until she was older?" suggested Mr Ridgeway, shrugging carelessly.

"They've been very thorough," Mr Crozer added, resting his elbows on the desk and flipping through pages. "They've listed not merely the names and addresses but also the forms of transport Bronte is to take. There are even some recommendations for restaurants and cafés where she might like to dine. Some of those are optional."

"She's ten years old," Aunt Isabelle repeated, more mildly. "She doesn't *dine*. In any case, how is she expected to *carry* a chest full of gifts?"

"Pack it in her suitcase," Mr Ridgeway advised.

There was a pause while Aunt Isabelle pursed her lips at him. Then she frowned. "Who *are* the recipients of these gifts?" she demanded. "I assume they all live here in Gainsleigh?"

Here both lawyers laughed aloud, and I got a glimpse of how they might have looked had they spent their days joking with the lions.

"No, no, certainly not! They're scattered throughout Kingdoms and Empires!" Mr Crozer handed Aunt Isabelle a piece of paper, and she angled it towards me so I could read it too.

It was a list of names.

They were the names of my ten other aunts.

At the bottom of the list, in tiny scrawl, was an "Addendum". My parents had initialled it.

No gift to be delivered to Aunt Isabelle — she got the cloudberry tea.

3

Aunt Isabelle cleared her throat. Her words, when she spoke, were like the thuds of falling books.

"Cloudberry tea," she said, "is all very well."

I knew what she meant. She meant that she had taken care of me since I was a tiny baby, and deserved a little treasure of her own. She meant that all this time the cloudberry tea had seemed like the sweetest gesture, a token of affection, but now it was nothing but a scrawl, an "addendum".

She squared her shoulders. "But Bronte," she continued, "is certainly not taking this journey alone. Far too dangerous for a child! There could be Dark Mages anywhere! If she must traipse around delivering treasure, the Butler and I will accompany her."

The lawyers tipped forward and both tapped the paper excitedly, as if playing a lively duet on the piano.

"It's quite clear," Mr Crozer said.

"She *must* travel alone," Mr Ridgeway added.

"Piffle," said Aunt Isabelle. "There has to be a way around that. The Butler and I will buy our tickets separately. We'll sit *behind* Bronte and keep an eye on her. You lawyers are the loophole experts, are you not? Figure it out and get back to me."

Now the lawyers looked sideways at each other.

"Ahem," said Mr Crozer.

"Madam," said Mr Ridgeway. "Look closely at that paper, if you please."

Aunt Isabelle sniffed. She lifted up the paper and studied it.

"Well?" she asked, after a moment.

"Do you see the border all around it?"

"Yes."

"Do you see that it has been cross-stitched?"

"Very pretty," Aunt Isabelle said. "Very fine."

"Look more closely," Mr Crozer instructed her.

"*Very* fine cross-stitch. Yes, I see that. But I do not see how—"

"What colour is the cross-stitch?" Mr Ridgeway asked.

Aunt Isabelle was growing impatient. "It's a sort of silvery-blue, I suppose, but quite honestly, I can't—"

"And touch it with your fingertips."

Aunt Isabelle sighed, and did so. "Very soft," she said. "Extremely soft."

"Yes," said Mr Ridgeway.

"Yes," said Mr Crozer.

There was a long pause. A clock ticked.

Aunt Isabelle looked up slowly. "It's not..." she breathed, and stopped. "It's not *Faery cross-stitch*?"

Both lawyers nodded firmly, cheerfully. "It is."

4

Here, I should interrupt my story to say that I am now twelve years old.

I am writing this in a hammock, while my dog, Will, sleeps in the hammock's shade. Back then, however, I was only ten. I knew plenty about good manners and cakes with lemon icing, but nothing about Faery cross-stitch – or practically anything, really. And I didn't even *have* a dog then.

The only thing I knew about magic was a passage from *A Children's History of the Kingdoms and Empires* that my governess, Dee, had once made me memorize:

Magic is worked by thread. Long ago, the thread was real, and you dug it out from a magic mine. In the first sort of mine, there was "bright thread". Silver-blue and soft as a cloud, bright thread was used by True Mages, such as Faeries, elves, and water sprites. In the second sort, there was "shadow thread". Black and red, thick and coarse, this was used by Dark Mages like witches and Sterling Silver Foxes. And in the third, there was binding thread. More string or twine than thread, and golden-green, this was used by Spellbinders to cast nets around Shadow Magic, and stop it from doing harm.

Over time, all the mages learned to do their magic with imagined thread. These days, they simply move their hands about as if they are actually sewing (or knitting, weaving, crocheting, et cetera). The mines have long since disappeared; nobody remembers where they were, and you rarely see actual thread these days except in a museum.

Or in lawyers' offices, it turned out. When your parents have found a Faery to cross-stitch bright thread around their will.

"They got ahold of bright thread," Aunt Isabelle muttered, shaking her head. "What were they thinking?"

The lawyers nodded gravely.

I was becoming annoyed.

"Well," I said. "But what does that mean?"

Both lawyers turned to me, their chairs creaking.

"It means, Bronte, that you *must* follow the instructions in this will," said Mr Crozer.

"If you don't," Mr Ridgeway put in, "you break the cross-stitch."

"And if the cross-stitch breaks," both lawyers chanted, "*so does your hometown*."

They waved their hands at the windows, indicating Gainsleigh, all around us.

"Breaks?" I was still annoyed. "My hometown *breaks*?"

"It is ripped apart," Mr Ridgeway clarified, "like threads torn asunder."

He jabbed his finger at the parchment. "See here?" he said. "In exactly three days, you must take the 7:15 a.m. train to Livingston." He paused. "If you don't, *roads will crack*."

Mr Crozer reached over to jab a finger too. "See here? On this day, you must take the Clybourne Overnighter to visit your Aunt Claire. Or *trees will be uprooted*."

"You must stay with each aunt for *exactly three days*," Mr Ridgeway intoned.

"With two exceptions," Mr Crozer said, still jabbing. "You stay with *these two* aunts on their cruise ship for a *month*, and you stay with *this aunt* for *two weeks*."

"If you don't," said Mr Ridgeway, "*bridges will fall*."

The lawyers' voices grew louder. They were punching the paper with their fists.

"The final aunt is Aunt Franny in Nina Bay!"

"Aunt Franny must hold a party, inviting family and friends, to celebrate your parents' lives!"

"Only when that party is complete, Bronte, are you free!"

"*Before* that party, you must follow these instructions *exactly*!"

"You must give the aunts their gifts at *the time specified*!"

"*Or windows will shatter!*"

"You must go to this café!"

"*Or roofs will cave in!*"

"You must order *cheesecake* here!"

"*Or buildings will collapse!*"

They were shouting now. Pounding the desk. The room was shaking violently. So was I.

"YOU MUST FOLLOW THESE INSTRUCTIONS PRECISELY, BRONTE!"

"*OR PEOPLE COULD DIE.*"

There was a sudden silence. Or not a silence exactly, because the lawyers were both panting. They dabbed at their sweaty foreheads with handkerchiefs.

"But she's only a child," Aunt Isabelle whispered.

I looked at her face. It was white as fresh snow — and now I was truly afraid.

5

Over the next three days, I did not breathe.

Well, I probably did breathe, otherwise I'd be dead.

But it really seemed as if there was no time to breathe.

We ran out of the lawyers' office, and then we kept on running.

Planning, packing, folding, zipping, visiting the seamstress for new frocks. I read my parents' instructions over and over, and had nightmares about losing them or spilling lemonade on them. "The ink has run!" I screamed in my sleep. "I can't read the words!"

Of course, we had to race to the bank to collect the treasure chest from the vault.

It turned out to be very small, the size of a large shoe box. For a moment, I thought it shimmered with jewels, but those were only glued-on sequins.

Accompanying the chest was a small sack of silver coins "for expenses" on my journey.

"Handy," sniffed Aunt Isabelle, but then she pivoted and ran out of the bank.

As we raced about, Aunt Isabelle drilled me on the dangers of Dark Mages.

"How can you tell if somebody's a witch?"

"They often look confused. They wear socks with sandals."

"Good. What do you do if you see one?"

"Stay quiet. Try to blend in."

"How do you know a Sterling Silver Fox?"

"Lots of jewellery. Sharp ears."

"What do you do if you see one?"

"Laugh loudly. They can't stand the sound of laughter."

"How do you know a Whisperer?"

I paused. A Whisperer was the most frightening Dark Mage. The others tended to leave you alone unless you bothered them, but Whisperers kidnapped children.

"But I won't see a Whisperer, will I? They're all safely bound in the Whispering Kingdom?"

"True." Aunt Isabelle nodded. "But what if a Whisperer escapes? How do you know a Whisperer?"

"They don't escape, do they?"

"Bronte. How do you know a Whisperer?"

I sighed. "They never cut their hair. You hear a voice in your head like burning steel."

"What do you do if you see a Whisperer?"

"Run."

"How fast?"

"As fast as I can."

"Faster, Bronte. Faster."

We went through all the other Dark Mages – ghouls, radish gnomes, fire sirens, and so on – and covered other dangers too. Getting my new frocks muddy. Forgetting to say thank you. That kind of thing.

In the middle of this, a telegram arrived from my grandfather. Now, I knew that my father had eleven sisters and that his parents had died before I was born. But I didn't know much about my mother's family. She had run away from home when she was fifteen, wanting adventures.

Her father, however, sent me gifts every birthday and some-times invited me to come and visit him. He always offered to send a carriage to fetch me. Aunt Isabelle had never allowed this, as he lived outside of Colchester, which is very far away, and as he was "a perfect stranger to us".

I AM HEARTBROKEN ABOUT THE DEATH OF MY ONLY DAUGHTER – YOUR MOTHER, his telegram said. BUT I SUPPOSE THAT'S THE KIND OF THING THAT HAPPENS IF YOU GALLIVANT ABOUT HAVING ADVEN-TURES WITH PIRATES. DO PLEASE VISIT ME, BRONTE! I HAVE MANY SPECIAL ITEMS THAT BELONGED TO YOUR MOTHER, WHICH I WOULD NOW LIKE TO GIVE TO YOU. I AM ELDERLY AND CANNOT TRAVEL, BUT I CAN SEND A FRIEND TO COLLECT YOU AT ONCE.

Aunt Isabelle telegrammed back to say that she was very sorry but I was going on a journey until the first of August. On that day, I would be in Nina Bay, visiting my Aunt Franny and attending a party to celebrate my parents. He was welcome to come along to that party himself, she added.

My grandfather replied at once. NINA BAY IS PERFECT. WILL SEND FOR YOU THERE AFTER THE PARTY, BRONTE. I HOPE YOU LIKE PLAYING ON THE BEACH AND EATING ICE CREAM!

"He sounds lovely," I said.

Aunt Isabelle said, "Hmph," and consulted her map.

"I suppose Colchester *is* very close to Nina Bay," she admitted, after a moment. "And I suppose the Butler and I will be there for the party ourselves. It *is* right that you visit him now, and see your mother's special items."

"So you will allow it at last?"

"I will allow it."

I smiled. At least there was one gleaming thing in my future.

I didn't see the Butler much in those three days, as he was so busy sending telegrams to aunts and checking timetables. Sometimes I would hear him and Aunt Isabelle talking in low voices in the study. The night before my journey was to begin, I passed the study very late and heard my aunt's voice: "Faery cross-stitch," she said. "What were they *thinking*?"

I paused and knocked on the door.

"Bronte," said Aunt Isabelle. "Why aren't you sleeping?"

"Another nightmare," I said.

They were sitting at Aunt Isabelle's desk, which was scattered with books and maps. Both held glasses of brandy and their faces glowed from the rich light of the fireplace.

The Butler took off his reading spectacles and reached into his pocket. "A gift for you, Bronte," he said, and handed me a little vial of pale pink liquid. It was marked **Gainsleigh Dewdrops**.

"They don't do much," he said. "But they're pretty. And they'll help you remember home."

I almost cried then, but Aunt Isabelle told me to skedaddle to bed.

✳

In case you need it spelled out for you, I was anxious about my trip.

I'd never been away from Gainsleigh before, you see, and never spent a night apart from Aunt Isabelle and the Butler.

I tried to pretend that I only minded because it was inconvenient. "I will have to miss my swimming practice," I sighed. "Not to mention my trumpet lessons."

"Yes," Aunt Isabelle sighed back. "*Extremely* inconvenient. I am continuing to consult with the lawyers about ways around the Faery cross-stitch, Bronte. Perhaps you will not need to go, after all?"

Interestingly, when she said that, I felt two things at once. Imagine that you are in a cosy room with a fireplace, and you catch sight of the end of a silk ribbon just outside the window. You step outside, pick up the ribbon, and realize you must follow it. You can see that the ribbon is long and winding, that it stretches across the snow and disappears into a distant forest.

Now, imagine that somebody calls you back into the cosy room, and tells you that they have consulted with the lawyers and that now you need not follow the ribbon, after all.

You might feel relieved to be safe from the blizzards and wolves outside, but you might also feel a jolt of disappointment – the loss of that fluttering ribbon of adventure.

As much as I was frightened, a tiny part of me, right in the centre of my heart, was also rather excited.

Anyway, Aunt Isabelle could not get me out of it after all, and early the next morning, I climbed into the carriage to go to the station.

My governess rushed up, passed a package through the window to me, and stood back, beaming.

"That will be the schoolwork I asked her to prepare," Aunt Isabelle said. "There's no need for you to fall behind while you are travelling."

But when I opened the package, it was only a few storybooks, along with a gift card:

Take a break from schoolwork, Bronte. Breathe the air, pick the flowers (if they are growing wildly, say in a forest), read stories, dream dreams! Fondly, D.

"Good gracious," complained Aunt Isabelle. "Why do we *pay* her?"

The Butler banged on the side of the carriage with his palm. "Hurry along," he said. "It's a quarter to seven already."

Aunt Sue

6

That afternoon, I arrived at the first aunt's home.

It was 2:30 p.m. in Livingston. The heat here was vivid.

Aunt Sue met me at the mailbox at the end of her driveway, one hand to her forehead for the glare. The other hand was deep in the mailbox, and I had the impression from her dreamy smile as she looked up at the approaching milk cart, and from the quick, startled expression that crossed her face when she spotted me there by the driver – I got the impression that she'd forgotten I was due. She'd come down to check for letters, and it was pure luck she'd done this at just the right time. You could hear her relief in this luck in the splendour of her welcome.

"Look at you, and the sight of you!" she shouted. "It is not young Bronte arrived for her visit! It is not!"

"It is," I corrected her, and the driver, beside me, clicking at his slowing horse, agreed.

"Aye. It is young Bronte. I've brought her to you as planned."

"And look at you!" Sue repeated, her voice bursting like rockets. "It is *not* Bronte!"

The driver nodded again. His quiet grey beard prickled across his chin and around his mouth.

"Aye, Sue, and it is. Perhaps if you learn to accept that fact, you'll raise a hand and help her from the cart?"

Aunt Sue rushed to reach her arms to me. The moment her hands touched mine, large and warm – from the sun I suppose – the moment her fingers curled tight around mine, the last three days seemed to fall through my body like a descending scale on the pianoforte. My feet hit the road with a thud and twin bursts of dust. I smiled at Aunt Sue.

"Good afternoon," I said politely, "Aunt Sue."

We walked the long driveway towards the farmhouse. I could see it emerging from the haze now. It seemed to have lost one of its chimneys. There was one tall chimney, and there was a sort of pile of rubble where another matching chimney should have been.

"Look at you and the walk on you!" Aunt Sue said. "Look at the walk on you!"

"Yes," I said politely. I looked down, trying to see what she meant. But it's tricky. You can't get the sense of your own walk.

I suppose she just meant I held my back very straight. I always do that when I'm nervous.

1

It was much cooler inside Aunt Sue's house. The floorboards had cracks and, if you looked closely, grit inside the cracks.

As soon as we stepped in, Aunt Sue sat on the floor and gestured for me to do the same.

I obeyed her, bewildered.

Perhaps this was a country-folk ritual?

Then I saw that she was wrenching off her boots – their soles were clumped with mud and bits of grass, so this seemed a good idea. She crammed the boots into a wooden crate that stood beside the door. It was already all a-tumble, this crate, with muddy boots of every shape and size, the laces intermingled.

Once Aunt Sue's boots were safely stowed, I made ready to stand again. But she was smiling down at *my* shoes in a friendly, patient way. I twirled my toes. It was the only way I could think to show her that the bottoms of my shoes were perfectly clean. But she only waited.

So I removed my shoes. I placed them on top of the crate and stood, feeling shy in my stockings.

Aunt Sue wore thick white socks and dungarees. With her knee, she inched my suitcase forward, and the floorboards creaked in such a wretched way that I jumped and said, "Sorry!"

"Look at you and the sight of you," Aunt Sue murmured. She

grasped my suitcase by the handle, swung it high, and marched down the hall.

The house was big and airy, filled with golden light, and the furniture seemed also big and golden. A spiderweb caught the light in one corner, and a lampshade was missing a jagged piece. We passed bedrooms crowded with colourful rugs and toys. A row of tiny undershirts draped the side of a cot in one room; a huge black dog stared out at me from another.

Aunt Sue opened a door at the end of the hall.

"This will be your room while you stay," she declared, and swung the suitcase onto a bed. It cried out beneath the weight just like the floor had.

"Oh my." Aunt Sue pointed at a patch of mould on the ceiling, but she quickly lost interest in it, smiling around at the stacks of boxes and suitcases instead. It was a storage room: there was a crumpled accordion, a basket of frayed towels, and a shelf crouching gamely beneath its overload of books and magazines. The bed was pressed against one wall. Lime-green coverlet and fat white pillow.

"And you'll be staying?" Aunt Sue inquired.

"Yes," I said, alarmed. There was any doubt?

"And you'll be staying...?" she repeated.

"Oh." I understood. "Two nights. And on the final morning, I'm supposed to drink a glass of juice squeezed from oranges that I myself have picked in your orchard. I hope that's all right... my picking your fruit... and I hope that... there *is* fruit... Aunt

25

Isabelle worried that you might not *have* the orchard any longer or that—"

"Hush," said Aunt Sue gently. "We still have the orchard. And aren't the oranges perfect to be picked as we speak? Aren't they perfect to be picked?"

"I don't know," I confessed.

Aunt Sue beamed, warming to her theme. "And aren't they the finest, brightest oranges in all of Livingston? Livingston! Listen to me and the sound of me! The finest in the kingdom? In *all* the Kingdoms and Empires!"

I congratulated her on her oranges, and she seemed pleased.

Then she frowned.

"Well, they're not so fine as oranges grown in the tiny Empire of Ricochet," she admitted. "Have you ever tried a Ricochet orange?"

"No."

"Well, don't."

"All right."

"They spoil you for all other oranges. They're so fine, they're so *ridiculously* fine!"

I blinked. Aunt Sue blinked back. "And are there more instructions?" she said next, giving her shoulders a little shake as if to shake the oranges of Ricochet from their branches.

"One other," I said. "There is a café I'm to visit tomorrow for my lunch. I have to walk along the river to reach it. I think it is called...the Upturned Chair?"

"The Upturned...Ha! You mean the Dishevelled Sofa!"

"Yes. That's it." I was embarrassed. "I think that's all."

"Nothing else?"

I glanced towards my suitcase on the bed and remembered.

"Yes," I said. "Of course. I am to give you your gift from the treasure chest on the final morning. Just after I drink the orange juice."

Aunt Sue nodded in a distracted way as if that was neither here nor there.

"And then I must depart at once," I said.

"At once," Aunt Sue repeated, falling into this phrase with great sadness. "Really at once?"

"The instructions are very clear," I said. "And if I don't follow them exactly, the Faery cross-stitch will start to break."

Aunt Sue frowned. "Yes," she said. "And Gainsleigh will begin to come to pieces. I can't think why your parents added the cross-stitch."

"Neither can Aunt Isabelle," I said. "Or the Butler."

Aunt Sue gazed down at me, her frown fading. "Oh, my child, your parents. Your dear, dear parents and their mad ways, and ah, look at you, and the sight of you, so much like your father, and like your mother too, so beautiful the pair of them, and you, just like them, with that sweet, bewildered smile, and the tiny not-quite-a-dimple here." She reached out to touch my cheek but seemed to change her mind, and grabbed me into her arms

27

instead. I wasn't prepared, so it was rather as if I were a rag doll being jigged about, but then I settled myself, and politely hugged her back.

Eventually, she straightened, and was cheerful again.

"You'll be longing to see your cousins!" she said, which surprised me. I wasn't really. I had imagined she was going to say I was longing to wash, or to rest, or to take refreshments. The usual things.

"I am curious to meet them," I allowed. I knew that there were four boys in the family, and that the eldest, Sebastian, was the same age as me. Also I knew that I *had* met him once before, when Aunt Sue visited us in Gainsleigh, but that was when Sebastian and I were babies. So I did not recall it.

"No," Aunt Sue agreed. "You would not." There was the sound of a slamming door, and she said, "Why, that will be the boys! Home to meet you!"

Now I could hear it too, a rush of footsteps and a blare of voices, tangled together like the laces in the crate.

We went directly to the kitchen, which had a big stove and an oak table. The table was jumbled with objects: a teapot, a picture book, a plate covered in pastry flakes, coloured papers, scissors, and glue – and that's just a sample. There was plenty more.

All but one of the boys were smaller than me, and all were noisier. They tore about, grabbing at this and reaching for that. One flung open a drawer and took out a large knife; another slid sideways along the floorboards – with pizzazz, like a dancer – and threw open a bread bin to grab a loaf of bread; a third wrenched open the refrigerator with such vigour that it rattled and shook; and a fourth – a very little one – was clambering from chair to chair, to what end, I was not sure.

"Boys!" said Aunt Sue. "Look and if it isn't your cousin, Bronte, arrived to stay!"

All four stopped, turned, and stared at me.

"Here's Sebastian." Aunt Sue indicated the boy now slicing bread.

I reached out my hand. "Sebastian," I said.

He seemed surprised, but remembered himself, wiped his hand on his trouser leg, and shook my hand firmly.

The one who'd slid along the floor with pizzazz now slid towards me so fast that I thought we would collide. His hand was out ready to shake.

"I'm Nicholas," he announced.

"Nicholas," I repeated.

Aunt Sue pointed to the boy by the fridge, a jar of raspberry jam in his hand, and to the little one on the chairs: "Connor and Benjamin," she said.

"Connor," I said. "Benjamin."

"She keeps saying our names," said the middle one by the fridge.

"She does," agreed another.

All four of them now looked at me, quizzically, as if awaiting an explanation.

"She's come all the way on the train from Gainsleigh," Aunt Sue put in, and there was a sort of "aaah" in the boys' expressions. They turned back to their activities.

A moment later, it seemed, the boys were all at the table eating jam sandwiches and making paper chains. They were very busy about it. I wondered if I was expected to help, but suddenly I was so tired that I could hardly blur them. They weren't even blurs through my eyes – they were shapes between blinks. No, not even shapes. They were the sounds that shapes make, and my head was bobbing, and Aunt Sue's voice was murmuring me down the hall and back to the bedroom and I was saying, suddenly clear and loud, "I must build you a new chimney!" and Aunt Sue was saying, "Hush now, hush, you'll be so tired, and I should have thought!" and then I was in the bed, fast and deeply asleep.

8

The next morning, there were buttermilk pancakes, bright red strawberries, a pot of coffee, and a lot of scraping and banging for breakfast. My cousins scraped their chairs back and banged the kitchen door behind them as they ran out to feed dogs or collect eggs or fetch the ball that had been kicked into the pigs' enclosure. Each of these tasks, the boys seemed to recall suddenly, with a mouth full of pancake and a proud little glance in my direction. Between all this, the boys kept a football skidding back and forth across the kitchen floor, in and out of chair legs. Meanwhile, Aunt Sue was busy at the stove, flipping pancakes with a dreamy smile on her face.

The table was now even more crowded, for along with the breakfast there were coils and coils of colourful paper chains. They must have been making paper chains until midnight! The littlest boy, Benjamin, had a pancake in one hand and the end of a chain in the other, and he was doing great loops around the room, dragging the chain behind him. It draped across shoulders and over the backs of chairs, and wound around people's ankles. Now and then an older boy would cry out, "Benji! Put that down! You'll break it!" and Benji would glance at that boy and carry on.

Uncle Josh arrived from somewhere outside in the midst of this, brushing leaves from his shoulders. He wore square glasses and had lots of curly hair.

"Look, Dad, it's Bronte!" the boys cried, pointing at me. "This is our dad," they informed me. "She's our cousin," they informed him.

"I am indeed," their father confirmed, "and she is indeed," nodding solemnly in my direction. "Indeed, and she is Bronte."

"You can call him Uncle Josh," a boy suggested. They all looked at me and waited.

"She's not doing it."

"Say his name," another urged.

Uncle Josh gave the ball a firm kick with the side of his foot, dragged out a chair, sat down, and turned to me.

"You've grown," he said. "The last time I saw you, you were as big as this little fingernail." He held up his smallest finger and pointed to the nail.

This seemed unlikely. I was ready to disagree, but then I saw he was joking. He had a dash of spark in his eye.

"It's a lucky thing you've grown," he continued. "Or we'd lose you in the cracks in the floorboards. We'd always be after finding you. We'd be saying, *Where's Bronte now? Is she in your pocket, Benjamin? You haven't gone and washed her down the sink, have you, Connor?*"

I laughed, and the boys laughed too, although then someone remembered, "The lambs!" and all of them – even littlest Benji, who now finally dropped the paper chain – rushed and banged out of the kitchen.

By the time they returned, Uncle Josh had asked me more questions than I had thought possible: he poured out questions the same way he poured maple syrup onto his pancakes, always with smiles or chuckles at my replies. I was so busy answering that I stopped wondering about whether I was supposed to cut the pancakes into little pieces (as the oldest boy seemed to do), or roll them up with strawberries tucked inside (as the two middle boys did). I simply ate them, even reaching for the maple syrup myself.

As the boys returned, scraping back their chairs once again, Uncle Josh carried on talking and my cousins looked from their father to me with interest.

The biggest cousin, Sebastian, interrupted with a question of his own. "Do you play a musical instrument?"

"Yes," I said. "Trumpet."

"I once played the piano," Sebastian told me. "For a year. But then I gave up, didn't I?"

"For a year!" exclaimed Uncle Josh. "You played the piano for a *year*, Sebastian! How tired you must have been!"

Everybody fell about laughing, including Sebastian, who stopped looking at me in his strange, fierce way. A tiny white fly landed on the edge of the water jug. I'd never seen a white fly before.

"Which aunt are you visiting next?" the second boy inquired. That was Nicholas, and he seemed the quickest and liveliest. He often flourished his hands as if dancing.

"Aunt Emma," I said.

"We've visited her," Sebastian told me, "on Lantern Island. It's good. You?"

"Never," I admitted.

"And then?" Nicholas pressed, jiggling about.

"Aunt Claire," I replied, then began to count them off, "followed by Aunt Sophy, Aunt Nancy—"

Here, the third cousin, Connor, interrupted. He was the most solid of them, and shared Sebastian's fierce gaze, but gentled by flicks of humour. "Have you already met any of the other aunts and cousins, or will they all be strangers to you? As we are?"

"Some of them," I began, "but—"

"What about the queen?" the other boys jumped in. Connor nodded as if this was the point he'd been driving towards.

You see, one of the aunts, Aunt Alys, had grown up to become a queen, and no, I had never met her, nor her son, Prince William.

"Neither have we," the boys all agreed, disappointed.

"Has *anybody* met the queen?" Uncle Josh demanded.

"Well, *I* have," Aunt Sue put in tartly, joining us at the table. "Isn't she my sister?"

"Sure, and you'll have met her," Uncle Josh agreed. "She is your sister, after all."

"But we hardly ever see or hear from her," Aunt Sue admitted. "Except for a telegram now and again, asking our advice about her son. He must be quite a handful."

I decided it was my turn to ask a question.

"Is there a reason you've all been making paper chains? Or is it just a hobby?"

This turned out to be the right question, because they rushed to answer. Today, or did I not know? Of course she doesn't know, she's from *Gainsleigh*! But isn't it a marvel that she's here for it! For that, *today*...!

34

Today, it turned out, the Festival of Matchstick would take place.

"The Festival of Matchstick?"

"A celebration of the elves," they all explained.

"You have elves here?"

Which ignited them again. And does she not know, of course she doesn't know! She is from *Gainsleigh*. I waited patiently. Eventually they explained.

When the first settlers came to Livingston, they accidentally brought along a handful of elves in a crate of lettuce. The elves scattered amongst the orchards and now formed a thriving community.

"They keep mostly to themselves," Aunt Sue told me. "Except for today, for isn't it the festival today?"

"It is," they all confirmed.

"The highlight," Uncle Josh added, "is the elven football match."

"The Darians will win," Sebastian declared.

"Sure, and they will not!" shouted Nicholas. "It will be the Glassrings!"

"The Glassrings! Not a chance!"

They clashed back and forth, slamming the table sometimes, Uncle Josh and Aunt Sue both joining in. There was talk of one elf having a sprained ankle and another a touch of fever, and talk of rain, little Benjamin pointing out that Glassring feet often got jammed in mud.

At that moment, I looked at the kitchen clock.

"My parents' instructions say I have to walk along the river this morning," I told them. "Before I do that, could I write a post-card to Aunt Isabelle, to let her know I am safe?"

The boys looked at me quietly, as if they found me both astonishing and not quite the thing.

"Of course," Aunt Sue said. "Onwards and upwards!"

This seemed a signal to everybody to leap to their feet and clatter plates and cutlery to the kitchen sink. Uncle Josh set me up at a desk in the corner of the room to write my card.

Dear Aunt Isabelle, I began. **It is rather noisy here.**

9

The Dishevelled Sofa was a small café, dim in the storm-cloud light. I chose a table by the window and ordered "Today's Special!!" without knowing what it was. (My parents' instructions recommended the home-made lemonade but didn't specify what I should eat.) Today's Special!! turned out to be a pot of lamb and vegetables, with huge croutons bobbing about like somebody's joke.

This was the first time I had ever eaten alone in a public establishment, and I felt very nervous. Strangely, so did the people at the other tables, it seemed: bright eyes, quick movements, and whispers everywhere. As if *they* were all dining alone for the first time too.

Phrases began to drift towards me: "The confectionary table is already full!" and "The scorekeeper must not fall asleep again," and "Yes, it is sure to rain, is it not, but it will pass, as rain does," and I realized that it was not nerves, but excitement about the Festival of Matchstick.

I ate my Today's Special!! and drank my home-made lemon-ade, and the clink of my fork, the clunk of my glass, the violent crunch of those croutons all began to seem much too loud. Embarrassed, I set down my fork and sat back in my chair.

I studied a painting on the wall. In the painting, a boy in a red jacket sat on a swing while a girl in a blue dress stood by a seesaw. The girl faced out of the painting, looking directly at me, it seemed. Almost as if she was demanding that *I* join her on the seesaw.

Well, I can't, I thought. *I'm eating lunch.*

I smiled to myself, turned to the window, and saw raindrops scattered over the glass.

"Not long and it will bucket down!" declared a voice at a nearby table.

I raised my hand for the bill.

It was raining steadily as I followed the path along the river back towards the farm. "Take an umbrella!" Aunt Sue had urged when I set off earlier, and she had pressed one into my arms. Now, as I opened it, I saw that it was bright yellow, with a pattern of ladybirds.

I liked it.

Across the river, a boy was also walking along, keeping pace with me. He had no umbrella, but he didn't seem bothered by this. His clothes were shabby, his feet bare. He glanced across at me and smiled. A friendly face. I smiled back.

I imagined how I must look, striding along in my new dress, which was apple green with a full skirt. So the boy was seeing a girl in a new green dress with a yellow umbrella, a girl who had just dined alone in a café, ordered food, and paid from her own crocheted purse. Of course, the boy could not know about the food and the bill, and he certainly can't have known about my crocheted purse. But I felt that he could *sense* how grown-up I was. Anyway, I was very happy.

I carried along on my side of the river and the boy continued on his. Now and then we glanced at each other and smiled again. The river was too wide to talk across, otherwise I think we might have chatted. I liked the fact that he was alone, like me, and not part of a big, noisy, paper-chain-making, football-kicking family. He might have been heading home to such a family, I supposed. But somehow I doubted it.

I reached the edge of the village and there were no longer roads or people. The river seemed pleased to be out amongst paddocks and orchards. *This is more like it*, it seemed to say, hurtling along.

The rain also pleased the river, I thought, for it was rollicking and turning this way and that, like a dog being vigorously petted.

It certainly *was* a slapping sort of rain, I realized, for it had been growing heavier. Now it was a regular downpour, the air crowded with water, the sky dark with low cloud. The path was no longer paved here, but dirt.

The rain and wind were making such a racket! Rather than walking, I seemed to be *pushing* myself through the noise. The path was no longer a path but a sort of muddy stream.

The river now seemed alarmed. It careened, foaming and white, hurtling branches and leaves along with it. Also rubbish: a single glove zipped by, a page from a newspaper, a bright-green basket, bobbing along the water at quite a pace. The basket's edges were trimmed in white.

The rain rushed from every angle, ignoring the umbrella, splattering my dress and bare legs. My shoes were soaked, my feet wet and cold.

I began to run, angry at my own foolishness in being outside in this weather. I *was* just a child! Who *cared* that I had ordered my own lunch at a café?! I should have stayed and waited for the rain to finish! No proper grown-up would get caught in such a storm!

I wanted to cry. The rain roared, the river roared back, and from somewhere amidst both came a thinner, higher sound. I ran along, my dress plastered to my thighs, and that thin, high sound persisted. Was it the boy across the river? I looked over and there he was, running along himself. But he seemed untroubled. He ran in a loose, easy way.

Up ahead, the green basket had caught on a snag in the centre of the river. A gust of wind, and my umbrella tore itself inside out. I closed it and jogged on, the rain now pounding my bare head. As I passed the basket, still caught on the snag, waves parting around it, I saw that it held a tumble of green and white material. It must be a laundry basket.

The high, thin sound was back again.

I stopped.

There was something else in the laundry basket.

A toy. A teddy bear? A doll?

It was impossible to see. I stepped closer to the river's edge, peered harder.

There was a baby in the basket.

A baby.

"A *baby*!" I screamed at the boy across the river. *"There's a baby!"*

"What?" he mouthed back at me, skidding to a stop.

I dropped my umbrella and bag, kicked off my shoes, and jumped into the river.

Such a burst of cold! And the river frantic to take me with it!

I fought it with my elbows. I kicked out with my legs. My dress clung and dragged me down. I'd taken second place in the Gainsleigh Junior Swim Contest the year before, I reminded myself. I could do this! I struck out, arms strong, feet kicking.

I gasped, splashing up, then struck out again. I was almost at the basket.

My hand reached out to touch it.

My hand almost touched it.

The basket bounced, sprang free from the snag, and hurtled onwards.

"No!" I swallowed a mouthful of water. I spluttered and struck out again. It was easier to swim with the current, of course, but I was tossed about, my dress still dragging. I swallowed even more water, and each time I looked up, there was the basket, rushing ahead, always out of my reach. It rocked violently as it rushed.

It would tip! It would hit another snag and the baby would be thrown into the river! The baby would drown!

I swam harder and harder, and the next time I looked up, the basket had halted. It still bobbed, but a branch was pressed firmly against it.

It was the boy from the other bank – he was lying flat on the grass, hands around one end of the branch. The rain plastered his hair to his head.

I reached the basket, wrapped my arms around it, and trod water. The baby was tiny, dressed in a white cotton suit, tears and rain streaming down its little face.

But how was I to get the basket to the riverbank now? I might fight the river on my own, but with my arms around a basket?

"Hold on!" the boy shouted. He was pointing to the branch. "I'll pull you in!"

I stretched around the basket, still kicking hard at the water, and managed to grasp the wood – slick and wet – with one hand. My other arm was firm around the basket. I turned back towards him. He nodded.

Slowly, slowly, we inched towards the bank. I could see the concentration on the boy's face as he towed us in, one arm over the other.

As we neared the bank, I took a chance and let go of the branch so I could use both hands, and flung the basket up towards him. At once, he reached out and caught hold of it, pulling it up onto the shore.

I was tossed along a little farther, but in a final furious surge, threw myself at the bank. Tufts of weed grew there, and I used these to drag myself closer and clamber out.

The boy was holding the baby close to his chest, talking to it. The green basket lay on its side on the grass.

"We need to get the baby out of the rain!" I cried, breathless.

The boy nodded, still soothing the baby. He looked up at me, then squinted out at the fields.

"The closest farmhouse is a good distance, I think," he shouted. Then his face cleared. "There's a festival! I saw people setting up tents for it earlier! This way!"

He began to jog along, cutting out across a field, the baby pressed against his chest. I ran behind him, tripping on ruts, my bare feet caught now and again by slurping patches of mud.

We crossed another field and turned along a lane, the boy running faster all the time. He stopped at a stile. I caught him up.

The rain had eased, so he could speak in an ordinary voice.

"I think it's along this lane," he told me, pointing, and then he pressed the baby into my arms. A bedraggled little form, soaked through.

"Hush," I said, cuddling it closer to my chest.

When I looked up, the boy had set off in the opposite direction.

"Wait!" I called.

He turned back. "Along the lane there," he repeated.

"But where are you going?"

The boy smiled. "Your swimming is champion!" he called. "I've never seen the like!" Then he turned again and strode away.

10

It had stopped raining, but everything still dripped.

I stood at the edge of a vast, muddy field. Somebody, some-where, was forging metal, and it was making a terrible shriek. At the opposite edge of the field, a row of brightly coloured tents drooped and trickled. As I watched, a man prodded at the roof of one of these tents with a long pole: a waterfall gushed over its edge. The man stepped smartly out of its way.

The baby in my arms was quiet now and looking up at me inquir-ingly. I touched its face with my palm, and its cheeks were very cold. I began to hurry and squelch across the field towards the tents.

As I drew closer, I heard people talking and shouting. They were gathered between the first two tents — a small crowd — and all seemed to be pointing in different directions. The metal-forging sound ran through all this at its awful pitch. But it wasn't forging at all, I realized: it was a woman screaming. She was in the centre of the shouting crowd, and she was lifting her face to the sky and lashing it with her screams. A few in the crowd set off running, and others kept up their shouting.

"Hello?" I called, hurrying now, afraid they'd all scatter before I reached them. "Hello!"

One or two in the crowd turned towards me, raising hands to foreheads.

"What's she got?" I heard somebody ask.

"Is that a baby in her arms?"

"Has she got him? She hasn't got him, has she?"

There was a sudden quiet, and then the screaming woman shot out of the crowd and ran towards me. The only sound now was the woman's heavy footfall as she ran.

Her face was terrible, all creased and pouched, her eyes pressed quite together, and then, as she drew closer, her run became a sprint, and she screamed once more, her face transforming, the creases vanishing and re-forming into a beaming smile. She launched herself at the baby in my arms.

"Oh, my baby, my baby boy," she cried, sinking to the grass and wrapping herself around the little one, kissing his cheeks, crying, and stroking his head.

The baby took all this in good grace, but after a moment, he made a small whimpering sound and the woman cried, "Oh, you're so cold! And aren't you cold?"

By now, most of the other people had crossed the field too, and the crowd had formed around us. There were cries of joy and relief, and people called to each other, "It's the baby!" and "The little girl here has brought the baby!" A few helped the woman to her feet and hurried her across to one of the tents, talking of blankets and dry clothes.

The others looked at me with great friendliness and interest.

"And who would this be, if she isn't a young hero, and you've

45

brought the baby back!" That's the sort of thing they said, all of them gazing at me.

I told them I was Bronte from Gainsleigh, here to visit my Aunt Sue and Uncle Josh ("Oh, Sue and Josh," and they all nodded to each other), and I told how I had seen the baby floating by in a basket.

"Oh, and you did not!" they all cried, but I did, I told them.

"And how did you come to get the baby out?" they prompted.

I explained about jumping in and swimming, and the boy with no shoes who blocked the basket with a branch and then towed us in.

"I don't know where the boy with no shoes went," I apologized, looking about me. They didn't seem to mind that. They wanted to tell me how the baby came to be floating down the river in a basket, and I must say I had been wondering this myself.

Here is what happened, they said, and what happened was this.

The baby had been taken by the elves.

"The elves!" I cried, astonished. I had always heard that the elves were a good and law-abiding race!

"Ah yes, and they are, and are they not? Generally speaking anyway."

It was a terrible misunderstanding, the people told me all at once. Each year, before the Festival of Matchstick, a gift was set out for the elves, wrapped in the elven colours of green and white. The elves always took the gift and immediately tossed it from a cliff or threw it into a fire or the river.

Strange way to treat a gift! I thought to myself, and this must have shown on my face. They assured me that it was the tradition, and that no offence was taken.

However, this morning, Tabitha Creaksay, as that works on the Matchstick Committee, had brought her little baby along, bundled up in his green-and-white blanket, and sleeping in a green basket with white trim.

She hadn't thought for a moment of the colours − although perhaps she *might* have, somebody said, for aren't they the elven colours every year? But others hushed this person: you must not be blaming Tabitha, they said, you must not.

In any case, Tabitha had set her baby down by a tent and set to work with decorations. After a bit, she had noticed the baby was gone, but she had not worried. *Oh, my sister must have the baby*, she had thought to herself.

But then the sister had strolled by and said, "No, no, I have not taken your wee baby, Tabitha," and Tabitha had begun running about looking for the baby, but still without much worry, for perhaps the baby's father, Royan, had come by to help.

Around this time, the Chief of Elves had approached the Chair of the Matchstick Committee, pulled on his trouser cuff, and performed the official Thank You Dance.

"Your dance is as lovely as ever, sir," the Chair had said. "But why are you dancing it now? We've not yet set out the gift! It's in the back of the wagon there − that basket of eggs and berries."

The Chief of Elves, annoyed to be interrupted in his dance, had said, "Why no, it's not eggs and berries, it's a bundle of blankets. We've taken it some good hour back!"

That's when the terrible mistake had come out, and Tabitha had begun her shrieking.

Now the crowd exclaimed at the wondrous luck of the elves not having tossed the gift over a cliff or into a fire this year. Next they exclaimed at the marvel of my having heard the baby's cry and what a swimmer I must be, to take on the river in a storm! The baby had been in dreadful danger, they all agreed, and surely would have drowned, for it is not far along that the river turns into the most violent rapids and then out it flows, into the sea.

"Oh," I said, horror-struck, shivering at this idea — at all of these ideas — and at last somebody noticed just how drenched and dripping I was.

I was rushed to Aunt Sue's house in the Chair's cart, and there were more cries of wonder from Aunt Sue and her family when we arrived and the story was told. Aunt Sue drew a bath for me and sent Sebastian to fetch my bag, shoes, and umbrella from the riverbank, and all of this was done in a fever — partly because everyone was excited that I had rescued a baby, and partly because we had to get to the festival in time.

II

The horn blew to signal that the festival was open, and then it blew again. The sky was now polished blue and bright, smiling fondly down on us as if it had never even *met* a raindrop.

My cousins darted away, vanishing into the crowds.

"Well," Uncle Josh said. "What do you say to our festival?"

I looked around, considering. Along with the tents I'd seen earlier, there were now stalls and stages, jugglers and fire-eaters, pens of farm animals, and apples bobbing in barrels. People wandered about, seeming very low.

"It looks good," I said. "But why is everyone sad? And where are the elves?"

"Ah," Aunt Sue said. "And have you not looked down?"

I had not. I did so now and the grass was alive with the hurry of elves, each wearing a tiny tin hat. It was as if hundreds of teaspoons had decided to dress up in colourful clothes and run about in a field.

"But they'll be crushed!" I said, alarmed.

Uncle Josh and Aunt Sue laughed. "No, no," Aunt Sue said. "They use their elvish intuition to avoid footfalls."

"And you see the care that everyone is taking?" Uncle Josh added.

I watched awhile, and the elves did seem to flow easily between the hurrying shoes. A boot fell perilously close to one little elf, but she gave it a jab with her elbow and carried on chatting with the elf by her side.

People, meanwhile, walked slowly, with downcast eyes, and this was why I had taken them to be sad.

"Shall we show you about?" Aunt Sue asked next. "Or would you prefer to wander your own way?"

"On my own, please," I said, so we arranged to meet at the football match, to take place at six p.m.

First, I explored the row of colourful tents. In each tent, elves competed in events involving paper chains or matchsticks: they sprang in and out of paper loops like tiny gymnasts; they raced to build ships out of matchsticks. It was quite mesmerizing.

Next, I bought a bag of cinnamon doughnuts and wandered around the stalls and stages outside.

Everybody seemed to know that I was the girl who had rescued the baby, and there was much pointing at me and whispering. I saw Tabitha eating corn-on-the-cob. Her eyes were still rimmed in red, and she threw her arms around me and snuffled, "Thank you, oh thank you!" into my hair. She introduced the man beside her as her husband, Royan. He was carrying the baby in the crook of his arm, but he shook my hand and thanked me too.

The baby held my little finger, then let it go. We all smiled at the baby. After a moment, he spotted a leaf that had got caught in his blanket, and he said, "Oh!" and offered this to me.

"*Thank* you," I said, and suddenly he gave me a huge smile. There were only two tiny teeth in his mouth, at the bottom.

I put the leaf into my coat pocket, and I would have it still if it wasn't for the incident with the flying teacups and avalanche at Aunt Nancy's. But that all happened much later.

The Festival of Matchstick carried on and the mood began to change. The chatter grew louder and more excitable, and everyone swarmed towards the far end of the field. *What for?* I thought, and then I realized it was nearly six.

I found Aunt Sue, Uncle Josh, and the boys. They were painting each other's faces with stripes of either crimson (for the Dariens) or blue (for the Glassrings). Others around us were doing the same.

"Which colour would you like?" Aunt Sue asked me.

"Which team should I support?" I responded, at which the

boys all shouted *Dariens* or *Glassrings*, back and forth, louder and louder. I should have guessed that would happen.

Uncle Josh said, "Hush now" to the boys, then he turned to me: "Dariens," he said sternly. "You must support the Dariens."

Aunt Sue smacked the back of his head, and the boys all started up their shouting again.

"Who usually wins?" I asked.

"It's about even," Uncle Josh said, "but the Dariens have won the last three festivals in a row."

"Then I shall support the Glassrings," I said. "Because it is their turn."

"It doesn't *work* like *that*," my cousin Sebastian said witheringly, but Nicholas took both my hands and swung me around.

"It's your choice," said Uncle Josh, sighing heavily.

The match took place on a platform painted with the usual lines and markings of a football field, little goals at either end. A whistle blew and a cheer went up, and I felt a rush of excitement.

And there was the boy with no shoes! He was on the edge of the crowd, and he caught my eye and sent me his friendly smile, but when I looked again, he was gone.

The elves tore around on the platform, kicking the tiny ball. It is quite strange to me now, to think of that tiny ball sliding back and forth on the platform, and how we all stared at it. But we did.

The Glassrings won. I felt proud of my team. My heart sang,

actually. The score was 3–2, and it was a great match, everyone agreed. Both teams *brought their best game.* The Darien supporters were good sports, and shook the hands of the Glassring supporters. Sebastian shook my hand, for example, and so did Uncle Josh. Then my cousins began to recreate the game, kicking their own ball around amongst the crowd, ignoring complaints from strangers. They were very good.

"Is that the end of the festival now?" I asked.

"Almost," my cousin Connor told me. "Only the prize ceremony left. In the big tent over there."

We trooped across to watch. It went on for quite a while, elves coming onto a little stage and receiving their medals, and they would weep and give heartfelt speeches. But they spoke in the elven tongue, so I did not understand. Many elves sat in a grandstand the size of a suitcase, and watched and nodded, applauding the speeches. The people stood about in a crowd.

The Championship Trophy was presented to the captain of the Glassring Football Team, and now the applause turned into a roar. I thought that would be the end of the day, but the elf presenter called for quiet.

"We have one final award," he cried. "It is the Elvish Medal for Bravery, presented only once in every century!"

Once a century! I thought. *This is important, then.* I wondered who could have been so heroic.

"A girl from Gainsleigh," the elf went on – and I suddenly

went cold. "A girl from Gainsleigh has rescued a baby from the river. To save a little baby? The baby of Tabitha and Royan? This alone deserves recognition!" The elf paused. Around me, people were whispering to each other, and turning to smile and point at me. "But this girl has not only rescued a baby," the elf declared, "she has saved the Elven People. For it was *us* who threw the baby in the river! Believing him to be our gift! A mere bundle of blankets! Which, I will say, we didn't think was much of a gift, but that is by the by. We were willing to let that slide. But it was a baby! Now, if the baby had drowned, we would have lived the next thousand years in the greatest of shame. All of us would have worn black, and you know how we love to dress in colours."

Here everybody agreed with this, both the people and the elves.

"Bronte Mettlestone! Bronte of Gainsleigh! Come forward and accept the Elvish Medal for Bravery!"

"No, no!" I whispered. I tried to find my voice. "I couldn't! All I did was—"

Did they not see? It was *lucky* that I had happened to see the baby floating by, not brave! Of *course* I had jumped in to get him! In the same way that I brushed my teeth each day, and said "thank you" when I bought my cinnamon doughnuts. But everyone was staring.

"It wasn't just me," I remembered. "It was also a boy. He held on to a branch to help. A boy with no shoes—"

Everybody looked about them. "Hello? Boy?" they called out. "Boy with no shoes?"

Nobody came forward, and I could not see the boy anywhere.

"Perhaps she could describe him," somebody suggested.

I tried to do so, but everyone either shrugged or asked questions I could not answer. "Does he have a little blister on his thumb?" "Is he studying science over at the village school?" "Was he at the post office earlier?"

In the midst of this, Uncle Josh leaned over and murmured to me, "You are a good girl, Bronte. And I think it would be a kindness to these elves if you accepted the medal."

So when people stopped looking for the boy and the elf presenter called again, "Bronte Mettlestone! Come forward and accept the Elvish Medal for Bravery!" I did so.

The medal was hung around my neck. It was strung on a soft ribbon, but the medal itself was a heavy, burnished gold. Everybody cheered, stamping their feet, and I worried again about an elf being crushed.

"Use that medal wisely," said a tiny breath of a voice, a whisper that tickled my ear. I looked down and an elf was standing on my shoulder.

"Use it?" I said, confused.

The elf held a finger to his lips, shaking his head. Then he scrambled down my arm and swung himself to the ground, joining in the clamour of cheering as if nothing had happened.

12

A strange thing happened that night.

It was especially strange because I was happy. We were sitting around the kitchen table at Aunt Sue's house, talking sleepily about the day. The boys and I had already bathed, and we all wore our pyjamas with robes. It was past little Benji's bedtime but he'd been allowed to stay, and he was sitting up straight, eyes big and shiny.

We drank hot chocolate and ate warm banana bread, the butter melting darkly. Nicholas had baked this earlier, his brothers told me proudly.

"You baked this?" I cried. "But it's delicious! Wonderful!"

Nicholas shuffled in his seat. "Thanks," he said, clearing his throat. "I like to bake. Can I see your medal?"

Everyone wanted to see it. It was passed around the table, each boy whistling and testing its weight in the palm of his hand.

"Do you know," Aunt Sue said, when it was her turn. "I think there's something special about this medal?"

"Of course it's special! What are you even *talking* about?" the boys all shouted. "It's an Elvish Medal for Bravery!"

Aunt Sue ignored them. "A story I've heard," she said, "but now what was it?" She placed the medal on the table.

"I've heard something too," Uncle Josh said. "Isn't it special in some way known only to the elves? Give it back to Bronte now, Sebastian. And, Bronte, I think you ought to wear it *all* the time."

I thought he was making one of his jokes, but he nodded gravely. So I lifted it over my head. The medal fell with a light thud against my pyjama top. "All the time?" I said doubtfully.

"I have the sense," Aunt Sue put in, "that your Uncle Josh is right. All the time."

"Indeed, and I *am* right all the time." Again, Uncle Josh nodded gravely.

"That is not what I meant, and he knows it," Aunt Sue sighed at the ceiling, but she laughed. "*Wear* it all the time is what I meant. You can slip it under your jacket so none can see."

I played with the medal, flicking it between my fingers. "All right," I said.

There was a thoughtful quiet.

"You're to pick oranges tomorrow?" Aunt Sue said to me.

"Yes," I agreed. "And then to drink the juice."

"Does she know where the orchard is?" Connor wondered.

"How could she know?" Sebastian demanded. "And how could she possibly know? Has she been here before? Has she?"

The boys seemed to speak to each other in this suddenly fierce way sometimes. I found it strange and alarming. But Connor shrugged, not seeming to mind at all.

"No," he agreed. "She wouldn't know. Shall I tell you, Bronte?"

"Please."

They all joined in his explanation. I had thought the orchard would be just behind the house, but no, it seemed to be along this laneway, and around that bend, and open this gate, and cross the cow paddock, and climb over this fence.

"No, she should go left at the lobelia tree," Nicholas argued. "It's quicker that way."

"Then she'd have to cross the creek!" Sebastian said. "And will it not be high after all the rain today?"

Connor grunted, irritated. "No, no. She'll not need to cross the creek! You're barmy!"

On went their arguments, Aunt Sue contributing now and then, until she stood up and began collecting plates and mugs. "We're to bed now, and all of us," she declared. "It was such a day! Such a day!"

Uncle Josh pushed back his chair and gathered Benji into his arms. The little boy had fallen fast asleep in his chair.

Aunt Sue stepped over and stroked Benji's hair. "Come along, boys," she said. "Bronte, do you know where to go now in the morning? To reach the orchard and pick your oranges?"

"Yes," I replied, although I didn't know at all. Only, I was tired and didn't want to hear more instructions about turning left at lobelia trees.

"And do you know which oranges are the best to pick?" Sebastian asked me.

They were all in the doorway now, Aunt Sue, Uncle Josh, and

their four boys, warm and tired, gathered close together, looking expectantly across at me.

"Of *course* I don't know," I said, and suddenly I was shouting: "I'VE NEVER EVEN *SEEN* AN ORANGE TREE, LET ALONE AN ORCHARD!"

Benji's eyes flew open. He lifted his head from Uncle Josh's shoulder and stared.

"Why is she shrieking?" Connor asked.

"I AM NOT!" I shrieked. "I NEVER SHRIEK!!" Then I burst into tears. "I don't know where the orchard is! I don't know how to pick oranges! AND WHAT EVEN *IS* A BLASTED LOBELIA TREE?"

"What's she saying?" Sebastian asked.

"Shhh," Nicholas urged. "I'm trying to understand."

"But you can't understand her," Connor said reasonably. "Because she's crying."

Somewhere behind me, Aunt Sue was dragging a chair around, and now she had wrapped her arms around me and lifted me right up. She sat on the chair and I was in her lap, as if I was a tiny child, rather than ten years old with my legs draping down towards the floor. "Hush, darling," she said, and "I know, I know," and "It's going to be all right, shhh, I know."

Stop crying! I urged myself. But I couldn't seem to do it. I kept right on crying, and Aunt Sue continued patting my head and saying, "I know."

Eventually, I stopped. I looked up.

The boys were all staring, fascinated.

"Give her a tissue," Nicholas suggested.

I wiped my nose. My face felt a mess of tears and snot.

"She certainly doesn't like lobelia trees!" Connor said forcefully. He sounded impressed.

Uncle Josh smiled at Connor. "I think this is not about trees, Connor," he said. "Or not exactly. Bronte has just started an adventure. She has to follow her instructions very carefully or else her own hometown will be torn to pieces."

Aunt Sue muttered at this, shaking her head.

"It must feel overwhelming," Uncle Josh continued. "Like she's about to enter a great, dark forest all alone. And here we are, confusing her at the very first trees!"

Aunt Sue hugged me tighter. "It's my fault. I'm so sad about losing your parents, Bronte, that I can't concentrate properly. I should have paid more attention to you."

"Yes," her boys agreed, nodding at their mother. "You should have."

Uncle Josh knocked on his nearest son's head. "Very helpful, boys," he said. "Luckily, we know Bronte is super brave and will fly though her adventure."

"But I'm not brave," I whispered.

"Not brave!" cried the boys. "You rescued a baby!"

"No." I frowned, trying to explain. "That wasn't brave. That was just like brushing my teeth."

The boys' eyes became round. "Show us your teeth!" Connor demanded.

Aunt Sue laughed. "She means she didn't think twice about it. But Bronte, the river in a storm is a dangerous place. Many *adults*, even strong swimmers, would not have ventured in there. They'd have called for help instead of jumping in."

"The fact that you didn't think twice," said Uncle Josh, "means you have bravery deep within your heart."

I looked down to my chest, as if to check my heart. There was the Elvish Medal for Bravery.

"Why did you come on the journey?" Sebastian asked suddenly. "I know the Faery cross-stitch would destroy Gainsleigh if you *didn't* come, so is that why? Is it because you love Gainsleigh?"

I stared at him. "Your question shows an extreme lack of insight," I said. "Of *course* I love Gainsleigh. It's my home! I love the harbour and the Botanical Gardens and the cobblestone streets lined with *gardenia* trees! Not lobelia, you see. But that is beside the point. Even if I didn't *know* a town — even if I hated it! — I wouldn't want to be the cause of its buildings and bridges crashing down!"

After a moment, Sebastian asked his parents what *an extreme lack of insight* meant.

"It means you asked a daft question," Uncle Josh told him.

"It means that Bronte has picked up many of her Aunt Isabelle's more cantankerous phrases" – Aunt Sue smiled – "in addition to her excellent manners."

"I wonder if the real Bronte is in the manners or the phrases," my cousin Nicholas mused.

I wondered the same thing myself. How could one tell?

"I'm sorry, Sebastian," I said now, recalling the well-mannered me. "I was impatient just now. And I'm sorry, everyone, about losing my temper. I was so loud!"

"*What?!*" the boys cried. "You think *that* was loud? You should hear *us* when we get mad. What you just did was nothing! A little chick cheeping!"

"Well, a bit more than cheeping," Connor admitted. "But in a minute, I'll show you how loudly *I* can shout when I'm angry."

"No, you won't," Uncle Josh and Aunt Sue said at the same time.

My cousins and I said good night in the hallway outside our bedrooms.

"Listen," Sebastian said quietly. "When you pick your oranges from the orchard tomorrow, do you have to go alone?"

I took out the instructions and found the place. "I have to drink juice squeezed from oranges I've picked myself," I read. "But it doesn't say anything about picking them *alone*."

"Well, then," Nicholas declared. "We'll *all* come with you in the morning and show you the way to the orchard."

The other boys nodded vigorously.

13

So that is what happened.

The boys helped me pick a basketful of oranges while the dogs ran around our feet, and then we came into the kitchen and squeezed a glass of juice.

It was fresh and delicious, its sweetness like very high notes. I put the glass back down and widened my eyes.

Everyone nodded and grinned at my wide eyes.

After that, I had to give Aunt Sue her gift. I went into my room, unzipped my suitcase, and there was the little treasure chest.

The lid creaked open on its hinges. Inside were small boxes, each gift-wrapped with a card and curling ribbon.

I found Aunt Sue's gift – *For Sue, with much love from Patrick and Lida,* said the notecard – and brought this back to the kitchen. Uncle Josh was frying eggs at the stove and Aunt Sue was setting out plates for breakfast. The boys were making coffee and toast. It was unusually quiet. Everyone turned when I entered the room, and then quickly went back to their task.

"Here it is," I told Aunt Sue.

Aunt Sue wiped her hands on her apron. "Thank you, Bronte," she said. She took the gift in a formal way, and hugged me. She set it on the table and regarded it. It looked very small.

"It's tiny," Connor announced.

"Hush," said Aunt Sue.

There was a hiss and sizzle from the frying pan. Uncle Josh wiped his forehead with the back of his hand, switched off the stove, and turned around to watch.

Aunt Sue pulled out a chair and sat down. She touched the notecard with her fingertips and ran her palm over the wrapping paper.

"Come on, then," Nicholas urged, and his brothers concurred.

So Aunt Sue opened the gift.

It was a small jar of honey.

"Honey," said Sebastian, and the other boys echoed him. "We've waited all this time and it's *honey*!"

"We've already *got* honey!" little Benji protested, dragging a jar out of the cupboard and holding it up.

"You can get honey at the grocery store!"

"Okay now, boys," Uncle Josh said. "That's enough." He stepped closer to Aunt Sue and squeezed her shoulder.

"It's honey from the hives of the Peppercorn Mountains," Aunt Sue whispered. "My favourite." Tears formed in her eyes and she smiled at me. "Your father used to love honey, Bronte. It's a Faery food, and he was always fascinated by Faeries. His best friend was a boy named Walter whom he met in nursery school, and Walter's family was Faery."

"I don't know any Faeries," I told her.

"Yes, they're rare. Anyway, that was when Patrick's interest started. I used to find him picture books about Faery lore, and read them to him as he fell asleep each night."

Her words dwindled as she spoke. I wanted to hear more, but right then, there was a knock on the kitchen door.

Aunt Sue wiped away the tears and opened the door. It turned out to be a telegram.

"It's from your Aunt Alys!" she said, a little proudly. "Wasn't I saying that I hear from her sometimes? She'll be wanting advice about Prince William again. He's ten now, but she still asks our views. Naughty corners, points systems, bedtime hours!"

"You'll get to meet William when you visit Aunt Alys," Nicholas told me. "You'll have to tame him."

"You'll be good at that, Bronte," Sebastian said confidently, and I wondered if I should be pleased or insulted.

Aunt Sue read the telegram, and her eyebrows leapt high on her forehead.

"Well, it *is* about William," she said. "But this time Alys says she's learned that pirates are coming to kidnap him! She asks what we think she should do." Aunt Sue stared around at us. "*I* don't know what she should do!"

"That is rather outside our area of expertise," Uncle Josh agreed.

We had a good chat about the problem, asking ourselves why pirates would want to kidnap Prince William, did they not know he was a handful? Ha-ha. Then we thought we shouldn't make jokes about it, as it was rather serious. At that point, everybody glanced towards me, and I remembered that my own parents had been killed by pirates.

You'd think that kind of thing would stay in my mind, and of course it *was* in my mind – only I was still seeing pirates in my old way, as almost-imaginary, adventure-story people with parrots on their shoulders, rather than the kind who shoot cannons at parents.

"I'm sure this will be sorted out long before you get there," Aunt Sue told me kindly.

"Probably just a false alarm," Connor put in.

In the end, we agreed that Aunt Sue should send back a telegram saying, OH, HOW DREADFUL! YOU POOR THINGS. STEP UP SECURITY IN THE PALACE. THINKING OF YOU, AND SENDING LOTS OF LOVE.

Later that day, the milk cart collected me at the end of the drive-way, ready to return me to the railway station. From there, I would take a train to Beenray and a ferry to Lantern Island.

"Young Bronte!" said the driver, tipping his hat as if I was an old friend.

Uncle Josh hoisted my suitcase onto the back of the cart, and Aunt Sue hugged me fiercely.

"You take very good care of yourself on this journey, will you not?" she said, sounding almost angry. "You are just a little girl, are you not?"

"I'm ten years old," I replied. "That's not so little."

She hugged me again, even more ferociously.

The boys all shook my hand and gave me friendly shoves or gentle kicks.

"I will write to you all!" I promised.

They seemed startled by this.

"We probably won't write back," Connor admitted after a moment. "Letter-writing's not really our thing."

"I can't even *write*," Benji said. "So it's definitely not my thing."

"Mine, neither," Nicholas and Sebastian said in unison.

"Pay no attention," Uncle Josh instructed me. "Of course they'll write back! I'll make them!"

"Try not to write too often," Nicholas urged.

Uncle Josh helped me into the cart and I sat up high looking down on them all.

"Will we ever see her again?" little Benjamin wondered.

"We'll see her at Aunt Franny's party at the end of her journey," Uncle Josh promised. "And later, I hope she will visit us again."

"She ought to," Sebastian said gruffly, "as she is our cousin."

"I will," I promised. "Goodbye, Aunt Sue, goodbye, Uncle Josh. Sebastian. Nicholas. Connor. Benjamin. Thank you for your kind hospitality."

"She's so polite!"

"And she did the name thing again!"

"Boys!" scolded Aunt Sue, then she shielded her eyes from the sun to look up at me. "And Bronte, listen," she called, suddenly urgent. "If you ever get a chance to try the oranges of the tiny Empire of Ricochet?"

"Yes?"

"Why, you must take it!"

"Aye, never miss an opportunity to try a Ricochet orange," the driver agreed, frowning slightly. "And why would you not?"

I told him about Aunt Sue saying I should never taste a Ricochet orange, as they spoil you for all other oranges.

At that, the driver laughed loudly, and then, still laughing, he twitched the reins and clicked at the horse, and away we went. The dogs barked and the boys ran alongside, kicking their football to each other as they did, waving and shouting at me, until eventually they grew tired and stopped.

 # Aunt Emma

14

A man was fishing from the wharf at Lantern Island when I arrived. There was a bucket at his feet, and beside that, a big knife, and he was smoking a cigarette. He watched me step off the ferry and set down my suitcase, and then he turned back to fishing.

"Thank you!" I called to the ferryman, but *he* was dragging the gangplank back onto the boat. There was a great clatter, and the ferry roared into reverse and away.

The water rolled and churned. Bright white lines of foam faded. Quiet settled. The wharf was just a wooden plank, swaying on the tide, slick with damp and algae.

There was no sign of my Aunt Emma.

I sat on my suitcase. The man fished. Birds remarked on this and that to one another.

After a while, I took out the packet of food that Aunt Sue had prepared for me that morning.

Cheese and pickle sandwiches and an apple. I ate these happily. The apple crunched.

The man lit another cigarette. He slapped a mosquito. He was a shortish man with crinkled grey hair and squinting eyes, and his arms were thick and muscular. He made a slight noise, and I saw his shoulders tense as he leaned over his rod, then he made another noise, this time disappointed, and relaxed again.

Across the water was another dark green island.

"What's that island called?" I asked the man.

"Tuttlecock," he replied, and then, as if our words had made this happen, a little boat emerged from around the side of Tuttlecock Island. A woman was rowing the boat in a strong, sturdy way, like somebody in a hurry. She wore a scarf and enormous sunglasses.

I breathed out. Here at last was Aunt Emma.

Perhaps she had been gathering colours at that island and forgotten the time? My Aunt Emma is an artist – she sends me paintings for my birthday every year – and I know that she likes to extract colour from plants, leaves, flowers, and stones.

Back when she first learned that I was coming to visit her on my journey, she telegrammed to say she was *very* excited to meet me at last, and she planned to paint my *portrait* while I was here, and would I please bring her a *very* small handful of those pebbles you find around the roots of the flowering movay trees in Gainsleigh Harbour? Since these make the most *marvellous* pinks, but *only* if there was room in my luggage, and she could not *wait* to meet me and we would have a *lovely* time together, dear child, *so much* love, your affectionate Aunt Emma.

"Oh, *Emma*," Aunt Isabelle had scolded, reading this telegram. "Do you think we have *time* to be gathering pebbles?!" Aunt Isabelle is the eldest sister in the family and becomes very bossy when she talks about the other aunts. But then she smiled and told me that Emma had not stopped painting since she was a babbling toddler. "She'd make art out of the peas on her plate and her mashed potato," Isabelle had said. "Out of her hair ribbons and the buckles on her shoes." She'd looked at the clock, said: "Get your coat, Bronte!" and we'd rushed to Gainsleigh Harbour to collect pebbles. These were now packed in a drawstring bag in my suitcase.

The rowboat was drawing closer. Ripples ran towards the wharf. The splash and swish of the oars were quite clear. I stood up and smiled, and Aunt Emma smiled back at me. The fishing man touched a finger to his cap, and Aunt Emma nodded.

The boat was so close now I could hear her breathing and her little grunts of effort.

I took a step forward. Was I supposed to help her tie the boat to the wharf?

The oars hit the water: *splash, whir, splash, whir.* Aunt Emma panted. The boat bumped against a pylon. Aunt Emma used an oar to push it away. She gave a great shove, her head down. She tucked the oars back into their rings, and set to rowing again. The boat slid across the water's surface and past the wharf. On it went, skirting the shore.

There was a tiny grassy beach not far from the wharf. Was Aunt Emma planning to stop there instead?

The boat slid past the little beach.

On it went, Aunt Emma rowing hard, leaning forward and back, her scarf swishing about, and there she went, hugging the coast of the island, around the curve, and around the curve, and then she was gone.

I stood and stared.

The man continued fishing.

"Where's she gone?" I asked.

The man startled. He turned to me. "Where's who gone?" he said.

"Aunt Emma!"

The man frowned. "Aunt Emma? Who's Aunt Emma?"

"That was Aunt Emma in the boat!" I said. Then I blinked. "Wasn't it?"

"In the boat that just went by?"

"Yes!" I said impatiently.

"That wasn't Aunt Emma," he said. "That was Sugar Rixel."

"Sugar Rixel?!"

The man nodded. "Yes. That was Sugar Rixel." He smiled to himself at the thought.

"What sort of a name is that?" I demanded.

"It's *her* sort of a name!" the man countered.

I turned around and looked at the stone steps leading to the woods.

"In that case," I asked, "where is Aunt Emma?"

"Where *is* Aunt Emma?" The man grinned, as if this were a game.

I remembered myself. "Bronte," I said politely, and held out my hand. "How do you do?"

He shook my hand. "Barnabas," he declared. "And I do all right. How about yourself?"

"Well, thank you," I replied. "But I am wondering about my Aunt Emma. Emma Mettlestone is her proper name. Do you know her, perhaps?"

Barnabas's face changed completely. His smile washed away and his jowls drooped.

"Emma Mettlestone?" he repeated hoarsely. "She's your *aunt?*"

"She is," I said.

"And you're her ... niece?"

I saw no reason to reply to this.

He set down his fishing rod. "You're the niece that was coming to visit her?"

I nodded firmly.

"So nobody has let you know?"

"Let me know what?"

"Your Aunt Emma," said Barnabas, grim and grey, "is in prison!"

15

Prison!

I threw open my suitcase, grabbed my parents' instructions, and riffled through the pages. But there was not a single word about what to do if one of the aunts was in prison.

I knew there wouldn't be, actually. I'd have remembered reading that.

Barnabas watched as I flicked pages back and forth, shook them violently, then crammed them back into my suitcase and closed it up.

I tapped my forehead with two fingers. This is what Aunt Isabelle does when she is trying to think. It didn't help. It only made my thoughts jump more violently.

"Will the ferry come again?" I asked.

"Not today. That was the last one."

I looked up at the steep steps. "Is there a post office? Where I might send a telegram to Aunt Isabelle?"

"Aunt *Isabelle*?" Barnabas smiled broadly. "I thought you wanted Aunt Emma!" He seemed relieved to be joking about aunts again.

"I *do* want Aunt Emma," I shouted. "But you just told me she's in *prison*! Aunt *Isabelle* is *not* in prison. At least as far as I know! Is she?"

Barnabas looked frightened again. "I don't know," he confessed.

"I don't know any Aunt Isabelle." He glanced back at the rod. I could tell he wanted to return to fishing.

A thought occurred to me.

"Why?" I said.

"Well, I've never met anyone named Isabelle, and so," he began, then paused. "I tell a lie. I *did* meet an Isabelle once. I was seven at the time. She came to my school in the second grade and she had a rag doll that she clutched under her arm all the time – like so – and she chewed on the doll's hair. I found that fascinating. How did it taste? I've never heard of her since, but she *might* have grown up to become an aunt and so I could know an Aunt Isabelle. I apologize."

I stared at him. "Not that!" I said. "Why is my Aunt Emma in prison?"

"Oh. She stole a pepper grinder."

"A pepper grinder!" I said. "From a shop?"

"From Sugar Rixel."

"The woman who just rowed by? With the scarf and sunglasses?"

"That's the one." Barnabas nodded. "They're friends."

I was already angry with Sugar Rixel for rowing by the wharf and not being Aunt Emma. But now!

"That's not fair! She sent her friend to prison for taking a pepper grinder? Aunt Emma probably just wanted to *borrow* it for a minute! To grind some pepper onto a slice of tomato or something! She probably tried to give it back but Sugar Rixel was rowing about the place so madly she couldn't *catch* her! Tell Sugar Rixel to stop rowing and stay *still*!"

Barnabas rocked back and forth on his boots. He shook his head slowly. "This pepper grinder," he said, "had sentimental value."

I gave him a look.

"It did!" he said. "Sugar Rixel got it from a water sprite, you see. She found him – the water sprite – washed up on the shore after a sword fight with his brother, and she carted him up to her house in a wheelbarrow. She put him in the laundry tub, sewed up his cuts, iced his sprains, gave him ginger tea for his headache, and generally took care of him until he got well. To thank her, the water sprite gave her the pepper grinder."

I still glared, but actually I could see that a pepper grinder that was a gift from a water sprite would be rather special. "Hmph," I said.

Water plashed against the wharf. The birds twittered and the frogs made their annoying sounds. Barnabas took one quick step towards his fishing rod, but I fixed my gaze on him and he stepped back again.

"I wonder," I said aloud. Barnabas waited obediently. My parents' instructions only said I had to stay in Aunt Emma's house for three days. They didn't say Aunt Emma had to *be* there.

"I wonder," I repeated, "if I might stay in Emma's house alone for a few days? I mean, is this island quite safe?"

Barnabas lit up at the idea. "Perfectly safe! Well, apart from robbers who steal pepper grinders, but she's in prison now so we're all good."

"Ha," I said coldly.

Barnabas looked remorseful. "Sorry. Just trying to lighten the mood. But yes, it's very safe here. None of your Dark Mages ever sighted here – not even a Sterling Silver Fox – and certainly never a Whisperer. Emma's place is just up the path, the cottage on the left. She always keeps it neat and tidy as a pin, so you'll find everything you need all right. The spare key's under the cushion on the porch swing."

How did he know where she kept her spare key?

"I live in the next house down from her," Barnabas explained. "Your Aunt Emma and I water the houseplants when either of us is on holiday. Or in prison," he added thoughtfully. "There'll be plenty of food for you. Emma was stocking up for your visit. She was *very* excited you were coming, you know."

I took a moment to be sad about this, but then cheered up. Perhaps Aunt Emma would not be in prison for long? It *was* just a pepper grinder, even if it did have sentimental value. She might be out tomorrow! I could wait for her!

"How long will she be in prison?" I asked.

"Fifteen years," said Barnabas.

"Oh," I said. "I couldn't wait that long."

"No. You'd get hungry. She didn't stock the pantry *that* well."

I nodded. "Plus, if I don't leave in three days, my hometown will be torn to pieces, of course."

"Of course," agreed Barnabas, and then he blinked. "It will?"

"Fifteen years!" I said, ignoring him. "They must be very strict about pepper grinders with sentimental value around these parts."

Barnabas tugged on his ear. "Well, it's also the kind of pepper grinder that grinds out gold dust," he said. "I forgot to mention that. That might be relevant."

"It might."

"It's an unexpected thing, the gold dust. One moment, you'll be grinding pepper, and the next? Here comes the gold! Water sprite magic, you see. You have to keep an eye on it or you end up with gold dust in your teeth."

"Sounds a nuisance," I said.

"Sometimes," he agreed. "Especially if it goes right back to pepper so you only get a tiny sprinkle of gold and you've got to sift it out and you think, *Well, is this worth the effort?* But sometimes the gold dust just keeps coming! Sugar got a bucketful once! She bought a piano."

I sighed.

Then, once again, I rallied.

I could still follow my parents' instructions. Stay at Aunt Emma's house and visit her in prison, on the third day, to give her my parents' gift! Only, was the prison far away?

"It's more a jailhouse," Barnabas told me, "than a prison. Well, to be quite frank, it's just the back room of the police station. Go up these stairs, walk down Main Street, past the ice-cream parlour, the wishing well, the library, and there it is on your right. You can't miss it. A five-minute walk."

"So close!" I said.

"On Lantern Island," Barnabas said, "everything's a five-minute walk."

At that moment, a wonderful idea occurred to me.

"I know what I'm going to do!" I said.

"What?" Barnabas returned my smile.

I picked up my suitcase and nodded at him. "You'll see," I said. "I have no idea why Aunt Emma had to go and steal her friend's pepper grinder, but at least I got to meet you, Barnabas. It's been a pleasure."

"It has!" he agreed.

We shook hands again, and I set off up the stairs.

"As for why she stole it," Barnabas called after me. "I'll bet she wanted to use the gold dust for *colour*, in a very special painting."

I paused and turned back. "A very special painting?"

"She's been in a red phase for a while," he said. "But she said she was going to break out of that to paint a portrait of her niece!" He stopped, realizing. "A portrait of you!"

I swung back around, lifted my suitcase higher, and hurried up the steps.

16

"I am here to bail out my Aunt Emma!" I cried.

I set my suitcase on the police station floor, unzipped it, and took out my sack of silver. This, I dumped on the counter. It jangled.

Behind the counter, an elderly man in uniform glanced up at me. He was writing. He carried on writing for a moment and then, slowly, placed his pen behind his ear and stood. He had soft white hair and a matching soft white moustache, all neatly combed. His nose was quite enormous. The nostrils flared now as he rested his arms on the counter and looked down at my linen sack.

"There's a hundred silver coins in there," I told him. "My parents gave them to me to cover expenses on my journey."

The old man studied the sack awhile. He looked up at the ceiling and blinked.

"When you say *Aunt Emma*," he said, "I take it you mean Emma Mettlestone?"

"I do."

"She is your aunt?"

People on this island seemed a bit slow on the uptake when it came to aunts. "Yes," I said. "I am her niece. My name is Bronte Mettlestone."

"And you're here to bail her out?"

"As quickly as possible, please."

The old man sniffed.

"Where did you get the idea," he said, leaning over his arms, "that you could bail her out?"

"It is a great idea, isn't it?" I agreed. "I was just on the wharf talking to Barnabas. He was fishing there. Do you know Barnabas?"

The old man gave a slow nod. "I do."

"Anyway, I suddenly remembered that you bail people out of prison! You just go to the front desk and hand over money, and you come out a little later with the prisoner, and you both look very serious. You shake your head and scold them and tell them this has got to be the last time."

"Uh-huh," said the old man.

"I know this from the cinema," I explained. "My Aunt Isabelle and I go there every other Saturday afternoon."

The old man looked interested at that. "The cinema, eh? Never been myself, but I hear it's a cracker."

"It is," I said. "Sometimes. Other times, it's exciting rather than funny. And once we saw a film that made both Aunt Isabelle and me cry all the way home. The Butler baked us chocolate scrolls to cheer us up."

The old man lowered himself back into his chair. I stood on tippy toes so I could see him. He was writing again. A name plate on his desk read **CHIEF DETECTIVE RILEY**.

"Are you Chief Detective Riley?" I asked.

He grunted and carried on writing.

"So?" I said. "Chief Detective Riley? May I bail her out?"

"No," he said. "You may not."

There was a long pause. Outside, children were playing, and a woman was speaking sternly to a dog.

Chief Detective Riley opened a drawer. He took out a pale-coloured folder. Very slowly, he stood again, placed this folder onto the counter, and opened it. He nudged my sack of silver along the counter to make room.

"This is the file on your Aunt Emma," he said.

"There's a file!"

"Yes," he said. "There's always a file when a person is convicted of a crime." He took a stack of photographs from the folder and spread these along the counter.

The first photo showed a wooden cottage set amongst fir trees, smoke rising from its chimney.

"This," said the chief detective, pointing, "is Sugar Rixel's cottage."

"It's lovely," I said.

The second photo showed the window of the cottage, open wide.

"This," he said, "is where the thief entered the cottage."

"Sensible," I said.

Chief Detective Riley looked at me.

"To use a window that's already open," I explained. "Rather than smashing one? That, at least, must be in Aunt Emma's favour."

He shook his head as if having a conversation with himself. "See this?" he said, pointing at the window ledge in the photo.

I peered closer. Smears of red stained the ledge, ants crawling all over them. "Blood!"

"No," he said. "It's the crimson sap of the tehassifer tree."

"Phew," I said, and he frowned.

The third photo showed a bookcase. It was smeared with the same red, ants everywhere again.

"And this is where the pepper grinder *used* to stand," he said, "before it was stolen."

"Sugar Rixel kept her pepper grinder on her bookcase?"

"She did."

"Strange."

The old man's brows became ferocious. "Sugar Rixel may keep her pepper grinder *anywhere she pleases*!"

"All right," I said. "Don't get in a twist about it."

The fourth, fifth, and sixth photos were all of paintings hanging on various walls. They didn't seem to fit into the story at all.

"Very pretty," I said, to be polite.

"It is *not relevant*," growled the chief detective, "that they are *pretty*. Look at the *colours* in these paintings!"

I looked again. The paintings were abstract – dashes, lines, and splatters – and every one was painted in red.

"These were all painted by your Aunt Emma," the chief detective told me. "She has, for the last two years, been favouring red."

I nodded. "Barnabas told me she was in a red phase."

The seventh photo was a pair of woman's hands, stained red.

"These," the chief detective said, "are your Aunt Emma's hands. On the day of the robbery."

"Hm," I said. "That doesn't look good."

"Caught red-handed," he pronounced.

I thought about this.

"But aren't there *other* artists living on the island who are *also* in red phases? So *they* might have had red hands that day and left red paint everywhere when *they* stole the pepper grinder?"

"No," he said. "Only your Aunt Emma is in a red phase. Three tehassifer trees grow right behind her cottage – the only ones on the island – and she uses the crimson sap for her paintings. She gets all the shades of red she needs from that sap."

"Oh."

"Caught red-handed," he repeated.

"Yes, yes," I said. "I get it."

The final photo was a close-up of the woman I'd seen rowing the boat: Sugar Rixel. Her eyes were downcast.

"Here is the victim of the crime," he said, "looking very sad."

"She does look sad," I agreed.

"Missing her pepper grinder," he added.

"Oh, all right," I said impatiently.

With one swoop, Chief Detective Riley gathered up all the photos, slid them back into the file, and closed it. It was very smooth, the way he did that, and reminded me of how my Aunt Isabelle and the Butler play cards sometimes. They can both shuffle cards like nobody's business.

Chief Detective Riley sat down again. "That," he said, from his seat, "is the evidence we used to convict your Aunt Emma of the crime." He sounded proud.

There was a pause.

"That, and the fact that she confessed." Now he sounded grumpy. I saw why. All that detective work and she goes and admits she's done it anyway.

I leaned over the counter again so I could see him.

"All right," I said. "But now I'd like to bail her out."

The old man rested his forehead on his fist, and raised his eyes up at me.

"Bronte," he said. "The trial has already *happened*. Yesterday, when the circuit judge came to the island. And the prisoner has been *sentenced* to fifteen years. There's nothing that a sack of silver can do."

"Nothing?"

"Nothing."

I looked at the sack. It seemed impossible that there was nothing a sack of silver coins could do.

"Who's in charge here?" I asked. "I'd like to speak to the manager."

"*I'm* in charge," he said.

"And Aunt Emma is locked up here?"

Chief Detective Riley looked over his shoulder. "Down the hall there," he said. "In a cell."

"Have you got the key?" I asked.

"Of course."

"So you could go down the hall and open her cell," I said, "any time you liked?"

He grunted.

"In that case" – I pointed to the sack of coins – "I will give *you* this sack of silver coins, and you can let her out!"

Chief Detective Riley studied the sack of coins. He studied my face.

"Think what you could buy with a sack of coins!" I urged him. "Meanwhile, Aunt Emma can go on the run. She can give me the pepper grinder and I can use the gold to carry on with my journey."

He tilted his head.

"Maybe do it quite quickly?" I suggested. "Before anybody else comes in."

The chief detective opened a different drawer. Looking for the key, I guessed. But instead he drew out a thick book and began to flick through it. Pages sprang back and forth. Eventually, he placed the open book on the counter and held his finger at a line.

I looked at him. He did not speak, but tapped the line again.

Sighing, I leaned forward and read it. This is what it said:

Criminal Code - Section 189

If a person offers, promises, or gives financial or other advantage to an Officer of the Law, intending to induce the Officer of the Law to perform an improper activity, that person shall be guilty of the offense of bribery.

Penalty: 10 years' imprisonment.

17

"Hm," I said.

My legs felt wobbly. My heart had become terribly busy, as if it had suddenly remembered just how much it had to beat.

"Are you an Officer?" I whispered. I cleared my throat. "Of the Law?"

"I am," Chief Detective Riley confirmed.

"And if I offered you silver coins," I said, "that would be a bit like ... offering you ... a bribe?"

"That's not what it would be like," he said promptly. "That's what it would *be*."

I looked at him. My eyes fell down to the book.

Ten years' imprisonment, it said.

"Do you want to put those coins away?" the chief detective suggested.

"All right."

"Do you want to withdraw the offer you just made?" he suggested next.

I blinked at him. "What offer?" I said. "I never made an offer."

Chief Detective Riley kept his gaze on me. "Good girl," he said at last.

My heart was still rushing around trying to catch up on all its forgotten beating, but I put my sack of coins back in my suitcase, smoothed down my skirt, and stood again.

"May I *visit* my Aunt Emma?" I asked, with dignity.

But Chief Detective Riley frowned at me suddenly. "Why did you say you'd take the pepper grinder with you?" he said. "Have *you* got Sugar Rixel's pepper grinder?"

"Why, no!" I said. "Aunt Emma has it, doesn't she? I only thought she'd lend it to me."

"What makes you think your Aunt Emma can do whatever she likes with Sugar Rixel's pepper grinder?"

I sighed. This man and his questions.

"Well," I said carefully. "She *stole* it, so it's *hers* now."

"It's not *hers*! It's Sugar Rixel's!"

"That can't be right," I said. "Aunt Emma is giving fifteen years in prison. She must get the pepper grinder in return. Otherwise, she's got nothing out of this bargain."

"It's not a bargain! It's the law!"

We glared at each other for a while. A clock ticked.

Chief Detective Riley frowned more deeply. "Actually, Emma refuses to tell us where she's hidden the grinder. I turned her cottage upside down, I'm here to tell you, but it's nowhere to be found."

"Well," I said, "that's something," which was a mistake, because Chief Detective Riley growled, "We will *find* that pepper grinder, I am *here* to tell you, young lady!"

I don't like to be called "young lady".

I lifted my chin. "I would like to visit my Aunt Emma, and say hello."

The chief detective shook his head. "Visiting hours are Saturdays, two to four."

"Saturday! But it's only Tuesday!"

He shrugged.

"I *must* give her a gift from my treasure chest," I told him, "in exactly three days! It's Faery cross-stitched!"

"Faery cross-stitch?" He raised his eyebrows.

"Yes!"

"Ah, well."

"And I'd like to see if she needs anything," I added, this occurring to me as something Aunt Isabelle might say. "I could check that she has enough paints and brushes and paper."

The chief detective leaned his elbows on the counter. "What makes you think she's painting back there?"

I stared at him. Of course she was painting. Aunt Emma did nothing *but* paint.

"No painting allowed," he told me firmly. "She must simply sit and think about what she's done."

My face gave a strange twist. Out of nowhere, I was going to cry!

I grabbed my suitcase, almost tipping to the floor with its weight, spun around, and ran out of the station.

18

The key was under the cushion on the porch swing, just as Barnabas had promised.

At first, when I opened the door, the cottage seemed very noisy.

But that was the sound of me panting — I had run all the way from the police station.

Next, the cottage seemed to be a complete and total shambles.

One big room, a row of windows at the back, and I honestly could not see how anyone could get *across* to those windows to close the drapes.

No pathway. Just a jumble of upside-down chairs, upturned drawers, scattered paintings, books, buckets, cups, brushes, ink pots, easels, hats, petals, and tins lying on their sides and spilling paint. Mostly red.

An upright piano stood in the middle of all this, but it was draped in boots, canisters, and tangled fairy lights, as if the piano was a very young child trying to play hide-and-seek.

In the opposite corner of the room, every cupboard and drawer in a kitchenette was wide open. Cutlery and crockery were helter-skelter in the sink; maple syrup ran in a stream to the floor from an upturned jar.

Across from the kitchenette stood a four-poster bed, its sheets and blankets wound around its posts.

"How does Aunt Emma *live* like this?" I wondered aloud.

She doesn't *live like this*, I answered myself slowly.

"I turned her cottage upside down," Chief Detective Riley had said proudly.

He had done this! Searching for the pepper grinder! Him and his giant nose and his frowns and all that standing, sitting, standing, and *what makes you think* and *young lady* and jabbing at things with his fingers! *"I turned her cottage upside down, I'm here to tell you."*

I was furious!

In fifteen years, when she got out of prison, my Aunt Emma would be so excited about coming home to her little cottage! She would run down the path and throw open her door! And what would she find? Chaos! Her heart would sink like an anchor! Actually, by then the place would be overrun with rats. More! The cottage would be a wildlife reserve! Possums in the pantry! A pony sleeping in her bed! An elephant standing in her bathtub!

That last part cheered me up a bit. A pony and an elephant. She might like those.

But then I remembered Barnabas telling me Aunt Emma keeps her cottage *"neat and tidy as a pin"*.

"And look at it now!" I cried. Nothing like a pin.

I took a deep breath. Through the windows across the room, I could see the darkening shapes of trees. It was late afternoon.

"Right," I said, and I got to work.

Hours later, I climbed into Aunt Emma's freshly-made four-poster bed. The floor was swept clean. Chairs stood around the table. Clothes were folded into the drawers. The kitchen things were washed and put away, the piano was pushed against the wall (luckily, it had wheels), the fairy lights were strung around the front door, the cracked easel leaned against the wall, and the paintings were hanging on hooks.

I might have put things in wrong places, but at least they were put. The floor was still streaked in red paint, and the rugs were still sticky with spilled syrup, but tomorrow I would find a scrubbing brush and get to work on these.

"What makes you think, Chief Detective Riley," I said aloud, "that it's okay to upturn a jar of maple syrup and walk syrup footprints everywhere?"

I blew out the lamp and fell asleep.

19

The moment I woke up, I panicked.

Aunt Emma was in prison! Detective Riley would not let me visit! And somehow I *had* to get the gift to her!

Well, I would have to break into prison.

Maybe I could smash the prison window? I gazed around Aunt Emma's cottage, looking for a rock.

Of course, I couldn't see one.

But at least the cottage looked tidy. As neat as a pin.

Or was it? How neat was a pin anyway?

I would look for a pin to compare, I decided. Did Aunt Emma have a sewing basket somewhere? I began opening cupboards and drawers.

There was a strange, crawling sensation at the edges of my vision. I kept rubbing my eyes to make it go away.

I knelt down and rifled through a drawer. As it was full of socks and stockings, a pin did not seem likely. I looked anyway. Carefully, in case the pin pricked my finger. But that scribbling feeling was still there in the corner of my eye. I could not concentrate!

I stepped towards the piano stool and my foot landed on something sticky.

Maple syrup, all over the rugs, of course. I'd forgotten that.

I looked down and there it was: the scribbling sensation.

Ants.

Each patch of maple syrup swarmed with them. Trails ran to and from the syrup patches. Ants hurrying to spread the word, I guessed. They skirted around the splashes of gluggy red paint.

Well, back to looking for a pin.

I wish I were an ant, I thought tearfully as I lifted the lid of the piano stool. *I could be eating maple syrup rather than looking for pins in piano stools.*

I stopped still. What exactly *was* I doing? Aunt Emma was in prison, the cross-stitch would be broken, and I was looking for pins? Crying about ants?

I was mad!

Then I realized that I'd been so busy cleaning, I'd forgotten to eat last night. I was *starving*. I often lose my mind when I don't eat.

I took breakfast out onto the porch at the back of the house. Toast with strawberry jam. There were bushes and trees, pieces of ocean in the gaps between, birds shouting at each other, and frogs croaking.

In the middle of the garden, three spindly trees stood in a row like a family. As I gazed at these trees, the sun swung its light onto them.

Hm, I thought.

I stood up and stepped over the dried bark and pebbles to the trees. Up close, you could see lines and patches of sap, some fine strands, some thick and bubbled, all in shades of red. These must be the crimson tehassifer trees. The sap was what Aunt Emma used for paint. I stared at these for a while and then I did something strange.

I went to the library.

Down the lane to Main Street I walked, past the ice-cream parlour and wishing well, and into the library.

It had flat green carpet and white walls. People wandered amongst the shelves or stood frowning at books.

At the front desk, the librarian beamed.

"A child!" she exclaimed.

I looked over my shoulder quickly. "Where?"

"You!" Her voice was full of vim. People turned to stare. "Oh, I love to have a child in my library! I've just finished redecorating the children's section, so this is perfect, dear child! Trust me! You are going to *love* it!"

She popped up from her chair, placed a hand on my shoulder, swivelled me around, and pointed.

CHILDREN'S BOOKS! cried a banner in the corner of the library. Below this were brightly-coloured bean bags, stuffed caterpillars, and a rocking horse.

"It does look very nice," I agreed.

"Go over at once!" she urged. "Sit on a caterpillar while you read!"

I was a bit dismayed. "Well," I said. "Thank you ... But may I look something up instead?"

"Research!" the librarian shrieked, and inside the library people cleared their throats. One woman shot a cranky *Shhhh!* in our direction.

The librarian looked guilty. "I make too much noise," she confided. "But I *love* it when people want to research! Do it! Dear child, you will *love* it! The catalogue is over there!" Her voice rose to a shout at the end. People muttered disapproval.

I found a great stack of books on the subject that I wanted, and sat down to read.

Now, I don't know about you, but I like a book to tell a story. These books did not. They told *about* things. It's true that this is what I needed them to do, and yet honestly. Did they have to? "Oh, just *stop*, you insufferable bore!" I murmured to the authors. (This is what Aunt Isabelle says to visitors who are being dull. They usually take it as a joke, but she is deadly serious.)

Also, I couldn't find what I hoped to find. So there I was, turning pages, turning pages, looking up to sigh. I let my forehead thunk against the table. There were three books left in my stack, but I only wanted to punch them.

I was done.

"Here," said a voice. I jumped. It was the librarian. She placed a glass of milk and a plate of cookies on the table. "Enjoy!"

I stared up at her, amazed.

"You're allowed to *eat* in the library?" I whispered.

"Oh, certainly not!" the librarian cried. "But rules make me so *mad* sometimes. Do you know what I mean? Just brush the crumbs off the pages, dear child," she advised.

"Thank you," I said.

The librarian saluted and hurried back to her desk.

I drank some milk. I took a bite of a cookie. It was chocolate chip.

Well, I thought, *might as well look at a book while I'm eating.*

I opened the next book.

And guess what?

There it was. Exactly what I wanted.

"Ha!" I cried.

"Hush!" hissed a woman at a nearby shelf, but across the room, the librarian gave me a double thumbs-up.

20

Sugar Rixel's cottage was only five minutes from the library. The librarian explained how to get there.

It looked bigger than it had in the photograph. But that was to be expected. Photographs are small.

I pounded on the door with my fists, then banged with my palms.

"Gracious!" came a voice from inside, and the door flew open.

Sugar Rixel blinked down at me. She was wearing an artist's smock that was splattered with colour, and her hair was falling out of its bun.

"My name is Bronte Mettlestone," I announced. "I am the niece—"

"Oh, you're the niece!" Sugar Rixel's face leapt from its startled expression into a beam, and her arms jumped into the air. "The child I saw on the ferry wharf! Of course! It is you! I should have realized! Come in, little one! Come in!" And she wrapped me in a hug, which actually *lifted* me from the ground, and then she swung me through the door and into the cottage.

I stepped back from her.

"Emma was so excited you were coming! As was I, for Emma is my favourite person in the world. I love many people, dear child, but I love your Aunt Emma most of all!"

I frowned. "It is good to love many people," I declared. "But it is not good to send those people to prison."

"No," she agreed, her smile vanishing. "It's awful. Dreadful. Would you like a glass of water?"

Refusing to be flummoxed, I looked around the cottage. An easel stood in the middle of the room, a half-finished painting of daisies clipped to it. On the floor beside this lay a plate of buttered toast.

"You'll step on that toast," I warned her, "if you're not careful."

"Yes," she said. "I do that *all* the time. Always got butter on my feet!"

Again I did not let myself be distracted even though now I wanted to look at her feet. But there it was! The bookcase from the photograph. The top shelf was still streaked with red paint, a few ants wandering around the red.

"This," I said, pointing, "is where you kept your pepper grinder?"

"Why, yes!" She seemed impressed. She was beside me now, handing me a glass of water. We both gazed at the rows of books on the other shelves.

"Why did you keep a pepper grinder on a bookcase?" I asked, suddenly annoyed about this.

"Oh, well, you see these books? They all belonged to my father. They have peculiar, magical properties."

"All books have magical properties," I told her sternly. (My governess is always telling me this, but in a dreamy voice.)

"No – well, *yes*, of course. But these ones are Faery books! If you are ever at a loss for words, you simply open a book, tip it upside down, and give a good shake. The words you need will sprinkle out."

I looked up at her, very interested.

"Really?" I said.

"Absolutely. And the pepper grinder sprinkled out gold, you see, so they were like cousins! The books and the grinder? Does that make sense?"

"I suppose," I began, but then I shook myself hard. "Stop trying to distract me!" I said.

"Oh, I *am* sorry," she said. "What was it you wanted, precisely?"

"This!" I said, and I took a step closer to the shelf.

I was trembling.

What if I was wrong?

What if it didn't work?

I looked at the glass of water in my hand. I looked at the bookcase.

Then I tipped the water all over the top shelf.

21

"*So* unexpected!" Sugar Rixel breathed.

"Hush," I told her. I was trembling violently now.

"Might I just get a couple of towels?" she asked.

"Wait," I said.

"It's just, I'd rather the water didn't spill onto the next shelves down and damage the books?"

"In a moment," I whispered.

And then it happened. The patches of red began to shrivel and then spread across the shelf. As they did this, they faded to a quieter, softer red.

Then, almost at once, they became deep pink.

A cheerful pink.

Pale pink.

White.

"This is fascinating!" Sugar Rixel exclaimed.

"Wait, wait," I said through gritted teeth.

Pale green.

Pale blue.

Blue.

Blue.

Still blue.

"*There!*" I said.

"Where?"

"It's not the crimson sap of the tehassifer tree!" I shouted wildly. "It's the blue oil of katamanchi kelp!"

Now an interesting thing happened to Sugar Rixel's face. It was a lot like the paint actually: her face seemed to shrivel then expand while different colours rose and faded on her cheeks.

Eventually, she looked straight at me. Her face was white now. She spoke in a hoarse voice: "The katamanchi kelp?"

"Yes!" I said. "In the ocean, it's blue, but if you take it out, it dries to red. You only have to splash water on it for it to go back to blue!"

Sugar Rixel gazed at the shelf. Absentmindedly, she began to mop up the spilling water with the edges of her smock.

"I got the idea from the syrup," I told her.

"The syrup," Sugar Rixel repeated politely.

"There were ants on the *syrup* at Aunt Emma's cottage, but none on the red paint. None on the sap of the trees outside either. But in the photos of your bookcase and your window ledge? Ants all over the red."

Sugar Rixel nodded vaguely, but I could tell she wasn't listening.

"So I went to the library to see if any other plants made a red paint. And there it was. Katamanchi kelp."

"Katamanchi kelp," Sugar Rixel said, in a strange voice, "grows only in the ocean, doesn't it?"

"Yes."

"In fact, it grows only in the secret forests of the water sprites." She was whispering now, almost to herself. "None who walks upon land may enter the secret forests."

"Exactly." I was impressed that she knew this. I had read it all in the book in the library just now. "Ants *love* the oil of katamanchi kelp," I added, hoping this at least was something she did not know. "They lap it up." I'd read that too.

Sugar wrung out her smock so that water dripped to the floor.

"It was the water sprite," she said in a voice of wonder. "He must have come and got his pepper grinder back."

"That's what I was thinking."

"I am astonished," Sugar said after a moment, quite forcefully, "that he would retrieve a gift."

"It does seem a bit rude," I agreed.

Sugar Rixel sighed. "Well," she said. "Perhaps it is a cultural thing. In the secret forests of the water sprites, maybe it is considered *good* manners to come and fetch your gifts back when you want them?"

"Maybe," I said, and then I was cross. She was always distracting me. "But the point is, Sugar Rixel, it was *not* my Aunt Emma who stole your pepper grinder!"

"It was not!" she agreed fiercely.

"And yet you have thrown her into prison!"

"Me?" Astonishment flew onto her face. "No, no, child! Not

me! I only *reported* the theft of the pepper grinder! I was very upset about it. It had sentimental value, you see, and the gold dust came in *so* handy. So Chief Detective Riley came and did his detective work with his magnifying glass and his camera and he was so excited about it! He loves detective work. And next thing you know, my dear *Emma* had been arrested!"

"You should have called the whole thing off right then," I told her.

"I tried! But Chief Detective Riley said it was out of my hands now, that the *law* had been set in motion, and none could stand before its churning wheels, and before you knew it, the circuit judge was here and they were locking dear Emma away!"

"He's a dreadful man," I said, "that Chief Detective Riley."

Sugar Rixel clicked her teeth. "Well, yes and no," she said. "He can be a real grump, but he's my godfather, you see, and he promised to take care of me when my father died, and he takes that responsibility *so* seriously! He knew I loved my pepper grinder."

"Hmph," I said.

Sugar Rixel fixed me with an earnest look. "Dear child, I have been so distressed about Emma! My tears have flown every which way!" She flung her hands around, demonstrating the direction of her tears. "And when I haven't been weeping, I've been rowing about, gathering the materials I need for a jailbreak."

For the first time, I was struck silent.

She nodded vigorously. "Yes, I'm planning to bust her out of there," she told me. "I've got ropes and disguises and crowbars. She can't stay! She can't *live* without her painting! Remember when I saw you on the ferry wharf yesterday? I was on my way to Carafkwa Island to get some expert advice on jailbreaks. They have a marvellous criminal element on Carafkwa. They were so helpful. Some of them have even worked with the great Gustav Spectaculo! You've heard of him, of course?"

"Of course," I agreed. Everyone knows the tales of Gustav Spectaculo. He was a master criminal. For years, he was pursued by a master spy known as The Scorpion. But when she caught him, she didn't put him in prison. She talked him into becoming her partner, and well-behaved. Together, they headed up the Anti-Pirate League, which did important work during the Whispering Wars, when the Whispering Kingdom, along with their pirate friends, tried to conquer all the kingdoms and the empires. But they retired when the peace treaty was signed.

"Anyway," Sugar continued. "One of the criminals offered me a gun in exchange for a painting of daisies. Hence!" She waved her hand at the easel. "The daisies."

"But a gun!"

"I thought it might be handy. The criminal element agreed. *Brilliant idea*, they said. Do you not think so, Bronte?"

"Well!" I began. Was a gun a brilliant idea when you were breaking somebody out of jail? I tried to give some thought to my answer, weighing up the pros and cons, but then I shook myself and cried: "Who *cares* if it would have been handy! Guns are *dangerous*!"

"But Detective Riley would have shot at me if I tried to break Emma out of jail. No question. So it would make sense to have a gun to shoot *back*."

"Detective Riley is a dreadful man," I said again.

"Yes, you said that but, as *I* said, he's my godfather and he's always so protective of me."

"You just said he'd shoot at you!"

"He would. That's why I had to get the gun. To shoot back."

"But then you would kill somebody! Your godfather!"

"Oh, no, just wound his foot. I was only planning to aim at his feet."

I was stern with her. "You could have missed."

"Well, that would have been all right, then. If I missed, no harm done."

"No! I mean you could have missed his foot and got him in the *heart*!"

"That would make me a dreadful shot," Sugar began, and then she paused. "We could argue about this for days. I expect you would win in the end, Bronte, as you seem very *committed*, but so much time would be lost. The *point* is, I was going to get a gun and that's why I'm painting daisies. Generally speaking, I'd never paint daisies. My flower phase is long behind me. But that is how far I was willing to go to free dear Emma."

Now her eyes shone. "But I won't need to finish the daisies! Or get the gun! My dear child, Emma is innocent! It was the water sprite! We will get Emma out of prison in a proper legal way!"

She grabbed my hands and began to dance me around the room. She laughed and I laughed and we spun around, and then, at exactly the same moment, we stopped. "But why did she confess?" we said.

22

We decided she must have been thinking about something else when she confessed.

"She *is* very absentminded," Sugar Rixel said. "Don't you find?"

"I've never met her," I admitted. "But Aunt Isabelle told me that Emma would forget her own feet if they weren't fixed firmly to her legs. She was always dreaming about her next painting, Aunt Isabelle said."

So that was all right.

Next we hurried out to tell Detective Riley that Emma was innocent. We were halfway up the path when Sugar paused.

"I wonder," she said, "if Detective Riley will *believe* us."

"He has to! We will take him to the library and show him the book I found! Then we'll take him to your shelf and I'll tip the water on it again."

Sugar Rixel looked thoughtful. "That's a lot of taking," she said. "I think maybe we should get the water sprite to write a *letter*, confessing. You can't argue with a letter."

She swivelled and began marching in the opposite direction, down towards the water.

"I'm a little irritated with the water sprite," she chatted as we marched. "Even if it *is* a cultural thing. He gave me the pepper grinder to thank me for looking after him! Now that he's taken it back, does that mean I *didn't* look after him?"

"I don't think time works like that," I said.

"Well, he shouldn't have made that flowery speech about the pepper grinder being his most prized possession, and how he wished he could give me a *thousand* of them, that's how grateful he was. I said, *Oh no, I wouldn't have room for a thousand*."

By now, we had reached the little beach I had seen from the ferry wharf the day before. There was Barnabas, fishing again. We both waved at him, and he raised a hand and nodded.

Seaweed and driftwood were scattered about the sand. Sugar Rixel sat down on a rock, pulled off her sandals, and waved at Barnabas a second time. She turned to face the ocean. Waves plashed gently against the shore.

After a while, I said, "Now, then."

"Oh, yes." Sugar Rixel roused herself. "I was just thinking of the day I found my water sprite on the sand here, all battered and bleeding, poor thing. He'd been in a sword fight with his brother. And then I was thinking that I'd quite like to paint that crab there, do you see it?"

A large crab scuttled across the sand and disappeared behind a rock. "It's gone now," I pointed out.

"Isn't that the way?" sighed Sugar Rixel.

I began to wonder how my Aunt Emma and Sugar Rixel ever *concentrated* long enough to be friends.

"Will we just wait here for the water sprite?" I murmured, as politely as I could.

Sugar pushed herself up from the rock and squinted around. "Here we go!" she said, and picked up a damp, twisty piece of driftwood. "Perfect." Her eyes scanned the sand, and then she pounced, dragging up another, bigger stick.

Next, Sugar waded into the water. She stopped when the water reached her knees, raised the sticks high, and began to beat them together. At first, it seemed as if she was just making a racket, but then a certain rhythm emerged.

Thwack-thwack-thwack
thwack ... thwack ... thwack
thwack.

Then the same pattern again, and again.

The sound echoed strangely on the beach. Over at the wharf, Barnabas watched Sugar Rixel. She lowered the sticks to her side, but the thwacking sound still drifted around us as echoes. The wharf creaked.

Barnabas turned back to his fishing.

There was a long quiet.

Sugar raised the sticks and began again.

Something troubled me. I took off my own sandals and waded into the water myself. It was cool and refreshing. "Is this how you call your water sprite?" I asked, once I was standing beside her. "Or are you just having fun?"

"Hm?" Sugar Rixel glanced at me, thwacking away.

Oh gosh, I thought. *She's mad.*

Then a water sprite was standing beside us, seawater streaming from his hair, down his face, past his smile.

23

I had never seen a water sprite before.

I wondered if they were all as handsome as this one. He looked a lot like a man — a shortish man, broad in the shoulders. His chest was bare and his skin was a rich dark-golden colour, seaweed dusting it, the way regular men are often dusted in hair. The seaweed thickened around his hips and became a sort of skirt.

"Sugar Rixel!" he said, and his voice had a deep, rough, friendly tone. It was difficult not to stare at his face, his eyes were so creased with his smile.

"That is all very well," replied Sugar Rixel tartly, and she was not smiling. "But why did you take your pepper grinder back? I call that mighty rude!"

The water sprite glanced towards the sky and then abruptly sank into the water again and disappeared.

"Oh," I said.

"Just wait," Sugar told me. "He needs to replenish often, you see."

The water sprite soared up again, with a splash.

"Good morning, young one," he said, turning his smile towards me. "My title is Cyphus, King of the Water Sprites, Division 32. May I know your title?"

He was a king! Nobody had told me that the water sprite was a king!

"Take no notice," Sugar Rixel declared. "There are dozens of kings amongst the water sprites. They've split themselves into that many divisions! It's more like he's a *chairman* or something. Cyphus, this is Bronte Mettlestone, and she is the niece of my dearest friend in all the world, Emma Mettlestone. And *you've* gone and got Emma locked away!"

Cyphus nodded along with all of this, very interested.

"One moment," he murmured, and back into the water he went.

When he re-emerged, he lay on the water's surface, hands behind his head, kicking his feet gently. I could see that his feet were large and flipper-shaped, the toes webbed, which was to be expected.

"Sugar Rixel," he said, "most beauteous marvel of all marvels, Sugar Rixel. I often plead with the stars to contain my adoration of you, beautiful marvel who dazzles to behold and who once saved my life. But the stars cannot contain it, try as they might."

We both looked at him.

"I adore you," he clarified.

"Oh pssht," Sugar Rixel complained. "Get to the point. Why did you take your pepper grinder?"

"But I didn't," he said, and he sank gracefully beneath the surface.

We only had time to glance at one another in consternation and then he was back.

"Please," he said, twisting and turning in the water. "Explain why you think that I did?"

So Sugar Rixel told him the story of her pepper grinder going missing, and red paint everywhere, which meant that Emma was accused, on account of her red phase, and so Emma was sent to prison, and then dear Bronte discovered that it was *not* the crimson sap of the tehassifer tree but the blue oil of the katamanchi kelp! Which is *only* available in the forests of the water sprites, so it *must* have been Cyphus! It must have!

I noticed that she skipped the bit about Emma confessing, which seemed sensible.

Cyphus bobbed up and down in the water. His face became thoughtful.

"Sugar Rixel," he said, raising his hands so that water rushed between his fingers. "I will return." And arcing like a dolphin, he dove into the water and was gone.

We stood side by side in the quiet.

The quiet continued.

Over at the wharf, I saw that Barnabas was watching us with open interest. He raised a hand in a kind of questioning shrug. Sugar Rixel shrugged back.

"When?" I said forlornly. "When will he return?"

Sugar Rixel sighed. "That's the question, isn't it?"

We waited. The water moved around our ankles. The sun was warm on my head and face.

I began to think we ought to head in for lunch.

"I am back!" And it was the water sprite again, only now his face was as ferocious as a gravel pit. "Come!" He pressed us both towards the shore. "We will rush to your police station! Your friend must be released at once! My dear Sugar Rixel, he will *pay* for this! He will pay!"

Sugar and I hurried along beside him, water splashing everywhere.

"But what do you mean?" Sugar Rixel cried. "Who will pay?"

"My brother." His voice was now so deep and grim, it seemed to rise up from a canyon. "My *brother* stole your pepper grinder, Sugar."

24

King Cyphus insisted on coming with us to the police station.

"No time to write a letter," he growled, when Sugar Rixel suggested this. "Your friend is *wrongly* accused!"

We ended up taking him there in a wheelbarrow. Seeing the commotion, Barnabas had put down his fishing line and joined us on the beach, and he ran to his place for the barrow. Now he pushed it, bumping along over the rough terrain, while Sugar and

I ran on either side, carrying buckets of seawater. We splashed the water sprite with these as often as we could.

"The injustice!" he shouted. "I cannot abide it!"

I'd rarely seen anybody so angry. Certainly I'd never seen anybody riding in a wheelbarrow this angry. Ordinarily a person in a wheelbarrow will laugh and whoop at the fun of it all. (Although now I remember that my Aunt Isabelle fractured her ankle once while gardening, and the Butler gave her a ride back to the apartment in a wheelbarrow. She did not laugh so much as wince and be pale.)

"He will pay for this! Oh, my brother will *pay*!" the water sprite roared, and: "Hurry, man, spin the wheels of this contraption faster! A woman is falsely accused!"

"Going as fast as I can," Barnabas panted, reasonably enough. The barrow tilted this way and that and Barnabas tilted with it, struggling to get it up the slope. He was dripping sweat.

Along the main street we ran. People stopped and stared, calling to their friends to come and see. Sugar ran ahead, threw open the door of the police station, and held it back while Barnabas manoeuvred the barrow inside.

Detective Riley rose slowly. He ran his eyes over us: the water sprite in the barrow, Sugar Rixel panting, Barnabas wiping his forehead, me splashing the water sprite and getting a little on the floor. He frowned down at the splashes, and frowned back up at us.

The water sprite spoke first. "My title is Cyphus, King of the Water Sprites!"

"Oh, you're all kings down there," Detective Riley muttered, and sat back down.

Sugar Rixel stamped a foot. "Uncle Riley, you will come out from behind that desk this instant, and you will listen to what we have to say!"

"He's your uncle?" I asked, surprised.

"I just call him that," she explained, "since we're so close. Uncle Riley! Come out, or so help me, I will drag you out by that enormous honker of yours!"

There was a sigh from behind the desk, a chair squealed back on tiles, and then Detective Riley was before us. He leaned an elbow on the counter, his eyes flashing to show he was in charge.

"Good," Sugar Rixel declared. "And I meant no disrespect. Your nose *is* large, but it is most distinguished. We are here to demand the immediate release of Emma! She is innocent! Tell him, Cyphus!"

The water sprite squirmed around in the wheelbarrow until he got himself into a sitting position.

"She certainly is," he proclaimed. "The pepper grinder was stolen by my *brother*, Serfpio, King of the Water Sprites, Division 93!"

"Told you they were all kings," Detective Riley said smartly. "And what makes you think your *brother* stole the pepper grinder?" He drummed his fingers, unperturbed.

"I have seen the pepper grinder! It is proudly displayed in my brother's gallery! I never swim by my brother's gallery, as we loathe one another, but I swam by just now and there it was!"

Detective Riley twisted his big nose this way and that.

"Why would your *brother* come and steal the pepper grinder?" he said, a little scornfully. "Anyhow, crimson sap of the tehassifer tree was all over the crime scene, and that proves it was *Emma*!" He made to return to his desk.

At this point, Sugar Rixel was splashing water onto the water sprite again, but she raised the bucket in a threatening way. "Stay right where you are!" she said. "It was *not* the crimson sap of the tehassifer tree! Bronte here figured it out with her detective work! It's the blue oil of the katamanchi kelp! Which is—"

For the first time, Detective Riley blinked. "Which is only available in the secret forests of the water sprites," he interrupted, frowning. "Go on."

"My brother is one of the finest artists of the water sprites," Cyphus announced from down in the barrow, sounding proud. "He makes sculptures and he paints every one with the blue oil of the katamanchi kelp. He *drips* with the stuff. Leaves a trail of it everywhere he goes! As soon as the beauteous Sugar told me about the blue oil, I guessed it must be him! You see, my brother believes that the pepper grinder is rightfully his."

Here, Sugar Rixel's mighty expression faltered. "The pepper grinder belongs to your *brother*?"

Cyphus shifted again to sit even taller. "Certainly not! It is *my* pepper grinder!" I splashed a little water onto his shoulders for him. "Thank you." He nodded at me, and then to Sugar Rixel: "My brother just *thinks* it's his. You see, our grandfather, the Great Deex, King of the Water Sprites, Division 422—"

Detective Riley cleared his throat meaningfully but we ignored him.

"Our grandfather, the Great Deex, lives and swims in the Sea of Varsity," the water sprite continued, "which is far, far, and even farther away from here. When my brother and I were very small boys, Grandfather visited us. One day, he reached into his luggage and drew out the rare and magical pepper grinder, the prize of the Sea of Varsity. 'Boys,' he said to my brother and me, 'play one of your games of Capture the Flag. Whoever wins will have this pepper grinder.'"

Here Barnabas spoke up. "Capture the Flag! I forgot all about that game! Used to love it as a boy! So you play it amongst the water sprites, do you?"

"Indeed we do." Cyphus smiled back at Barnabas. "And on this particular day, we had a fierce and mighty game of it, my brother and I, which I won! And so the pepper grinder belongs to me."

"So why does your brother think it belongs to him?" Barnabas asked.

"Oh, well, he thinks *he* won, you see. But he didn't! I *tagged* him! It matters not that I tagged him on the seaweed skirt! It was a fair tag! Anyhow, my grandfather laughed and tossed the pepper grinder at me and said, 'You two figure it out between you,' and then he began his journey home to the Sea of Varsity, and I said, 'Well, nothing to figure, it's mine,' and I took it and kept it. We've been fighting ever since."

We all considered this.

"You could get a legal ruling on who won," Detective Riley suggested. "There must be codes about it? Water sprite codes."

"Oh, yes," Cyphus said. "But the code is ambiguous. The Supreme Water Court wouldn't hear our case. They said it was childish."

Again, we all considered.

"Wait," said Sugar Rixel, slowly. "When I first met you, you'd been injured in a sword fight with your brother."

"Yes."

"Was the sword fight over the pepper grinder?"

"Yes."

"But then you gave *me* the pepper grinder!"

The water sprite nodded. "For safekeeping. He'd never find it there! Or so I thought. And I was very tired of fighting him for it."

Sugar Rixel dropped her bucket of water on the floor, where it crashed sideways, spilling water everywhere. "You *gave* it to me as a *thank-you* gift!"

"Yes. It served a sort of double purpose."

Before Sugar Rixel could finish taking in a furious breath,

Detective Riley sniffed and said: "Sword fighting, you say? That's illegal. I'll write you up. You'll be locked away for years, I shouldn't wonder. Wait and I'll get my codes." He made to go back to his desk.

"Oh, for goodness' sake," Sugar Rixel scolded, letting out the great breath of air in an instant. "That sword fight was ages ago. Stop it, Uncle Riley. The point is that Emma didn't do it! Go and let her out at once!"

"Could I have a little more water?" the water sprite asked politely. "I'm drying out here rather."

"Not from me." Sugar Rixel pointed the toe of her shoe at the spilled water.

"And I'm running out." I raised my almost-empty bucket.

The detective frowned deeply at us all. "Emma Mettlestone is staying where she is," he growled. "She confessed to the crime!"

"She did?" exclaimed Cyphus.

"Oh," Sugar Rixel said. "I forgot about that."

"But the brother did it!" I was suddenly angry with them all. "So who *cares* that she confessed!"

"Go and fetch Emma," Barnabas urged. "And *ask* her why she confessed."

Detective Riley scratched behind his ear. Then he shrugged and said: "I'll bring her out." He glanced at the water sprite and reached for my bucket. "Give me that," he grumbled, "and I'll refill it as well."

25

Nothing happened.

We waited silently.

Nothing continued to happen.

Then a number of things happened all at once.

Detective Riley returned, the bucket in one hand (water sloshing), a chain in the other hand, and a woman trailing behind him, her hair wild, face pale, manacles on her ankles and her wrists.

This must be Aunt Emma, I thought. *She is beautiful, but she looks quite unwell.*

"Emma!" Sugar Rixel cried in horror – and the door of the police station burst open.

A water sprite stood in the frame.

We stared.

He shouted: "She didn't do it! *I* did it! *I* stole the pepper grinder! She is innocent! My darling Emma!" He snarled at Detective Riley, "You will pay for this, you swine!" and then he started again with, "She didn't do it! *I* did it!" but his voice choked on itself, and he hunched forward, coughing.

This water sprite looked very much like King Cyphus, only with darker colouring and flashing black eyes. And his skin was patterned like cracked porcelain. In fact, a faint crackling sound ran right across his body. He looked up from his coughing, eyes wild and staring.

"You must be the brother," Sugar Rixel said. "But don't tell me you've come all the way from the shore without any water!"

"Of course," the new water sprite said hoarsely, slumping against the door frame. "I had to save dear Emma. It was me! Arrest me!" and he crumpled, coughing again.

"Great Ocean!" said Cyphus, turning white. "He will die before our eyes!"

Now Aunt Emma wrenched the chain out of Detective Riley's hands and rushed towards the coughing water sprite with much clanking. "Oh my love, my love!"

She threw her arms around him and began to drag him, stumbling, across the room. Barnabas stepped over to help, and between them, they carried the water sprite down the hall. We heard more cries and coughs and clanks, and then the sound of rushing water.

Cyphus cleared his throat. "There is a good, strong water supply down the hall there?" he inquired.

"There is," Detective Riley agreed gruffly. "A bathtub."

"A tub." Cyphus nodded firmly. "Just the thing." His voice quivered a little.

"He'll be all right," Sugar Rixel murmured.

"They'll fill it up in no time," Detective Riley added.

From down the hall, there were more low groans and sharp cries, and Aunt Emma's voice shouting, "Move him this way!" and

Barnabas's voice lower, "Just help me here?" and Emma shrieking, "Oh, these cursed chains!"

"Do you think you might—" Sugar Rixel began, but Detective Riley was already sorting through keys and marching down the hall.

We heard more cries and the loud clanging of chains being pulled aside and clanked out of the bathroom.

"I'll fetch the doctor," Sugar Rixel declared.

"Nothing that a doctor can do at this point," Cyphus told her. "There is no medicine but water. Of course..." He paused. "Of course," he repeated, more forcefully this time, "it may be too..."

Again he stopped. Sugar Rixel and I looked down at him. Faint cracks were appearing around his collarbone. I splashed a little water on them, and they faded.

"It may be too..." he tried again in a soft voice.

"It *won't* be too late," Sugar Rixel said firmly.

Down the hall, the water blasted on and on.

26

Sugar Rixel and I leaned against the counter, waiting. We took turns splashing water onto Cyphus and he kept trying to smile up at us, without quite managing.

"No! No!" we heard Emma wail at one point. Cyphus started up in the barrow. Then we heard Barnabas's voice, low and calm.

"It's all right. Look. His chest is moving. He's still breathing."

Detective Riley reappeared from down the hall. His eyes flickered towards us, then away again. "I'll just..." he began, and he strode outside.

Minutes later, he was back, rolling a huge oak barrel. He tipped this to a standing position. Then he hurried out again, returned rolling a *second* barrel, stood this up, and left again.

We watched, bewildered.

Next, Detective Riley brought in a garden hose and began filling the first oak barrel. From down the hall came the sounds of more rapid conversation between Aunt Emma and Barnabas, something to do with the tub overflowing, and then the rush of water stopped. There were now only the sounds of splashing.

"Here we go," Detective Riley told Cyphus eventually. "Why don't you step into this barrel?"

The water sprite breathed in deeply. "Sir, I thank you," he said.

With Sugar's help, he clambered out of the wheelbarrow and hoisted himself quickly into the oak barrel. There was a splash. The barrel was big enough for him to crouch, immersing his head completely. After a moment, his head rose up again and he said, "Aaaah. That *is* better."

Detective Riley was filling the second barrel. "This," he said, "will be ready for your brother when he's better. We'll have a celebration afternoon tea *right* here. I'll just run to the bakery and get provisions."

Cyphus nodded, but his lips trembled. Abruptly he plunged under the water.

Detective Riley strode out of the station, carrying the hose.

"Are you *sure* there's nothing else that could help your brother?" I asked Cyphus when his head reappeared. "Nothing but water?"

Cyphus nodded. "Water is the only thing."

"Should it be seawater?" Sugar Rixel asked suddenly. "I'll run and fill the buckets from the sea!" She had already grabbed them, but Cyphus shook his head.

"In fact," he said, "fresh water is better at a time like this. He'll be all right."

"Oh yes," Sugar and I said quickly. "Yes, he will!"

But down the hall, there was a terrible silence now, and only occasional splashing.

I bounced on my feet. I pulled on my ponytail and re-buckled my sandals.

I couldn't stay here a moment longer.

Before anybody could stop me, I ran to the station door and out onto the street.

27

The librarian shouted, "Dear child! You're back! More research?"

I nodded quickly, looking over her shoulder at the catalogue, my eyes running around the library, up and down the shelves of books.

"Excuse me," I said. "Are *you* good at research?"

"Not so bad," she replied modestly.

"Only, this is a sort of an emergency," I explained.

Abruptly, the librarian leaned towards me. "Tell me!" she said, eyes sparkling.

I told her. She peered hard at me.

Then she was gone, moving so fast she was a blur. Silent as a bicycle.

She was back while I was still blinking, setting a great pile of books onto the desk.

She threw open the first book, leafed through to the index, ran her thumb down the page, shook her head, and placed the book onto her chair. This all happened in the time it takes to *think* about breathing. She picked up the second book. The same thing happened. Same with the third.

With the fourth, she paused. Her eyes flickered. Her thumb touched the index and stopped. She nodded. The pages flew back, forth, back, then stopped.

"Here," she whispered, and she tapped at the top of a page.

Water Sprite Dehydration is generally treated with immersion in fresh water. While this is effective in a small proportion of cases, Dehydration is an extremely serious condition and almost always fatal.

I looked up, my eyes widening. But the librarian gestured for me to continue reading.

> However, a recent study carried out in the *Travails of Endiva* found that when a drop of Pure Liquide is ADDED to the fresh water, survival rates were markedly improved.

"Pure Liquide?" I breathed, turning to the librarian, but she had gone.

She was back beside me while I was still realizing she had gone. An enormous volume thumped onto the desk.

"Pure," she murmured to herself, her fingers turning pages like a concert pianist, "pure, pure … here!"

She smoothed out the page and pointed. We read together.

> Pure Liquide
>
> Pure Liquide is an essential vapour, distilled in the fifth winter of the fullest moon, by the radish gnomes of Takejby Bay, available only in the midnight markets of Bay Ten.[172]

"Oh," I said.

But the librarian was now pointing to the bottom of the page. There was a footnote.

172. Effective substitutions for Pure Liquide include a cup of water from the Helmet Cascades in Rafern, a single Gainsleigh dewdrop, or the tear of a mountain seal-frog.

"Hm," the librarian murmured. "I have a cousin who lives in Rafern. I *think* she's not far from those Helmet Cascades. I will telegraph at once and she—"

But my heart was clattering like a locomotive.

"A Gainsleigh dewdrop!" I said. "I have a *vial* of Gainsleigh dewdrops! The Butler gave them to me!" and then I was tearing from the library, shouting, "Thank you! Thank you!"

"GOOD LUCK!" the librarian bellowed, and there was a chorus of *shhhhs!*

I was back at Aunt Emma's cottage.

I was skidding across the floorboards.

Wrenching open my suitcase.

My fingers trembled so much that I had to shake my hands hard to stop them.

I threw everything out onto the bed. Not this, not this, my dresses kept tangling together and getting in my way! Where *was* it, had I *lost* it? And there it was!

I was holding the vial of Gainsleigh dewdrops.

Now I was dashing through the streets of Lantern Island again.

Past the ice-cream parlour, the wishing well, the library – and then I was throwing open the doors of the police station.

Nobody was there.

The two oak barrels were empty.

Nobody behind the counter.

Then, from down the hall, came sounds. Somebody was weeping. A hoarse voice was saying, "His face, keep water on his face," and another voice grimly: "It's too late."

I ran down the hall and skidded around the corner into the bathroom.

It was crowded in there.

Detective Riley and Barnabas both stood, their faces grim. Aunt Emma leaned over the bathtub, sobbing. Sugar Rixel crouched beside her, a hand on Emma's shoulder. Cyphus also knelt by the tub. He was draped in sopping wet towels. Both his hands were in the water, splashing his brother's face: "His face, keep water on his face," he was saying, over and over.

And inside the tub, Cyphus's brother lay perfectly still, eyes closed, skin like a sheet of paper that somebody had scribbled on, over and over, with angry black lines.

Barnabas saw me and shook his head sadly.

I opened the vial, stepped forward, and tipped the whole thing into the tub.

The water fizzed faintly.

Sugar Rixel looked up at me, puzzled.

The fizzing grew. It crept across the surface of the tub. It picked up speed and *swept* across the surface.

The bathtub fizzed! It bubbled and foamed!

"What's *happening*?" Aunt Emma cried.

"Yes," said a voice. "What *is* happening?" And the dark-haired water sprite sat up in the tub, in a great wash of froth and bubbles.

28

After that, we had a celebration afternoon tea.

Well, first everybody shouted with amazement, and asked the water sprite, Serfpio, if he was all right? He said, yes, perfectly all right, thank you.

"But are you *alive?*" Aunt Emma cried.

And he said patiently that he doubted he would be perfectly all right if he were not alive, so there was that. Aunt Emma agreed that there was that, and she half fell into the bath, hugging him and sobbing.

He still looked dreadful, though. When Aunt Emma sat back again, sudsy water dripping everywhere, we could see the web of black cracks covering his face.

"More!" Cyphus cried. "Everyone! Toss this fine and bubbled water all over my brother!"

So we did. It was like a water fight where everybody has decided to gang up on one person, and that person is being a good sport about it. Serfpio sat back smiling and laughing as we threw the fizzling bathwater over his face and neck, his arms and toes. Slowly, the cracks faded to smoothness.

Now everybody wanted to know just *what* I had put into the tub?

I told them the story, and they all hugged me madly, Aunt Emma most of all. She also cried, *Welcome to Lantern Island, dear, dear niece!* and *Oh, you are like your father! I loved him so much! I have not stopped weeping about your parents, dear child. I love you most of anybody in the world!*

Then Detective Riley said, "We must have a celebration afternoon tea!" and I asked, "May I invite somebody?" They looked puzzled but agreed, so I ran to the library and invited the librarian. I told her what had happened and she was pleased. She left a sign saying, "Back soon! Make yourselves at home!" and we ran to the station together.

"Look," I said, "this is the person who actually saved Serfpio!" Everybody praised her research skills.

And *then* we had the celebration afternoon tea.

The water sprite brothers splashed about in the oak barrels and Detective Riley dragged chairs into a circle around the low table. He set out the pastries and peach tarts he'd bought earlier.

"I never thought we'd be eating these!" he told us cheerfully. "I was at the bakery and I thought to myself: *This is a total waste of money. He's never going to make it.* That bothered me a bit," he admitted. "I don't like waste. But here we are!"

We all talked fast, with bright eyes, the way people do when a catastrophe turns out well.

Aunt Emma and Serfpio told how they had met in the sea, when Emma was bathing under moonlight one night. After that, they had swum together often, talking of their art and their favourite foods and exchanging poetry, and all the time sinking slowly into love, until they loved each other most of anybody in the world.

One night, while they were swimming and chatting, Aunt Emma had mentioned her friend Sugar Rixel, and told Serfpio about Sugar's pepper grinder. Emma wondered if Serfpio knew the water sprite who'd given it to her? His name was Cyphus? Then Serfpio roared that Cyphus was his brother!

The roaring confused Emma, as it struck her as a lovely coincidence that the two water sprites she and Sugar knew were brothers.

But Serfpio told her he'd been lurking around this island ever since his sword fight with his brother, wondering what Cyphus had done with the pepper grinder, which is how she had happened to meet him. They had a small tiff then as Emma said, "I thought you came here every night to see me!" and he said, "Well, to see you *and* to keep an eye out for the pepper grinder," and Emma was upset. He assured her that he loved her more than all the pepper grinders in the world, so she was happy.

However, now that he knew where the grinder was, he continued, he must get it back! And would Emma please get it for him? Maybe when her friend Sugar was facing the other way, she could slip it under her shirt and run out?

Emma became wretched, wishing she had never opened her big mouth about Sugar's pepper grinder. But Serfpio said no, no, we should tell each other *everything*, for that is what lovers do, without restraint. So Emma told him, without restraint, that she was sorry he had lost his pepper grinder, but that Sugar Rixel was a great friend of hers, and she could never steal from a great friend.

"How *loyal* you are!" Sugar Rixel cried, throwing her arms around Aunt Emma. "I love you most of anyone in the world!"

"I love you most too," Emma agreed.

I thought this was interesting, as I was sure Emma had just said she loved Serfpio most, and back in the bathroom, she had definitely told me she loved me most. But nobody else commented, so I let it go.

"So I stole it myself!" Serfpio declared. "I rolled myself in waterlogged bandages and ran up from the ocean and took it! Sorry about that, Sugar Rixel," he added humbly.

Sugar Rixel said she understood.

"I had *no* idea that Emma would be blamed," Serfpio went on. "Or I'd never have taken it! She hasn't been in the moonlit sea these last few days, but I thought she must have a cold! Or maybe that she was angry with me for our little disagreement, and that time would cool her down. Then my brother swam by the gallery today and bellowed something about, *You have stolen the pepper grinder! And an innocent woman named Aunt Emma is now in prison!* I came as fast as I could. I didn't even stop to wrap myself in water-soaked bandaging."

Barnabas frowned. "Didn't you realize you'd get the Dehydration and die?"

"Of course I did," Serfpio replied. "But the only thing that mattered was rescuing my Emma."

We all smiled gently, thinking about the greatness of love and sacrifice.

"But Emma?" Barnabas said next. "Why did you confess?"

"I had to," Emma said simply. "I knew at once that Serfpio must have done it. I myself was on Ringtail Island with the Fruits of the Forest Club the day of the robbery, and I knew that Detective Riley would eventually hear that and realize I was innocent. Next thing you know, Serfpio would have been arrested and locked away, which surely would have killed him! I could never allow that! So I confessed."

We sighed, thinking once again about the greatness of love and sacrifice.

Detective Riley announced that he would now charge Serfpio with the theft of the pepper grinder, and that Serfpio would certainly be given fifteen years, if not more, and he stood up ready to get his codes.

This took the mood down a little.

"But the pepper grinder *belongs* to Serfpio!" Cyphus declared from inside the water barrel. "So there is no crime!"

"Belongs to me?" Serfpio's head popped up over the side of his barrel.

"Yes, dear brother," Cyphus said in the same warm tone. "Enough of this terrible feud. The grinder is yours."

Detective Riley sat down again, disappointed, but he took it in good grace.

Now Sugar Rixel threw her arms around Cyphus and said, "Oh, I'm so proud of you, dear Cyphus! You are such a good sort!" and everybody agreed that Cyphus was a good sort.

After a moment, Serfpio announced that, "No, *you* won that game of Capture the Flag, Cyphus, fair and square. You *did* tip me. The pepper grinder is yours."

"Mine?" said Cyphus.

"Yours," he agreed.

"Well," began Detective Riley, standing up again. "In that case, it *doesn't* belong to Serfpio, so Serfpio *did* steal it, so—"

But here the librarian bellowed, "Oh, *hush*, Detective Riley," and he did.

Aunt Emma pointed out that the pepper grinder actually belonged to *Sugar Rixel* now, as it had been given to her as a gift.

Sugar Rixel said, "Well, I didn't like to say anything, but this is true."

Serfpio considered and said, "You are quite right."

Then Sugar Rixel suggested that she could share the pepper grinder with Aunt Emma, and they could take turns with it, what did everybody think?

Everybody thought that was brilliant. Cyphus said he was happy that the pepper grinder would be with his greatest love, Sugar Rixel, part of the time, and Serfpio said that he was happy it would be with his greatest love, Emma Mettlestone, the other part.

Once we had finished our afternoon tea, Detective Riley said that he'd better lock Emma up again.

This was startling. The detective explained that he could not possibly release her without an order from the circuit judge. He was confident that he *would* get such an order, but it would not be until the circuit judge was back on the island in a month. And so, come along, Emma, let's go.

There was an uproar and Detective Riley burst out laughing and said he was joking. He would just make a call, he explained, to get an ex parte order of release, and it would only take a minute. He went off to make the call.

Everybody was stern with him when he returned, and told him that it wasn't funny, that sort of a joke, especially coming from him, as usually he *meant* it. Yes, he said, usually I do. He smiled proudly, taking no notice of the scolding.

Then Emma sighed and said, "Oh, I can't wait to get back to my cottage!" and Detective Riley's proud smile faltered. "Oh," he said. "Your *cottage*."

I said, "It's all right. I cleaned it up last night."

Detective Riley swung around and looked at me.

"You cleaned up the cottage?"

I nodded.

Detective Riley put his hands behind his back and studied me. "How old are you?" he barked suddenly.

"Ten," I said. I cleared my throat to say it more clearly: "Ten."

His face was now fierce. "Bronte Mettlestone," he said. "I am not a man who often gets things wrong."

"Pssht," said Sugar Rixel, and the others giggled.

Detective Riley ignored them. "Nor," he said, "do I like to *admit* it when I get a thing wrong."

"Oh, well, *that* part's true," Sugar Rixel said, and there were more snickers.

Detective Riley blinked but did not look away from me. "It seems to me," he said, "that I've been making a giant mess of this case. In more ways than one. And it seems to me that you, Bronte Mettlestone, have been running around cleaning up the mess. Would that be fair to say?"

I wasn't sure how he wanted me to respond, so I just sort of shrugged.

"It would," he confirmed, answering for me. "In fact, it would be fair to say, Bronte Mettlestone, that you are the finest ten-year-old ever to set foot on Lantern Island." He leaned towards me, still frowning. "Thank you, Bronte Mettlestone," he said. "May I shake your hand?"

"All right," I said, and we shook hands.

29

The next day, I stood on the wharf again, my suitcase beside me.

Barnabas was fishing, Aunt Emma was chatting, and the ferry was approaching.

I wished it would not come so quickly.

The previous afternoon, Aunt Emma and I had rowed her boat all around the bay. I had given Emma the pebbles from the roots of the flowering movay trees at Gainsleigh Harbour, and she'd shown me how to crush them. She'd painted a portrait of me, let it dry in the sun and wind, then rolled it up and taken it to the post office to mail to Aunt Isabelle.

"Isabelle will be missing you so much, dear child," she told me. "Hopefully this portrait will cheer her up a little."

I hadn't really thought of Aunt Isabelle missing me. It was an interesting idea. I bought a postcard with a picture of Lantern Island on it and wrote to Aunt Isabelle and the Butler that I was having a splendid time. There was no need to tell them that Aunt Emma had been in prison when I arrived, I thought. Emma agreed there was no need.

"Isabelle is a worrier," she said. "Now your *parents*, they were different. Always loved adventure. You know, they probably wanted *you* to have adventures too? I expect that's why they used the Faery cross-stitch. So that Isabelle would *have* to let you come on this journey. She'd never have allowed it otherwise."

That was an even more interesting idea.

While we were chatting, the postmistress was bringing out a stack of mail that she'd been holding for Emma. We sat on a bench and ate ice-cream cones while Emma opened this.

There were mostly bills, and Emma put these aside "to throw away". But then there was a telegram — "I wasn't allowed to give that to you in prison," the postmistress called apologetically. It was from Aunt Alys, the same one she'd sent to Aunt Sue about pirates wanting to capture Prince William.

"*I* don't know what she should do about that!" Aunt Emma complained.

"That's exactly what Aunt Sue said when she got the telegram!" I said. In the end, Emma decided to send a pocket-size painting of a frog to Aunt Alys to cheer her up, along with a note that said:

Hope it's all blown over by now. Much, much love.

The final piece of mail was an invitation from Aunt Franny:

You Are Cordially Invited to a

Marvellous Party

To Celebrate the Lives of

Our Dearly Beloved

Patrick and Lida

1st of August 2:00 p.m.

24 Jarrah Avenue

Nina Bay

Aunt Emma's hands trembled as she held the invitation, then her shoulders shook and she was sobbing. I patted her back until she stopped.

"Darling child," Aunt Emma said. "Your wonderful, adventurous parents! At least we still have you. I'm already counting the days until I see you again in Nina Bay."

"So you are coming to the party?"

"Of course! I would not miss a celebration of your darling parents, darling. Besides, I've never visited Franny since she moved to Nina Bay, and it's a *thrilling* area. Dragons, pirates, and any number of Dark Mages and criminal sorts. There's a small Empire of Witchcraft nearby, and a colony of radish gnomes. Why, the Whispering Kingdom's only an hour away."

I widened my eyes at her. "Whyever would Aunt Franny have moved to such a dangerous place?"

"Oh, she was always one of the edgier sisters. Needs excitement, see?"

My head was racing. "My grandfather lives near Nina Bay," I said. "Outside Colchester. No wonder Aunt Isabelle has never allowed me to visit him!"

"Colchester's pretty placid," Aunt Emma said. "But yes, I don't blame Isabelle. It's only five years ago that the Whispering Kingdom was *properly* spellbound – with the Majestic Spellbinding."

"Majestic Spellbinding?"

"Done by Carabella-the-Great. She's the most powerful Spellbinder ever, apparently. Before *she* bound the Whispering Kingdom, the bindings were mediocre. Torn bits, ragged edges. You never knew when a Whisperer might slip out and steal a child."

A shiver ran down my spine at that, but then Aunt Emma leapt to her feet and proposed a picnic on Tuttlecock Island.

Now I could see Tuttlecock Island across the bay, the ferry rounding it and growing larger. Aunt Emma began to cry again, saying she would never let me go. But I knew she would. She had to.

There was a shout, and Sugar Rixel came rushing down the stairs. She held a book in one hand and waved it in the air. "Almost forgot!" she bellowed. Barnabas looked up at her, blinked, and turned back to his line.

"I wanted to give you this!" she puffed, staggering onto the wharf. "I've never run so fast! It's one of my father's magical books. If you're ever at a loss for words, you just shake it!"

"That is very kind," I said. "But I cannot accept it. It is special to you."

Aunt Emma laughed. "That's exactly what Isabelle used to tell *me* to say. I suggest you ignore exactly *half* of what Isabelle has taught you."

"Agreed," Sugar Rixel said, and she pressed the book into my hands. "The point is, *you're* special to me, Bronte! You saved me from a life of painting daisies."

I thanked Sugar Rixel, and pointed out that there was only one daisy painting I'd saved her from, not a lifetime. Sugar Rixel said, "Pssht, let me have my exaggerations."

The ferry bobbed shyly towards us, lining itself up with the dock. I opened my suitcase, slipped in the book, and took out the treasure chest.

The ferryman was dragging out a gangplank for me. "Oi," he said. "No time for packing now. We're on a schedule."

But so was I. *As the ferry docks,* it said, *give the gift to Emma.* And *my* schedule was Faery cross-stitched.

I handed Emma her gift. Barnabas called to the ferryman, "Carp biting your way lately?" and the ferryman said, "Nah. But I heard around at Seracuse Bay..." and their conversation continued. Fish and where to catch them. Sugar Rixel joined in. I think they were distracting the ferryman to give us time.

Emma opened the gift.

She became very still.

A strange expression crossed her face.

"What is it?" I asked.

She gave me a quick smile and looked back at the gift.

"Cinnamon," she whispered. "It's a little jar of cinnamon."

"Is that ... not a good thing?"

Aunt Emma crouched beside me. "I was a girl about your age," she murmured, speaking quickly, her eyes bright. "And my brother – your father – was eight." She paused again. "We stole a great sack of cinnamon together from a warehouse down by Gainsleigh Harbour. He scrambled up the wall and into a tiny window – he was such a climber, Patrick! And he opened a latch for me to get in, and we took the cinnamon between us and carried it home, running all the way, and into our bedroom! We were so excited! We'd made it! Only, we left a trail of cinnamon behind us. So it was a simple matter for the police to find us. We got in so much trouble! Everyone was going to the opera that night, and we had to stay home as our punishment."

She smiled at me. "It was wonderful! We hated the opera, Patrick and I. We laughed the whole night long, and ate sweets from the back of the pantry. And we had tipped out enough cinnamon from the sack before they caught us to..." She looked at the cinnamon jar in her hand. Her words became so quiet now I had to press close to hear her. "We wanted the cinnamon to colour my painting of a bear," she whispered. "Patrick always loved my paintings of bears."

Her face twisted oddly, and she wiped her eyes fast.

"Enough chitchat!" called the ferryman suddenly. "All aboard!"

I hugged Aunt Emma as hard as I could, and then Sugar Rixel too. Barnabas stepped forward and shook my hand: "Bronte Mettlestone," he said. "It's been a pleasure."

"It has," I agreed.

At that moment, there was a splash and the water sprite brothers burst from the sea in two great fountains. One golden, one darker, both of them shimmering under the sunlight, both grinning and waving.

"Farewell, young Bronte! Thank you for saving my life!" cried Serfpio. "Hello, beauteous Emma!"

"Farewell, young Bronte! Thank you for saving my brother's life!" shouted Cyphus. "Hello, beauteous Sugar!"

Aunt Emma and Sugar Rixel waved back madly. Barnabas made a low *hmph* in the back of his throat and returned to his fishing.

I stepped onto the ferry.

Aunt Claire

30

By now you'll be thinking that every visit to every aunt would end with me doing something clever or brave.

That's what I was thinking.

Here we go, I sighed to myself. *What's next?*

But listen to what happened with the next three aunts.

First, there was Aunt Claire in the busy metropolis of Clybourne.

From Lantern Island, I took the ferry to Curly Bay, bought a very good caramel-vanilla ice cream with extra sprinkles (as instructed by my parents), and boarded the Clybourne Overnighter. I slept with my head leaning against the window, which bumped and rattled through my dreams, and when the coach arrived in Clybourne, I looked sleepily out onto the morning.

A black motorcar stood across the street. I had only seen motorcars in the cinema before – we don't yet have them in Gainsleigh. Aunt Claire, in elegant hat and tailored suit, leaned against this car and nodded at me. I could see at once that the edge of her coat was caught in the door, so I waved through the window and pointed. She looked down, opened the car door to set the coat free, and nodded at me again.

Aunt Claire is a professional Events Coordinator. She dresses sharply and swings her umbrella as she strides about, and she laughs loudly when things go wrong. But then she turns away, frowning to herself. I already knew her well because she often comes to Gainsleigh to organize events. Whenever she's in town, she takes me out for lemonade and cakes at the Arlington Tea Room.

So we were very cheerful to see each other, and she shook my hand firmly and said, "Here she is! Hop aboard!"

Motorcars turned out to make a roaring sound, like tigers, and slid along at a terrific pace. I tried to be nonchalant, but I could not stop watching the road spinning by, buildings and trees skidding sideways like frocks in my wardrobe when Aunt Isabelle is swishing through them.

We drove directly to a hotel where Aunt Claire was organizing an event.

"Here it is," she said, hurrying up a flight of stairs. "I'm afraid you'll have to sit in on the sessions."

"That's all right," I began – but then I read the sign.

The Annual Convention of Mathematics Teachers

An Investigation of Long Division, Long Multiplication, and the Careful Placement of Numerals in Columns

"Perhaps I could just read a book?" I suggested.

But now Aunt Claire was striding along a corridor. She took out a key, opened a door, led me along another corridor, opened a *second* locked door, and stopped at a third. Two enormous security guards blocked this one.

"I mean, if it was long *addition*..." I was saying. "That might be one thing, but—"

"Hello, fellows," Aunt Claire said, and she gestured towards me. "My niece."

The security guards stared hard at me and then nodded. One

pressed several buttons on the handle of the door, until it *clicked*. He stood aside.

Aunt Claire swept through.

Now we were in an immense room lined with tables and chairs. Men and women sat at these tables, scribbling on notepads. At the front, a grey-haired man in spectacles stood at a lectern, waiting for the scribbling to finish.

"Right," he said. "Shall we get on?"

I sighed.

Aunt Claire indicated two empty seats. I slumped in mine.

"A radish gnome," said the teacher, "is a right little rascal with claws like a set of steak knives."

I straightened up.

"It's not *actually* a mathematics convention," Aunt Claire whispered, leaning close to me. "It's a Convention of Spellbinders. Always top secret. Spellbinders have to keep their identities strictly hidden, otherwise Dark Mages come for them in their sleep. Come after their friends and family too."

I nodded slowly. I'd never thought about that before, but it made sense. When you see pictures of Spellbinders in the newspaper, they're always wearing capes with hoods that hide their faces. I used to think they did this to look stylish.

"Mint?" Aunt Claire whispered next, pushing a bowl towards me. I took one. The day was looking up.

Over the next three days, Aunt Claire had to hurry away often, to check lists and scold people. (This is called "organizing".) Meanwhile, I sat and listened to different professors teach classes on Dark Mages and Spellbinding.

Some lessons were very technical and dull, so I counted mints or fell asleep during those. Or I looked around at the Spellbinders sitting at their tables. They acted just like regular people, picking their teeth and sighing, or scratching at marks on their trousers or skirts. This seemed strange. Even though I'd always known that Spellbinders were ordinary people who'd inherited Spellbinding powers, I still expected them to be sparkly. Or at least to have extra big muscles.

Almost every professor talked about "the most powerful Spellbinder of all time", Carabella-the-Great, which was funny. I'd never even heard of this Carabella-the-Great before Aunt Emma mentioned her on Lantern Island, and now she seemed to be flying at me from every direction. It was like when you learn a new word, such as *cantaloupe*, and suddenly everybody you meet is singing songs about cantaloupes, or wearing them as earrings.

Nobody showed a picture of Carabella-the-Great, of course, so I had to imagine her. Long jet-black hair, I decided, and blasts of magic shooting from her nose like sneezes. "She disappeared right after completing the Majestic Spellbinding of the Whispering Kingdom," one professor said. "And has never been heard from since. Such a *tragedy*!" The students all nodded sadly.

"Doing the Majestic Spellbinding would have worn her out

completely," another professor said, "so it made sense for her to take a *holiday*. But it's been five years and not a word!"

This particular teacher was a favourite of mine. She was a very old woman who called herself Prattle, and she snapped her fingers and rolled her eyes as she talked. This made people laugh. Her class was on the binding of Whisperers.

"Why do we need to learn this?" a skinny girl asked. "Aren't all the Whisperers trapped behind the Majestic Spellbinding?"

Prattle had been pacing up and down, but now she stopped still. She lowered her voice. "Have you not heard?" she breathed. "The Whispering King has been boasting of a Whisper he heard long ago from the future. That this very year, his own grandchild would step forward and help *release* the Whisperers from the Spellbinding!"

A chill ran through the room and lodged itself in my stomach. The evil Whisperers could soon be wandering the Kingdoms and Empires again? Around me, people shook their heads. Some cursed quietly to themselves and then remembered that a child (me) was in the room and bit their lips. I didn't mind. I have heard the Butler cursing when he can't get the lid from a jar and doesn't know I'm there.

"But there are rumours that the king has also heard *another* Whisper," a man in a corduroy jacket called nervously. "That another child, ten years old and also of royal blood, will cause *great difficulties* for the king's grandchild. The king is supposed to be very annoyed by *that* Whisper."

Now people turned to each other, raising eyebrows.

"Can it be true?" they murmured.

"Let us hope so," Prattle said. "Let's hope that this second Whisper is more than just a rumour. And that this child indeed exists."

At that moment, Prattle's eyes landed on me. *I* was ten years old. If only, I thought suddenly, if only *I* could be the child who *caused great difficulties* for the Whispering King's grandchild!

But I was not of royal blood, so I could not be that child. Secretly, I was rather relieved by this.

For a moment, it seemed as if Prattle's face was going to collapse into its wrinkles, but then somebody dropped a pen and she was suddenly pacing again.

"Nutmeg!" she cried. "Mix nutmeg into your potions! Potions make your bindings stronger, and nutmeg is the secret ingredient Carabella-the-Great discovered. Nutmeg! Write that down!"

Everyone scribbled.

"Underline that!" the teacher commanded. "Put circles and daisies around it! Nutmeg! Remember that!"

Next, she had the class practise net-making using a shuttle and gauge, a clamp, and real, ordinary string. "The more you do this," she said, "the more the movements of Spellbinding will come to you instinctively. You should all take up fishing and make your own nets!"

I sat at the table watching, but Prattle suddenly clicked her fingers at me. "You too, child! Up you get!"

"But I'm not a Spellbinder," I explained. "I'm just watching."

"Who cares?" she said, which made everybody laugh. So I got up and tried net-making. After that, we had to close our eyes and move our arms, working with imaginary tools and twine. Peculiar at first, but soon the air seemed to turn to water, my hands moving through it like a new swimming stroke.

It was fun. Prattle gave out folders of Spellbinding potions at the end, and I packed mine away in my suitcase.

I hardly saw Aunt Claire, she was so busy. But on the last day, I gave her the gift from my parents. We were in the hotel lobby café and had just shared a slice of cake. She studied the card for a while. Then she opened the box in her neat, careful way, and lifted out a little packet filled with tiny red flakes.

"What is it?"

"I don't know," Aunt Claire replied, raising her eyebrows. She turned the packet over and read the label: **Dried Chilli**. "Ha!" she chuckled. "Spicy! Of course! When we were young, your father and I used to compete to see which of us could eat the spiciest food," she explained to me. "I once consumed an Empress Black Chilli. My finest hour. Ever tasted one?"

"No."

"Don't. Took me a month to get sensation back in my mouth. Patrick drank a jar of Sartorial Hot Sauce in response. *His* finest hour. Most impressive. Not long after that, he and your mother, Lida, started dating. I took the pair of them out to dinner one night. They were in low spirits that day, as Lida had received a message from home. You know your mother was a teenage runaway, I suppose? We knew *nothing* about her family, so I was that curious to find out. I thought if we had a blast, they might tell me. But not a word. Never even found out what the message was."

I told her that I was going to visit my grandfather at the end of my journey, after Franny's party in Nina Bay, and perhaps he would tell me?

"Perhaps," she agreed. "Anyway, they cheered up and we ended up having a fine and hilarious night. One of the best. Turned out Lida could take us *both* on. *She* munched on a Vast Diego Pepper without batting an eyelid!"

Aunt Claire stood, placed the chilli flakes in her handbag, and said, "Right, then! Best skedaddle!" Which was her way of saying, "Let's go."

And that was the end of my visit with Aunt Claire. I hadn't done a single thing that was clever or brave.

I suppose it had been helpful of me to point out that Aunt Claire's coat was caught in her car door when I arrived. But she would've noticed that herself, in a moment, anyway.

 # Aunt Sophy

31

Next, I took a dray cart to visit Aunt Sophy in the outskirts of Straw Bridge. Sophy is my youngest aunt, and is a veterinarian – she lives in an animal hospital. I already knew that, as she had visited Gainsleigh before and told me.

After she hugged me in welcome, we stopped outside the animal hospital. It was huge, like a barn. Aunt Sophy turned to me. "You know how certain things are famous throughout the Kingdoms and Empires for being dangerous and wicked?" she asked.

"Yes," I replied.

"And you know how it often turns out that, in fact, they are perfectly lovely?"

"Well," I said. "No. No, I've never heard that."

"Hmm," she said. "Well, trust me. It often does."

Then she told me that her animal hospital specialized in dragons.

All enormous creatures, like whales and tamarind elephants, have a magical impossibility about them. Your heart flares with astonishment to see them. They are so *big*, like buildings, and yet warm and alive, which is not like buildings. Dragons have that big-creature magic, of course, but they also ripple and glimmer with colour, on account of the gemstones in their scales.

So, yes, they are beautiful.

On the other hand, they have teeth like daggers, tails that can crush, and breath that could burn you alive.

I was petrified.

But Aunt Sophy was so kind and bossy with her dragons, moving quickly between them, spooning medicine into one dragon's open mouth, scratching the chin of another, scolding the next for having torn up its pillow, that I soon forgot to be afraid. It helped that some of the dragons could speak human language. Once you start chatting with a monster about the weather, you begin to forget that it's a monster.

Aunt Sophy speaks fluent Dragon, of course, which is a curious language. You speak it by making sounds that are sort of crunchy, or sometimes a bit like bicycle bells: *brrrring! brrring!* But you combine the sounds with gestures.

So if you want to say, "Sleep is the best thing for you, Dragon Sayara, and when you wake, your throat will feel much better," you make these noises: *grrrrr eek! eek! brl, grl, brl,* and at the same time, you bend, touch your toes, straighten up, then punch yourself in the stomach.

At night, Aunt Sophy and I had cocoa and cinnamon toast and

slept in bunk beds. I don't know if you have ever slept while dragons sighed and snuffled; if so, you will know that, on the first night, you have terrifying nightmares about dragons ripping you to pieces in your sleep. But, on the second and third night, there is a deep and comforting earthy smell, and the air glows and flashes with the warmth of their dreams.

During the day, Aunt Sophy set me to work shovelling dragon poop, boiling potatoes and peas (they work wonders for dragons with flu, Aunt Sophy told me), cutting up bandages, and disinfecting needles.

One of the older dragons, Dragon Great Damian, taught me some words and phrases in Dragon. He had a sprained hoof and was reclining, his hoof propped on a mattress with an ice pack the size of a flour sack. He chuckled often at my Dragon, sometimes cackling so hard that steam snorted from his nostrils. But each time that happened, he apologized and said, "No, but you're doing very well, Bronte! Very well!" Afterwards, he told Sophy that I had given him the best laugh he'd had in years, and quite taken his mind off his throbbing hoof.

Dragon Great Damian had grown up in Nina Bay, he said, and I told him I'd be visiting my Aunt Franny there at the end of my journey.

"Watch out for Whisperers," he said to me. "They steal children."

"It's safe now!" Aunt Sophy called from the baby dragon pen.

"They've got a Majestic Spellbinding all around the Whispering Kingdom, Damian."

"Ah, yes," muttered Dragon Great Damian. "My memory is not what it was." He chuckled. "As a young dragon, I used to fly over the Whispering Kingdom, you know, trying to see what it was like."

"And what is it like?" I asked.

"No idea," he said. "You can't see a thing. Wild ocean on one side, Impenetrable Forest on the other, and a witch-made Mist Shroud stops you from getting in – or seeing *anything* at all – from the air. The road, of course, is blocked by the Whispering Gates. They're a very secretive people – plus they have several diamond mines and need to keep out thieves."

"I think there are three Whispering Gates?" Aunt Sophy inquired, coming to join us, a baby dragon in her arms.

"Correct." The big dragon nodded. "Only Whisperers can get through the Whispering Gates – they Whisper them open. I have heard pirates speak of a legend that there are keys to the Gates hidden somewhere – pirates and Whisperers were allies in the Whispering Wars – but otherwise, nobody can enter."

"Why would anybody *want* to get through the Whispering Gates?" I asked.

"Excellent point," Aunt Sophy agreed. "Come, Bronte, would you like to learn how to feed this little guy?"

Bottle-feeding the baby dragon was my favourite part of the

visit. He snuggled himself into my lap and slurped on the bottle, staring steadily up at me. Newborn baby dragons are about the size of a cat, and their scales are still soft. They haven't even got their milk gemstones yet.

On my last day, I gave Aunt Sophy the gift from my parents. It turned out to be a tin of sugar cubes.

She smiled in the same soft way that she smiled at the baby dragons, and she told me that she and my mother, Lida, had been great friends as teenagers.

"Lida arrived in Gainsleigh with nothing but her shoulder bag," Aunt Sophy told me. "Not even a pair of shoes, and hair that fell into her eyes and all the way to her waist. She and I became friends.

"We both loved animals. We used to visit wild forest horses on the outskirts of Gainsleigh after school," Aunt Sophy continued. "We held sugar cubes out on the palms of our hands, hoping to win over the horses. Eventually, the horses began coming to us for sugar every afternoon. One day, we noticed that a horse had red nettle poisoning. Well, the only cure for *that* is blue chrysanthemums, but those are deep in the forest. Do you know what your mother did, Bronte? She persuaded another wild forest horse to carry her into the forest to find it!"

I blinked at that. As far as I knew, nobody had ever ridden a wild forest horse and lived to tell the tale.

"Another day, my brother, Patrick — your father — asked if he could please come along on the visit to the wild forest horses? He began to come all the time, bringing funny stories to tell the horses, glancing often at Lida's face as he told them to see if she might smile. She did. Your father was hilarious. Lida would practise her cartwheels and high flips in the forest, and *she* would glance at Patrick to see if he was impressed.

"In such a way, I was the first in the family to know that your parents were falling in love," Sophy told me proudly, and then she tilted her head and crouched beside me. "Do you want to know a secret about your mother, Bronte?"

I nodded. The question was a little foolish. "Of course."

"She told me never to tell anybody this, but she was a princess, you know."

I smiled. "An imaginary princess?" I asked. "Or do you mean that she was quite beautiful? Or that she liked things to be just so?"

But Aunt Sophy shook her head. "She told me that her father was the king of a tiny, distant kingdom, and that she ought never to have run away, for she should have been queen one day."

My heart was beating quickly now. "But her father is my *grandfather*," I said. "And he's an ordinary man who lives outside of Colchester and telegrams to invite me to stay and have ice cream on the beach! I'm visiting him at the end of this journey! You'd think he would have *mentioned* if he was a king!"

Aunt Sophy laughed. "I know," she said. "I have wondered

about that myself. But I think that your grandfather must have left his kingdom – or perhaps it was taken from him? Probably this happened not long after your mother ran away. And now he has moved to Colchester and is no longer any kind of king."

I frowned. "Or perhaps my mother was only pretending?"

Again, Aunt Sophy smiled. "Perhaps." She nodded. "I believed her when she told me. But she did have a good imagination."

At that moment, a great wind blustered in through the open door of the hospital. We hurried outside, Sophy pressing the sugar cubes into her pocket. An immense dragon hovered, scales alight in the afternoon sun. Aunt Sophy shouted greetings while the dragon landed and folded his wings. "It's Dragon Carpy," Sophy said to me, "here to visit his wife. He'll have to come back later, I'm afraid. I've given her a sleeping dram that'll last the day."

She gave Dragon Carpy an update on his wife's health. I understood fragments, but she was so quick, her hands twirling above her head one moment and patting the soles of her feet the next. Then she turned and looked at me thoughtfully.

"What do you think of Dragon Carpy giving you a ride to Blue Chalet Village?" she asked me. "He passes directly over it on his way home, and it would save you the long ride in a dray cart? I noticed in your parents' instructions that the dray cart is only a *suggestion* for how to get there. I wondered why it was written like that, and now I think maybe they were hinting at this?"

I stared at her. "Ride a dragon? I could do that?"

"Sure! I mean, you'd never ride a dragon without first asking his permission, of course. That's bad manners. Do you remember how to ask?"

It seemed to me that she was missing the point. This wasn't about manners, it was about the possibility of falling from the sky or getting char-grilled and eaten. "I think I'd rather..." I began, but then I remembered that my mother had once ridden a wild forest horse. "All right," I said instead.

To ask for a ride on a dragon, you have to take a handful of dried leaves, crumple them between your palms, clap four times, and say, *"Crch, crch, shhh, vip, crch?"* Easy.

I did that, and Dragon Carpy smiled and presented his neck.

"Hang on, we'll have to get her bag first," Aunt Sophy told him, in Dragon. "And I'll call your Aunt Nancy, Bronte, to make sure she can meet you earlier than planned."

Back inside, I ran around saying goodbye to the dragons and stroking the babies one last time and thanking Dragon Great Damian for his lessons. I could hear Aunt Sophy on the telephone explaining things to Aunt Nancy. "So she'll get there at *two* instead of *four*. Is that okay? You'll be there to meet her at *two*? By the fountain in the village square as planned, yes, but *two*, not four. All right?"

Over and over she said, "Two, not four. You got it?" and I could hear the voice on the other end of the phone beginning to sound impatient. "*Yes*," I heard, "I *got* it!" I didn't blame Aunt Nancy. Aunt Sophy was overdoing it.

"Well, that's done," Sophy said eventually, hanging up. She frowned at the phone, though, as if she might want to call back and say it one more time. It struck me as interesting, the way that people who are calm and sensible among animals can fall apart when it comes to other humans.

We hurried back outside and Dragon Carpy bowed, crouched, and lowered his neck again. Aunt Sophy demonstrated to me how you climb aboard a dragon, and how you cling to the tops of a dragon's wings without hurting him. I climbed on very cautiously, and the great dragon moved warm and slow beneath me. Aunt Sophy hooked my suitcase over Dragon Carpy's claws. My heart was beating very fast.

As the dragon rose into the air, I waved to Aunt Sophy and thanked her for my visit. It occurred to me that, once again, I had not done a single brave or clever thing my entire visit, although I supposed I'd been helpful. Then Dragon Carpy tilted a little, and I clutched his wings with both hands and leaned forward in the way Aunt Sophy had told me, and we sailed higher and higher into the blue, the wind fresh and free, my knees pressed against the dragon's flanks, and I found that I was laughing aloud. My father loved Faeries and told funny stories! My mother was a gymnast, and perhaps even a princess! Which, I realized suddenly, would make *me* a royal child of ten years old, so that perhaps I *would* be the child who caused great difficulties for the Whispering King's grandchild! This made me laugh more loudly, for I did not think my mother *was* a princess: more likely, she was a storyteller, like my father, and Aunt Sophy had fallen for her tales.

My parents had sent me on this journey to have adventures – small adventures, such as dining alone and trying out new foods, and bigger adventures with elves, a boy with no shoes, water sprites, Spellbinders, and dragons. They had sent me on this journey to hear my aunts tell stories about my parents themselves – reading Faery books, stealing cinnamon, eating spicy foods, turning cartwheels in forests – a basketful of memories to comfort me. Now I soared through the air, my heart glowing golden, and a thought flung itself at me.

I have never been so happy.

 # Aunt Nancy

32

Next, I visited my Aunt Nancy in the mountain village of Blue Chalet.

While I was there, I started an avalanche. I cannot imagine anyone calling that clever or brave. It's not even helpful.

33

I suppose I should tell you about the avalanche. I was thinking I could use that short chapter to skip straight over it and onto the next aunt. But no, that would only be annoying of me.

Here is what happened.

Dragon Carpy flew into the Blue Chalet Village Square about ten minutes before 2 p.m. He set down my suitcase and waited while I slid myself from his back. It was a long drop; I skidded a little on the icy cobblestones, but Carpy reached a wing to steady me.

I remembered my Dragon for "Thank you so much! Have a

great flight home!" and Carpy beamed and began to tell me a long story in rapid Dragon.

"I'm sorry," I said to him. "I only know a *tiny* bit of Dragon." Dragon Great Damian had urged me to practise this phrase as often as I could. "*Oftener,*" he had said, chortling.

"Oh," Dragon Carpy replied, and I could see he'd been excited about chatting. He was probably lonely without his wife. I told him that I had enjoyed the flight enormously, and that I hoped his wife, Dragon Bree, would recover soon.

Dragon Carpy nodded along politely as I spoke, but I could tell by the little dimple in his snout and the spark in his eye that I was making mistakes. I expect I was speaking mainly nonsense. Still, he seemed to get the point, and he thanked me for my kind thoughts, and folded his wings in a gesture of friendship. I folded my arms in response, and we both bowed. Then Dragon Carpy crouched low, spread his wings wide, and soared away.

I watched him sailing above the clock tower and rising up and up towards the mountains, past the mighty snow-covered peak of Mount Opal, and then he was gone.

So I hurried over to the fountain, placed my bag on the cobble-stones, and turned my attention to the village square.

At first, to be honest, I didn't notice anything strange about it. I was still elated by my dragon flight and the crowds of dragon memories from my days in Aunt Sophy's dragon hospital, and new memories about my brave and interesting parents. In fact, I was trembling with happiness.

Bong! ... Bong! said the clock tower, so now it was two o'clock. I looked around expectantly for Aunt Nancy. Would the girls be with her? Aunt Nancy has three daughters, two a little older than me and one a little younger, and my heart was thudding quickly about these cousins. I had spent so much time with grown-ups lately. They had all been very pleasant, of course, but it doesn't matter how pleasant grown-ups are, they're not children. I don't blame them for this – there's not a thing they can do about it.

I really wanted to spend some time with children now.

I stood alongside the fountain, stamping my feet and thinking, *Please be nice* about my cousins. Children who are unkind are even more useless than grown-ups.

Aunt Nancy was fifteen minutes late now. I remembered waiting on the wharf for Aunt Emma. Maybe Aunt Nancy was in prison too? Well, I would have to do detective work and get her out! I laughed to myself at that, and stamped my feet again.

After a while, I noticed what was strange about the square. It was empty. There were patches of snow and ice here and there, and icicles dripped from the eaves of all the shops, but nobody was hurrying into a shop or out of one. Nobody was standing looking up at the clock (except me, of course). No children played by the fountain, and no parents called to them to hurry up, it was time to go home.

I also noticed that I was stamping my feet. This was because it was cold. The sky was blue and there was a patch of sun in the shape of a triangle across the square, but the fountain was in deep shadow. I buttoned my overcoat right up to my chin and wrapped my arms around myself tightly.

BONG! said the clock, and it was 2:30 p.m.

I walked across to the triangle of sunlight and stood in it, facing the fountain. I would be able to watch out for Aunt Nancy from here, and the sun was now warm against the back of my neck. I felt my shoulders relax. There was a good view of Mount Opal from here too, rising up from behind the clock tower, bright with snow.

Nearby was a bakery. CLOSED said a sign on the door. Another notice hung directly beneath that, handwritten on a scrap of paper. I stepped closer to read it. **Due to Avalanche Risk**, it said.

"Avalanche risk!" I laughed. I thought it was a joke.

I stood rocking back and forth on my heels in the sunlight. *Bong!... Bong!... Bong!* said the clock. So now it was 3 p.m. My triangle, I noticed, was shrinking.

I waited. The triangle of sunlight disappeared. I looked around the square, but it was all in shade.

My teeth began to chatter.

3:30 p.m.

I sneezed.

I jogged on the spot, but my feet slid out from under me and I landed on my bottom, hard. I stood up again. I decided to walk briskly (yet carefully) around the square until Aunt Nancy arrived.

CLOSED DUE TO AVALANCHE RISK! said the sign on the bookstore. Closed - Avalanche, said a scribbled paper stuck to the butcher's shop window. I frowned. I looked towards the peak of Mount Opal. It looked right back at me, perfectly innocent. Its snowcap fitted snugly.

"Avalanche," I scolded the shops as I carried on around the square reading sign after sign. CLOSED DUE TO AVALANCHE RISK. "There's not going to be an avalanche!"

My voice echoed across the square. My fingers and toes burned with cold. I strode a little faster, skidded on a slippery cobblestone, but caught myself in time. I slowed down, watching my breath blow out its steam.

Around and around the square I walked. *Bong!* said the clock, over and over. CLOSED DUE TO AVALANCHE RISK, said every single shop. I passed a signboard painted with a map of the village and stared at this awhile. Mount Opal was sketched into the map, and somebody had pinned a little notice to *that*: AVALANCHE RISK: EXTREMELY HIGH.

4 p.m.

5 p.m.

The sky was a deep, dark blue now, the shadows in the square a deep black, and my whole body shook with cold. My hands and feet throbbed. My nose ran and I sneezed once, twice, three times, and sneezed again.

Suddenly, I understood. Some terrible accident must have happened to Aunt Nancy. Perhaps she had driven to the square to collect me in an automobile and it had crashed! Or in a horse and buggy, and it had skidded on ice and landed in a ditch! Maybe the girls were injured! Maybe Aunt Nancy and all three girls were trapped beneath the buggy in deep snow, and it was all my fault! They had been on their way to fetch me! And now they were slowly dying and here was *I* pacing around the square!

What was wrong with me?!

I threw open my suitcase and fumbled for my parents' instructions. I had to take off my gloves to turn the pages, and my fingers were a vibrant blue. I found Aunt Nancy's address: *The Dime House, Furrier Lane, Blue Chalet*. I packed the suitcase again and ran across to the signboard with the village map.

Furrier Lane! Where was it?

There it was, quite high in the hills. It joined Steep Road, which ran all the way down to the square, so that *had* to be the route they had taken.

I grabbed my suitcase, skidded out of the square, and turned onto Steep Road.

34

Steep Road should have been called Steep and Also Covered in Slippery Ice Road. Or maybe The Road on Which You Take Two Steps and Slide Down Five.

But it was only called Steep Road.

I clambered and slipped my way up using a sort of crawling motion with my elbows and knees as wedges. An icy wind played with me all the way, diving under my collar, slithering up my sleeves, and dusting me with gritty bits of ice. I kept careful watch for carriages upturned in ditches, but I saw no vehicles at all – not the upturned kind, nor the kind that travel on their wheels. Once I thought I saw a person facedown in the snow, and I cried out, "Aunt Nancy!" and rushed over, leaping into deep snow. It turned out to be a tattered old scarecrow.

By the time I reached Aunt Nancy's house, the sky was scattered with stars. DIME HOUSE, said a wooden board hanging from a letter box. The windows were orange golden.

I tried to knock on the door, but my arm was frozen solid like a piece of wood and wouldn't work. I tried thumping with my suitcase instead.

A long silence.

I thumped again.

"What *is* that noise!" came a voice from inside. Then footsteps, and the door flew open. It nearly tripped me backwards.

A tall woman frowned down at me. *"Yes?"* she demanded.

Had Aunt Nancy moved? Was this the wrong address?

Now what?

"Aunt Nancy?" I tried hesitantly.

"Bronte!" she said. "What on . . . ? Come inside! Quickly! Of all the . . . ?"

She shut the door firmly behind me, and we both stopped in the hallway. I stood shivering, and she stood staring.

"What are you doing here already?" she asked eventually.

"I arrived at two," I said.

"Two? No, no. Sophy *specifically* told me it had been changed. Ten, she said. I've organized the chair to collect you! Oh, blast, now that's for nothing. I'll have to cancel it." She smiled brightly at me. "Never mind," she said. "Don't blame yourself. I'll just go cancel that chair."

I followed her down the hall and we turned into a kitchen. There was a fireplace in the corner, but it had not been lit. A window was ajar, and the icy breeze was using it to come inside and flutter the tablecloth.

While Aunt Nancy made her telephone call, I pulled off my boots. My stockings were drenched. Snow showered from the boots onto the floorboards along with melting slush.

"Oh!" I said.

Aunt Nancy turned, still talking into the phone. She furrowed her brow at the snow on the floor, then pointed out a towel that was hanging from a hook. I slid over to get it and wiped up the snow as well as I could.

"Well!" Aunt Nancy said, hanging up her telephone. "Let's have a look at you. But you're still wearing your coat! Funny thing. Take it off! You're inside now."

I looked over at the open window. "Could we close that?"

"Oh dear, no. Fresh air clears away the germs. Now, I'm right in the middle of preparations for tomorrow's meetings." Aunt Nancy pointed out stacks of papers lined up on the table. "This is terrible timing, your visit, dear – I have meetings for the entire three days. Lots of people will be coming here – but you must *not* blame yourself for that. Only, I'll have to keep working as we talk, I'm afraid. But you won't mind that. I can't think why you've arrived now, at what is it?" She looked at her watch. "Nine o'clock! You're an hour early! Sophy specifically told me ten. Never mind, it's all worked out in the end."

"I got here at two," I said. "I waited in the village square, and then I walked up."

"Whatever did you do that for? Sit down, won't you, and make yourself at home. Take off your gloves at least!"

I pulled off my gloves, which were soaked through, and set them on the table. A puddle formed around them.

"Now then, would you like a glass of water?"

I stared at her. A glass of water? Surely I should be changing out of my wet clothes? Not adding *more* water to the mix.

"It's not a trick question!" Aunt Nancy grinned. "Yes or no!"

"All right, then," I said. "Yes, please."

She hurried over to the sink and turned on the tap. As she did that, I tried to solve the puzzle. Aunt Sophy had said *two* on the telephone. Very clearly. Many times. I had *heard* her.

The answer occurred to me. Aunt Nancy must have a hearing problem, and *that* was why Aunt Sophy had repeated herself so much.

How could I find out for sure?

I would speak very softly, and see if she heard me.

"Do you have a hearing problem?" I whispered.

Aunt Nancy swung around from the sink, glass of water in her hand. "No, I most certainly do not!" she said. "My hearing is excellent! What a funny thing to say." She set the water down before me, her face rushing with frowns, which settled back into a smile.

"Now, then," she said, swiping papers from each of the stacks. She straightened edges and stapled the papers together: *CLUNK!* "I've been on the telephone with your other aunts today, and I've heard all about *your* adventures! Your Aunt Sue says you've been jumping into rivers! Your Aunt Emma says you've been arguing with the police! Your Aunt Claire says you ran around going to conferences! Your Aunt Sophy says you've been gallivanting with dragons! What a funny thing you are!"

I sneezed seven times in a row.

Aunt Nancy laughed. "You've gone and got yourself a chill, and no wonder! Jumping into rivers! What a funny thing to do!"

I wanted to say that I had jumped into the river *ages* ago and that, if I did have a chill, it was from waiting in the village square for her. But that didn't seem polite.

"Well," I said instead. "I only jumped into the river because there was a baby in there."

"Oh yes, my girls like babies too," Aunt Nancy said. "They're always wanting to play with babies."

"I didn't want to *play*—" I began. *CLUNK*, said Aunt Nancy's stapler. I took a sip of water. It was icy cold. I felt it all the way down my throat to my chest. "Where are the girls?" I asked. The house was very quiet. Perhaps they were sleeping?

"The girls?! Why, they're at boarding school, of course! And your Uncle Nigel is on one of his research trips, as usual. Honestly, he works so hard, his hair has fallen out! Completely bald he is now. I kept telling him to slow down if he wanted to keep his hair, but he only laughed at me. He loves his work writing history books, you see. But that means it's just you and me, I'm afraid. Didn't you know that the girls go to boarding school? Gosh. Isabelle doesn't tell you much, does she?"

"She might have told me," I said quickly. I didn't want her thinking Aunt Isabelle had failed me. "I just forgot."

"Oh, yes, my girls forget things all the time too! Ribbons,

cardigans, bracelets. They leave a trail of possessions behind them wherever they go! And they're always *going* places too, just like you! It would be just like my girls to take it upon themselves to walk all the way up from the square! You funny thing!"

"I'm actually quite good at looking after my things," I said, and I heard my voice becoming fractious. "And I waited for a *very* long time in the square. I thought there must have been an accident. I thought you were dead in a ditch! I *saw* you, dead in a ditch!"

"Excuse me?"

"But it turned out to be a scarecrow."

Aunt Nancy burst into laughter. "You thought I was a scarecrow!" She laughed even more loudly. "Oh *my*!"

The laughter went on.

I sat at the kitchen table, shivering and listening to the laugh. I thought about how laughter can be warm as a dragon's breath, or cold as a big block of ice. In some ways, Aunt Nancy's laugh reminded me of Aunt Claire's laughter when things went wrong at the conference – a raucous ha! ha! ha! – only with Aunt Nancy, the tone was a notch along. Just one notch was enough to change a thing from warm to cold.

I thought of my other aunts and all their different laughs: Aunt Sue's soft murmurs as she helped her boys make paper chains, Aunt Emma's sudden giggles, Aunt Sophy's low chuckle as she stroked a dragon's nose.

Then I thought of home, and Aunt Isabelle and the Butler

playing cards in the study, all the different tones and notches of their laughter.

My father had made my mother laugh among the wild forest horses. I tried to imagine how my mother's laugh sounded, but I couldn't hear it at all.

I looked across at the empty grate in the fireplace, and waited.

Eventually, Aunt Nancy's laughter slowed, and she sighed contentedly and picked up the stapler again.

I felt cold right through to the centre of my being.

"I wonder," I said, "if I could have a bath?"

"Well!" Aunt Nancy cried. "If you'd arrived at the time you were *supposed* to, this afternoon at four, instead of changing it to *ten p.m.* you could have had a bath! But the hot water's done for the day now."

"Oh," I said.

Aunt Nancy frowned at me. "Come on," she said. "Cheer up! What's up?"

"It's just, I'm rather cold."

"Oh, there's an easy solution to that. Hop into bed, why don't you? The covers will warm you up! Take any of the girls' rooms! You can have your pick!"

I stood up and waited, but Aunt Nancy remained sitting at the table. She picked up another pile of papers.

I should find the girls' rooms myself?

I walked to the kitchen door and paused. Left?

"Not that way!" Aunt Nancy called. She was grinning and pointing right. "*That* way! Funny thing."

"Is there a bathroom this way?" I inquired.

"Of course there is! You think we have no bathrooms up here in the mountains! City girl through and through!"

"I only meant..." I began. "May I have a towel. To dry myself? I got quite wet walking here."

"I'm not surprised! Yes. There's a towel on the hook right – oh, where's it gone? Ah! That's right. There."

The towel I had used to wipe the spilled snow still lay on the kitchen floor. Aunt Nancy picked it up with the toe of her shoe and flung it in my direction.

"Nice catch!" she said.

35

Over the next three days, I wore every single item of clothing in my suitcase.

Aunt Nancy's house skittered with icy draughts. Windows were cracked open in every room and the fires were never lit, although each was stacked with wood. I asked once if she would like me to light one for her? "Oh gosh!" she said. "A fire! You are accustomed to grandeur, aren't you! Funny thing! Honestly, though, it's not your fault." Then I had to wait again, while she laughed a whole storybook of laughter. After which she walked out of the room.

So I wore layers. All my dresses and cardigans, scarves and gloves, four or five pairs of stockings, my summer coat and my winter overcoat too. Still, I shivered. When I think of Aunt Nancy's house, all her furniture seems to tremble and jitter, and that is because I was seeing it through shivers.

On the first morning, Aunt Nancy was frying sausages when I walked into the kitchen. They smelled warm and delicious. My eyes watered happily at the smoke and spit of them.

"Late riser!" she said when she saw me. "Sausages for breakfast?"

"Yes, please!"

"How did you sleep?"

"Very well, thank you," I said politely, although I had found the mattress as hard as a board, and I had shivered and tossed under the thin blanket, eventually creeping down the hall and taking the blankets from the other girls' beds. Even then, I had been too cold to sleep. Eventually, around dawn, I had drifted into dreams of ice-polar bears.

"Oh, good!" Aunt Nancy said, beaming. "Yes, I thought you would sleep well. The girls all have the *best* beds. We splurged on them. Orthopedic SleepWells. You get the *best* sleep, don't you think?"

"Mm," I said, and sneezed. Aunt Nancy smiled at me. "Here," she said, "make yourself useful and get the toast going, will you?"

I found the bread and the toasting iron and got to work, breathing in the smell of sausages.

"Well, let's have a look at it, then!" Aunt Nancy said suddenly.

Confused, I held up a piece of toast.

"Ha-ha! No, not the toast! I mean, this gift that your parents have for me. Aren't you here to deliver it?"

"Oh," I apologized, replacing the toast in its stack. "I'm supposed to give it to you on my third day here, just before I leave. My parents put that in their instructions. They also suggested I go to the Mountain View Café after I give it to you, and order a hot chocolate. Is that far?"

"Of all the things," Aunt Nancy cried. "You funny thing! I can't say I'm a fan of the place myself." She looked at her watch. "Oh, the time! I know what I'll do," and she reached for a slice of my freshly-made toast, popped a sausage onto it, and folded it up. Then she switched off the pan and tipped the remaining sausages into a container. She sealed this tightly, and put the whole thing in the refrigerator.

I blinked.

"Butter for your toast is over there!" she called through her mouthful of sandwich as she hurried from the room. "The sausages will be perfect for everybody's lunch! Lucky you didn't want any!"

"But I did," I whispered.

I sat at the table and ate my buttered toast. I thought about taking the container out of the fridge and getting a sausage for myself, but that would look rude if she caught me. And what would everybody have for lunch?

Now and then, Aunt Nancy hurried in and out of the kitchen, grabbing papers and muttering to herself. She seemed very excited about her meetings. I began to be interested to see what would happen.

In fact, the meetings were unbelievably dull. People kept arriving, unwinding their scarves, and calling out droll things to each other, which I could not understand. Then they would gather in the living room and say things like "protocol" and "funding cuts", and "You know, those make excellent talking points but is this the time to talk?" Or: "I'm going to go ahead and stop you right there, because is any of this legitimately productive?"

There were men with deep voices and coughs, and women who leaned forward, frowning and tapping their fingers on their chins.

After a while, the group would stand up and troop to the front door, winding their scarves back around their necks, calling more droll things, and slamming the door behind them. A few moments later, another group would arrive and do the same.

They were all "subcommittees", it seemed, and Aunt Nancy was the "chair" of every one. After the sausage incident, I had decided that she must be one of those absentminded people. But in the meetings, she seemed sharp as a tack. She kept reeling off regulation numbers, and the others always said, "Precisely. Good point."

Meanwhile, I wandered around the house, blowing my nose and shivering. I read the storybooks my governess had packed for me, and then looked along the bookshelves in the living room for something else to read. But there were only Uncle Nigel's history books. I was so bored I even tried to read those.

Now I want to tell you about one surprising thing that I found amongst Uncle Nigel's books. It was ancient and tattered and it was called:

The Whispering Kingdom: A Travel Guide

That's why I pulled it out. I saw the title on the spine and thought it must be a joke book. Nobody would want to visit the Whispering Kingdom! It's full of evil Dark Mages! *This will give me a good laugh*, I thought – but then I read the first page:

The Whispering Kingdom is a tiny realm of gentle, private people who do not much like social interaction. To visit, you first need to seek permission of the king or queen. If accepted, you will be given an appointed time, and the Whispering Gates will be opened for you.

Once inside the kingdom, you will find picturesque gardens, cobblestone streets, and a mild and musical people. Of course, Whisperers have the power of persuasion/suggestion and can whisper thoughts into your head. You may find yourself stepping into restaurants or cafés, sitting down to order, then wondering: "Now why did I come in here? I don't even LIKE pizza!" However, you will quickly get to know the tickle of a Whisper, and will learn how to shake it off.

Whisperers are very sensitive people and can often pick up on your thoughts or emotions. So don't be surprised if a Whisperer suddenly offers you a hug on a day when you're feeling low. Some Whisperers can even pick up on "whispers" from the future: if you see a fortune-teller in the marketplace, you are likely to find out exactly what is going to happen!

I stopped reading there. I was too chilly to sit still any longer, and too confused to turn another page. If this was a joke book, it was not very funny. It seemed to be perfectly serious. In fact, it was dangerous. Everybody knew that Whisperers were Dark Mages: if you went into the Kingdom, you would never come out. Whispers didn't "tickle", they *seared* into your brain! Most probably the book had been published by the Whisperers themselves, to lure people into their kingdom. A shiver zigzagged down my spine and I quickly shoved the book back onto the shelf.

I kept expecting Aunt Nancy to notice that I was wearing all my clothes at once – I resembled a tree stump and could hardly fit through doors – but she never did.

"This is my niece Bronte," she told the men and women as they arrived. "All the way from Gainsleigh for a visit!" and the people would be kind and say, "Gainsleigh! You're a long way from home!" Then they would ask how old I was. After that, they seemed to run out of conversation, and would go back to making jokes with one another before settling into their meeting.

The committees had breaks for morning tea, lunch, and afternoon tea, and Aunt Nancy set me to work buttering piles of bread and opening packets of biscuits to set out on plates. During these break times, people would sometimes think up more questions to ask me. Did my parents mind me travelling all the way from Gainsleigh to visit my aunt? they often asked. Then Aunt Nancy would step in and answer for me by telling a story. Over and over, she told this story as she hurried around serving tea and coffee. She swished the story behind her like a raincoat on a blustery day.

"Well, you see," she began. "I was one of twelve children. Eleven were girls but the youngest, Patrick, was a boy. Oh, he was a mad, wild thing. Like a puff of dandelion, our mother used to say, blown about in pieces on the breeze. And we were that surprised when he settled down with his girlfriend and married her! *What a turn of events*, my sisters and I wrote to one another – for, by this point, most of the sisters had grown and moved across the Kingdoms and Empires, and many of us didn't even have Gainsleigh accents anymore.

"Anyhow, Patrick and Lida rented a little cottage by the Gainsleigh Memorial, but they were *never* there. They kept running off on adventures! Still, they found time to have a baby girl and name her Bronte. And guess what happened next?"

"Oh yes," people said, sipping their tea and reaching for biscuits, "Mm, hmm," and "Oh my," and "What?"

So then Aunt Nancy told them how my parents had left the baby in the lobby of Aunt Isabelle's building and gone off to have adventures.

"No!" people cried, but in a delighted way, as if the story was getting really good now.

"Yes! That was just like them, you see. Now, if Patrick and Lida had just told us all in *advance* that they wanted adventure *sans* child – well! We could have set up a sort of roster system for Bronte! Bundling her from here to there. Which would have been so great for her complexion. But no, the issue of what to do with the baby had *apparently* slipped their minds until they were approaching the docks. They must have panicked! *What shall we do with her? Let's drop her off at Isabelle's with a note!* Which, again, was *exactly* like them."

"Oh my," people murmured, wide-eyed.

"The note was addressed to my eldest sister, Isabelle, and the child *was* left in Isabelle's building, which meant that she was responsible."

"I suppose so," the others agreed.

"Anyway, then a very sad thing happened. Patrick and Lida were killed by pirates."

At this point, the people would all turn from Nancy to me, their faces so sad and aghast that I had to cheer them up.

"It's all right," I said. "I never knew them."

"No, you didn't," Aunt Nancy agreed. "But I did. And I am absolutely devastated. Anyhow, they left a will that instructs Bronte to deliver gifts to all her aunts! So! Here she is! On a journey of delivery!"

"What a story!" people said. "And what gift did you get, Nancy?"

Then Nancy said, "Oh, she refuses to give it to me until her very last day here! Just before she leaves, so she says!"

At which everybody laughed and said, "Isn't she a darling?" and they looked at me and smiled.

"It's not *funny*!" I said. "It's Faery cross-stitched!" But they were busy with their papers again and didn't hear me.

36

On my last morning at Aunt Nancy's place, I took her gift from the treasure chest and carried it into the kitchen.

"Good morning," I said, and my voice rasped so strangely it made me jump.

Aunt Nancy grinned at me. "Up then, are you? Another lovely sleep?"

"Not bad," I agreed, still rasping. I touched my throat. There was an ache deep inside it. I thought I could avoid the ache if I just never swallowed again.

"How did *you* sleep?" I asked, more to hear my own voice again than because I was interested. This time I sounded like a barrow being dragged over gravel. It also *felt* that way.

"Perfectly," Aunt Nancy replied, bowing to her papers again.

A sudden, powerful image came to me of my Aunt Isabelle. She was frowning and pressing her palm against my forehead. She was turning to the Butler – "You had better fetch the doctor" – while she took my hand and hurried me to bed.

I shook the image from my mind, and placed my parents' gift on the table. Aunt Nancy glanced at it. "Aha!" she said. She pursed her lips. "May I open it now?"

I nodded.

Aunt Nancy reached out with both hands and tore off the wrapping.

She pulled out a tiny box and peered at its label. "Well," she said. "They've got that wrong anyway. Dried rose petals. A nice thought, except that they're pink! I've always had a fondness for the *red* ones. Never mind! You mustn't blame yourself, dear." She pushed the box to the side and carried on working. Her face looked a little stern, but then she blinked the sternness away and smiled.

"You're having your toast, as usual?" she asked.

I moved towards the bread but the idea of toast crumbs in my throat was too awful to imagine. Instead, I pulled out a chair.

"Is there somewhere I could buy a postcard?" I inquired. "I'd like to send one to Aunt Isabelle."

"Oh, gosh! You didn't think to bring stationery with you, did you? *Just* like my girls! And why ever doesn't Isabelle get a telephone? Far too old-fashioned!"

I coughed, took a breath, and tried to speak *around* the rasping. "I *did* bring stationery," I said. "Only I promised Aunt Isabelle I would send her a postcard from every place I visited."

"Rash promise! And I'm afraid that'll be a no-go here. The village shops are all closed because of the avalanche risk. Oh gosh, I must book the chair for you! It will take you to the station, and I think you get a train to the Jumian Wharf and then join the cruise ship there. What time will you be ready to leave, do you think?"

I fetched myself a glass of water. It ran down my throat like an icy flame.

"Well," I said. "First I'm supposed to go to the Mountain View Café and order a hot chocolate, remember?"

"Oh, the Mountain View Café, I'm not a fan of the place. Why would you go there?"

"It's in my parents' instructions."

"Oh. Compulsory, then? The Faery cross-stitch?"

"No. Just a recommendation."

"In that case, skip it."

"But they *want* me to go."

Aunt Nancy burst out laughing. "Oh my," she said. "Trust me, child, you don't need to go to that café!"

"I'd like to go," I said.

"Skip it! What have your parents done for *you*, besides running off and then tying you up with Faery cross-stitch? I'll get the chair to come and fetch you straight to the station," and she stood, still laughing to herself, and reached for the phone.

Everything changed colour for a moment. My eyes went flash! flash! flash! and the room went blue! purple! red!

I felt floaty. I watched Aunt Nancy pick up her telephone and begin to dial a number. My eyes filled with tears. *Sorry,* I thought towards my parents, *I've failed you.* I imagined the hot chocolate they wanted me to have. How smooth and warm in my throat! I imagined it tipping sadly away into the snow, without me. The tears slid down my cheeks.

Another image came to me. Aunt Isabelle frowning. *"You've a very strong will there, Bronte!"* she scolded. And another. Aunt Isabelle beaming. *"You've a very strong will there, Bronte!"*

I swiped the tears away and jumped to my feet.

"No, Aunt Nancy," I declared.

She was waiting for someone to answer the phone. "Shhh," she told me.

"*No*, Aunt Nancy," I repeated. "I *am* going to the Mountain View Café."

Aunt Nancy chuckled. "No, you're not," she said. "I'm calling you the chair."

"Yes, I am."

"No, you're not. You won't even like it!"

"Yes. As a matter of fact, I am."

Aunt Nancy chuckled again. "Listen to you! Funny little thing!"

"Kindly do not *chuckle*," I said in a low and crackling voice. "My parents might have left me and tied me up with Faery cross-stitch. But I'm *sure* they had reasons. They want me to go to the Mountain View Café, and I *will* go there. Right this instant. Arrange for a chair to collect me if you like, but I will *not* be here to take it."

I strode out of the kitchen and down the hall.

Behind me came an icy, cool silence. The telephone clicked.

I returned to the kitchen, carrying my suitcase. Aunt Nancy was standing with folded arms.

"Thank you for your hospitality," I said. "Goodbye for now."

I walked out the front door.

37

I didn't have a clue where the Mountain View Café was, of course.

I stood outside Aunt Nancy's front door. The sky was blue and the snow was bright. I squinted to the left. There, the road ran to

Steep Street, and on down to the village. I squinted right. There, the road ran up into the mountains.

Both directions were silent.

"Mountain View Café?" I called, very softly.

It didn't answer, of course.

Hmm, I thought to myself.

Then I realized something. Even if I knew where it was, it would be closed! Like everything else! Because of the avalanche risk!

I had just wasted my will.

Behind me, the door opened. "Goodness me!" Aunt Nancy said. "You *are* the funniest thing. Well, if you must go to the Mountain View Café, it's up that way." She pointed right. "They're open because the avalanche risk is mild there." She tilted her head, examining my boots. "It's quite a walk. Can you manage?"

"Yes, thank you," I said.

"All that way carrying your suitcase! Funny thing. Ask the people at the café to order you the chair to the station. That suit you?"

"Perfectly, thank you."

"Just follow the road, then," she declared. "And eventually you'll see a signpost. It's quite a famous café. Everybody *loves* it, although I *cannot* think why. But don't blame yourself, dear."

I looked at her. "I don't," I told her frankly. "Thank you again for my stay."

Aunt Nancy beamed. "As long as you've had a *really* lovely time!" she said.

I wasn't at all sure how to answer that, so I turned around and set off.

And when I got to the Mountain View Café, of course, I started the avalanche.

38

This is how it happened.

First, I found the café. It was a long, steep trek up the road, and then a longer, steeper trek up a snowy track through the mountains. By the time I arrived, I was breathing in and out like this: *crackle-HUFF! crackle-HUFF!*

A wooden platform, crowded with chairs and tables, rose from the snow on thick wooden stumps. It was empty except for one table, where a rugged-up family sat eating and drinking. They were perfectly silent. A little boy put a spoon into a bowl of ice cream and it clinked. "Shhh!" hissed his mother.

I stopped to get my breath. My eyes ran from the platform along a path to a log cabin. Huge block letters were painted on the side of this cabin: MOUNTAIN VIEW CAFÉ, and beneath that: Order Inside.

I *crackle-HUFF*ed my way to this cabin and pushed open the

door. Inside was another little cluster of tables and chairs, a picture window, and a fireplace. No customers at all in here, but a young woman stood behind a counter.

She pointed to a sign on the counter. BE QUIET! it said.

I nodded.

We looked at each other. I set down my suitcase. We looked at each other a little longer.

"Yes?" the woman prompted.

Now I was confused. I pointed to the sign.

"Oh!" She smiled. "You're allowed to speak. Just don't *shout*. We need to be careful of loud noises around here, because of the avalanche risk. Got a pair of cymbals in that suitcase? Whack them together, why don't you? And *then* we'll have a show!" She grinned, and then shook her head quickly. "But don't," she said. "Don't do that."

"I haven't got any cymbals," I assured her.

She smiled. I ordered my hot chocolate.

"Inside or outside?"

Now, on this particular day I made three bad decisions. The first one was now. I looked at the fireplace in the corner, and then I looked at the big blue sky in the window and thought of the platform and its tables. "Outside," I said.

"Leave your suitcase in here, then," she suggested kindly. "Sit anywhere you like, and I'll bring you the hot chocolate."

I thanked her and turned to the door.

"Would you mind taking these along with you?" the woman called softly.

I turned around. She was holding a tray of teacups. "The family out there have ordered a pot of tea," she said. "I'll make it now, but it would be a huge help if you carried the cups out for me?"

I hesitated.

"Don't worry if it's too much trouble," she added.

This was my second bad decision. "Not too much at all," I said. In fact, I was pleased that she trusted me with the job. I reached for the tray.

The empty teacups sat elegantly on their saucers, each painted with matching flowers. They jingled a little as I walked along the path. From up on the platform, the family looked across at me. I slowed down.

Here came my third decision.

I could feel a cough in my chest. It rose slowly to my chin. The cough wanted me to cough, but I kept my mouth firmly closed. *No,* I thought to the cough. *I will not make a sound.*

That was the bad decision. I should have just coughed.

As it was, the cough grew steadily. It billowed and surged inside me. It pulsated in my cheeks. It grappled at my scalp, plunging its nails into my knees.

If you haven't had a serious cough for a while, you'll think I'm talking a lot of nonsense. But I'm not. That's exactly how coughs feel when you refuse to let them cough.

Steadfastly, I walked on, the tray held out before me. *You MUST let me cough*, the cough commanded, and I replied, *I will NOT!* The cough got its shoulders right up against the inside of my chest and shoved as hard as it could. I pressed my mouth tightly closed and then, without me making a decision, the cough *exploded into being.*

It turned out it didn't need my permission after all.

By now, of course, it had grown so big and powerful that it was a shouting cough, a bellowing cough, the kind of cough that takes you by the shoulders and shakes you wildly. I stumbled. I hit a patch of ice on the path. My feet flew up beneath me and the tray of teacups soared into the air.

39

People ask me, "What was it like to be tossed down a mountainside in an avalanche?!" They are so eager to hear, but I don't have a clue how to describe it.

So I tell them about the curtains.

Once, a great storm blew through Gainsleigh, and the windows in the drawing room were open. Aunt Isabelle and I ran in to close them, but we both paused a moment, struck by the chaos. The rain was splattering the carpet but, more than that, the curtains were under attack. The terrible wind was dashing them, wringing them, slamming them up against the glass, against the wall, against the ceiling. It was beating them, tossing, slapping, and twisting them. I always remember those curtains and how desperate and helpless they were, how they swung towards us and seemed to cry, *Help!* but the wind plucked them back again, away from us at once.

That was me on the mountain. I coughed, hit a patch of ice, the teacups flew – and then I *was* the curtains in the wind.

My teeth rattled, my cheeks ached, my arms and legs twisted and flailed. *Help,* I cried, reaching out to Aunt Isabelle, for there she was in the doorway of the drawing room, watching me. *Help!* I called, but I was flung back against the glass. *Help, Aunt Isabelle!* I sobbed.

Help! I called to my parents. But they were very busy. *What shall we do with her?* my father asked. *Just drop her here with a note?*

The wind slammed me up against the ceiling. *Help, Aunt Isabelle,* I whispered deep inside me.

The wind took a fist and punched me quite through.

Just drop her here in this ditch, said my mother, *with a note.*

Here, said my father, *wrap this cross-stitch all around her so she can't escape the avalanche.*

Over and over, I whispered or sobbed, *Help me, help me,* twisting and flailing in a thicket of trees, somewhere in a ditch, on the mountainside, lost.

Until something fell upon me like the window slamming fast: the curtains dropped, lifeless and still.

40

I dreamed that I was warm.

I remember this! I thought. I decided to stick with the dream.

But then I opened my eyes and saw the warm orange glow of a fireplace, overlapping rugs on warm wooden floorboards, a tall, warm clock saying *tick, tock, tick.*

I am *warm,* I thought in amazement.

I fell asleep again.

The next time I woke, three girls stared down at me. Each had dark-gold braids.

"Are you awake?" said one.

"Shush," said the second. "You'll wake her."

"Not if she's already awake," the first countered.

"Are you awake *now*?" inquired the third, archly. "I mean to say, have my sisters woken you?"

I stared up at each face in turn.

"It's so warm!" I said.

"You're too hot!" one cried, and the second bellowed: "Turn the fire down!" The third rushed to the fireplace. "How do I do it?" She seized a poker.

"No, please!" I said. "I *like* being warm!" I tried to sit up.

"Lie down!" they all cried in horror. The girl holding the poker dropped it with a clatter, rushed over, grabbed my shoulders, and pushed me back down. *Bounce*, went my head against the pillow.

"Don't be so rough!" the others scolded her.

"I was being firm," she explained. "Not rough, just kind and firm."

The others swung to look at me. "Was she rough?"

I considered. They waited patiently.

"I'm very confused," I said eventually.

The three girls looked at one another. They widened their eyes. Then they beamed.

"Of *course*," said one. "She doesn't know where she is!"

"She probably doesn't know who we are!"

"She might not even know who *she* is," breathed the third.

The others scoffed at that. "I'm sure she knows who she is."

I thought about it.

"Bronte Mettlestone," I said. "Pleased to meet you."

They beamed again. "*Well* done," they said warmly.

"And do you know what happened to you?" one inquired gently.

Up until that point, I had only been happy to be warm. But instantly, I remembered. The warmth fled like scattering mice. I took a great breath in and I couldn't breathe out. Sobs rushed at me. I was nothing but a tangle of sobs.

"Oh no!" the girls exclaimed. "Don't cry! Darling, don't cry!" All three of them clambered onto the bed, all their hands and arms wrapped round me. "Hush now," they murmured, all at once.

"I'm getting very wet," one said politely.

"The avalanche!" I wept.

"No, darling, from your tears."

The others hushed her. "Yes," one said. "You were in an avalanche! It must have been so scary!"

"No wonder you're crying. Poor thing."

"But the people! The people!" I was sobbing again.

They patted me and smoothed my hair until I quieted down again.

"What people?" one murmured eventually.

"The people at the Mountain View Café! The family! The waitress! I caused an avalanche! I killed them all! They're all dead!"

"Oh, they're *fine*," the three girls scoffed. "Are you thinking they got hurt? The avalanche thundered down right between the cabin and the platform. It took you with it."

"It carried *you* for miles! It's *astonishing* you're alive!"

"And a night out in the snow? It's *miraculous*! You nearly died, you know. You had a terrible fever."

"When the doctor brought you in, he said, *I don't like her chances.*"

"He did say that. We specifically heard him: *I don't like her chances.*"

"And when he came back the next day, he said, *Well, she's proved me wrong!* He sounded a bit annoyed with you for proving him wrong."

"No, he didn't, Imogen. You're inventing. He sounded very pleased."

"And then you just slept. You've been sleeping this last week!"

I stopped crying. "The people are all right?"

The three girls nodded vigorously.

"Only everyone's annoyed with that waitress for asking you to carry a tray of teacups. She says she thought you were older than ten. Because you seemed so sophisticated. And self-assured."

I was quite happy about that. Sophisticated and self-assured. I still feel happy now, remembering.

"Everyone's all right?" I whispered again, and the three girls whispered, "Yes."

Then I began to laugh. I laughed until I cried, and at once the girls began their patting and smoothing and hugging.

After a while, they sat back and regarded me again.

"You are to rest for at least another week," one told me. "And we are not to upset you."

They raised their eyebrows at each other then. "So much for that promise," one said. "She's been crying her eyes out."

"I'm all right," I assured them.

I leaned back against the headboard. I felt tingly with cheerfulness now. Everyone was okay! I looked at the room more carefully.

There were lamps lit, and arched windows. On the wall were paintings: a jester juggling coloured balls, a woman on a picnic rug with a slice of cake on a plate.

A white feather quilt lay on my bed, and this was covered, at a diagonal, by a patchwork blanket.

For the first time, I wondered where I was.

"She still doesn't know who we are," one of the girls whispered.

"We should introduce ourselves," another whispered back.

"I'm too shy," said the third.

All three giggled. The bed shook.

"*I'll* start," one said boldly, and she reached out to shake my hand. "My name is Imogen," she said. "Pleased to meet you."

"I'm Esther," said the second.

"I'm Astrid," said the third.

"Imogen, Esther, and Astrid," I said. I shook their hands in turn. Imogen was the tallest, and her forehead was quite high. Esther was the middle one and her nose had a tilt. Astrid was the smallest and liveliest.

They gazed at me. I gazed back.

"Imogen, Esther, and Astrid," I repeated. Something went *click-click-click* as if the names were the cogs in a turning wheel. "Imogen, Esther, and Astrid! I have *cousins* with those names!"

The girls smiled.

"Do you indeed?" Imogen inquired.

"The funniest thing," Esther added. "*We* have a cousin named Bronte."

Astrid bounced on her knees. "It's us!" she said. "We're your cousins! This is our boarding school!"

"The avalanche carried you all the way to the woods by the school gate! The groundskeeper found you!"

"Your suitcase was still in the café!"

"That's how they figured out who you were. Your name is on the suitcase! The café sent it down for you."

At that moment, a bell jangled somewhere in the distance and Astrid said, "Whoa, that's the time?"

Then they sprang from the bed and ran from the room, blowing kisses behind them. "Don't sob again," Esther called over her shoulder, "or not until we're back anyway."

41

Let me be honest with you. My week at the Katherine Valley Boarding School for Girls was one of the most pleasant of my life.

But let me be honest again. That first day, I fell out of bed.

After the bell rang and the girls ran from the room, I lay down smiling, pulled the covers higher, then sat straight up with a gasp.

The instructions!

My heart tumbled out of place. Or anyway that's how it seemed. It was probably still right where it belonged.

I have been here for a week?! I thought. *I need to stay another?*

Impossible!

What was I supposed to be doing right now? Not lying in a bed, that was for sure! But what? My mind flew around like a bird trapped in a classroom. Then I remembered. The ship! I should have boarded it at the Jumian Wharf! I should be sailing the seas right now!

The *Riddle and Popcorn* cruise ship, it was called.

It was captained by two of my aunts, Aunt Maya and Aunt Lisbeth.

"Two aunts for the price of one," the Butler had remarked with approval when we talked about this part of the itinerary. "Handy!" Aunt Isabelle and I had laughed.

But the ship would have sailed by now, and *I was not on it!* I did not have two aunts for the price of one, I had NO AUNTS! For the price of none! Which was *not* funny.

I had broken the Faery cross-stitch.

What would happen? What had *already* happened? Was Gainsleigh in pieces? Were Isabelle and the Butler clinging to cobblestones, swept along streets that had been torn in two?

I had to obey the instructions at once! Before any more damage could be done! I *had* to get onto that cruise ship!

At this point, I was breathing fast and loud like someone in a race.

I heard the voice of my governess in my head. *Come on, Bronte! You can solve this problem!*

Another voice swooped in. *Come on, Bronte!* Now it was my swimming coach. *Swim!*

Of course!

I would swim.

Swim across the ocean to the ship. I was a good swimmer. Second place in the Gainsleigh Junior Swim Contest.

First, of course, I would have to bust out of this place. If only I had the criminal element from Carafkwa Island to help. Or, even better, Gustav Spectaculo and The Scorpion, former leaders of the Anti-Pirate League! I knew they wore black masks and suits, decorated with pictures of exploding skull-and-crossbones. (I'd been to plenty of costume balls, dressed up as one or the other of them.) I imagined them knocking on the window, their eyes bright behind their masks. "We've come out of retirement to bust you out!"

Well, I could be a criminal alone if I wanted. I would need ropes to climb down from the window, and maybe a gun? No. I would never want to shoot anybody. Also, this was a school, not a prison. I would need my suitcase, though! It had the gifts in it! Where was it?

There it was. On top of that wardrobe. A very tall wardrobe.

Well, I would drag the bedside table over, stand on it, and reach up for my suitcase. I looked at the bedside table now. A glass of water stood on it. I would have to move that glass before I dragged the table, of course, or else the water would spill. Actually, a shimmery puddle sat beside the glass of water now. Somebody had already spilled it.

In fact, now that I looked more closely, the shimmery puddle was not a puddle. It was an object. I reached out to touch it. It was my Elvish Medal for Bravery!

I would need that. I couldn't remember why, and then I could. Uncle Josh at the table in Aunt Sue's house. *"And Bronte,"* he had said. *"I think you ought to wear it* all *the time."*

I picked it up by its ribbon and slipped it over my head.

This was when I noticed I was wearing a nightgown. Difficult to swim in. It would weigh me down, and get tangled around my legs.

Another easy problem to solve. I would change into my bathing suit.

So. Here was my plan: Move glass of water. Drag bedside table across room. Climb onto bedside table and reach for suitcase. Find bathing suit. Change into bathing suit. Find rope. Climb out of window. Walk through the snow in my bathing suit to the wharf. (Where was the wharf? Figure that out.) Swim across the ocean until I reached the cruise ship.

Chilly! But perfectly possible.

Well, I would do it.

Only, now that I thought about it, moving the glass of water seemed like *very hard work*.

I lay down again to consider this. As far as I could remember, moving a glass of water was usually a pretty simple thing.

Come on, Bronte, I heard Aunt Isabelle say. *You can do it!*

I pushed back the covers – and fell out of bed.

Right at that moment, the door swung open and a song burst into the room.

The song was sung in one of those rich, deep, dramatic voices that could be someone being very funny, or someone who believed he had extraordinary musical talent and belonged on the stage.

The song stuck halfway through a word.

"Hold the horses!" said the voice of the singer, now sounding like an ordinary man. "Where's she got to?"

"Why, she's on the floor!" a woman's voice replied. The woman's voice sounded melodious itself, as if she was singing without meaning to.

Two faces looked down at me. A man wearing spectacles and a plump woman. Both had wispy grey hair, and both appeared to be very interested.

"What was wrong with the bed?" the man asked. He pushed on the mattress with the palms of his hands. "Good springs! Seems a fine bed to me. Why depart it?"

"Oh, stop now," said the woman. "She's fallen out, any fool can see. Come on and I'll help you up, dear girl."

"No!" I said. "I mean, thank you, but no. You see, I've got a schedule. I'm just getting my suitcase so I can change into my bathing suit, and then I'll be climbing through that window there, and down into the snow, so I can swim to the cruise ship."

They both seemed even more interested now. They looked at each other.

"Oh blast," I said. "Now I've gone and told you."

But, in a way, I didn't mind that I'd been sprung. It seemed a lot more relaxing to lie on the floor than to drag a bedside table around.

"You've still got a touch of fever," the man said, his hand against my forehead.

"Clearly," laughed the woman. Then she got her hands under my arms and hoisted me up and onto the bed. I fell onto it with a *plong!* It was good to be back. The woman pulled the covers up and under my chin.

"I'm the Matron," she said, "and this is Dr Saurelis here to check on you. Bronte, you have *nothing* to worry about except resting."

"Thank you," I said. "But I'm afraid you are wrong."

"I'm often wrong," the Matron nodded. "About all manner of things. Here's an example. I was wrong to advise my husband, Kenneth, to pursue his dream of becoming a ventriloquist. Turns out he's *terrible* at it. You can see his mouth move all the time!"

"Oh, not all the time," the doctor said. He had opened a black bag and was now listening to my heart through a stethoscope. "Not when he pauses 'cause he's forgotten his lines."

They both laughed.

"Anyhow, yes, I am often wrong, Bronte, but not today." The Matron folded her hands together. "I've been on the telephone with your Aunt Isabelle. I like her very much. No nonsense, that one. She wanted to swoop in to see you when she heard about the avalanche and your illness, but there's still an avalanche risk around here. So, no visitors allowed. We persuaded her to leave you in our care."

"We'd best not tell her you've been sleeping on the floor," the doctor put in. Now he'd taken a bottle of medicine from his bag and was holding it up to the light.

"I have a schedule," I said. "Thank you for your concern but I need to be on a ship. I was thinking I'd swim for it, but now that seems wrong. Girls don't swim across oceans looking for ships, as a rule. Or do they?"

"You're in a muddle because you've been very ill," the Matron said. "As for the cruise ship, we know all about it. Your aunts – don't tell me – Maya and..."

"Lis—" I began, but she snapped her fingers at me.

"Lisbeth!" she said. "You are supposed to be on a cruise ship with your aunts, Maya and Lisbeth. To give them a gift from your parents. You see? You think we know nothing but we've been talking to your Aunt Isabelle, and we know a great deal more than nothing!"

"Only a little more," the doctor said sunnily. He shook the medicine bottle hard, opened the lid, and tipped some into a spoon. "Here you go."

I didn't like the look of it.

"It tastes like sunshine and cherries," he coaxed.

"Really?"

"No. Not really. But drink it anyway, would you?"

I drank it. It was horrible. Like charcoal and soap.

The Matron handed me the glass of water, and they both waited while I drank.

"It's all been sorted out, Bronte," the Matron continued. She pulled the pillow from behind my head, puffed it up a bit, and put it back. "You were supposed to spend a month on the cruise ship, yes? Well, now you'll meet it when it docks at Saranchi instead – you can take a wagon there once you're well. And you'll spend a fortnight on the ship, not a month, and the schedule will be all right again."

"But it's already broken," I said fretfully. "Things must have happened to Gainsleigh already!"

"No, no," the Matron soothed me. "Faery cross-stitch only breaks if you *decide* to break it. There are exceptions for accident and misadventure. I mean, it's not like Faeries use *Shadow Magic*. Faeries are very reasonable people. Marvellous people, actually. Remarkable. Gorgeous."

"She's got Faery in her," the doctor explained.

"On my mother's side." The Matron nodded. "Not on my father's. He was a goat."

"A goat!"

"Not an actual goat. I just mean he was a bit of a fool. Anyway, I've been talking to your lawyers too, and they agree that the cross-stitch isn't broken yet. If you'd started the avalanche on *purpose*, that could be a different story. As it is, two weeks on the cruise will be fine."

"It's probably for the best," the doctor put in, closing his bag with a snap. "A month on a cruise ship would be far too long."

"Oh yes," the Matron agreed. "Play one game of shuffleboard, you've played them all."

"Not *so*!" said the doctor. *"Not so!"* and he broke into a bellow-ing song about all the splendidness of shuffleboard.

"I'll tell you what I like," the Matron mused, once the song was done. "A game of quoits."

"Then I shall sing about that!"

"No, you shan't," the Matron replied. "For we must let Bronte rest." She stroked my hair a moment, and touched the medal that was lying against my chest. "I see you've put your Elvish Medal for Bravery back on. We had to take it off for fear you would strangle yourself in your fever."

"You were right to put it back on," the doctor told me. "You should always wear those things if you've got one. Only, I don't know why. Do you know, Matron?"

"Of course, I do," she replied. "Didn't we just discuss my Faery blood? I can tell you about your medal if you like, Bronte. Only not so the doctor can hear."

"Then I shall stand over here by the window," he declared, "and sing very loudly."

And this is what he did. He sang about chandeliers and swimming pools while the Matron knelt by the bed and murmured the secret of my Elvish Medal for Bravery to me.

After that, they both suggested I not make any plans to climb out of windows, nor swim across oceans, nor even fall out of bed. They wished me sweet dreams and closed the door behind them, and I fell into a deep and lovely sleep.

42

After that, I was free to be happy in a big white bed by a fireplace for a week.

Once or twice I tried to get up, and then I felt a strange, misty swirling in my head, and my whole body ached, so that I was glad to lie back down.

"No wonder you ache!" the Matron said. "You were that bruised and battered by the avalanche!"

She came in all the time, holding her palm against my forehead or stoking up the fire or standing at the window and chatting to me about her husband, the ventriloquist, or about the ways of the Faery folk. She brought me croissants and hot chocolate each morning. For lunch, I would get something like a hearty, flavoursome soup with crusty bread, and for dinner, roast chicken with mashed potatoes, followed by ice cream.

From my bedroom, I listened to the sounds of the school: bells clanging and footsteps running up and down the stairs, and teachers shouting, *"No running, girls!"* I drew pictures in a big sketchbook that Matron gave me one day, along with a box of fine-quality crayons. Also, I wrote to Aunt Isabelle, working my way through a stack of Katherine Valley Boarding School for Girls postcards.

One day, the school principal sent me a handwritten note:

"I think she's got you mixed up with a princess or something," Imogen told me, when I showed her.

This gave me a start. I had almost forgotten Aunt Sophy telling me that my mother had been a princess. I thought about sharing this with my cousins now, but worried they would only laugh at me before I got a chance to explain that I did not believe it myself.

"Yes," Esther agreed, reading the note. "Otherwise, why's she so honoured?"

"Just enjoy it," Astrid advised. "Act like a princess and she'll never know the difference. Hold your nose when you speak so you sound snooty." She demonstrated, holding her own nose.

"It's a good plan," Esther agreed. "But Principal Hortense may as well be honoured to have Bronte here. And us too. I mean, we're all *related* to royalty too, aren't we? Aunt Alys is a queen! So our cousin William is a prince! We just don't go on about it."

"Which is more noble of us," Imogen said.

"Have you visited Aunt Alys yet, Bronte?" Astrid asked. "Did you know some pirates want to steal William? Aunt Alys sent our mother a telegram asking her advice."

I told them I had heard about the pirates.

"Our mother wrote back that if Aunt Alys wanted to avoid her child being at risk from pirates, she ought never to have become a queen," Esther put in.

"Helpful," murmured the others, and snickered.

"Aunt Alys is next on the list," I said, "after the cruise with Aunt Maya and Aunt Lisbeth."

This led to a long conversation about whether they, as sisters, would ever want to captain a ship together. They decided it would be all right for a week, but after that, they'd need space to be their own true selves.

In a family, they explained to me, you get a sort of identity. "Imogen's the bossy sister, and Esther's quirky, and I'm the scatty one," Astrid explained, and her sisters nodded wisely.

"So if *I* ever want to be scatty, say?" Imogen said. "And take a break from being bossy? I'd need a cruise ship all to myself."

I wondered what my identity would have been if my parents had been my *parents,* rather than running off to have adventures.

"Well, but you had Aunt Isabelle as your family, didn't you?" Esther asked.

"Yes," I realized. "And the Butler."

"So what's your identity?"

I thought about it. Those two were the "adults" and I was the "child", and that was it really.

"Oh, that sounds perfect, darling," Esther said. "You can be what you want. Bossy, quirky, scatty. Anything. As long as you're a child."

"What about when she's had *enough* of being a child?" Astrid pointed out. "And she might be lonely? Are you lonely, darling? Do you want to have a cry?"

I didn't, but thanked her for the offer. And so the conversation carried on.

Sometimes my cousins brought me books to read. Most were storybooks, but one day, they gave me a history book written by their father. They seemed quite proud of their father, so I thought I should try reading it to be polite. It was called *The Origins of the Whispering Wars*, and I thought it would be boring enough to put me to sleep.

However, the first two sentences startled me awake:

> What many people do not realize is that Whisperers have not always been Dark Mages. They were once a gentle, private people.

Here it was again! Just like that old travel guide I'd found, the idea that the Whisperers were *gentle*! I shook my head and kept reading. My Uncle Nigel seemed to write in a very chatty way.

215

But when the current king took the throne, it turned out that he was more ambitious than other royals. Right away, he sent people out searching for MORE diamond mines! They already had five, but oh no, that wasn't enough. He wanted to be SUPER wealthy.

So off they went digging. But they didn't find more diamond mines. Guess what they found?

Go on. Guess.

Well, I will tell you.

They found something remarkable. Something you would not BELIEVE.

An ancient trove of shadow thread, buried beneath the Whispering Kingdom!

Now, Whisperers were not Dark Mages, so the shadow threads seemed useless to them. Couldn't do the knitting and sewing, et cetera, could they? The king nearly sold them to the nearby Empire of Witchcraft.

But then he discovered something incredible. The shadow threads could be woven into wristbands.

Guess what happened when the king wore one?

Go on. Guess.

Oh, I can't wait around all day while you're thinking. I'll tell you.

His Whispers were magnified many thousand times!! His Whispers became a force that was impossible to resist!!

Now, around this time, the king lost his beloved wife – she died not long after the birth of their daughter – and he was WILD with grief. Furious with it. He ordered every Whisperer in the kingdom to wear shadow wristbands. So now they ALL had supercharged Whispers. Next thing, he's sending out teams of Whisperers to infiltrate major kingdom and empire associations, security forces, and military organizations. He's annexing neighbouring principalities.

And with the incredible power of shadow-strengthened Whispers? This was easy. A piece of cake.

Of course, if you wear shadow threads close to your skin, the dark magic seeps into your bloodstream. Before you knew it, every Whisperer had become a Dark Mage. Did the king know this would happen? Not sure.

Shadow threads get frayed and worn over time, so the king needed people plucking the shadow threads from the trove and weaving them together day and night. Well, doing that REALLY hurts. You get blisters and burns. It's also very tricky unless you have small fingers.

And that's why the Whisperers began stealing children. All across the Kingdoms and Empires, children were taken and brought back to the Whispering Kingdom to work.

This practice continued even AFTER the Whispering Wars, right up until the Majestic Spellbinding was put in place.

I stopped reading there. Or anyway, I tried to keep reading, but I was upset about the children's burned and blistered hands. Plus, the next bit had words like *negotiations*, *escalations*, and *alliances*. My uncle tried to make it fun with "guess who?" bits, but I quickly fell asleep.

43

Another thing my cousins brought me was Cendra Delite chocolate, which was my favourite back then. They sat on my bed and made me tell them stories about my journey so far, as payment for the chocolate.

Their favourite story was the one where I rescued the baby, mainly because they were fascinated by the boy across the river with no shoes. "*Why* did he have no shoes?" they kept asking. The question seemed to miss the point.

Another question they liked to ask was *why* my parents added Faery cross-stitch to their will? Again, I had no clue.

"Maybe it's because they had no experience of being parents?" Imogen suggested. "So they didn't realize you can just *tell* the child what to do, and the child has to do it. They thought you had to use magic."

"Hmm," I said. "Maybe."

One day, Esther, the middle sister, came to visit me alone. She sat on the edge of my bed, twisting her hands together and glancing back at the door.

"Did you know there is a full moon tonight?" she asked eventually.

"I heard." I nodded.

There was another long quiet while she twisted her fingers.

"You deserve to know this," she said suddenly.

"Oh yes," I agreed at once. "I do."

I waited to find out what I deserved to know.

"Only, there's something I have to tell you. I overheard my mother telling my father this, when I was hiding behind the couch one day and listening in on their conversation."

I nodded.

Esther checked the door again. She opened the wardrobe, looked under the bed, and lifted my pillow.

"There's nobody under my pillow," I promised. "I'd have noticed."

"It's just that this is a secret," she explained. "I mean, my mother should never have known it *herself*, except that she used to hide behind couches and listen to other people's conversations when she was young. Terrible habit," she added thoughtfully.

"Terrible," I agreed.

Eventually, Esther whispered, "You know your father?"

"Not really," I replied.

"Well, he was a Spellbinder."

That made me jump as if someone had burst a paper bag behind my head. If I'd had the hiccups, it would have cured me.

"No!" I said.

Esther nodded. "He was. My mother heard him talking to *your* mother about it when she was behind a couch. Nobody else knew. Apparently, he was planning to start the training when he turned twenty-one."

I felt a bit floaty. Being born a Spellbinder is very rare and special. It made my father rare and special! He could defeat Dark Mages! Save people! For a moment, I wished I'd paid more attention to his picture in the wedding photo.

"Anyway, it means it's in our family," Esther continued. "Between us, I'm hoping I've inherited it myself, but so far no signs. I thought you should know because *you* could be a Spellbinder too. If you are, don't tell me because you're supposed to keep it secret. Although, if you *wanted* to tell me? I'd swear not to tell."

"I'm not," I said.

"Well, but are you sure? Sometimes you don't get any symptoms until you're sixteen."

"What symptoms?"

"Your toenails turn blue."

I stared at her. "But that happened to me once!" I breathed.

"All of your toenails?"

"No, just the big one. After I dropped a hammer on it."

Esther laughed. "That doesn't count," she said. "That was a bruise. It's all the toenails that turn blue, and it happens in a flash and then the blue fades away. Then you know you're a Spellbinder." She lowered her voice. "I've heard that the blue thing happens most often on days when there's going to be ... *a full moon.*"

We widened our eyes at each other. I pulled my feet out from under the covers and Esther pushed off her school shoes. We both sat awhile staring at our toes. Nothing happened.

Eventually, a school bell rang and Esther had to go.

Later that night, as the full moon shone across my face, I lay in bed thinking again of the Whispers that the Whispering King had heard. How his own grandchild would help him to release the Whisperers, and how another royal child would cause *great difficulties* for that Whispering grandchild.

If Aunt Sophy was right and my mother was a princess, then I *could* be a royal child, and now, if Esther was right and my father was a Spellbinder, then I could also be a Spellbinder! It would mean I had the power to Spellbind the shadow magic of the Whispering grandchild! I could defeat him! Or anyway, cause him difficulty.

My heart thudded quickly and softly. Most probably I was *neither* a princess *nor* a Spellbinder.

Still, it never hurt to be prepared, my governess often told me. So I tried to remember the Spellbinding movements I had learned at Aunt Claire's Convention.

No use. I'd forgotten them all.

But then I closed my eyes, let my hands move through the air, and it turned out my *hands* remembered what to do. It felt good, like stretches for my neck and shoulders, but not especially magical.

Next, I hopped out of bed and dug out the folder of Spellbinding potions I'd been given at the convention. I flicked through it, reading by moonlight, thinking that something in the words might jump out and tell me that I was a Spellbinder. But nothing jumped. The words sat on the page looking exactly like words.

Actually, they looked like recipes. One, A Potion to Bind the Whispering King, was like a recipe where you had to *guess* its ingredients. There was a note that explained:

> This potion was sent to the Spellbinding Committee by Carabella-the-Great not long after she completed the Majestic Spellbinding. It arrived so water damaged that we could scarcely read it. Nobody has seen or heard from Carabella-the-Great since then, and we only include it here for sentimental reasons. Of course, it is useless.

It certainly was. Combine a spoonful of − n − , it said, with a pinch of - i − a − . And so on until: Finally, add a cup of − − − − − −.

I snapped the folder closed and returned it to my suitcase.

Probably, I thought, you only inherited Spellbinding from fathers who were actually *around*.

I sat on the edge of my bed. The moonlight washed its silvery light across the room. I looked at my bare feet.

For the faintest moment, my toenails turned blue.

44

The next day, my toenails were their regular colour again and I decided I had dreamed their being blue.

That was the day the cousins taught me how to play a game called poker.

One interesting thing was how completely the girls changed whenever we played this game. Usually they giggled, called me "darling," and inquired whether I needed to cry again. But when the cards came out, they were suddenly clipped and fierce, narrowing their eyes, nodding slowly to themselves, and raising sly eyebrows at each other.

They stopped speaking altogether except to say things like, "I'm in," or to explain to me in quick sentences how the rules worked. I learned what a full house was, and a royal flush, and how important it is to keep your face blank. That way nobody can tell you're "in the swamp without a paddle," Imogen explained. She meant having useless cards, I think.

Astrid was the best player, and this seemed to be because she had the talent of knowing what her two older sisters were thinking, even though their faces were like stone walls.

One day, when we had finished playing and the girls were packing up to leave, I asked how they had learned poker.

"Our mother taught us," they said.

"Oh," I said. "Aunt Nancy! Of course. I forgot that she was your mother." I tried to keep my face blank, but I must not have learned the "poker face" well enough, because all three threw themselves back onto my bed and said, "What? What were you going to say?"

"Nothing!"

"You were! I can tell!" Astrid crowed. "You had a *terrible* time staying with our mother. It's all over your face!"

"Not at all," I said. "I was not well with a cold, but otherwise, the stay was—"

"Horrible? You poor darling, and you're trying to pretend you like her!"

I wasn't sure what to say. I worked on my poker face by thinking of snow.

"I'll bet she didn't come in time to fetch you," Imogen said. "She's always late."

"Well," I admitted. "I did wait in the village square for a few hours."

"You didn't!"

"That's probably where you got the chill!"

"And she doesn't *notice* anything! Once, Imogen came home on school vacation with a patch over her eye from an infection, and Mother didn't say a *word* about it all week!"

"And when we mention it now," Astrid put in, "Mother laughs and says, *Oh what nonsense, Imogen's never had an eye infection.*"

"It's the worst when she laughs," Imogen reflected.

225

"She's very critical," Astrid added. "And she hides the criticism in her laughter." They were all quiet for a bit.

"Dad says she *means* well, she's just absentminded without realizing she is. He says it's because she's so busy, but honestly, Dad's busy too, running around doing his history research. But he still calls us each week and remembers what subjects we're doing and which of our friends are annoying and which ones are good at public speaking – that kind of thing. Our mother doesn't even know we *have* friends."

"Poor Bronte," Imogen said. "You were there in that house all alone with her."

"I expect she was worse than the avalanche," Astrid put in.

Then the bell rang, and they all hugged me and ran down the stairs.

✳

Strangely, after that conversation, I felt better than I had in days.

"You've turned a corner, haven't you?" the Matron said, coming in with my medicine. "You'll be all right to get on with your journey tomorrow! I can see all that in your eyes. For I've a little Faery in me, have I mentioned it?"

We both laughed then, as she mentioned it all the time. Now she hurried out of the room, promising to be right back with a surprise. When she returned, she gave me a slice of Faery cake. She had baked it herself, she said. It was treacle orange and coconut, and very good.

"That'll set you right now," she said.

"Is it a healing Faery cake?" I asked.

"Indeed it is."

We were both quiet, and I sat in the bed, eating the cake.

"You'll be wondering why I didn't just give you this cake the first day you arrived?" the Matron said now.

"Well," I said.

"It seemed to me," she said, "that you weren't quite ready to be healed, and needed a good rest first." There were footsteps on the stairs at that moment, and a song billowed up. "Anyhow," the Matron added, "it's good for the doctor to practise his medicine."

The door burst open and the doctor sang, "And how is our young patient today? Are you ready to leave us yet?"

"I think so," I said, and I felt both excited and sad.

Aunt Maya and Aunt Lisbeth

45

The *Riddle and Popcorn* cruise ship was grand and crackling with fun, and so were my Aunt Maya and Aunt Lisbeth.

"Tour of the ship!" Aunt Maya exclaimed, after they had welcomed me aboard and instructed me to spin around so they could appraise me.

"Top-notch niece!" Aunt Lisbeth concluded. "I like her. Also, top-notch idea, Maya! On with the tour!" She plucked the suitcase from my hand and spun around herself. "Games Room first."

"Ripper of a plan," Aunt Maya declared. "But the Games Room is *this* way," and she took Aunt Lisbeth's shoulder and spun her back.

Aunt Lisbeth blinked. "So it is!" she said, and burst out laughing. Aunt Maya joined her in the laughter, and they both looked at me, shaking their heads. I laughed too. Their laughter was the kind that you feel bubbling inside your own chest.

There was a lot of striding after that, and I had to run to keep up. We went out onto the deck, below all the full, white sails, and passed a heated swimming pool, crowded with people – both adults and children – dive-bombing and hooting, tossing balls and riding on big inflated toys. We passed a thrumming dance floor and jazz band, a class of women doing energetic calisthenics, and any number of games of quoits and shuffleboard. These were played so closely together that they kept getting tangled up, which led to good-natured arguments and jokes.

People made zippy comments to each other and laughed at the sky. People waved at my aunts as we passed, or tipped their hats and said, "Hello, Captain! Hello, Captain!" and my aunts called back, "Whoa! Nice shot, Lolly!" or "Sweet dance moves there, Garry!" And to some, they said: "Look, it's our niece, Bronte, come to sail with us!"

"Welcome aboard!" people said to me, and a man in a striped swimsuit called, "Ahoy there, Junior Captain!" That got taken up by everybody, and I spent the entire two weeks of the cruise being referred to as Junior Captain, which I enjoyed.

Inside, there were swooping staircases, men in black tie gazing fiercely at machines with jangling lights, and elegant women sipping colourful drinks. The aunts showed me my cabin, which they called a "stateroom". I was very pleased with the dark walnut walls, the big bed beneath a swinging chandelier, the neat little bathroom, and the large porthole looking out to sea.

"This room is all for me?" I asked.

"You'll be all right on your own?" Aunt Lisbeth worried. "Our rooms are right along the passageway there, and see the telephone by your bed? You only need to lift that receiver and there'll be a voice."

"Not just a voice," Aunt Maya elaborated. "But a *person*, speaking with a voice. And the person will answer any queries you may have."

"Let's say you're wondering about the price of purple grapes? Or the most daring feat of Gustav Spectaculo and The Scorpion when they headed up the Anti-Pirate League? Pick up that receiver there and ask."

"Although," Aunt Maya put in, "if you ask too many general knowledge questions, they might get impatient with you."

"But do," Aunt Lisbeth urged. "If you want to."

"Thank you," I said.

We left my case on the bed and went striding along the passageways again, until we found the Games Room. Through the door of this enormous room, I could see table tennis, billiards tables, and giant stacks of board games in snazzy boxes. We were about to enter when I noticed, right alongside the Games Room, a door festooned with balloons. KIDS' CLUB, said a multicoloured sign.

"Hold your horses!" Aunt Lisbeth had followed my gaze. "You're a kid yourself, aren't you, Bronte?!"

"Why, I believe you might be right!" Aunt Maya said. "Ma'am, may I inquire your age?"

"Ten," I replied.

"Ten!" Aunt Maya turned to Aunt Lisbeth. "Now, just refresh my memory. If a person is *ten years old*, is the person a child?"

"Undoubtedly." Aunt Lisbeth nodded. We all laughed.

Aunt Maya raised an eyebrow and jutted her thumb towards the Kids' Club. "Want to get acquainted with the kids in there? Only, we couldn't come in with you, I'm afraid. Kids' Club. Adults not allowed."

"Apart from Randwick," Aunt Lisbeth said. "His job is to take care of the kids."

"Speaking of *jobs*," Aunt Maya put in. "I suppose you and I *should* get on with the business of sailing this ship," and Aunt Lisbeth said, "*Knew* there was something we were forgetting."

I was a little bewildered by this, as the ship seemed to me to be sailing already. We were cruising along the coast of the Oski Empire, and blue water rushed by the windows, patterned with white foam. In the distance, beaches and woods appeared and faded, appeared and faded. So wasn't this rather dangerous? To be sailing without any captain? Were my aunts completely mad?

"It's okay." Aunt Maya smiled at me kindly. "We're kidding. We have co-captains! I recommend them! They do all the work."

They both chuckled at this, and then Aunt Lisbeth clicked her tongue and said, "Oh, but I suppose we do have to deal with the whatsit."

"Not to mention the hoozit," Aunt Maya agreed. They nodded at one another solemnly and turned to me.

"Want to follow us around while we work, Bronte?" Aunt Lisbeth inquired. "Or prefer some time with the kids?"

I said that I'd be glad to meet the children, please, so they opened the door of the Kids' Club. It must have been tucked into the very front of the ship – you call that the prow – because it was shaped like a curving triangle, and it had portholes all around, lined with window seats. A gathering of children, many around my own age, were crowded together in the middle.

"Randwick!" my aunts called. "Come and meet Bronte!"

Randwick sounded like a noble name, and I straightened my shoulders, ready to be polite. But then Randwick popped up from the circle of children. He was bouncy, bright-eyed, and his hair stuck up in pointy bits all over his head.

"You will *love* it here," he promised me, springing over and shaking my hand vigorously. "These kids are *hip to the jive*! And I can tell right away that *you* are too!"

As I didn't have a clue how to be "hip" or what "the jive" was, I tried to smile politely.

"Now, this one's been terribly ill," Aunt Lisbeth told him. "So she ought to take it easy."

That was a relief. A reprieve from being hip to the jive.

"Holler if you need us, won't you?" Aunt Maya told me, tousling my hair. "We'll see you at dinner at the Captain's Table, Junior Captain Bronte!"

They both saluted and strode from the room.

The children all looked at me with interest, and Randwick explained that I was just in time, as they were about to begin a treasure hunt.

"Teams of three," he said. "Everyone form into threes! Here, Bronte, you team up with Taylor and Billy."

Taylor was a girl with narrow eyes and long black hair, which she'd scooped up into a very high ponytail. It was like a fountain on the top of her head. She held her palm in the air and said, "High five."

"Oh, Taylor," said Billy, who turned out to be a boy in a starched white shirt with a crisp accent. "Nobody *ever* knows what you mean by that, and yet you persist, what?"

Taylor shrugged, took ahold of my wrist, and raised up my arm. "You just slap my palm," she explained. "It's like a way of saying hello?"

Randwick, meanwhile, was bouncing between groups, handing out clues on little squares of cardboard.

"On your marks!" he cried out, and the other children jostled excitedly. "Get set! Go!"

There was a stampede for the doorway.

"Let's not run," Taylor said comfortably. "Let's take a leisurely approach to this thing."

Overhearing this, Randwick laughed. "At least have a look at the clue," he suggested.

So we did.

> *Go to the Place*
> *where Dreams*
> *Go*
> *to Play the Guitar.*

Oh my, I thought.

I suddenly remembered a conversation between Aunt Isabelle and the Butler over breakfast one morning, long ago, back when I was at home. Aunt Isabelle was frowning at a newspaper headline. "*Foundation Laid for New Shopping Mall Complex*," she read aloud, and then she *tch*ed: "For goodness' sake, whatever *is* a shopping mall?"

The Butler stepped forward and replied, "A shopping mall? It's the place where dreams go to die."

Aunt Isabelle snorted at that, and the Butler got the little dimple he gets sometimes, to the right of his mouth, and stepped back. That was after he had broken his nose, I remember, having run into the pantry door, and it was good to see the twitch of a smile beneath the large white plaster.

Anyway, so I *had* heard the expression, *where dreams go to die*. But where did dreams go to play the guitar?

"That's an easy one," Billy declared, brushing off the collar of his fancy shirt. "The band that plays in the Checkers Club on Deck Five is called The Dreams. *They* play guitar, what?"

"This way." Taylor set off, her ponytail splashing around on her head.

"Welcome aboard, what?" Billy said to me as we strolled along beside her. "Which deck are you on?"

"You might be wondering why he keeps saying *what?*" Taylor put in.

"Oh, am I doing it again?" Billy stopped, crestfallen. He looked at me earnestly. "It's an affectation. I add *what?* to the end of practically everything I say. People find it infuriating, and I truly don't blame them. I'm trying to stop it."

"Just give him a little pinch whenever he does it," Taylor advised.

"Hm," I said, "I don't think I *will* pinch Billy. I don't want to, I'm sorry."

This seemed to delight both of them, Billy because he wasn't keen on being pinched, and Taylor because I had surprised her.

"Most people obey me," she said. "I seem to have that nature. I'm a real spitfire."

"She is," Billy agreed. "She was a stowaway on this ship, do you know? Such moxie! The captains found her in a linen chest. They also admired her moxie and gave her the stateroom next to mine. Now I *am* travelling unaccompanied, but *my* ticket was arranged

235

by my mother, and I'm under the official care of the captains. No moxie here, what?"

"You almost got through that whole speech without doing it, Billy, and then you fell down at the end," Taylor said. "Come on, let's go win this treasure hunt." And suddenly she took off at a sprint.

46

We won the treasure hunt.

I hadn't believed it likely, as we had started off so slowly. But it emerged that Billy had been onboard for weeks, and knew the ship inside out and upside down.

"Like the palm of your hand?" Taylor suggested, and Billy said, no, he had only the vaguest idea what the palm of his hand looked like. He'd never paid much attention to it. Whereas he'd done nothing these last few weeks but explore this ship.

So Billy solved all the clues in a flash and also knew the quickest routes and shortcuts. Taylor, meanwhile, was agile and athletic, so if a clue was hidden on a high shelf, say, or pressed behind a light fitting? She scampered up the wall like a lizard and grabbed it.

"She's on her way to join a circus," Billy told me proudly as Taylor collected yet another clue. This time it was tucked behind the curtain rail in the Theatre. "That's why she stowed away, what? Hertfordshire is one of our ports of call, and Taylor plans to meet up with the Razdazzle Moonlight Circus there. Have I got that right, Taylor?"

"You've got it right, Billy," Taylor agreed, hanging upside down from the beams and swinging sideways with an outstretched hand. "My special skill is tricks on horses, only I couldn't bring my horse along. Wouldn't have fit in the linen chest, see? You ride yourself, Bronte?"

She landed beside me with a thud, handing Billy the next clue.

I told her that I did ride, and that I have a horse named Tully at home, a chestnut with soulful eyes, only I hadn't brought him along on my journey either – actually, it had never come up as an option – and that I didn't know how to do tricks on him.

"No trouble," Taylor said. "I'll teach you. Where to now, Billy?"

"The Formal Dining Hall," he announced, studying the clue, "where that historian gives lectures every night."

"Any good?" I asked.

"Fascinating," Billy replied, while Taylor said, "Deathly dull. Give them a miss."

I promised I would and off we ran again.

I felt a bit useless for much of the hunt, since Billy and Taylor were doing all the work, but then the final clue said, "Betwixt firm binds live other worlds," and Billy frowned, stumped. Taylor did a handstand and spoke from near my feet: "Say again?"

Billy repeated the clue: "Betwixt firm binds live other worlds."

"That sounds like what my governess would say," I said. "About books. Is there a library on the ship?"

And they both flew away, shouting, "Yes! There is!"

Another team of children was running towards the Library, so the three of us zoomed past them, skidded around the corner, and through the Library door.

"There!" shouted Billy, pointing to a glint of gold at the top of a bookshelf, and Taylor scrambled up, grabbed it, and held it up to us. It was a small golden chest with a lid.

The three of us were panting, laughing, and gasping for breath when Randwick arrived in the Library, followed by hurrying groups of children, who sighed or shrugged when they saw us with the chest.

"And this is what *taking it easy* looks like?" Randwick said to me archly, but then he smiled and said, "Good work, team."

"It was Bronte got the final clue," Billy told everyone, and Taylor added, "It was. Nicely played, Junior Captain."

"But these two did *everything* else!" I told the crowd, and Billy said sternly, "Credit where it's due, Bronte. You have earned our thanks, what?"

We opened the little gold box and it turned out to be full of sweets and chocolate bars.

The other children suggested, quite earnestly, that we ought to share the treasure with them, as that was only fair.

"In what way, fair?" Randwick demanded. "Did you people win?"

Nobody had an answer to that, but we let them have some of the sweets anyway. There was still plenty left for the three of us.

Maybe we would have become friends anyway, but winning a treasure hunt makes you so fond of each other. We had a midnight feast that night in Billy's stateroom, to celebrate.

Lying at the bottom of the treasure chest were six chocolate bars marked **Maywish of the Riddle Empire**. Taylor and I had never heard of this brand, but Billy gasped to see them. Once we tasted this chocolate, he assured us, it would be our new favourite for all time. In the future, we would find ourselves dreaming of Maywish Rose and Black Pepper chocolate at unexpected moments.

"Not a chance," Taylor declared. "My favourite is Carrols Chocolate Cherry, and that will never, ever change."

"Mine is Cendra Delite," I said.

"Nice." Taylor nodded her approval. "But Carrols Chocolate Cherry defeats all. I bet you a thousand silver, Billy, that you are wrong about this Maywish Rose and Black Pepper – I mean, *rose and black pepper*, for a start! Who puts *rose* in a chocolate?! It's a *flower*! And black pepper? Are you kidding with me? Burns your mouth. Makes you sneeze – anyhow, nothing will *ever* shift me from Carrols Chocolate Cherry."

"Very well," Billy said calmly. "A thousand silver."

Then we ate the chocolate, and Billy turned out to be right.

"I'm going to have to write you an IOU for those thousand," Taylor apologized. "The moment I make my fortune, you will have it. Give me another of those chocolate bars, meantime. Rose and black pepper! Genius."

Billy said he'd waive the debt and Taylor said he was the bee's knees, and we carried on eating sweets and chocolate until we fell asleep amidst the wrappers.

The next few days were a dazzle of fun. Sometimes we were in the Kids' Club, playing games with Randwick and the other children. Sometimes we ran around the ship, exploring alone. As we were the only three "unaccompanied minors", I think the other children were a bit in awe of us, and we enjoyed that.

We ate meals together at the Captain's Table, all dressed up in elegant clothes with our hair combed neatly – Billy had the most immaculate shirts and pressed trousers and little bow ties, and Taylor seemed to have brought along a collection of dizzily coloured circus outfits when she stowed away in the linen chest. Aunts Lisbeth and Maya asked us to describe our days and seemed delighted by everything we said. Then they told big, laughing stories about the adventures they themselves had had in their cruise ship, what with the sea monsters and finfolk.

Aunt Maya told about the day a passenger spotted a little merchild caught in the tentacles of a giant squid. Aunt Lisbeth, without a thought, had dived into the sea and rescued the child. Aunt Lisbeth told the story of how Aunt Maya had skated out onto an iceberg that was threatening to stave the ship's hull, and bravely reasoned with the berg-troll until he agreed to move along.

The farther north we sailed, the fewer icebergs we saw, and the warmer grew the days. Taylor, Billy, and I swam in the pool or stretched out on the sun loungers and chatted. I told them about my journey to visit the aunts, and they were very interested to hear that the next aunt, Aunt Alys, was a queen.

"She has a son, Prince William," I said.

"Same age as you?" Taylor asked. "Will you be friends?"

"I doubt it," I said. "I hear he's quite a handful."

"In what way?" Billy inquired.

"Just a brat, I think. I plan to try to tame him."

"You'll be good at that," Taylor said.

"Oh yes," Billy agreed sunnily. "You'll be excellent, what?"

"You did it again, Billy," I pointed out.

"Thanks ever so."

Billy taught us how to play billiards in the Games Room – he was very excited about the "gyroscope", a device that kept the table level even in stormiest seas – and Taylor tried to teach us how to do tricks on horseback. This was difficult, as we didn't have a horse. However, one stormy day, when the sea was huge with waves and the ship pitched and yawed, swinging people sideways, Taylor said: "Perfect!" She made us climb onto the deck railings and practise standing on one leg.

We got in trouble for that, as we could easily have fallen overboard.

"No, no," Billy said. "We made sure to fall onto the *deck*, you see, when we fell?" And he pointed to the bump that he had gotten on his head, doing just that. It made no difference: we still got into trouble.

The next day it was calm again, and Taylor said she would teach us some tricks in the corridors – only Billy reminded us they were called passageways – so that the next time the seas were wild, we could do *cartwheels* on the railing.

"Oh," I said, interested. "Even though we got into trouble last time?"

"She's not at *all* bothered by authority," Billy explained. "Trouble washes over her like soap bubbles. It makes me quite giddy, what?"

"Before I start," Taylor said, "let's see what you can do. Can you stand on your hands, Bronte?"

It didn't seem likely. That would make me upside down.

"Just try," Taylor coaxed. "Like this." She demonstrated a few times.

So I tried. I fell forward onto my palms, threw my legs in the air, and without even thinking, I found myself running along *on my hands*. Then, because it felt right, I swung my legs over my head and sprang back up to a standing position. It was easy.

"Great *turkey*!" shouted Billy.

"Jeepers," said Taylor, and whistled loudly. "*Junior Captain*, you're a natural! You have circus performers in your family?"

"No!" I laughed, but suddenly I remembered my Aunt Sophy's tale about my mother. How she had impressed my father with gymnastics in the wild horse forest.

"Oh, that's it, then," Taylor said. "You've inherited it. It's in your blood."

A strange thing happened at that moment. I looked down at my hands, and the veins on them, and at my arms and legs, and I saw myself, for the first time, in a completely different way. I was the child of Patrick and Lida Mettlestone.

"Okay, Billy," Taylor said. "Let's see what you can do!"

Billy was a bit hopeless, to be honest. He kept flinging himself onto his *head*, instead of his hands, and then falling back, groaning in agony. But he tried his best.

47

Sometimes the ship would dock in a port, and people would debark and explore a seaside village for the day. Then everyone would come back on board with bags full of souvenirs, faces flushed from the windy shore, brimming with stories of their day.

One balmy Sunday, we arrived at the village of Lasawftk, and word went around that the Lasawftk Markets were under way. "Marvellous markets!" everybody said. "What luck!" and there was a general bustle towards the gangplanks.

However, Taylor had twisted her ankle that morning and wanted to rest it, and Billy was caught up in an intense game of billiards with a financier from Clybourne. So I ended up going to the markets by myself.

At first, I wandered around the stalls wondering just what it was that adults found so *great* about markets? Really, they're just shops out of doors. Perhaps adults don't get enough fresh air? And that's why the excitement?

Anyway, these markets had colourful fruits and vegetables, fresh bread, jewellery, paintings, and oils from every kingdom and empire. Exactly the kind of thing you get at the market at Gainsleigh Harbour and every other market I have ever visited. It was perfectly pleasant, but I thought I might return to the ship and watch Billy's game.

I was standing at a stall, picking up pots and vases and things, while I had these thoughts. I wasn't paying much attention to the pots; I was pretending to be interested by them. I pulled the lid from a tall, slender bottle and squinted inside it — as part of this pretending — and then I noticed that the man behind the stall was standing very still, watching me.

I looked at the bottle in my hand. It had the swooping, ornate appearance that you associate with genie bottles. "Is there a genie in here?" I joked, for something to say.

"Not any more, there's not," the man said, his voice as still as he himself was. "You've just let it free."

"What?!" I almost dropped the bottle in my shock.

He raised his eyes from the bottle to my face. "No," he said. "I jest." Then he smiled, the faintest smile, an echo of a smile, and I had the strange thought that his *original* smile, his *real* smile, had been lost somewhere, far in the past.

"That genie," he added, "was freed many years ago."

His eyes were sad, and suddenly I knew that he himself had once known the genie from this bottle. Maybe he'd even been *friends* with that genie, and his original smile, his real smile, was lost in the time of that friendship.

A woman's voice spoke up beside me. "Is it right to sell a genie bottle that contains no genie?" she asked tartly. I hadn't realized she was there, and I started and turned to look at her. She was all got up in the sort of reds and crimsons that you usually see as lipsticks. Shawls were draped over her in every direction, and she seemed to be holding her arms up high, as if on purpose to show off these shawls.

"Not at that price," the man retorted, pointing to the tag on the bottle. It's true that it was very cheap, only a few copper coins. The man turned away, as if to help another customer, but there was nobody else to help.

Now the woman beside me gave a little shiver and disappeared, and then I realized that *she* was the genie herself.

"Oh!" I said, and the man turned his sad face back to me. He shrugged.

"She returns to say hello now and again," he said. "She brings me fruit." And he indicated a large basket of fruit that had just appeared on the table.

"That's nice of her," I ventured.

I would have liked to hear more about the genie, but the man was now peeling a banana from the basket. "You could buy the bottle if you like," he said, taking a bite. "It's very cheap."

"It is," I agreed, but I was thinking that really, as the genie herself had intimated, there was not much use in a genie bottle without its genie.

"An empty genie bottle has a very peculiar power," the man said, guessing my thoughts.

"What power is that?"

He took another, larger bite, chewed a while, and swallowed. "It helps you dream the dreams you are meant to dream."

"Complicated," I observed.

"No." He shook his head. "At night, when we sleep, we mostly dream a lot of nonsense, but sometimes we dream just as we ought."

I thought I knew what he meant, but wasn't sure.

"This bottle." He picked it up and placed it in my hands. "This bottle, if placed by your bed while you sleep, will direct you to the right dream."

"Every night?"

He shook his head quickly. "Just once."

"Hmm." I looked at the price tag again. One proper dream didn't seem worth it. "If I bought the bottle," I said, "would the genie bring me fruit?" That would be handy.

But the man shook his head again. "She has long ago left this bottle. It no longer has any hold on her. She visits *me* and brings the fruit because we have...a past." Then he smiled again, even more faintly, the echo fading.

In the end, I bought the bottle from him and returned to the ship.

48

Buying the genie bottle had felt like a dream *itself*, I told Billy and Taylor. The way I had somehow *known* that the man's smile was an echo, and that he had been friends with the genie, and that the woman was the genie, and so on.

They took all this in their stride and asked if they might borrow the bottle sometime so that they could have a dream they ought. Billy was especially cheerful, having won the game of billiards against the financier, but Taylor was glum, as she was tired of icing her ankle.

We agreed to take turns sleeping alongside the genie bottle, and I let Taylor go first on account of her glumness. She returned it to me the next day, furious about her dream. In it, she had climbed a tree and was crawling out onto a branch, when the branch began to crack.

That's it. *Bam*. Woke up. Dream done.

"What's *that* all about?" she demanded. "So short! No action! No plot twists unless you call a branch cracking a twist, which I do *not*. No resolution! No respect for my intelligence, because I am *not* the sort of girl to climb tree and choose a branch that will crack!"

"Maybe it means something symbolic?" I suggested.

"What, I shouldn't try new adventures? Because things will come crashing down? Ridiculous!"

"So you didn't dream the dream you ought?" Billy asked tentatively.

"Not a chance."

Billy took a turn the next night and he was very happy to report that he had dreamed he was locked in a cage and that a dog had explained to him how he should escape.

"Talking dog?" Taylor asked, impressed. "Nice."

"Yes, and the odd thing was that the dog was actually *me*," Billy added. "I realized that the moment I saw him. I'm allergic to dogs, as a rule. But not in this dream! Lovely, big, reddish-brown, woolly dog, and an expert in escapology."

"Was that the dream you were supposed to dream?" I asked, and Billy said, "Search me, what?" but he put his hands in his pockets and did a sort of sliding-back dance step, grinning all the way.

Finally, that night, it was my turn with the genie bottle.

I placed it on the chest of drawers by my bed, shifted it around until it seemed to be in the right position – not too close to the bed in case I swung my hand out in my sleep and knocked it over, and not so far away that it would forget to send me a dream – and got under the covers. Taylor, Billy, and I had played water polo in the swimming pool that day under a bright sun, so I was very tired.

I fell asleep almost at once.

I dreamed that I was standing outside the Gainsleigh

Nightingale Club. Aunt Isabelle and I had attended many balls and parties in this club, and watched plays, musicals, and magic shows, so I was immediately excited. It was twilight, and people were rushing along the path in gowns or suits, drawing tickets from their handbags or pockets. *But where was Aunt Isabelle?* I wondered. *Where was the Butler?* I looked around anxiously and a handsome man in a tuxedo was striding towards me.

It was my father.

"Oh good, there you are, Bronte," he said. "Come quickly, we must rescue your mother."

"She is in danger?" I cried.

"Rescue her from a deathly dull conversation, is what I mean," he said. "With a meteorologist. Your poor mother. This way!"

And he hurried down a dark alleyway I hadn't seen before. We reached a wooden gate and my father pushed this open, revealing a garden lit by lanterns. A cocktail party was under way, people spilling words and laughter, wineglasses catching flashes of moonlight.

"Oh, help," my father said, surprised. "Where's she got to now? Vanished!" and he himself faded, and was gone.

I sat up, wide awake and trembling with rage.

49

Here might be a good time to tell you this.

I lied when I said it didn't bother me when I heard that my parents were dead. Of course it bothered me! I had no memory of my parents! When I looked at the photograph my aunt kept on the mantelpiece, I paid more attention to the trumpeter than them *on purpose*, to defy them!

Because they had run off without me.

In the dream, I felt annoyed with them for disappearing at the party, but the instant I woke, I fell straight into fury.

They had always been gone, but now they had truly vanished and could never come back for me. Killed by pirates, of all things!

Sure, I'd been happy to hear the memories my aunts were sharing on this journey, but these were not *my* memories! They belonged to my aunts! Even though *I* was the child. *I* was the child of Patrick and Lida Mettlestone! There would never be a chance for *me* to get some memories all my own! To make paper chains, watch an elven football match, then stand in a kitchen doorway with my parents.

I tossed and turned in ferocious temper for the rest of the night. I did not care that they had probably not intended to be killed by pirates, or that it was likely more the pirates' fault than their own, I was just plain *mad*!

Strangely, I woke to the news that pirates had been sighted in the area, and were steadily closing in on our ship.

50

I could see the pirate ship.

Taylor, Billy, and I were in the Kids' Club with Randwick, only we weren't playing games. We were on the seats by the portholes, watching the ocean hurtle by, while in the distance, the pirate ship grew larger.

We were very quiet.

That morning there'd been bustle and excitement at first, as everyone rushed to their muster stations, many still wearing pyjamas. But then a co-captain had addressed us in such a low, serious voice that the laughter faded and stopped.

"We have confirmed," the co-captain said, "that the *Dagger and Serpent* pirate ship is in pursuit. Please listen carefully to everything I am about to tell you. For your own safety and that of everyone else on board, follow my instructions precisely."

We had to put on life jackets and lock ourselves in our staterooms. We should be prepared for instructions to evacuate. *If* we were instructed to evacuate, *all* possessions were to be left behind, and we were to *immediately* proceed to Deck 7. Each of us was allocated a lifeboat number.

"Captains Lisbeth and Maya are two of the greatest sailors in all the oceans," the co-captain concluded. "They have escaped pirates before." He cleared his throat. "However, the *Dagger and Serpent* pirate ship is one of the most ruthless and cutthroat of them all. These pirates are no laughing matter, my friends. This is deadly serious."

All the other children were now locked in their staterooms with their families, but Randwick had collected the three of us and brought us to the Kids' Club. It turned out to have a double-security system, which he quickly slid closed and padlocked.

"We're perfectly safe," he said, pointing to the padlock. "That's an iron door! What do you say to a game of cards?"

Only we didn't want to play cards – we wanted to press against the portholes and watch as the pirate ship loomed larger then faded, loomed larger then faded, its black sails tall and tight. When it faced us directly, its stem seemed as sharp as an arrow.

Our ship, meanwhile, was moving very fast. We could hardly hear each other talk, the ocean was in such a roar of speed.

"The captains have set all sail," Billy told us. "I was on deck this morning and saw. Stunsails, gallants, topgallants, royals, everything."

"They have," Randwick agreed. "Well done on the terminology, Billy. If anyone can get us out of this, our fine captains can. Now then, let's see what rations we might have for lunch."

But at that moment the ship gave a mighty lurch and tipped

abruptly sideways. Games and toys slid and crashed against the bulkheads, and both Taylor and Billy toppled to the floor. I fell forward, banging my nose hard against the glass.

There was a groaning noise, and the ship slowly righted itself again. Now we were sailing in a different direction and skimming along even faster. The pirate ship had vanished.

"We've lost it!" Taylor declared.

"Just out of our sights, I expect," Billy apologized. "Here she is, what?"

There it was again, farther away and in a different porthole now, but a solid black shape on the horizon.

And so it went on for all that day and into the darkening night. We sailed out into the open sea, so far from the shore that we could no longer see the coastline from any of the portholes.

We ate biscuits and watched the rush of foam in the water below, moving around the seats and then back again. Often our ship would change direction, and we'd slither to the floor, clutching on to each other while biscuits careened every which way. Sometimes the ship must have caught a good wind, and we flew so fast our voices vibrated when we spoke. Other times we bounced up and down, up and down, as if we were in a carriage and the horses had taken fright and bolted, dragging us along a rutted road.

The pirate ship would fade into the distance, becoming the tiniest toy, and we would all begin to be desperately hopeful. But then it would creep towards us again. Once it drew so near we could see the shapes of pirates, some rushing around, others standing on the deck: very still they seemed to be, hands to their foreheads, or resting on the hilts of their swords.

"Come!" Randwick said after that happened. "Let's have hot chocolates. I see provisions here!"

None of us wanted one, and eventually Randwick sat back down again. I saw that his forehead was damp with sweat. He wiped his hands over his hair and it stood up even more spikily than usual.

Eventually, we began to see the great, black loom of cliffs on a distant shore.

"Are we going to make landfall?" Taylor wondered.

"That would seem frightfully foolish, what?" Billy replied. "And whatever *is* this land? It's not the Oski coast."

"I know where we are!" Randwick said suddenly. He peered out into the night. The cliffs surged closer and strands of light crossed the water, forming patterns. A lighthouse, high on a cliff, was beaming these patterns down at us. In the glimpses of light, jagged rocks and boulders rose from the sea, all clustered at the base of the cliffs.

Yet still the ship rushed onwards!

"Have the captains fallen asleep?" Taylor demanded. "We'll crash!"

"It's all right," Randwick murmured, but he was moving from

porthole to porthole as he spoke. "They're sailing us into the Demon Playground, hoping to lose the pirates that way. Risky, very risky." Then he looked at us quickly. "But don't worry. The captains know exactly what they're doing."

Things became even more terrifying then, for we had slowed down to navigate the reef, and the pirate ship now soared right towards us. Through some portholes, we could see the twisting, sharp-edged shadows of rocks, harsh and broken, piercing the air, craggy and broad, or hulking low, as if in wait. Through the other portholes, there was the skull-and-crossbones flag, shivering stiffly from the deck of the pirate ship. Now we could even see the *faces* of pirates, illuminated by the beam of light from the shore, their mouths set in grim lines, eyes narrowed. One held a musket on his shoulder, and it seemed to me for a moment that he was aiming it directly at me. But he lowered it again.

"On the floor!" Randwick shouted suddenly. "They can *see* us in here!"

And we all crouched, breathless.

Taylor made to stand up again, but Randwick pulled her down.

On and on the night groaned, our ship veering and tilting, the hull shrieking as it scraped against rocks, the four of us curled together on the floor. More than once, I touched the medal hanging around my neck, but each time, I remembered the elf who climbed onto my shoulder and whispered: *Use that medal wisely.* Would it be wise to use it now?

Eventually, I must have fallen asleep, for I woke suddenly to a pounding on the door. I scrambled up, breathing hard, sure that this was pirates. Billy and Taylor were already sitting up, eyes wide with fright. Randwick wrapped his arms around all of us and whispered, "Hush."

The pounding started again, and then again.

"It's all right," Randwick said eventually, his arms relaxing now. "That's the code. It's one of the co-captains."

He stood and unlocked the padlocks, opening the door.

At once, a beaming face pushed his way into the room. "All clear!" the co-captain said. "The pirate ship has been wrecked in the Demon Playground, but *we're* through to the other side and have not sunk!"

"We haven't sunk?" Randwick asked, pretending surprise, and then he laughed at his own little joke. But his hands, I noticed, were shaking violently.

51

The dining hall was loud with a different sort of chatter than usual, alert and jangly, somehow. I heard fragments of talk about just how many ships had foundered in the Demon Playground, and just how many people had been killed by the pirates of the *Dagger and Serpent*.

Others wanted to know why the pirates hadn't fired their cannons. An elderly man explained that the *Dagger and Serpent* never fired except in battle, for fear of damaging treasure that might be aboard. Instead, this man explained, they sailed close enough to board themselves, and then they shot or stabbed all passengers and crew, gathered all the treasure they could find, set fire to the ship, and departed.

Some people were crying and others comforted them. The waiters came around pouring juice and coffee, serving waffles and pancakes, or smoked salmon and eggs, and today, rather than simply nodding as the food appeared, I noticed passengers looking up and smiling warmly: "Oh, thank you!" Some even conversed with the waiters: "How did you get on last night?" or "Wasn't it dreadful? I so admire you serving us food after a night like that. I know *I* couldn't do it. My heart is *still* beating like a racehorse! Are you all right?"

About halfway through breakfast, Aunt Lisbeth and Aunt Maya came through the door, talking quietly to each other. I think they meant to slip around to the Captain's Table without being noticed. But whispers and nudges rushed around the dining hall – *the captains are here, the captains are here* – and a hush fell on the room like a blanket.

My aunts could not help but notice. They paused, about to take their seats. Then, all at once, a mighty applause exploded into the room, every person clapping. And everyone was pushing back their chairs so they could stand, raising their clapping hands high. I was applauding too, as were Taylor, Billy, and Randwick, and I clapped so hard that I can still remember the burning and stinging of my palms. The shout came up, "Three cheers for the captains!" and a roar of cheers like crashing waves.

Then a man gave a passionate speech about how he had sailed on many a cruise ship before, and been chased by many a pirate ship, and every blooming time, the pirate ship had caught up! Never before had the ship been able to out-sail or out-manoeuvre the pirates! As a consequence of which he had lost many a gold watch and diamond cuff link, and once even a doll that he had bought for his baby daughter in Cathrew Square. However, luckily, for him, it had never been the *Dagger and Serpent* in pursuit of his cruise ship before, since, if so, he'd also have lost his life by now, and wouldn't be here to tell this tale.

"Indeed," everyone murmured, and somebody said, "Get to the point."

Then the man said, "My point is this. This is my first journey on the *Riddle and Popcorn* cruise ship, and I will never sail on any other vessel again. This, I swear. In all my days, I have never *seen* such sailing! To out-sail pirates – and *such* pirates as these! – for a full day in open sea! And to negotiate the Demon Playground, with pirates – and *such* pirates – in pursuit! Captain Maya, Captain Lisbeth! I salute you. Indeed, I am at a loss for words!"

"Well, not really," someone pointed out.

"Three cheers for the captains!" another voice shouted, to shut the man up, I think, and the cheers started up again.

Eventually, Aunt Lisbeth made a short speech about how grateful she and Maya were for our kindness, and what a top-notch bunch we were, the way we'd followed the co-captains' instructions, and how patient we'd all been, locked away, a day and night.

She paused, and I noticed how tired her eyes were, and how pale both she and Maya appeared. Then she continued. "I hope you can be patient for another day. As you might have noticed, we've anchored at a little port called Braewood, so as to carry out repairs – a topsail was ripped yesterday, and the hull took a beating. Go ahead and visit Braewood if you like. There's a fishing community here that does a ripper of a lobster supper, and you might even come across a Faffle-Toed Turtle, if you're lucky, as they come ashore here. We'll make sail again this afternoon, and should be back to our scheduled route by morning."

Then she made us give three cheers to ourselves, and three cheers to the co-captains, and three cheers to the Demon Playground for offering such a slammer of an escape route. Everybody laughed. Word had come through, Aunt Lisbeth added, that those pirates who had not drowned had been picked up by the local constabulary and arrested. The Anti-Pirate League had been notified and would soon come and collect them.

We cheered at this news without being asked, then she had us cheer things like the wind and the currents, and silly things such as Sfaray Champagne and a-good-game-of-tennis-on-a-sunny-afternoon.

Finally, Aunt Lisbeth had us applaud the cooks, for preparing this sumptuous breakfast, and she suggested we *eat* the breakfast, or else the cooks would be asking themselves just why they'd gone and bothered?

So everyone laughed and got on with breakfast. The atmosphere was more relaxed and festive now, less jangled. Everyone disappeared, to wash and dress, I supposed, and Aunts Maya and Lisbeth came and hugged us all – Taylor, Billy, and me, I mean. They had a quiet word with Randwick, which I think was to thank him for taking care of us, and both gave him a hearty slap on the back. He nearly toppled over from it.

52

It was an overcast day and drizzling, so most grown-ups stayed onboard.

However, most children went tearing down the gangplank and out onto the beach, where we raced each other, collected shells and pebbles, waded in the ocean, and generally shouted a lot.

Taylor turned flips in the air so that children stopped to watch her. After a bit, she landed on her feet, put her hands in her pockets, and turned to Billy and me.

"I wonder if they've got horses on this island?" she said.

Billy lit up. "Capital idea, what?" he said. "Let's see if we can't snag ourselves a horse, so that Taylor can get on with teaching us her horseback tricks!" Which was very sporting of him when you considered how bruised and battered his head already was from Taylor's lessons.

We decided to explore the island, keeping an eye out for horses (and for Faffle-Toed Turtles, we remembered, in a dutiful way).

It didn't take long for us to find ourselves wandering on a windswept, rocky moor, adrift in shades of grey and perfectly suited to the weather. There was nobody about at all. We carried on aimlessly, climbing over rocks and tripping into shallow holes. The clouds were low and the drizzle had picked up, so that there was a steady patter on our heads and dripping down the backs of our necks.

"This is getting stupid," Taylor said eventually. "And *I* can't see any horses."

"Can't see any turtles either," I said. "Should we go back to the ship and get some lunch?"

"Good plan." Taylor nodded.

Billy was facing the opposite direction to us. "Do you know," he said, "I believe these holes we keep falling over might be

Faffle-Toed Turtle holes? I'm sure I read that they sleep in shallow holes in the moors."

Taylor and I made noises like: *huh*. Interested, but only just. It didn't change our decision to turn back.

But Billy was squinting at something and, as we waited, he began treading purposefully away from us.

"Ship's this way," Taylor told him.

"Turn around, Billy," I advised. "Or else just start walking backwards?" Taylor and I giggled.

But Billy ignored us and kept walking. "I think there might actually *be* a turtle in that hole over there," he called back after a moment. "Let's have a look, what?"

In the distance, there *was* a dark shape in a hole. It could easily have been a shadow or a rock, and was two or three football fields away.

"Oh, jeepers," Taylor said.

We both sighed. "It might not be a turtle at all, Billy," I called to him.

"But it might!" he called back gustily.

"I guess a Faffle-Toed Turtle is a pretty rare thing," Taylor admitted.

"I wouldn't mind seeing its faffle toes," I said.

"What *are* faffle toes?"

"No idea. That's why I want to see them."

We ran to catch up with Billy.

The three of us tramped along chatting, but as we drew closer to the dark shadow, we slowed and grew quiet. There was definitely something in that hollow, and we didn't want to scare it away.

"It's dead," Taylor whispered.

"Sleeping," Billy whispered back.

The closer we got, the more we crept, until we were practically on tiptoe. Eventually, we stopped, a little distance from the hole.

We stood peering.

"*Is* it a turtle?" Billy murmured, doubtful, and suddenly all three of us rushed forward.

It was not a turtle. It was a boy. Curled up, bruised, bloodied, barefoot, clothing all torn and wet, hair all a-tangle with grass and twigs, eyes closed, face a bluish colour and streaked in rainwater.

"He *is* dead!" Taylor cried.

The boy opened his eyes. He looked up at us, blinking fast. "Not dead," he said, but his voice sounded as ragged as he looked.

I stared. I knew this boy.

"I *know* you," I said.

"You do *not*," Taylor scoffed.

But I did.

It was the boy with no shoes.

53

The boy was too bedraggled and broken to chat about the coincidence, so I didn't mention it.

Taylor surprised us by being very soothing. "There now," she hummed to the boy. "It's all right. You're all right now."

"He's not, though," Billy declared, looking across the vast, rugged moor and up at the rain, falling even more heavily now. "He needs a doctor, and pronto!"

"Is there a hospital around?" Taylor asked the boy. "There now. Hush. You'll be all right." She stroked his hair. It was strange seeing her like this, and I found it hard not to giggle.

"I don't know," croaked the boy.

"Well, we will take you to your parents. Do they live far from here?"

The boy shook his head. "No parents."

"All right, then, your family. Your friends. The people who take care of you?"

Again he shook his head. "No people."

"Oh, jeepers," Taylor said, losing interest in her soothing tone. She straightened up. "Are you even *from* here?"

"No," said the boy. "I came from the sea."

"You're a water sprite!"

Now *I* shook my head. "He's not a water sprite. He's a regular boy."

"Oh." Taylor was disappointed. "Are you sure? I've never met a water sprite."

"I've only met two," I said. "They looked like regular people mostly, only they had webbed feet and look, he's got regular feet."

"Yes, well," Billy said. "This is no time for chitchat. This lad needs our help! I say we help him back to the ship and have the ship's doctor take care of him. She's brilliant, the ship's doctor. She's taken any *number* of splinters out of my fingers since I've been aboard, and I scarcely felt a thing, what?"

"And the ship could give him a ride home," Taylor agreed. "Where's that, anyhow?"

But the boy's eyes had closed again, and he had sagged back into the hole.

We asked him if he could walk and he nodded, without

opening his eyes. But once we got him on his feet, he crumpled straight back down again. There was something very wrong with him, I realized; his face was such a bluish-purple. None of us looked at each other. We crouched down and picked him up.

Between us, we carried him back to the ship, sometimes half dragging, sometimes hoisting him quite high. He was silent, although I noticed him bite his lip and wince often. I was pleased each time I saw this because, even though it meant we were hurting him, it also meant he wasn't dead.

People stared as we drew closer to the ship, and a crowd gathered as we carried him up the gangplank. We ignored all the questions – we couldn't have spoken anyway, as we were out of breath from carrying him so far – and we took him straight to the infirmary, where the doctor, who was reading a novel and eating a muffin, put both down at once and hurried over to help, brushing her hands.

54

After that, we weren't allowed to see the boy again.

The doctor told us to fetch the captains, and the captains went into the infirmary for a time. They came out looking grim.

"Top-notch job rescuing him," Aunt Maya told us. "But you may have been too late, I'm sorry to say. The doctor will do what she can."

They had to hurry away themselves then, as repairs were complete and it was time to set sail. Taylor, Billy, and I went and sat on deck, talking about the boy and wondering how he had come to be on the moor all smashed up like that.

"I wonder how he got all the way here from Livingston?" I added, and they both said, "What?" so I told them about the incident with the baby in the river.

"That must have been a different boy," Taylor pronounced.

"No," I said. "It's the same one."

"Couldn't be. He can't have got this far. Also, too much of a coincidence."

"Well, *I* got this far," I argued. "So why shouldn't he have? Plus, coincidences *do* happen."

"Let's not fight, what?" Billy said.

But Taylor and I ignored him and carried on snapping at each other until Billy stood up and walked away. Eventually, Taylor and I also flounced off. To be honest, I think we were all a bit tired after a night pursued by pirates. And shocked by having found a near-dead boy in a hole.

I was so cross I had supper sent to my stateroom that night, and ate it sitting on my bed. I kept expecting Taylor or Billy to knock on my door, wanting to make peace, and I imagined how I would consider whether to accept their apologies or not, with my chin in the air, but they never did.

The next morning, I went to breakfast ready to make peace

myself, but I could not see them in the dining room. I sat at the Captain's Table as usual, and half listened to Aunt Maya, who was addressing the room again.

"As some of you might have noticed," I heard her say – but I only heard this vaguely as I was buttering a slice of toast, "we made a brief stop at Hertfordshire at dawn this morning, to take on supplies and to allow some passengers to disembark."

Hertfordshire.

I straightened up. Aunt Maya was still talking. She hoped people were not disappointed about missing out on seeing Hertfordshire – we were supposed to stay there for half a day, but skipping the stop meant we were now back on schedule.

"Hertfordshire is actually two peas in a pod with our next stop along, Oxfordshire," Aunt Maya added, "so we could all just *pretend* we're in Hertfordshire when we get to Oxfordshire, if we like."

People laughed but I was still only half listening. There was something important about Hertfordshire.

Hertfordshire, Hertfordshire, Hertfordshire.

And then I heard Billy's voice speaking to me, the day I first met him and Taylor. *"Hertfordshire is one of our ports of call,"* he had said, *"and Taylor plans to meet up with the Razdazzle Moonlight Circus there."*

My heart slipped sideways in my chest.

Taylor had not *gone*? Without saying goodbye? Surely she was still asleep in her stateroom?

269

At that moment, Aunt Lisbeth leaned across the table and touched my wrist. "I'm so sorry, Bronte," she murmured. "But Taylor had to disembark at Hertfordshire. The circus she wants to join was there. There was no time for her to wake you to say goodbye."

"Oh!" I said. It was all I could think of to say.

"There's more," Aunt Lisbeth said. "Billy's mother was coming through Hertfordshire herself, and wanted to collect him."

I stared. "Don't tell me Billy's gone too?"

"Billy's gone too." She nodded, and she gave me such a sympathetic look that I had to press my eyes together hard to stop the tears.

55

You might think it foolish of me to be so sad about Taylor and Billy. After all, we had only known each other a week and a half.

But when important things happen between new friends – winning a treasure hunt, getting in trouble for walking on railings, dreaming genie-bottle dreams, being chased by pirates, and stumbling across a boy dying on a moor – the friendship stretches and billows, and dives deep into your heart. On the *Riddle and*

Popcorn cruise ship, the three of us had been a family. And now they were gone.

Both had scribbled notes for me. Taylor's note said:

> Keep up practice on ship railings. Wait for next big seas to do it. Miss you already.
>
> T.
>
> P.S. No way he's your boy with no shoes.

This was Billy's note:

> Have fun on the rest of your treasure-delivery journey, what? Such a lark to meet you, Bronte. I bet you a thousand silver coins we will meet again one day. Affectionately, Billy

For a moment, Billy's note made me warm and glad. We would meet again one day! He had bet a thousand silver coins!

But then it only made me more miserable. How could we meet again one day? We hadn't even exchanged addresses! There was a vast world of Kingdoms and Empires out there, and we were three lost children wandering its ocean and lands. Also, the bet was worthless. If we did *not* meet again one day, how would Billy ever pay me the thousand?

So I was glum and irritable for the last three days of my cruise. I hovered outside the infirmary quite a bit, hoping for good news about the boy, but the doctor said that his body had been so badly damaged that he had fallen into a coma. *He might never wake up*, she told me sorrowfully. *Better not wait around out here.*

Randwick tried to cheer me up by inviting me to join games in the Kids' Club, and Aunt Maya and Aunt Lisbeth kept flying to my side and making jokes or telling stories of adventures. I tried to be polite, but inside my head I was fed up.

On the final night, I sat in my stateroom. I was supposed to give Aunts Maya and Lisbeth their gift at dinner. *"To Lisbeth and Maya,"* said the card. It seemed they would have to share a gift, just as they shared their cruise ship. I hoped they would not mind.

But instead of going to dinner, I was staring through the porthole.

I'd had enough of this journey. It was all very well for my parents to order me about, delivering little boxes of spices and other edible treats, but what exactly had they ever done for me?

I looked back at the treasure chest, still sitting open on my bed.

I made a decision.

I replaced Lisbeth and Maya's gift, closed the chest, and picked it up.

Out of my stateroom, down the corridor, and up the stairs I walked, the treasure chest under my arm.

On the deck, the wind blew my hair across my face. I wove around people playing quoits, or drinking sundowner cocktails on deck chairs.

I stopped at the ship railings.

The sun was setting and the water was a deep, quiet blue. Directly below, it rushed by in frothy white.

I propped the treasure chest onto the railing.

The only aunt who had told me the truth was Aunt Nancy. Maybe unkind people recognized unkindness? "What have your parents done for *you*," she had said, "besides running off and then tying you up with Faery cross-stitch?"

My parents were not kind people.

I tipped the treasure chest forward. *Thunk, thunk,* went the gifts, tumbling forward inside.

In Gainsleigh, roads would crack, trees would be uprooted, bridges would fall, windows would shatter.

But that would be my parents' fault, not mine.

I opened the treasure chest.

My hometown would be ripped apart like thread torn asunder, but that's what my parents had done to my heart.

The gifts skidded towards the opening. One teetered at the edge. It tilted, paused – and fell.

The ship bell rang out for dinner.

I plucked the falling gift from the air and jumped back from the railing with the chest.

I sighed.

Of course I wasn't going to let Gainsleigh fall to pieces.

But that was for Gainsleigh. Not my parents.

56

Maya and Lisbeth did not mind sharing a gift in the slightest, they assured me.

They said, "One, two, three!" and both ripped it open at once.

It turned out to be a package of cranberries.

"From Seacliff Mountain?" Aunt Lisbeth asked.

"Wait." Aunt Maya studied the label underneath. "Yes."

They both shouted with laughter.

Then they told the whole Captain's Table a story about my parents' wedding. "Patrick and Lida had the maddest circle of friends," Lisbeth began.

"Ripper bunch," Maya declared. "Top-notch eccentrics."

"You never had so much fun as when you went to a party at Patrick and Lida's! I tell you, they were the duck's quack. Artists, musicians, fire-eaters, and every one of them crackers."

"That means crazy," Randwick told me in an aside.

"Anyhow, one of these friends," Maya continued, "was a chef by the name of Peng-Lee."

"Oh, *Peng-Lee*," Lisbeth put in dreamily. "The feasts he threw together at the drop of a hat! Remember that spun-toffee pin-wheel with meringue-strawberry crush, Maya, that he made while we were pumping up his bicycle tyres?"

"Who could forget? Anyhow, he was the official wedding chef, of course, and he got it into his head that he'd make roast duck with cranberries and pistachios."

"But of course…" Lisbeth reached for the wine and refilled the adults' glasses. "He had to have the *best* cranberries. And those are—"

"The cranberries of Seacliff Mountain," a man in a sherbet-orange suit pronounced.

"Got it in one," Maya said. "Did you know that already, or make an educated guess?"

The man tried to look mysterious, and everyone laughed.

"So anyhow," Maya went on, "Peng-Lee puts in an order at the local importer, and they *promise*, they *guarantee*, they'll have the Seacliff Mountain cranberries in plenty of time."

"But do they?" Lisbeth looked around the table.

We all shook our heads. "No?"

"No!" shouted both Lisbeth and Maya, and then Maya took up the story.

"Shipment got detoured or derailed or eaten by rats – can't remember what now – but two days before the wedding and Peng-Lee was in a *whirl*. The wedding is *ruined*, he said. The wedding cannot *go on*! And such things."

"Bit of a nuisance for the bride and groom," Aunt Lisbeth pointed out. "Their wedding being cancelled by the chef."

"I would think so," many at the table agreed.

"So anyhow, Patrick sent word to all his sisters, asking if

anybody might have Seacliff Mountain cranberries lying about. Ha. Not likely. They're super rare, those cranberries. However, Maya and I were at sea at this point, on our way back to Gainsleigh for the wedding. We wired Patrick and Lida. We were sailing right *by* Seacliff Mountain on our route, we said, and we would pick some up."

"Perfect," said the man in the sherbet-orange suit. "Problem solved. Easy."

Aunt Lisbeth and Aunt Maya giggled.

"That's what we thought," they said. "Easy."

"Easy," Aunt Lisbeth repeated. "All we have to do is dock at the base of Seacliff Mountain and pick up the cranberries."

"Only we can't," Aunt Maya declared. "Because guess what, it's winter, and there's been a snap freeze. Seacliff Mountain is locked in. Ice as thick as your head there, Bo."

Bo was the man in the sherbet-orange suit. He was very cheerful to be called thick-headed by my aunt, and knocked on his own head as if to prove it.

We all turned back to the aunts.

"Called in a favour from a friend with an ice-breaker," Lisbeth said.

"He hightails it over, breaks the ice for us."

"So we dock. *Where are the cranberries?* we ask. *Oh, up in the village,* they tell us. *The store is smack bang in the middle of town. You can't miss it.*"

"So we look for the road to the village."

"Only that's been wiped out in a mudslide. Now you have to scale a *cliff* to get to the village."

Aunt Maya and Aunt Lisbeth grinned at each other.

"So we called in a favour from a *different* friend. She hightails it over with climbing gear: boots, ropes, picks, and so forth."

"We made it up the cliff," Aunt Maya says. "I scraped a heap of flesh off both knuckles. Lisbeth twisted an ankle. But we made it."

"Headed straight to the centre of town – me limping now – and there it is: *Ashurst: Purveyors of Fine Local Cranberries.*"

"Brilliant," said Bo, heaping his fork with jasmine rice.

"Only problem—"

"CLOSED FOR REPAIRS. Turned out the store had been *flooded* just the night before."

Bo set his fork down again, the rice spilling back onto his plate. "No!"

"Yes." My aunts nodded. "So what now?"

"What?" I asked.

"Well, we waded around the shop," Lisbeth said. "Knocked on windows and doors."

"People next door told us the Ashursts had gone to their cottage. Making a vacation out of the flood, it seemed."

"Oh, now, that's madness," a woman in a fancy floral jumpsuit put in. She gestured with her bread roll. "Stay where you are and *clean up* after a flood."

"Agreed!" Aunt Maya said. "Mop and bucket! Keep selling your cranberries!"

"Turned out their cottage was the other side of a lake."

"Was it frozen?" Bo inquired. "Like the sea?"

"It was," Aunt Lisbeth told him approvingly. "We thought, no trouble, we'll skate across the lake."

"And so we did," Aunt Maya said.

"Except that, middle of the lake, the ice was not so frozen as we'd thought."

"Fell right through, didn't we? The pair of us."

"Darn near drowned."

"Oh, that water was cold! Still makes me shiver thinking of it."

"How did you get out?" said an elderly lady with multiple strings of pearls. "Did you call in a favour from a friend?" She grinned wickedly and everybody laughed.

"You kick your legs, get horizontal, drag yourself out, roll yourself away from the hole. That's what we did."

"Turned up at the cottage like a pair of wet rats."

"Shivering so hard I chipped a tooth."

"They gave us dry clothes, whiskey, and their last box of cranberries! They're the bee's knees, that family!"

"Got ourselves back across the lake with the cranberries."

"Got ourselves back down the cliff with the cranberries."

"Got ourselves back into the ship with the cranberries."

"A day behind schedule now. Had to *hightail* it, ripped a couple of sails, called in a favour from a friend, and got a permit to short-cut through the Sfajdji Waters."

"Made it to Gainsleigh on the *morning* of the wedding."

"Tore through town to the Gainsleigh Nightingale Club, carrying the cranberries."

"That's where the wedding was held?" I asked. "At the Gainsleigh Nightingale Club?"

"You bet. Lisbeth had to hop the whole way, what with her twisted ankle – turned out to be fractured, later, but we didn't know that then – anyhow, she can hop like a demon when she needs to."

"Flew into the kitchens."

"And there's Peng-Lee, still sulking, still refusing to cook a single thing for that wedding."

"There are Patrick and Lida. Trying to persuade him to get started. Please, just get started. Offering him the second, third, fourth-best cranberries from all the Kingdoms and Empires."

"*We're here!* we shouted."

"Slid the box of cranberries along the countertop to him."

"Both of us gasping for breath."

"Peng-Lee looks up. You can tell he doesn't believe it."

"He picks up the box."

"He reads the label. *Seacliff Mountain Cranberries*, it says, clear as day."

"*You got them!* he crows. Now he's tearing open the box."

"We're all grinning. Patrick and Lida are mouthing, *thank you, thank you* at us. They're ready to hightail it out of there to get themselves dressed for the wedding."

"And then Peng-Lee stops."

"*Wait,* he says, frowning. *Are these from the east or the west face of Seacliff Mountain?*"

"We stare. Gobsmacked. *No clue,* we say. *Does it matter?* Peng-Lee is turning the box around and around. Studying the label. *There,* he says, and he's grim as granite."

"He points to a teeny-tiny line. *East Seacliff Mountain,* it says."

"He looks up at us. *The east side of the mountain?* he sneers. *Useless to me. I need cranberries from the west!* And he tosses the box into the trash."

57

Everyone at the table exploded into laughter, including me. Caught up in the story, I'd forgotten my mood.

"Patrick grabbed the box right back out of the trash," Aunt Maya continued, "and then both Patrick and Lida got stuck into Peng-Lee. Before that, they'd been gentle and coaxing, see, but now they were blasting him."

"That was something about your parents." Aunt Lisbeth looked over at me. "Most of the time, they were sunny and fun, but when they got mad, they *both* got mad at the exact same moment.

Turned themselves into a hurricane of shouting, their shouts piling up and overlapping."

"*They've got your blazing cranberries!* Patrick bellowed."

"*They've been through so much to get them!* Lida roared."

"*You ridiculous, ungrateful git!*"

"*Look, Lisbeth's even fractured her ankle!*"

"We hadn't *told* Lida what we'd been through, by the way," Aunt Maya added. "Not even that Lisbeth had *hurt* her ankle. But those are some of the things they shouted at Peng-Lee."

"A doctor confirmed my ankle was fractured later that night," Lisbeth put in, "after I danced on it for hours at the wedding. It swelled up like a zeppelin!"

"Your mother seemed to just *know* things, sometimes," Maya added, smiling at me now.

The rest of the table also smiled at me, and then turned back to my aunts. Aunt Lisbeth carried on.

"Anyhow, they were hopping mad! You'd think they'd have been hopping mad *before* this, what with Peng-Lee ruining their wedding, but it was only when they thought Maya and I had been mistreated that they lost it."

"In the end, Peng-Lee hugged both Patrick and Lida (while they were still shouting), shook our hands, and promised to make the grandest banquet in all the Kingdoms and Empires."

"Which is exactly what he did," Aunt Lisbeth concluded. "The gourmet pages in the *Gainsleigh News* wrote a feature on it."

"Still dream about that feast," Aunt Maya sighed. "Especially the roast duck with pistachio and cranberries."

"The cranberries were excellent," Lisbeth noted. "Afterwards, Peng-Lee told Maya and me that all this time he'd been mistaken. That we'd opened his eyes to the actual superiority of cranberries from the *east* side of the mountain."

They both smiled down at the package on the table before them.

"And where are *your* cranberries from?" said Bo.

The aunts studied the fine print, until Maya pointed.

"East," Lisbeth said.

"Of course," Maya whispered.

Everyone, still smiling, got back to eating dinner.

58

I was packing my suitcase early the next morning when Aunt Maya knocked on the door.

"Top-notch news," she said. "The boy from the turtle hole's awake."

I had to think for a moment what she was talking about. "The boy from the turtle hole" sounded to me like a boy with a long neck and a shell.

Then I remembered. "The boy with no shoes! He's all right!"

"Still a ways away from all right, Junior Captain. Still buried deep under the weather, you might say. But doc says he'll likely pull through. All packed? Shall we walk to breakfast together?"

I told her I needed another quarter of an hour, and we agreed to meet in the dining hall. But as soon as her footsteps faded, I slipped out and ran to the infirmary.

The doctor bit her lip when she saw me. She set aside her paperback novel. "Oh, honey, no," she said. "He's not ready for visitors. He's awfully weak."

"It's my last chance," I pleaded. "I'm disembarking this morning."

So she said that I was to be very quiet, and only stay a minute, then she pulled open a curtain and there he was.

He was propped against pillows, and his bright, black eyes looked right into my eyes. His face did not have the bluish corpse look anymore, but he was still grazed and bruised and bandaged.

"Here's Bronte." The doctor smiled at him. "She's the niece of the captains, and one of the children who found you and brought you aboard."

Now the boy's eyes brightened even more. "I am glad to meet you," he said. His voice was a little raspy. "You saved my life, you and your friends, and I thank you." He had an accent I couldn't place.

"It was nothing," I said.

We studied each other for a moment. I was waiting for him to mention the baby we'd rescued from the river, but he didn't. In fact, everything about his expression suggested that he was only meeting me properly for the first time now — that I was just a girl who had carried him half-conscious across the moor.

So perhaps I was wrong after all.

Disappointment like cold tea spread all around my body, down my arms to my fingertips, down my legs to my toenails.

Strange, I know. I hadn't realized that sadness could move like cold tea. And I hadn't realized how much I wanted this boy to be *my* boy with no shoes. Not just because that would prove me right and Taylor wrong. Although that was a scratchy part of it.

The doctor said she had to run out for a moment and would I look after Alejandro, please, while she was gone.

"What sort of looking after does he need?" I panicked, but she laughed and said, "Oh, give him a glass of water if he wants one," and ran out the door.

"Would you like a glass of water?" I asked. "Alejandro?" Trying out his name.

"No, I thank you," Alejandro replied, and he grinned in such a friendly way that I was sure, all over again, that he was the boy with no shoes.

"How are you feeling?" I asked next.

He shrugged. "I am right as rain." Looking at him, and all the violent purple bruising on his collarbone, I found that unlikely.

"If I may," I began. Then I stopped. I was trying to recall how Aunt Isabelle would phrase this. "If it is not too forward of me," I tried next. "May I inquire how you came to be − in such a wretched state − in the shallow hole of a Faffle-Toed Turtle?"

Alejandro laughed, but flinched and touched his chest. "Cracked ribs," he explained, but still smiled. "It is like this."

I sat down on the chair by the bed and waited for Alejandro to begin.

"It is like this," he said again. "I was raised on a pirate ship. The *Dagger and Serpent*, so called."

"You're a pirate!" I gasped.

"Well." He considered this. "I suppose. As I was brought up by pirates and lived aboard their ship. You will be wishing you'd left me in that turtle hole to die, won't you now?"

I hadn't thought that far. I was still caught in the surprise of his being a pirate.

"And I would not blame you," Alejandro continued. "For I am thinking you were on this ship as it was pursued by the *Dagger and Serpent*? You must loathe pirates now above all others!"

"Chased by pirates, yes," I said thoughtfully. "There's also the matter of my parents having been *killed* by pirates."

I was only reflecting aloud, really, rather than meaning to strike a dagger in his heart − I was still trying to catch up with him as a pirate (and therefore, *certainly* not my boy with no shoes) − but he recoiled as if I *had* struck him.

"I am truly sorry," he said. "On behalf of all pirates, I am sorry. Your parents!"

"It's all right," I said. "It was the *Thistleskull*. Not your ship."

"The *Thistleskull*." He nodded, and then his eyes went up to the ceiling. "The *Thistleskull*, you say? The *Thistleskull*."

"Yes."

I thought it was perhaps insensitive of him to keep repeating the name of the ship that had ended my parents' lives. But his eyes were so bright and his accent so beguiling that I didn't mind all that much. Perhaps this was falling under a pirate's spell? I had heard they could be bewitching.

"Only, I don't know that pirate ship," he apologized. "And I thought I knew them all. The pirates used to quiz me. But not the *Thistleskull*." He seemed disappointed in himself. "Must be a new one." Then he shook himself and said, "Again, I am sorry."

"Don't give it another thought," I said. "I hardly knew my parents. Keep on with your story."

He looked doubtful but took up the story again.

"I never did any pirating," he said. "I was sent belowdecks to play, at first, and then later to read my pirate manuals, or carve things of wood, or feed the parrots. So I never really knew what went on."

I was a bit dubious about that. "Everyone knows what pirates do," I said.

"Pirates themselves do not discuss it," Alejandro explained. "It's a sort of code."

"Well, what did you think they were *doing* when they chased ships and went aboard and came back loaded down with treasure?" I was getting a bit scornful. "And didn't you say you read pirate manuals?"

Alejandro smiled at my tone. "This is fair," he said. "But the pirate manuals are only statistics about *ships*, not about thieving and killing. And you see, these people were family to me – all that I had. You don't imagine your family are out slaying innocents and setting ships alight, you see?"

This seemed a fair and interesting point.

Alejandro gave me a rueful look. "I even looked forward to turning twelve, and being able to join in the pirating. But then, of course, on my eleventh birthday, my training began."

"And then you knew."

"And then I knew. They told me everything. I wanted none of it." His smile had vanished. "But would they allow that? No. *This one's got empathy,* they laughed at each other. *What sort of a pirate ship raises up a boy with empathy! We've made him soft!* They kicked me around, trying to beat the softness out of me."

"Oh," I said, my voice small.

He didn't seem to notice. He was grinning wryly. "In time, I saw that the only thing for it was to run away. The first time I did it was about six weeks ago. We'd set anchor a way off coast. The nearest big town was Livingston, and some were going ashore to pick up provisions."

287

"Livingston!"

"Yes. Livingston. I slipped away. Took nothing but a handful of coins."

"To Livingston?"

"Yes," he said patiently. "First, I followed the river into the town of Livingston. I wanted to send a telegram, to warn a certain Queen Alys of the pirates' plan to kidnap her son, Prince William. I had heard of this plan and did not like it."

"Queen Alys!" I said. "And Prince William!"

He nodded.

"But those are my aunt and my cousin!"

"Yes," he said thoughtfully. "I have told my story to the captains, your Aunts Maya and Lisbeth, and they exclaimed this same way. Anyway, once I telegrammed, I set out to return to the docks, to find work on a regular ship. I know plenty about sailing, but that is all I know. So I headed back along the river."

"Along the river?"

"Yes. There was a terrible rainstorm that day. And—"

"A terrible rainstorm?"

Alejandro studied me a moment. "I mean no offence," he said, "but you put me in mind of the parrots on my ship."

I laughed. His bright eyes and smile made this less insulting somehow, more funny. And it was a fair comment.

But my heart was pattering, because if it was Livingston, the river, the rainstorm, then it *was* the boy with no shoes, it *must* be.

But he did not recognize me. He didn't know I was the girl who'd been across the river from him.

I felt an odd twist at that – at having been forgotten.

I found my way around the twist to ask, "So you ran along the river?"

"Yes," he said, patient again but raising an eyebrow. "But it occurred to me I should allow time for the *Dagger and Serpent* to sail away. There was a festival that day and I decided to go to it."

"The Festival of Matchstick," I said.

"That is the one," he agreed, but he did not seem to register anything strange in my knowing. Caught up in his story, I supposed. "I saw a game of football played by elves."

Yes, I thought, *and I saw* you *at that game. I caught your eye and you grinned at me.*

"By nightfall," Alejandro continued, "I thought to myself, well, it will be safe now, ahoy for a sailor's life – I was trying to be positive – and along I went."

"And was it safe?" I asked doubtfully. For a boy raised aboard a pirate's ship, he seemed to know very little about pirates. You can't simply step off a pirate ship and start a new life. They never allow it.

"No," Alejandro replied. "Not safe at all. I had been a fool in thinking it. They were lying in wait. They took me back aboard and locked me in the ship's dungeons, and there I've been ever since."

"You haven't," I breathed.

"I have," he said, quite mildly. "They thought they'd wear me down."

"And then your ship was wrecked?"

"Torn all to pieces in the Demon Playground. Your aunts! They make the *finest* sailors I've ever known."

"They do seem rather good," I said, modestly.

"*Rather good,*" he chuckled, teasing again. "Anyhow, I thought I was certain to drown in the dungeon as we sank, except the hull was breached by the Demon rocks, and the waves poured in, and took me out with them, and eventually I washed up on the beach at Braewood. I crawled all the way to the moor, looking for help, and that is where you found me."

Again, he smiled, but it was slowly unfolding to me, how he came to be so battered – that his pirate friends had beaten him, and he'd been smashed against the rocks in the Demon Playground, his bones broken, his skin torn, nearly drowned, and here he was grinning about it.

Alejandro's eyelids began to sink. He tried to blink them open.

"You sleep now," I said. "I only wanted to say hello."

I stood up. Already he had sunk back down to the pillow. I must have worn him out, asking for his story.

I watched him sleeping and felt very small. All I had cared about was his being the boy with no shoes. And then I'd been so bothered that he'd forgotten *me*.

But his story was so much bigger and bolder than anything I had encountered. And here he was, teasing me gently, as he lay bruised and broken in his bed.

The doctor had come back in while we were talking, I realized. She was reading, head bent, at her desk in the opposite corner.

I crept towards the door.

"Bronte?" said a faint voice – a whisper – from behind me.

I turned and Alejandro's eyes were open again. "Was the baby all right?" he said.

"The baby?"

"The baby in the basket? In the river?"

"In the river?"

He chuckled. "Your swimming was champion that day," he murmured, almost to himself. "I have never seen the like." Then his eyes closed again, and he slept.

 # Aunt Alys

59

A carriage stood waiting at the wharf. It was the grandest I had ever seen, so gold and jewel encrusted that it dazzled your eyes when you tried to look at it. Six noble horses, midnight black, stood tall in their harnesses.

"That's not it, is it?" I asked my aunts nervously.

We were standing on deck, looking down.

"You bet it is," Aunt Maya replied. "See? On the door? Coat of arms of the Mellifluous Kingdom. The violin bow crossing the drumsticks."

"And look!" Aunt Lisbeth pointed. "There's Alys herself waving from the window!"

Lisbeth and Maya began leaping up and down, waving their arms madly. They were pulling hilarious faces, dragging down their lips, and blowing air into their cheeks. I was a bit worried about them.

Then I peered more closely down at the carriage window and saw that a woman had stuck her head right out now, and was waving and pulling similar faces! She crossed her eyes and stuck out her tongue.

After a moment, they all stopped carrying on and simply smiled at one another.

"Oh," I said, staring. "She's beautiful! When she stops making faces, I mean."

Maya and Lisbeth laughed. "She was always the beauty of the family. Cheekbones, willowy neck. Never seemed to notice it herself."

"Wasted on her," Lisbeth agreed.

"No wonder she caught the heart of the King of the Mellifluous Kingdom," I said, feeling grown-up about this comment.

Maya and Lisbeth turned to me in surprise. "Who told you she married a king?"

"Well." I frowned. "How else did she end up as a queen?"

"Why, she happened to be visiting right when they had a vacancy!" Maya said.

"Took up the reins of power and, by all accounts, she's been doing a *ripper* of a job running the place."

"Top-notch queen, that one. And I can't say I'm surprised. She was always bright, and she's got that quiet sort of authority. Works wonders. Come on, Junior Captain Bronte, let's go meet her!"

And they tore down the gangplank, waving madly again. I followed, swinging my suitcase.

There was a lot of hugging and prancing around between my three aunts. They were like children. Aunt Alys had tumbled out of the carriage when she saw us coming, and she shook my hand and smiled at me very warmly, then she, Maya, and Lisbeth started the hugging and prancing. There was also much chattering. I couldn't follow it. All three whispered occasionally, and all three wiped away tears. I supposed they did not see each other often.

Security guards hovered nearby, looking stern. After a bit, these guards muttered to Aunt Alys in an urgent tone, and she thanked them for their concern and went on chattering, laughing, and whispering for another fifteen minutes.

Eventually, Aunt Alys sighed and gave her sisters one final hug each.

"Shall we get going?" she said to me.

I thanked Aunts Maya and Lisbeth for the cruise, and they took turns swinging me around.

"You were a dream," they said to me. "Look after this one, Alys, she's the cat's pyjamas."

Alys said, "Of course she is," and took my hand to help me aboard.

But I had only taken one step when all three aunts said, "Hey! Will you be going to—" and stopped, because of the coincidence of speaking at the same time.

"To the party for Patrick and Lida?" Aunt Alys finished for them.

Maya nodded. "Of course."

Aunt Alys said she would see them there, and we stepped aboard. The guards clicked fingers and clapped their hands together. The driver said, "Ahead!" in a firm, stately voice, and we rolled smoothly away.

Aunt Maya and Aunt Lisbeth removed their captain's hats and waved these at me exuberantly.

60

If you have been imagining the interior of Queen Alys's coach to be luxuriously appointed, with puffy silk cushions and soft brocaded curtains, and if you have pictured this coach sliding along country roads through bright green fields – spotted with curly sheep or glossy cows, and neatly divided by quaint stone walls

– past thatched cottages with colourful doors, by occasional shining ponds and lakes, through cherry orchards whose trees were thick with clusters of rich-red cherries, and then into a little town, wide streets lined with placid trees, boxes of flowers on every window ledge, and on through wrought-iron gates into elegant grounds, past a rotunda set up with circles of chairs, musical instruments resting on these chairs, flower beds radiant with roses and camellias, all of this eventually leading to a picturesque stone castle, lively with turrets – if you have been imagining all this, dear reader, well, you have the most uncanny imagination.

For you are perfectly right.

Sometimes life turns out to be exactly as you hope, only better. All along the journey, I bounced on the puffy cushions and exclaimed at how pretty it all was.

"It *is* lovely, isn't it?" Aunt Alys agreed. She herself spent most of the journey scribbling on stacks of cards. But whenever I exclaimed, she glanced up and smiled and, now and then, pointed out a particularly interesting pond or mill. When we passed the cherry orchards, she said, "Cherries are our primary export: we are famous for our cherries." And when we passed the rotunda of instruments, she asked, "Do you know how the Mellifluous Kingdom works, Bronte?"

"No," I said.

I was a little confused by the question. Did kingdoms "work"? Wasn't that what *people* did?

"This is a kingdom built of music," Aunt Alys explained. "See the instruments in that rotunda?"

We were moving fairly slowly at this point, and I peered through the window. I could see a grand piano, a number of violins, a double bass, a row of saxophones glinting in the sun, and then we took a curve in the driveway and I lost sight of it all.

"Those are the ancient Mellifluous Instruments," Alys continued. "Each evening, musicians play them as the sun sets. In such a way, our kingdom remains in excellent repair. All the buildings freshly painted, roof tiles repaired, and so on. If we need a bigger school, say, or a new hospital? The music knows this, without being told, and the necessary buildings slowly grow themselves, over several days of playing."

I stared at her. I'd never heard of such a thing.

"I didn't believe it either when I first came here," she told me. "I was touring the kingdom with my jazz band. We all laughed when the locals told us. I mean, we thought we knew a thing or two about music: it *sounded* good, but it wasn't a handyman! However, the morning after we arrived, there was a terrible storm, hailstones as big as your head, Bronte. It lasted three days, and nobody dared come outside. The orchestra could not play the Mellifluous Instruments and, once the storm was over and everyone emerged into the streets again, you should have seen the state the town was in! Buildings battered! Doors sagging off their hinges! Because they hadn't been playing."

"Surely the storm caused that," I said. I was trying to keep my voice polite, but honestly. Nobody had told me Aunt Alys was daft.

We had reached the castle entrance now, but we remained sitting in the carriage while Aunt Alys considered my question.

"Yes, that's what we thought too," she said. "But near sunset that day, a voice shouted up and down the streets, *Is there a drummer anywhere?* It seemed the kingdom's drummer had been killed by a falling branch during the storm, and they urgently needed a new one. Well, my band found that very insensitive. We thought the town should grieve the lost drummer rather than run around shouting for a new one. But I was also curious. I stepped out of the hotel lobby and called, *Yes! I am a drummer!* And I was rushed to the castle grounds and led to the drum kit, and somebody hastily explained what we were to play.

"And then, the music began."

Here, Aunt Alys's eyes became distant and dreamy, and a slow smile formed on her face. But before the smile had completed itself, she blinked and looked at her watch. "Anyway, only a few days later they were advertising for a new queen, and I applied and got the job. It's near sunset now, Bronte. Time for the orchestra to play."

She stepped out of the carriage. A cluster of men and women in smart suits surged forward to greet her. To one of these people, she handed the stack of cards she had scribbled on during our journey. To another, she offered my suitcase, and requested that the Emerald Guest Room be made ready. A third was instructed to bring refreshments to the rotunda.

All the time, her voice remained calm and measured.

"Ten minutes until sunset, I estimate," she said, studying the sky. "Shall we go, Bronte?"

And she reached into the back of the carriage, drew out a picnic blanket, and set out back along the driveway. I hurried to keep pace with her.

61

Aunt Alys, I should have mentioned earlier, was not wearing a crown. Nor was she wearing a sequinned gown. However, she *was* wearing a very slight frown. I noticed this as we sat down.

Ha-ha. I did not plan to make that paragraph a poem – it turned into one on its own.

We were sitting, Aunt Alys and I, on a picnic rug, while the orchestra tuned up on the rotunda. The sky was still blue, but the softer blue of twilight now, as if it was getting sleepy.

A steady stream of families trooped through the gates and set up picnics of their own on the grass around us. As they arrived, they called polite greetings to my aunt: "Evening, Your Majesty," or, "Fine day, was it not, Your Royal Majesty?" Aunt Alys nodded and said, "Evening, Roger," or "Indeed it was, Barb" – she called everybody by name – and when small children passed by, she asked them things like how their wobbly tooth was going, or whether they'd done any more marvellous paintings for her to hang on the palace refrigerator.

I wondered about my cousin Prince William. Was he going to join us, or was he too much of a handful to attend a picnic concert?

I was also thinking how unexpected it was that Queen Alys was *not* wearing a crown or gown, but a loose linen suit, pale mint green, with sandals to match. Now she pulled off the sandals and pressed her toes into the grass.

One of her assistants approached, carrying a picnic basket, and Aunt Alys said, "Ah, here we are. Thanks, Dirk."

Dirk bowed. "Your Majesty."

"Let's see what we've got," Aunt Alys said to me, opening the basket. Salmon fish cakes, a cheese-and-bacon tart, roast chicken drumsticks, and a potato salad.

Two plates, cutlery for two, two cloth napkins, and two plastic cups.

So it seemed that Prince William wasn't coming after all. I felt disappointed, but I was only pretending that to myself. In fact, I was relieved not to have to start taming him.

"There's also a chocolate cake for after," Aunt Alys said, peering deeper into the basket. "Oh, and here's a jug of lemonade."

Now, she was smiling all this time, but there was always that slight frown in her forehead.

I wondered if this was because a part of her knew that musical instruments did not actually build and repair kingdoms.

But then Aunt Alys looked across at the rotunda, and the frown deepened.

"See there," she said, pointing. "We have no trumpeter."

It was true that a trumpet sat untouched on a chair, but the drums were also unattended.

"Maybe late?" I said.

"Our trumpeter resigned the other day," Aunt Alys explained. "Poached by the Gainsleigh Philharmonic. We've advertised for another, but so far no takers."

I was eating a slice of the cheese-and-bacon tart, and it was delicious. Flaky pastry drifted about. "I'm sure you'll find a new one soon," I told her.

Aunt Alys nodded. "Yes, we will. I'm just worried what effect this delay might have on our kingdom. My advisers tell me that we have a good strong brass section, and they doubt a week or so with no trumpet will make any difference. But I'm not so sure."

More and more people arrived, and the grass became a patchwork of picnic blankets. The sky began to flower into oranges and pinks.

I was just thinking that the orchestra took rather a long time to tune up when there was a sudden shout.

"Your Majesty!"

Everyone turned. The shout was coming from somewhere along the driveway. "Your Majesty!" it came again, accompanied by running footsteps.

Aunt Alys rose, brushing down her trousersuit, and squinted into the dim light.

The footsteps pounded louder, and then a large man, bearded and broad-shouldered, was thudding across the grass towards us. In his arms was a huge plant pot.

He reached us and bowed, but he was breathing so noisily that the bow did not seem all that respectful.

"What is it, Carl?" my aunt inquired.

"It's this!" And he thrust the pot towards her.

Alys peered into the pot, and so did I. A twig in soil.

"It's a sapling," Carl gasped. "A cherry sapling. This morning, it was thriving. And now?"

We looked again. The twig was gnarled. It looked quite dead.

"It's happening to *all* the cherry trees," he wheezed.

Now there was a buzzing from the crowd around us. Word flew from one group to another. Two of Aunt Alys's assistants-in-suits stepped smartly towards her and hovered.

"My niece and I passed the orchards on our way here from the docks," Aunt Alys told the bearded man. "The cherries seemed to be in good form."

"It's happened in the last half hour," the man said. "Cherries are rotting. Leaves are curling up."

The buzz around became louder and more anxious.

Queen Alys looked at the man's face. At the dead tree in the pot. She looked up at the rotunda.

"It's the trumpet," she said firmly.

There was another rise in chatter now, some agreeing, others disputing the idea. "But the music is for *buildings*," I heard people saying. "It's never been for plants and trees!"

"It's the trumpet," Alys repeated, ignoring all the talk. She raised her chin and spoke over the noise. "We need the trumpet played. Immediately. Can anybody play?"

There was only more clamour in response, and Alys spoke quickly to her assistants. They began to move about the crowd, addressing groups in turn.

"Can anybody play the trumpet?" Aunt Alys called again.

All around, people were shaking their heads.

"It doesn't matter how badly," she said. "We just need it played."

She turned to the bearded man, his arms still wrapped around the pot. "Are they all failing?" she said.

"Every tree."

Aunt Alys raised her voice again. "We are going to lose the entire crop," she said. "Unless we get the trumpet played immediately."

The crowd was quiet now. Everyone was staring at Queen Alys.

"I ask again, is anyone here a trumpeter?"

Silence.

"Can anyone play the trumpet?"

I could hear my own heart beating violently.

"Even a *little*?"

More silence.

I had sticky fingers from holding a chicken drumstick, a mouthful of potato salad, and my heart was going mad.

"Even if you've just had *one lesson*!" Aunt Alys shouted.

I put down my chicken drumstick and stood up.

"I can play the trumpet, Aunt Alys," I said.

62

Which was how I came to play a Mellifluous Instrument at sunset.

I was terrified.

You see, I'd only been playing trumpet for a year. I never practised much, and hardly ever did the lip buzzing exercises. My teacher had told me to do those for half an hour each day ("Is he mad?" the Butler had asked).

This explains why I didn't leap to my feet when Aunt Alys asked for a trumpeter. I can't *really* play. I'm a beginner. I explained this to Aunt Alys, but she simply beckoned me to follow her.

And so, as Aunt Alys and I walked towards the rotunda and the crowds watched in silence, fear was running fine lines up my spine, over my shoulders, and right down into my stomach. There, the lines met one another and knotted up.

I thought Aunt Alys was walking me there as moral support, or to point out where the trumpet was – or maybe to make sure I didn't run away – but she seated herself at the drum kit.

Her posture was perfect.

I picked up the trumpet and then put it back down again so I could wipe my sweaty hands on my dress. I tried again. At least I remembered how to hold it. My fingers rested on the valves – or not so much rested as *trembled* on the valves.

I reminded myself that my teacher had said my embouchure was quite good for a beginner, and then I panicked, trying to remember what embouchure was. (It's just a fancy word for the way you hold the instrument in your mouth.)

Don't blow your cheeks out, I recalled. *Teeth a little apart. Lips firm at the edges.*

A saxophonist handed me a stack of sheet music.

"I can't read it," I whispered, and she took a pen from behind her ear and quickly scribbled the numbers for the fingering below each note.

"It's not about how good you are," a violinist said, turning to look at me. "It's just about playing. Honestly. It'll work even if every second note you play is wrong."

The cellist spoke up. "Still. Try *not* to play every second note wrong."

I promised to try. "But I've only been learning a year," I admitted. The cellist grimaced. And then a conductor was standing in front of us, and the music began.

I played my very best.

I remembered not to raise my shoulders when I breathed. I remembered to hold each note for a good, clean tone.

To be honest, I made plenty of mistakes, but the music around me was so good and proud and loud, it never seemed to matter.

I played and played – and there it was. The magic. I felt it open up and splash into the twilight. I understood Aunt Alys's dreamy smile now: it seemed as if the bright blue sky of earlier had slid into my heart, the glowing pinks and oranges of sunset too.

There was a movement to the side of the rotunda, and there was big Carl, hefting the plant pot up so everyone could see. The twig had become a little tree, crowded with dark green leaves, and even a single cherry.

I glanced over at the drums, and Aunt Alys, who was tossing her hair about as she drummed up a storm, caught sight of Carl and the pot and threw me a beautiful smile. She followed this up with a high-speed, grooving drum solo, and then pointed her twirling drumsticks at me so that the crowd broke into wild applause.

63

Much, much later, Aunt Alys tucked me into bed.

This seemed funny to me. I had been putting myself to bed so often on this journey, I'd forgotten it was possible for an adult to pat your pillow and pull the blankets around your shoulders, and even sit on the edge of the bed and smile down at you.

We had played for hours, and word had arrived that the orchard was saved. The other musicians had shaken my hands, and the cellist even said that perhaps I had some small potential. I don't know if I believed him. I doubt he could hear me playing: Aunt Alys's drumming had been extremely loud.

Now I breathed in happily. I had expected to spend this visit with a difficult cousin, and instead I'd spent the first night saving cherry trees.

"Will I see Prince William at breakfast in the morning?" I asked.

"Oh, I'm sorry, Bronte," Aunt Alys said. "He's not here. I've sent him away, because . . ."

She paused and bit her lip.

I saw what she was trying to say. I helped her out: "Because he's such a handful?"

Aunt Alys blinked.

"No," she said. She scratched her neck. "No, what makes you . . . no, it's because I had a telegram letting me know that pirates were planning to kidnap him."

"Oh!" I said. "That was a while ago, wasn't it? And I met the pirate boy who sent that telegram, and his ship was wrecked and all the pirates arrested! So William is safe now. You can bring him home."

I was talking quickly, trying to talk myself away from my comment, but Aunt Alys was still back with it.

"Yes," she said, absentmindedly. "Lisbeth and Maya told me. And I'll bring the prince home as soon as the pirates have been collected by the Anti-Pirate League. I'm sure the local constabulary are good folk, but those pirates could still overcome them . . . But listen, a handful?" she said. "What makes you think my boy's a handful?"

This was confusing because it had become so clear in my head that Prince William was a handful. I hadn't thought there'd be any question.

"Well, *isn't* he?" I tried.

"Not at all! He's lovely! I mean, he's not perfect, but then what child is? I think you and he would have got on wonderfully if he'd been here, Bronte."

I doubted that, but didn't say so. Aunt Alys was clearly still waiting for an explanation. "It's only," I said, "that you send telegrams to the other aunts asking for advice on how to bring him up. So, the other aunts think – well, they think he must be giving you … trouble."

At this, Aunt Alys burst into laughter. It was the first time I'd heard her laugh, and it was different from all the other aunts' laughter: a sweet laugh, like a little phrase of music in a simple, major key.

It made me smile.

"Oh no, I've gone and ruined my poor boy's reputation!" she said, and laughed again. "I only ask them because I want to do the best job I *can*, bringing up my boy. I have advisers to help run the kingdom, but I know nothing about raising children! I mean, he has a tutor, of course, and an elocution coach, but it's only really me raising him, you see – his father was a palace gardener who has long since moved on to other kingdoms – and so all the decisions are mine. I don't believe in books of advice about parenting. But I do believe in my sisters."

"And you listen to their advice about Prince William?"

"Well," she said doubtfully. "I take about *half* of the advice that

309

your Aunt Isabelle sends me. No offence, Bronte – I can see she's done a great job raising you. It's just a sister thing, really. We all take notice of half of what Isabelle says. And when your Aunt Nancy recommends something, I send back a message saying, 'Thanks! Brilliant!' and then I do the exact opposite." She grinned and then looked anxious. "I shouldn't have said that. You won't tell Nancy, will you? She'd be terribly insulted."

"Aunt Nancy offered me sausages for breakfast," I said, "then put them away in the fridge. I think you are doing exactly the right thing in not taking her parenting advice."

We smiled at each other again, and then my mind turned a somersault and I scrambled out of bed. I almost knocked Aunt Alys to the floor.

"I almost forgot! I have to give you my parents' gift *tonight*, before I go to sleep!"

Aunt Alys waited patiently while I drew out the treasure chest – I was trembling a bit about almost having forgotten – and found the right package.

She opened the gift with her perfect fingernails. It was a small box of dried lavender, tied with a pale purple ribbon.

Aunt Alys made a small sound, like a breath of laugher, and stroked the sides of the box. When she turned to me, there was a tear poised on the edge of her eyelash.

"I went home to Gainsleigh for a visit once," she told me, gazing down at the box of lavender, "when I was pregnant with

William. I'd only been queen here for a year or so then, and I was still nervous – and my romantic affair with the gardener had just gone wrong. So I went home for a visit.

"Anyhow, your mother was pregnant with *you* at the time. One day, she and I went for a walk along the Gainsleigh River. Lida said she wanted to collect lavender – to bake lavender cupcakes, she said – and we gathered armfuls, chatting about our babies and imagining their being friends one day. At the end of the day, guess what she did?"

"What did she do?"

"She handed the basket of lavender to me. 'No clue how to make lavender cupcakes,' she said. And then she said I should take the lavender back to the palace and have it dried, and whenever I felt worried or lonely, I should take a deep breath of lavender and ask for help. She said I tried so hard to be perfect, I always forgot to ask for help."

Aunt Alys set the little box on the bedside table and folded the wrapping paper carefully.

"And *that* is why I ask my sisters for advice," she said. "Now, you tell me something about yourself. What made you play the trumpet? I'd have thought Isabelle's choice of instrument would be piano?"

"It is," I said. "Only, I always wanted to play the trumpet, on account of the trumpeter in my parents' wedding photograph."

"The trumpeter?"

"Yes."

Aunt Alys looked thoughtful, then her face cleared. "Oh, that will be Walter! He was a brilliant trumpeter. He was your father's best friend all through school. A marvellous face. He has Faery in him, you know – plump people often are Faery – no wonder he caught your eye."

"Well," I said, "yes..." and then I admitted that I paid attention to the trumpeter – to Walter – because I was angry with my parents. As soon as I said this, I felt ashamed. How selfish and spoiled I sounded, how *childish*.

But Aunt Alys was nodding at me vigorously. "Good!" she said, which was very surprising. "No, seriously, I'm pleased with you. Of *course* you should be angry with your parents! *I'm* angry with them! I loved them both so much. And they disappeared! And then they died! I'm *furious* with them for that!"

I stared at her. The light in the room was dim but her face seemed sincere.

"The whole thing," she said, "is strange. I cannot *think* why they had to run off like that and disappear."

"Oh, I know why," I told her.

"You do?"

"Well, I was thinking it was because they were unkind – but then Aunts Maya and Lisbeth told a story about them being kind, and *you* just did the same thing. So it must be my fault. They didn't like me." Aunt Alys was making a peculiar face, but I was thinking hard. "It's probably because I'm boring," I decided. "And that's what my dream meant. You see, I dreamed about my mother finding a conversation *deathly* boring, but now I see it meant they found it *deathly* boring looking after me. So they had to run away. And that's probably why they did the Faery cross-stitch: to make me have adventures and learn to be less boring."

At this, Aunt Alys surprised me again by bursting into tears. Not just one perfect, poised tear, but a rush of them, her face quite crumpled.

"It's all right," I murmured.

"It's *not* all right," Aunt Alys wept. "It's all *wrong*." She hiccuped. "I promise you, Bronte, that you are not the least bit boring, and your parents didn't run off because they didn't like you. Your mother was fascinated by every single thing about you when she was pregnant. She and I *loved* to discuss our babies in detail, little feet kicking, little elbows prodding."

"You did?"

"We did. Now that I think about it, when we were collecting lavender that day, your mother stopped very suddenly and said, 'I think the baby just blew a raspberry!' "

"She said that?"

"She sat down and hunched over, trying to blow a raspberry back to you – I mean, back to her own stomach, hoping you'd get the message."

"But maybe when I was born and she saw me, she thought, *Oh, I've made a mistake, she's actually quite boring*."

Aunt Alys smiled. "If you think it's fun to blow a raspberry at your own belly, then try blowing a raspberry at a *baby's* belly! It's the most fun you will ever have."

She stood up then, wiping her eyes and cheeks, and picked up the box of lavender.

"In any case," Aunt Alys said thoughtfully. "It's a good thing for our kingdom that you *did* look at the trumpeter in the picture instead of your parents. It's ended up saving our cherry orchards." She smiled to herself. "Walter," she said. "I'd forgotten all about him. I wonder if he still plays?"

Then she kissed the top of my head and said, "For the next two days, you can explore the palace, picnic with me in the evening, and play the trumpet as the sun sets. How does that sound?"

"Perfect."

"Sweet dreams, Bronte. And that's a royal order."

 # Aunt Carrie

64

Three days later, I arrived at Stantonville Post Office. The Mellifluous royal carriage had brought me to the coach station in Yearsdale, and from there, I'd taken the 73B Coach and Four to Stantonville.

My parents' instructions became quite detailed at this point.

I was supposed to go into the diner next door to the post office, choose a window table, and order a cheese-and-ham sandwich, a fruit frosty (*Whatever* that *is*, I thought), and a slice of cheesecake.

While I waited for my order to come, I studied the view from the window.

A dusty field. A broken-down wagon sagging in the middle. In the distance, low hills. A man sitting on a fence and smoking a pipe.

Why did it have to be a window table? I asked my parents, inside my head. *Nothing to write home about in* this *view.*

Still, I took out a postcard and wrote home about the view anyway.

The fruit frosty turned out to be a frozen watermelon drink that was so delicious I added a postscript to Aunt Isabelle's postcard: **P.S. Just had the best frozen drink ever – cheesecake also v. good. Not as good as the Butler's, but close. Love to you both. B.**

Next, I was required to buy a posy of violets for Aunt Carrie from the florist's shop on the other side of the post office. No other aunt had been given flowers. I wondered if that was fair. It didn't seem fair.

I decided not to think about it.

At last, I was supposed to walk to Aunt Carrie's cottage. I had met Aunt Carrie once before, when she was visiting Gainsleigh, and I was excited about seeing her again. There was a little map drawn into the instructions, with a scribbly line going across the fields, over a hill, through a gate, and past a few trees.

I set off, swapping my suitcase and the posy of violets back and forth from hand to hand. It was hot and dry. When I reached the top of the hill, I stopped to catch my breath and noticed a small, hand-painted sign nailed to a post:

RICOCHET ORANGES: THIS WAY ↪

I took no notice, as the arrow was pointing in a different direction from mine. But the word *ricochet* made me think of Billy teaching us billiards on the cruise ship: "And do you see how the

316

ball *ricochets* at an angle of — what would you say, sixty-seven point five degrees there?" he asked us once, and Taylor and I fell about laughing. I laughed now, tramping down the other side of the hill. What was a Ricochet orange, then? An orange you could roll across a billiard table?

I stopped. I was almost at the bottom of the hill. *Ricochet orange.* I had *heard* of that before.

Oh well, I thought. *Who cares?*

I took another few steps, and stopped again.

I cared. *Where* had I heard of Ricochet oranges? I tapped my forehead to try to tap the memory back. This never usually works, but today, it did.

It was Aunt Sue in Livingston. She had told me never to try an orange from the Empire of Ricochet, because they spoil you for all other oranges.

That's all right, then, I thought. *I'm not going to try one.*

But then I remembered Aunt Sue calling to me as I left: *"If you ever get a chance to try the oranges of the tiny Empire of Ricochet? Why, you must take it!"* And the cart driver had agreed: *"Aye, never miss an opportunity to try a Ricochet orange."*

I set the suitcase down on the dusty road and placed the violets on top of it.

Now what was I to do?

Aunt Sue had told me I must try a Ricochet orange. My parents' instructions said nothing about detours to buy oranges.

Was I *allowed* to make a detour? Even though that was not in the instructions?

Well, the instructions did not tell me to breathe. And yet here I was, breathing.

I sneezed. Too much dust.

Had my parents *told* me to sneeze? No.

I turned around and headed up the hill again.

65

The path took me by a couple of old barns and a children's playground. A boy and a girl were in the playground – not running, playing, or even talking, but perfectly still. They stared at me as I passed.

I reached a little shack with a sign out the front: ORANGES FROM THE EMPIRE OF RICOCHET. FOR SALE.

"Are these really from the Empire of Ricochet?" I asked.

A woman with a green scarf tied around her neck breathed out sharply. "Why would we have a *sign* if not?"

I saw I had made a mistake in asking. "It's just that the price is good," I explained. But that was a mistake too.

"Too reasonable for you, is it? Would you be happier if I doubled the price?"

I said no, thank you, that I was very happy with the price as it was, and I bought a huge sack of oranges. I'd only wanted one.

While the woman watched, I packed the sack into my suitcase. I had some trouble buckling it again, but used my knee to force it closed. Then I headed back the way I'd come. The posy of violets was looking bedraggled by now, and the suitcase was dragging my shoulder right out of its socket. Or that's how it seemed.

As I passed the playground again, I saw that the boy and girl were in exactly the same positions. They hadn't moved. The boy was sitting on a swing, but he wasn't riding it, or even twisting it around, or kicking at stones. He was simply sitting. He wore a red jacket, the collar turned up. *Too hot for a jacket*, I thought. The girl, wearing a blue dress, was standing by the seesaw and staring at me.

There was something hostile in the way she stared.

"Hiya!" she called suddenly.

I stopped. "Good afternoon," I replied.

She continued staring. I waited. Nothing happened, so I carried on walking.

"Oi!" she called now.

I turned back.

"Is this long enough, do you think?" she demanded.

I considered her question.

"Is what long enough?" I countered in the end.

The girl looked left and right, and then she strolled over to me. I put my suitcase down to wait for her.

"We've been doing this for an hour or something," she said. "It's getting boring."

"Yes," I said, trying to be agreeable. "I can imagine."

"So." She squinted at me. "Can we stop now?"

Again, I considered. "Can you stop what?"

"Stop standing by the seesaw and sitting on the swing. Or at least, can we *swap*? So I get to sit down for once. My legs are hurting."

"Of course you can stop," I said. "Or swap."

"Thanks," she replied.

She sniffed and looked at my suitcase.

"What made you think you couldn't?" I ventured.

"The letter?" the girl said. "My brother and I got a letter saying we'd get paid ten silver pieces each if we went to the park and wore clothes in these colours and did this thing until a girl came by with a suitcase."

That gave me a start. "Whoa," I said. I don't know if I'd ever said *whoa* before, but I couldn't think what else to say. I thought of an alternative. "Who sent you the letter?"

"Nobody."

"Nobody?"

"No name. No return address."

We stared at each other a little longer.

"That's mad," I said finally.

"Right?"

I looked across at the swing. The boy was still slouched there, although he had set it swaying slowly side to side.

"Hello!" I called to him.

He raised a hand.

I looked back at the girl.

"Bronte Mettlestone," I said to her.

"What?"

"That is my name. Bronte. May I inquire as to your name?"

"What?"

"What's your name?"

"Who wants to know?"

I took a break from this conversation to sort it out in my head. "I do," I said eventually.

"Okay. But our names were in the letter that came to us. So."

"I didn't send the letter," I told her.

She shrugged.

"All I can think," I said after a moment, "is that my Aunt Carrie sent the letter to you, hoping we'd run into each other as I passed, and make friends. Although, I only came this way to get the Ricochet oranges, so I could easily have missed you."

The girl sighed deeply now.

"I guess we could be friends," she said at last.

Our friendship didn't seem to be getting off to a promising start.

"What shall we do?" I tried.

The girl looked around vaguely. "There's a pony in the field over there," she said eventually. "I could draw a picture of it. You could catch it and hold it still for me while I draw?"

Well, that seemed like nonsense to me. Unfair both to me and the pony. Even unfair to the girl somehow, depending on how much she liked drawing.

This wasn't working out.

"It's been a great pleasure meeting you," I said, and put out my hand. "But now I must get on to my Aunt Carrie's house."

The girl looked at my hand in the air. After a moment, she raised her eyebrows and shook it. Her palm was quite dry.

She turned around and kicked her way back to the seesaw. "Oi," she said to the boy on the swing, and she pointed to the seesaw.

I set off, leaving them slowly creaking up and down.

66

It took so long for Aunt Carrie to open the door that I began to think she wasn't home.

Her cottage seemed to have been eaten by crawling vines. I had to push them aside to knock. A stone bench sat crumbling by the door, and some of the vines were working on eating that too. There was also a broken umbrella and a pair of dusty rubber boots.

The door opened slowly, and there was Aunt Carrie, shielding her eyes from the sun.

The last time I saw Aunt Carrie, when she had visited Gainsleigh, I had been six years old. I remembered her as big and boisterous, with eyes the colour of violets, thick hair piled on the top of her head and pinned in place with a silver clip. She had laughed enormously when I told her a joke I had learned from the Butler, and I had felt so pleased that I ran to find the Butler and asked him for another. Aunt Carrie laughed even louder at my second joke and announced that she would "Take this one out for tea and cakes, right away, if that suits you, Isabelle?"

At the tea room, she had sung songs with me loudly, not caring about people at other tables. The whole thing had seemed wicked, but also wonderful.

Something had burned in the kitchen of the tea room, I think, as the tea room had become smoky, so a waiter had begun opening windows. One of the windows was jammed shut, and Aunt Carrie had held up a finger – "Hold that thought, Bronte" – skidded over, and hoisted the window open for the waiter.

"You are *strong*," he had told her, amazed, and she had replied, "Why yes, young man, I *am* strong," and then she'd grinned at him.

Now, as she blinked down at me from her cottage door, the only thing I recognized was the colour of her eyes.

She was wearing a nightgown and she was as thin, faded, and small as a bedraggled cat. Her hair had been cut short and lay in a sort of tatter on her head.

"Bronte," she smiled, her voice also thin and faded. "Have you been knocking long? Only, I fell asleep just now. So sorry. Please."

She reached for my suitcase, but her shoulders were so bony I doubted she could lift it.

I handed over the violets instead.

"Oh," I said, realizing. "Your eyes are the colour of violets. That must be why I had to get them for you. I'm sorry they're so ..."

It occurred to me that wilting was exactly what *she* was.

"Let me put them in a vase," she said, and she drifted into her kitchen and began opening and closing cupboards.

At every window, the drapes were tightly closed, so the cottage was dark. As my eyes adjusted, I saw that it was crowded with stacks of cardboard boxes.

"Have you only just moved in?" I asked.

"Been here years," she said vaguely.

She was still opening cupboard doors and rummaging around so that plates and glasses clattered and clinked.

"Let me get you some lunch," she said finally, giving up on the search for a vase. She put the violets in a water glass instead, and ran the tap to fill it.

"No, thank you," I replied. "I've already eaten."

Aunt Carrie moved slowly across the room, stepping over stacks of newspaper. She opened a door to a tiny room that she called her "guest room" and invited me to put my suitcase inside.

"Now then," she said next. "Shall we play a board game?"

This was unexpected.

"Good idea," I said, to be polite, and she crawled along the floor to reach the lowest bookshelf, and drew out a dusty game. Next, she swept a lot of clutter from the table to the floor, and we sat down opposite each other.

We played the game for the whole afternoon. It was a dull game, one of those ones where you roll dice and then move a counter. Now and then you jump over a square, or move back two squares. Sometimes she won, sometimes I did. It was pretty even.

Eventually, it grew so dark that Aunt Carrie turned on a lamp. "Now then," she said. "Dinner."

She crept around her kitchen, opening cupboards, turning on the stove, and sighing. At last, she placed a pot of macaroni and cheese in the middle of the table, along with two spoons.

"Just eat it from the pot," she said.

She took a very small spoonful for herself and sat back and watched me eat. After I'd had enough, she said, "Did I forget dessert? I used to make a good fruit... what's it called? Fruit crumble?"

"I've got Ricochet oranges!" I remembered.

At this, there was a brief glimmer in her eyes. "You've been to Rawsons' stall?" she said. "They get Ricochet oranges in sometimes."

That reminded me. "Aunt Carrie," I said. "Did you send a note to two children and tell them to wait in the park for me to pass?"

Aunt Carrie blinked. "No," she said. "Was I... supposed to do that?"

I took out the oranges and Aunt Carrie smiled, but she still only ate half a wedge. She twisted the other half around in her palm. I ate the rest of her orange myself, and then I peeled another. I could have eaten the whole sack. Aunt Sue had been right: these oranges were like happy new friends who will laugh at your jokes and sing songs with you. Every time I took a bite, I found myself beaming. I tried to catch Aunt Carrie's eye with my beam.

She smiled ever so faintly, and set the half wedge down.

I'll tell you what it was like. It was like she was not there. She was not at the table. She was not sitting opposite me. I was sitting in this cottage, eating Ricochet oranges, alone.

"Aunt Carrie," I said, "I think you must be ill. Could I fetch a doctor for you?"

Again, Aunt Carrie smiled her wispy smile.

"Dear Bronte," she said. "I am not ill. Or anyway, not with an illness that a doctor can cure."

"Oh, I think they can cure most illnesses," I told her breezily. I didn't know that for certain, but I thought it only fair to give a doctor a *go* at curing her. "Do you know what it's called?" I said. "Your illness?"

Aunt Carrie began to gather the orange peels. "Yes," she said. "It's called sadness."

I considered that. I'd been sad myself at times. So far it had never made me skinny. If anything, it would have been the opposite, since the Butler baked meringues or chocolate éclairs whenever I was low.

"We should look into what's making you sad," I said. "And fix it."

My aunt smiled again. "A broken heart," she said. "Can't be fixed. Believe me, I have tried."

I frowned. It seemed to me that most things could be fixed eventually. If you tried once and it didn't work out, it only meant you had to try again.

"It was somebody you loved?" I asked.

"It was," she said. "A long time ago. He was so *big*, Bronte. And his hair was *wild*! Curls springing out here, and here, and here!"

327

Her hands pranced around on top of her head. It was the liveliest I had seen her. Then her arms dropped to her side again. "And I let him go, Bronte. I let him go, and lost him."

"Oh, well," I said. "Let's find him."

Aunt Carrie smiled mistily and suggested I have a bath, brush my teeth, and put on my pyjamas. So I did this. The cottage sat quietly all the while, so that the noise I made moving around seemed like garish colours.

Once I was in bed in the guest room, Aunt Carrie came in, kissed the top of my head, and told me that she would have to work each day of my stay. She worked as a filing clerk in a nearby office, and hoped I would be all right.

I told her I would be fine, thank you, but I wondered what I could possibly do each day for the next two weeks. (Aunt Carrie was the second exception to the three-day-visit rule. My cruise ship aunts had been the first.) There was nothing around except fields.

After a while, all the lights went out and I heard a slight creak, which I guessed was my aunt climbing into her bed in her room.

I lay in the darkness. A tap was still dripping in the bathroom in a *clip-clop* way, like a horse trotting along at quite a pace. I got up, turned off the tap more tightly, and went back to bed. So now there was not even a friendly horse to keep me company.

67

In the middle of the night, I woke up in a panic.

I sat straight up in bed, my heart beating wildly. I was frantic.

Only, I didn't know what I was frantic about.

I took deep breaths, as Aunt Isabelle had taught me to do whenever I got in a state. And I asked myself the same question that Aunt Isabelle would have asked: "Whatever is the matter, Bronte?"

The answer placed itself neatly before me.

I had *seen* them before. The children in the playground. The boy in a red jacket, sitting on a swing. The girl in a blue dress, standing by a seesaw.

I *knew* them.

This only set my heart beating faster. It made no sense! I climbed out of bed and started doing jumping jacks — something else that Aunt Isabelle had taught me to do when riled up.

I tried to jump softly so as not to wake Aunt Carrie.

Thump, went my feet.

But how could I know them? I had never been to Stantonville before!

Thump.

I *did* know them. I had seen them on this journey! I was sure of that.

Thump.

But *when* on this journey?

Thump.

There were so many aunts!

Thump.

I would have to go through them. I would go backwards.

Thump.

Aunt Alys, Aunt Maya, Aunt Lisbeth.

Thump.

Aunt Nancy, Aunt Sophy, Aunt Claire.

Thump.

Aunt Emma, Aunt Sue—

I stopped.

I sat on the edge of the bed.

From Aunt Sue's place, I had walked to a café called the Dishevelled Sofa. I had eaten Today's Special!! and drunk the home-made lemonade. I had been nervous. I had stared at a painting, to calm myself down.

The painting had been set in a children's playground: a boy in a red jacket seated on a swing, a girl in a blue dress standing by a seesaw and staring at me.

68

The next morning, I found a loaf of rye in Aunt Carrie's bread box and made myself toast. Aunt Carrie was still sleeping, so I set out into the day.

It was early but it was already hot again. I walked quickly past the trees, through the gate, over the hill (the sign for Ricochet oranges was still there, but somebody had tacked a piece of paper to it saying SOLD OUT), across the fields, and back to the post office.

I sent a telegram to Aunt Sue in Livingston.

I had never sent a telegram before, but it turned out to be quite easy. You just say, "I'd like to send a telegram, please?" and the man asks who you want to send it to, and what you want to say. So you tell him those things and then you hand over some money.

My first-ever telegram said this:

HELLO AUNT SUE, DID YOU SEND A LETTER TO TWO CHILDREN IN STANTONVILLE ASKING THEM TO ACT OUT A PAINTING THAT HANGS ON THE WALL OF THE DISHEVELLED SOFA CAFÉ? IF SO, THANK YOU. (AND ALSO: WHY?) IF NOT, NEVER MIND. LOVE, BRONTE (STANTONVILLE POST OFFICE).

The post-office man suggested I could use abbreviations for many of these words, to save money, but that seemed impolite.

I was so pleased with myself for sending a telegram that I decided to send another. This one to the Dishevelled Sofa Café itself.

GOOD MORNING. I ONCE CAME TO YOUR CAFÉ AND HAD TODAY'S SPECIAL!! IT WAS DELICIOUS! (I LOVED THE GIANT CROUTONS!) ANYWAY, THERE'S A PAINTING ON THE WALL OF YOUR CAFÉ, OF TWO CHILDREN IN A PLAYGROUND. WOULD YOU PLEASE TELL ME THE ARTIST'S NAME? THANK YOU. BRONTE METTLESTONE (STANTONVILLE POST OFFICE).

I went to the diner next door and had another fruit frosty and slice of cheesecake to reward myself for sending telegrams. Then I returned to the post office and asked if there'd been any reply.

"Not yet," I expected the man to say. *"Bit too soon, eh?"*

In my head, I could hear him saying this very clearly.

But he didn't. He handed over two telegrams.

The first was from Aunt Sue.

NO! I DID NOT! R U LIVING AT THE POST OFFICE NOW? ALL GOOD WITH U? SEE U AT THE PARTY AT FRANNY'S! AUNT S.

The second was from the café.

INTERESTING QUESTION. ARTIST IS RONALDO C. TORRINGTON. GLAD U LIKED THE SPECIAL! COME AGAIN. DSC.

332

"DSC stands for Dishevelled Sofa Café," the post-office man told me, reading over my shoulder.

"Yes," I agreed.

I sent a reply to Aunt Sue telling her that no, not living at the post office, ha-ha, and I looked forward to seeing them at Aunt Franny's.

Then I looked at the second telegram for a while.

"Is there a library around here?" I asked the post-office man eventually.

"Not in Stantonville. There's one in Mosman Village. About two hours' ride from here."

I thought about that.

"May I send another telegram?" I asked.

"You don't need to telegram ahead to the library," he said. "You just go there. You have a horse?"

"No," I said. "Not with me, anyway." And I explained that, in fact, I wanted to telegram a *different* library, one I'd been to before, on Lantern Island.

"Lantern Island?" he said. "Much too far. About ten days' ride from here. And you'd have to get your horse onto a boat."

"I don't have a horse," I reminded him. "And I don't want to go to the Lantern Island Library. I just want to send the librarian a telegram."

At last he relented and let me send the telegram.

HELLO, IT'S BRONTE METTLESTONE. REMEMBER ME? YOU
HELPED ME SAVE THE WATER SPRITE! (THANK U AGAIN.) I
WONDER IF U HAVE ANY INFO IN YOUR LIBRARY ON AN ARTIST
NAMED RONALDO C. TORRINGTON? E.G. IS HE STILL ALIVE? IF
SO, IS THERE AN ADDRESS WHERE I CAN CONTACT HIM? PLEASE
REPLY TO ME AT STANTONVILLE POST OFFICE. I DON'T LIVE
HERE AT THE POST OFFICE, I'M JUST NEARBY. BRONTE X P.S. I
STILL DREAM ABOUT THE CHILDREN'S SECTION IN YOUR
LIBRARY!

It wasn't true that I dreamed about the Children's Section at
the Lantern Island Library. In fact, I'd completely forgotten it. But
it came back to me as I wrote the telegram.

The librarian replied within five minutes. Dear child!
she wrote, and then she said that everybody on Lantern Island
missed me, which I found unlikely. I hadn't even *met* everybody
on the island. She told me that she was an "ardent admirer" of
the art of Ronaldo C. Torrington herself, and had a print of one
of his paintings in her kitchen, and then she gave me his postal
address.

"11 The Picturesque Way, Carnegie Waters," I read aloud.
"Sayer Empire. Do you know where that is?"

"Two kingdoms west of here," the post-office man replied.
"About six hours' ride. You have a horse, you say?"

"Still no."

334

I chose a postcard and wrote a message to Ronaldo C. Torrington.

Dear Mr Torrington,

A few weeks ago, I saw one of your paintings in a café in Livingston. Two children in a play-ground - one on a swing, one on a seesaw. Anyhow, just yesterday I happened to pass a playground in Stantonville and there it was! Your painting! Come to life! The boy, the girl, same clothes, same positions, similar playground!

Now, this might just be a funny coincidence, but the girl told me she had received a letter offering silver coins if she and her brother would wear those clothes and take those positions until I walked past!

Mysterious!

Is it common for people to bring your paint-ings to life in this way? If you know anything about this, perhaps you could write to me? I'm staying with my Aunt Carrie Mettlestone for

the next two weeks. Her address is 2 Thurston
Lane, Stantonville.

Thank you and kind regards,
Bronte Mettlestone

Next, I bought a stamp and mailed the postcard. I thanked the man in the post office for his help and said I hoped I would have a horse with me the next time I saw him. He seemed baffled by that.

I walked back to the playground. It was empty now, but I wandered around, sat on the swing, and swung awhile. I waved at the pony in the field behind the playground but it only flared its nostrils and carried on eating the grass.

Nothing else happened, so I headed back to Aunt Carrie's.

69

When I arrived there was a note from Aunt Carrie:

Hello Bronte, I've gone to work. Back at 5:30 p.m.
- we can play the board game again. C x

"No!" I half shouted at the note. I tried to be more polite. "No, thank you," I said to it instead. "I don't want to play the board game again."

I looked around the dark cottage. It seemed to me that it was probably my job to make Aunt Carrie happy and interesting again. I had read plenty of stories about children meeting grumpy older people and cheering them up. They did this by being delightful and sunny themselves, and also by opening all the curtains. At first, the grumpy people found the child irritating, but then they could not help but be charmed.

I wasn't sure how to be delightful and sunny, but I could open curtains.

Anyone can.

I ran around the cottage, pushing open all the curtains.

Once I'd done that, I wondered if I should close them. The light bursting into the room was not very strong because of the creeper vines covering the windows, but it was strong enough to illuminate dust and mess everywhere. Even the furniture seemed to cower.

Well, I had cleaned Aunt Emma's cottage for her on Lantern Island, so I could do the same for Aunt Carrie.

I would knock it over in an afternoon, I decided.

But that was nonsense. I worked all afternoon, but I'd scarcely made a difference by the time Aunt Carrie arrived home. She seemed alarmed by the opened curtains and hurried to close them all again. Then she looked around for the board game, but I had hidden it. She sat down on the couch, saying, "Let me just have a think where it could be, Bronte," and fell fast asleep.

I remembered that in many of the stories about children and grumpy people, there's a part where the child gets mad. The child shouts something like, "Buck up!" or "Snap out of it, you grumpy old git!" That sort of thing.

I've always been surprised that shouting at somebody will cheer them up, but it works in the books. (You can also slap the sad person across the face with your glove.)

So I went and shook Aunt Carrie's shoulder. *I'll be good at this part*, I thought.

"HEY!" I yelled. "WAKE UP! CHEER UP AT ONCE!"

Aunt Carrie half woke and said, "Oh, darling, I'm sorry, I've fallen asleep, haven't I? Shall we get the board game?" and then her eyes closed again.

I sat down beside her. In the dim light, I could see that great purple shadows looped under her eyes, and that the bones stood out sharply in her cheeks.

Shouting at Aunt Carrie would never make a difference.

There was nobody there to cheer up.

The only thing, I decided, was to make Aunt Carrie's cottage as pleasant as possible. So that she might have a *reason* to come back and be here.

After that, the days fell into a pattern.

In the mornings, I went to the post office to see if there were any telegrams. I ate morning tea in the diner and walked to the playground to see if there were any children or clues. There were never any telegrams, nor children, nor clues.

Then I came back to Aunt Carrie's place, opened all the curtains and windows, and cleaned. Each evening, Aunt Carrie would come home, close the curtains, and look for the board game. She never found it. (I'd hidden it under the wood box.) She would sit on the couch and fall asleep. Much later, she'd wake and say, "Oh, you must be hungry. Did I fall asleep?" We would share macaroni and cheese and a Ricochet orange, and go to bed.

The more I cleaned, the more reckless I became. At first I was careful not to touch any of Aunt Carrie's boxes, or open cupboards or drawers. But I saw that this would get me nowhere.

So I took everything out of every cupboard and drawer, threw it all away (it was grimy and chipped, broken and mouldy), and scrubbed the empty surfaces.

Next, I opened the cardboard boxes and unpacked them. I hung dresses in the wardrobe in Aunt Carrie's bedroom and folded cardigans into her drawers. I'd only seen her wearing a nightie or a plain grey dress, but the boxes were full of shimmery, silky gowns and velvet capes with hoods. There were also shiny sets of cutlery and fine dinnerware, which I placed in the kitchen cupboards. They made me feel less guilty about having thrown away the chipped plates. Some of them had only had a tiny chip, actually.

I found a gramophone and a stack of records, and placed these on a side table.

Outside, I threw away the broken umbrella, rinsed the dirty rubber boots, cleared the vines from the windows, and washed all the glass.

Inside, I mopped the floors and stood on chairs to polish the light fittings.

On my last day, I tipped out the bin of macaroni. This was very wasteful of me, but I was so tired of macaroni and cheese. Aunt Carrie must surely feel the same, I thought. Maybe that was why she only ate a spoonful each night?

I went to the local grocery store that day and bought as many colourful foods as I could find: tomatoes, carrots, red and green peppers. I filled up Aunt Carrie's pantry with fruits and vegetables, jars of bright herbs and spices, vinaigrettes, a carton of eggs, a side of ham, and a loaf of fresh bread. I also bought an entire cheesecake from the diner and placed this on the countertop. (I took it out of its box and put it on a cake plate, as if I'd made it myself.)

Next, I picked bunches of wildflowers and placed these in vases all around the cottage. The wildflowers were tricky to find, since most of the fields were dusty and dry, but the vases had been packed in one of the boxes.

At 5:25 p.m. I chose a record, placed it on the gramophone, and set it playing.

I looked around the cottage. Perfect.

Almost.

I slid the curtains from every curtain rod, folded them, and put them in a cupboard.

Now everything was perfect.

I could hear footsteps on the path outside.

Wait! One more thing.

I tipped the couch upside down.

The door opened.

10

Aunt Carrie ducked her head, as she always did, when she saw how bright her cottage was. She turned to the nearest window, reaching out her hand.

There was no curtain.

She frowned and moved to the next window along, reaching again.

She stepped to the third, arm outstretched.

Gosh, I thought. *When's she going to figure it out?*

At last, her hands dropped. She patted her sides, puzzled. Then she glanced back at me.

"Bronte," she said. "I can't seem to find the curtains. Let me just sit down and think what could have—" She started. "The couch," she murmured. "It's ..."

"Upside down," I prompted. She blinked at me.

She looked at the windows. At the couch.

Her eyes swivelled to the dining chairs. Quickly, I hurried over and tipped them all over.

She stared. Her face trembled.

Oh dear, I thought. *I've broken her.*

And then she erupted into laughter. It was alarming at first, like the roar of a volcano, but then she was slapping her thighs, hooting and shrieking. It was a very comprehensive laugh, high, low, sideways, musical, and everything in between.

It was also the kind of laugh that catches you, so I was laughing too. We laughed madly for a long time, and Aunt Carrie began dancing her laughter all around the cottage, pointing at things, opening drawers and cupboard doors – "It's clean!" – "The boxes are gone!" – "The floor is clean!" – "There are flowers everywhere!"

Oh, well, I thought. *I'm glad you find it funny, but it was actually quite a bit of work.*

But Aunt Carrie was still spinning – "Look at all this food!" she cackled from the open pantry door. "Oh, where's the macaroni?"

"Threw it away."

A scream of laughter.

"And the board game? Did you throw that away too?"

"It's under the wood box."

I thought she'd suffocate herself on that guffaw.

She was burbling in her bedroom now, shrieking about the dresses in the wardrobe, and then she was back in the living room, wiping her nose and eyes.

Eventually, she quieted, giggling now and then until even the hiccups faded.

The gramophone played quietly. Aunt Carrie looked across at it in surprise and I thought she might be about to laugh again, but her eyes returned to me.

"Oh, Bronte," she murmured. "Look what you've been doing. And I never even noticed."

Then she burst into tears.

We had a colourful dinner that night. Aunt Carrie spent much of it laughing and crying and praising my hard work.

She had to blow her nose a lot, and she still ate very little, but at least she was *there*. You couldn't really miss her.

After we'd eaten some cheesecake and shared the final Ricochet orange, I took out my parents' gift. Aunt Carrie was chortling again as she opened it – "You turned the couch upside down!" – then the gift rolled out along the tabletop, and she stopped.

It was a jar of nutmeg.

Aunt Carrie sat back. She rested her elbows on the table. She studied the jar.

I waited patiently. Now she was going to tell me a story about my parents. Maybe my father had made an excellent pumpkin pie for her once, and added a sprinkle of nutmeg? Maybe my mother advised nutmeg as a cure for the common cold?

But Aunt Carrie's silence spilled out across the table. It spilled across the cottage floor and seemed to hit the gramophone – it was only that the record happened to finish at that moment, but that's how it seemed.

At last, she spoke.

"He was so big," she said.

"He was?" I hadn't heard anybody call my father "big" before. He looked fairly standard size in the wedding photograph.

"And his hair, it stuck out – here, and here, and here!" Her hands shot out from her own head, and I thought: *Oh, this is not my father. This is the man she lost, the one who broke her heart.* "He was so big that I used to call him Bear."

She stopped speaking then.

I decided it was time to be stern. "Well, Aunt Carrie," I said. "I'm sure there are plenty of *other* big men around. Some might even have messy hair. Go find one and call *him* Bear."

Aunt Carrie's gaze drifted around the room.

"Not in here," I said firmly. "Out there. In the world." I pointed to the window.

But Aunt Carrie's eyes were on the upturned couch. *Oh, here we go,* I thought. *She's realizing she could turn it right way up again, and she's going to lie down.*

"Anyway," I added, to distract her. "Perhaps this *Bear* of yours should have *combed* his hair."

She laughed softly. "No, no," she said. "I loved it like that. I loved everything about him, Bronte, every detail. And he loved me. *What are the chances?* we used to say. *What are the chances of us finding each other?!* Then we'd throw our arms around each other."

"Hm," I said. I wondered if I should remind her that I was ten years old.

345

"I used to travel all over the Kingdoms and Empires for my work," she continued.

"As a filing clerk?"

"I was a different sort of filing clerk then," she said, reaching for the jar of nutmeg. "I filed big things. Dangerous things. It made *me* dangerous, and one day I decided that it wasn't safe for Bear. This was not long after I had tea with you in Gainsleigh, Bronte. From there, I went to do a huge job – a *huge* filing job. And I came home shattered and very dark. The darkness was under my fingernails, in my hair. As big as Bear was, he wasn't safe with me. I told him it was over. I told him he must marry somebody else."

"Well, I *hope* he took no notice," I said, stern again.

Aunt Carrie shrugged. "I insisted. I gave him no choice. He left. And so I lost him. And then ..."

Her voice dwindled.

"And then I realized my mistake. I couldn't live without him. I tried to work at home, but my tears made the ink run on my papers. I looked for Bear and learned he'd married somebody else, just as I'd told him to, so I sold the house, packed up, and moved here to Stantonville, to hide."

She rolled the jar of nutmeg back and forth. "And now," she whispered, "we've lost Patrick and Lida too. Oh, I'm tired. Shall we go to sleep, Bronte?"

She was gone again. I knew it at once.

In bed that night, I thought about the different ways there are of being sad. Just as there are different ways of laughing. All my aunts were sad because their brother and his wife had died. But this meant that Aunt Sue couldn't concentrate, Aunt Emma sobbed, Aunt Claire worked extra hard, Aunt Sophy hugged baby dragons, Aunt Nancy was cross – the Whispering King had been *furious* with grief when his wife died, I had read in Uncle Nigel's history book – Aunts Maya and Lisbeth told stories, Aunt Alys was quiet, and Aunt Carrie—

Well, Aunt Carrie disappeared when she was sad.

However, the next morning she made a special effort to be there.

I could see it in the way she looked directly at me when I came out of my bedroom. She was frying eggs in the kitchen, and she had brushed her hair.

"I'm taking the morning off work," she told me, "so I can see you off." She was eating something as she spoke, and now took another bite. There was a shower of crumbs. "Where'd you get the bread? It makes perfect toast."

"Will you get into trouble?" I asked. "For taking the morning off?"

"Yes!" She set plates down on the table. "My boss is a dragon!

Not a real one, Bronte, that's just an expression. I'll probably get fired."

But she seemed very cheerful.

"If not," she added, "I'll quit. My job bores me senseless, but I never have the energy to quit. Being sad makes you so tired." She yawned. "See that? I'm already tired again. I'll have to quit fast, before I fall asleep."

I opened the drawer where I'd put away stationery. "Write to your boss now," I suggested.

So Aunt Carrie scribbled:

> I quit!
> Yours sincerely,
> Carrie Mettlestone

Aunt Carrie said that other people would probably use more sentences to say the same thing, but that she believed in getting to the point.

"Will you go back to your old job now?" I asked, as I ate my eggs. "Did you like that one?"

"Oh yes," she said. "I loved it. But I won't be strong enough to do *that* work again for a while. Eat up now – you can't miss the coach."

I finished breakfast and went to pack my suitcase. I wondered why Aunt Carrie needed to be strong to do filing. *I filed different things,* she had told me. *Big things. Dangerous things.*

It was very mysterious.

"What exactly *did* you file?" I called from my room.

There was no reply.

I carried my suitcase out into the living room. Aunt Carrie was waiting by the open front door. *Big things*, I thought again. *Dangerous things*.

"You're a *Spellbinder*!" I cried.

Aunt Carrie flinched and looked behind her. I remembered that Spellbinding was meant to be a secret.

"Are you a *Spellbinder*?" I asked, this time whispering. "My father was a Spellbinder – Esther told me. So it's in the family! You could be one too! And you have velvet capes with hoods!"

Aunt Carrie smiled sadly. "Used to be," she admitted. "I was quite a good one."

She studied my face, then beckoned me over to her.

"Take off your shoes," she said.

I was too surprised to argue. I pulled them off.

"And your socks?"

I did as she asked.

Aunt Carrie leaned over and studied my bare feet. I studied them with her. They seemed like perfectly ordinary feet.

And then my toenails turned blue.

Every single one.

"There," said Aunt Carrie. "You're a Spellbinder too."

I was still staring, openmouthed, at my toes. The nails switched back to their regular colour and stayed that way.

"So I didn't imagine it," I breathed, "when it happened on the night of the full moon. But how strange for it to happen right at that moment!"

Aunt Carrie shook her head. "Not strange. It's because I was looking. My Spellbinding is very strong, you see, and yours responded. Congratulations, Bronte. Put your shoes back on now. We'd best get going."

She pushed the door wide and beckoned me outside. "Don't try to do any Spellbinding," she warned me. "You're much too young."

What about the Whispering King's grandchild? I found myself thinking. *How am I supposed to cause him great difficulties if I cannot Spellbind?* Aunt Carrie was shaking her head at me, as if she was reading my mind.

"If you want to work as a Spellbinder one day," she said, "training starts when you turn twenty-one. It's dangerous, as I mentioned, and you must never feel obliged. Plenty of time to consider."

We walked along, side by side, past the trees and through the gate. There was a strange, zingy feeling in my heart. I was a Spellbinder! Of *course* I would work as one! I would conquer Dark Mages one day!

I knew the darkness would be scary. Aunt Carrie had said it got under her fingernails and into her hair after her last job. I wouldn't like that.

But I could just wash my nails and hair.

A *huge* filing job, Aunt Carrie had done – now I knew she meant a huge Spellbinding, of course – and she'd come home shattered and told Bear to leave. I wondered what the huge job might have been.

We had reached the top of the hill. The sign for Ricochet oranges was lying on the grass now. I gave it a friendly kick as I passed.

"I went to a Spellbinding Convention when I stayed with Aunt Claire," I told Aunt Carrie as we crossed the fields. "And teachers talked about how Spellbinding wears you out. They said that doing the Majestic Spellbinding on the Whispering Kingdom must have practically destroyed Carabella-the-Great."

Aunt Carrie gave a half shrug. She was walking a little more quickly now, and I had to hurry to keep up with her.

"The teacher also said that Carabella-the-Great discovered a secret ingredient she used in potions," I added. "Only I can't remember what it was. Did you use that ingredient, Aunt Carrie?"

Aunt Carrie was even farther ahead. I could see the back of her head, the silver clip in her hair.

And then I stopped.

It was as if somebody had tugged down on a blind and it had sprung straight up and let in light.

I put down my suitcase.

"Aunt Carrie?" I said.

She turned.

"My parents' gift to you was nutmeg."

She nodded.

"Carabella-the-Great's secret ingredient was nutmeg."

Aunt Carrie looked at me steadily.

"Did *you* do the Majestic Spellbinding? Was *that* the huge filing job? Are *you* Carabella-the-Great?"

For a long moment, Aunt Carrie studied me. Then she winked.

13

We stopped in at the post office so that Carrie could send her *I quit!* letter. The man behind the desk said, "Carrie Mettlestone! I thought you must be dead!"

"No," said Aunt Carrie, and tapped her own head. "Alive."

"I've got a stack of mail waiting for you here!"

He handed it over and Aunt Carrie sifted through while we waited. There was the invitation to Franny's party. "Will you come?" I asked, and she said she would try, but might not be strong enough for visiting yet.

There were two letters for me in her stack: one from Aunt Isabelle and one from the Butler. Both just chatted about the weather and games of charades.

"Nothing else for me?" I asked.

"Were you expecting something?"

I shrugged. "Not really."

The artist had probably thought I was crazy and thrown my postcard away. Most likely, I would never know who told the children to pretend to be a painting, or why.

"Heading home, Bronte?" said the post-office man, leaning out the door.

"First seeing my Aunt Franny at Nina Bay," I said. "And *then* home."

"Nina Bay," the post-office man said. "A day's ride. Got your horse?"

At that moment, the coach approached, clattering down the highway.

"Oh," said the post-office man. "The coach, is it?" He turned back to his shop, disgruntled.

"Thank you," I said to Aunt Carrie. "I've had a lovely stay."

"No, you haven't," she replied. "You've had a terrible stay. But you've woken me up, Bronte. You've saved me."

Just like the children in the storybooks! I thought. And *I* had woken Carabella-the-Great, much better than any regular cranky person!

But then sadness misted over Aunt Carrie's eyes, and I panicked. I hadn't saved her at all. She would return home and fall asleep on the couch.

The coach pulled up.

"Remember when you visited me in Gainsleigh, Aunt Carrie?" I said urgently. "And we went out for tea and cakes? The waiter couldn't open the window, so you opened it for him?"

"Vaguely." Aunt Carrie frowned.

"You did," I told her. "And the waiter said: *You are* strong! And what did you reply?"

"What?"

"You said: *I* am *strong!*"

Aunt Carrie gazed at me. Her eyes crinkled.

"Coming or staying?" called the coach driver.

I picked up my suitcase.

Aunt Carrie leaned down and kissed my head. "Goodbye, Bronte," she said. "I will *definitely* see you at Franny's party."

And I got onto the coach.

 # Aunt Franny

14

I have no idea what the scenery was like in the early part of that coach trip. Probably just fields. But I stared through the window without seeing anything, my heart pattering like happy rain.

I was a Spellbinder! Just like my father!

It was a magical secret, like a gift just for me from him.

Also, Aunt Carrie was Carabella-the-Great! A mighty Spellbinder! Maybe I would take after her one day and be mighty too? She had made the Majestic Spellbinding that had finally, completely bound the Whispering Kingdom. Because of my Aunt Carrie, children were safe from escaping Whisperers.

I was very proud – of myself (in an embarrassed sort of way) and of my aunt.

Now I smiled as I thought through all my aunts and their strange talents and daft ways. Even Aunt Nancy made me smile, although only for a second – then I frowned.

The coach pulled over at an inn, and two women climbed aboard. They settled themselves down in the back.

Aunt Franny was the final aunt. I had met her a few times in Gainsleigh: she was one of the older aunts, and she was always either smoking a pipe or gnawing on a carrot. Her voice was rough and her arms were muscled. I used to find her a bit scary when I was small, but now that I'd travelled across Kingdoms and Empires, ridden on a dragon, and been chased by pirates, I didn't think I'd be so frightened.

Also, there would be a party with all the other aunts, and *then* a holiday with my grandfather. Ice cream and playing on the beach.

The coach pulled over again. The driver held the reins loosely and stared straight ahead. Minutes went by.

"What are we waiting for?" one of the women called eventually.

"Passenger," the driver called back. "See?"

I looked in the direction he was pointing, and here came a large man, pounding along the road. His face was big and soft, with the sort of cheeks that jumble about when you run, and he was running with huge footsteps, his hair flying out behind him. A large black case swung from his hand.

There was something very familiar about him. I felt as if he was an uncle I'd met long ago, only I couldn't remember his name or anything about him. Which made no sense. It was very strange. The closer he got, the more sure I was that I knew him very well, yet not at all.

Then he stepped into the coach, panting noisily and saying, "Thank you kindly for waiting," and I knew who it was.

The trumpeter. From my parents' wedding photograph.

75

The trumpeter sat in the seat across the aisle from me, his case on his knees.

I stared at him, as politely as I could.

It was definitely him. The dark skin, the golden-green eyes. Only, his face looked more lined than it had in the photo, and much more serious. His jaw was clenched, and there was a long, fine scar above his eyebrow.

He glanced across at me, then away again. The coach swayed along, and the trumpeter and I swayed with it.

Again, he glanced at me, and then again.

"Bronte?" he said suddenly.

"Pleased to meet you," I replied, remembering my manners. "Yes, my name is Bronte Mettlestone. I believe that your name is Walter?"

He slapped his hands on his knees. His whole face changed. There were dimples now and lights in his eyes.

"I believe that your name is Walter," he mimicked, shaking his head. "Oh, Bronte Mettlestone, I am sorry to tease. But you're a treat. I

knew it was you – it just had to be. You're Patrick and Lida in one. Do you mind if I sit there so we can get acquainted?"

I nodded and he shifted over. "Bronte," he said. "Let me guess. You're on your way to your Aunt Franny's place in Nina Bay? Don't look so startled, I'm not a mind reader. I'm heading there myself. To go to Franny's party for your parents. I was your father's best friend, you know. But tell me all about *you*?"

A difficult question to answer. Should I start with my date of birth and move on to my favourite brand of cheese?

Instead, I told him about my journey. He was a great listener, often widening his eyes or slapping his knees. When I reached the part about playing trumpet in the Mellifluous Kingdom, he raised his black case and said, "Guess what's in here."

"Your trumpet?"

He blinked at that. "You know I play trumpet?"

I explained about my parents' wedding photograph. Then, because he was so friendly, I admitted that I often looked at *him* in the photo, instead of my parents, on account of being mad at them.

"Because they ran off to have adventures," I explained.

Three lines folded themselves into Walter's forehead. "To have adventures?" he said. Then he muttered to himself. "Of course. That *is* what you'd all think." And he turned to look through the window. At this point, our trip had become picturesque. Bright blue ocean appeared and disappeared on one side, green fields steady on the other. Sometimes, a dragon glided by.

"Not adventures, Bronte," he said, turning back from the window abruptly. He glanced towards the back of the coach, where the only other passengers, the two women, had fallen asleep, their heads leaning together. Then he spoke in a low, slow voice: "But trapped in the Whispering Kingdom."

16

Outside the coach window, a girl was riding a midnight-blue horse across the fields. My heart seemed to gallop at just the horse's pace.

"My parents were captured by Whisperers?" I breathed.

But Walter shook his head. "They *went* to the Whispering Kingdom. Right after they left you in Isabelle's lobby as a baby."

I was annoyed with him now. He had seemed bright, but he was daft. "You don't *go* to the Whispering Kingdom," I scolded. "Anyway, it's surrounded by Spellbinding! You can't get in!"

"The Spellbinding stops Whisperers from getting *out*," Walter explained. "It's never stopped people going *in*."

I frowned at the window. The girl on the horse was still keeping pace with the coach.

"There are Whispering Gates!" I remembered. "Even if you *can* go through the Spellbinding, nobody can get through the Gates!"

"Whisperers can," Walter said.

"So what?" I began, but then my eyes widened. "Do you mean my parents had a *Whisperer* help them in?"

Walter's head tilted, a sort of sideways nod.

"I knew where they were going," he said. "I swore to them I wouldn't tell a soul. But months went by, and they didn't return, so I guessed things had gone wrong. I tried to find out. Whisperers are friends with pirates, of course, so I asked them. I went to some shady places, I tell you, in search of information." He touched the scar above his eyebrow. "Years went by and it was dead ends everywhere. Eventually, though, I learned they were in prison. I wrote to them. They replied."

"You can send mail to and from prison?"

"Of course. Prison guards check it closely, though, so you can never say much, and they couldn't have contacted any of Patrick's sisters. But Patrick and I had a secret language from our childhood, so we used that."

I considered. "But can mail get out of the Whispering Kingdom itself?"

Walter nodded. "The Spellbinding has always had a postage chute," he said. "It's lightly spellbound so Whisperers can't post *themselves* out – or send *Whispers* through – but it means they can carry on trading with the rest of the Kingdoms and Empires. Couldn't cut them off completely, or leave them without supplies." Walter sighed. "Your parents' letter asked me to go see your Aunt Carrie. I don't know why they thought she could help, but when I did track her down, she was so ill she hardly even recognized me."

I nodded. "I've just come from visiting her."

"I was desperate," Walter continued. "Tried to find pirates willing to help them escape."

His face settled back into its grim expression, jaw clenching again.

"And then, a few months ago, your parents sent me their will and asked me to get it to the family lawyers. I figured they were planning an escape themselves, and knew how risky it would be. They didn't want to leave you with no word at all, Bronte." His own words had slowed down again. All the spark had gone from his eyes. "They were right about the risk," he said. "They must have escaped with pirate help and been ... it must have happened on their way home to you, Bronte."

He covered his face with his hands. "I'm so sorry, little one."

I looked through the window again. Outside, the girl on the horse was jumping fences, but she was doing this very blurrily.

That was my tears.

I blinked hard and swung around again. This *was* a sad story, but it also made no sense.

"But *why*?" I demanded. "Why would *anybody* go to the Whispering Kingdom!"

Had they decided they needed a holiday? Had they read that

361

old travel book and not noticed it was *old*? Had they *forgotten* the Whispering Wars?!

Just how barmy were my parents?

Walter dropped his hands from his face. He played with the buckles of his trumpet case, snapping them open and closed.

A new idea came to me. "They went to the Whispering Kingdom to rescue stolen children!" I said. "Back then, Whisperers were still escaping, weren't they? And capturing children? My father was a Spellbinder – I don't know if you knew that, Walter, but he was – so he planned to spellbind Whisperers while my mother found the children!"

Of course, I reflected, their plan had failed drastically. But at least it had been a good and noble plan.

"Is that what happened?" I checked.

Walter chewed his knuckles.

"My stop's coming up soon," he said, peering through the window. "I'm staying in a hotel just outside Nina Bay. Bronte, it's not *quite* what happened. I'll explain when I see you at Franny's party."

I remembered my strong will again.

"No," I said. "Explain now."

Walter raised an eyebrow. And then he shrugged.

"You know that your mother ran away from home when she was young?" he asked.

"Yes."

"And she arrived in Gainsleigh with nothing, her hair down to her waist."

"Yes."

"But nobody knew where she had come from?"

"Right."

"Shall I tell you where she had come from?"

"All right."

"From the Whispering Kingdom. Your mother was a Whisperer, Bronte. Her father is the Whispering King. He's the one who summoned her home."

Then Walter stood, slapped the side of the coach, and called, "Driver! This is my stop!"

11

I sat on a bench in Nina Bay Square and waited for Aunt Franny.

She was late. The third aunt to be late.

The sky was busy with swooping dragons and the square was a mess of painted billboards, tobacco smoke, and food and drink stalls. Angry, squabbling people crowded around these stalls.

They seemed angry, anyway. It might just have been their loud, rough voices. The men had whiskery faces and the women were missing teeth.

Beside me, an elderly woman sat hunched forward, a bag of

sweets on her lap. She kept reaching into this bag, pulling out a sweet, and sucking noisily.

The sucking annoyed me, but I was glad that Aunt Franny was late. It gave me time to think about what Walter had just said.

My mother was a Whisperer, he'd said.

Could this be true?

No!

Well, but it was true my mother had come to Gainsleigh from somewhere mysterious just after the Whispering Wars ended, which is when the Spellbinding was still weak. So she could have escaped.

It was also true she had long hair when she arrived.

But long hair doesn't mean you *must* be a Whisperer! You could also be a runaway who hadn't had the time to cut your hair!

I tried out the idea of my mother as a Whisperer, juggling it like a ball between my hands. Maybe it was exciting? Having a Dark Mage for a mother! The daughter of the evil Whispering King! Truly a princess, as Aunt Sophy had said, but an *evil* princess! It gave her another dimension. One moment she was prancing around picking lavender, the next she was using her wicked powers to control minds!

On the other hand, the travel book suggested that Whisperers had once been a *gentle* people. And my Uncle Nigel's history book said they *became* Dark Mages only after wearing the shadow bands. What if my mother never wore the band? Perhaps she refused her father's order, and that's why she'd run away?

364

That made her more of a hero than a villain, which was also something.

I craned my neck, searching for Aunt Franny, but I only saw a woman toss a beer mug high, the beer spilling out in a wild froth. The mug shattered on the cobblestones.

If my mother was a Whisperer, then *I* was a half-Whisperer. Did that mean *I* had the power to whisper ideas into people's minds? Or sense people's thoughts? Or even hear Whispers from the future? Handy!

I glanced at the old woman beside me. *Give me a sweet*, I commanded her, inside my mind.

Nothing happened.

Were you supposed to *literally* whisper?

"Offer me a sweet," I whispered softly.

The woman swung her head around. "Did you say something?" She frowned.

I stood up, extremely embarrassed, and looked for Aunt Franny again. There were billboards advertising cough medicines, the Razdazzle Moonlight Circus coming to town, and a new sort of horse whip "for use on wayward children" – I decided not to be *wayward* while here in Nina Bay (whatever *wayward* meant). But there was no Aunt Franny.

Why had my mother been summoned home, anyway? And why had she and my father ended up in prison?

I slumped back onto the seat. This entire journey was wearing out my brain. I couldn't wait for the party to be done and for my holiday with my grandfather to start. Nothing to worry about then, except playing on the beach and eating—

I felt as if ice cream were melting down my chest and into my stomach. *Her father is the Whispering King.*

So my *grandfather* was the Whispering King?

But it wasn't true! He lived in Colchester! He had *invited* me to stay with him there!

Unless he did not live in Colchester.

Outside of Colchester, he always said when he invited me. We thought that meant that he was *just* outside the main town, somewhere by the sea. What if it meant he was *way, way* outside Colchester? In a whole other kingdom, say?

"I am elderly and cannot travel," he always said, *"but I can send a friend to collect you."* We thought that meant he was too old to travel. What if it meant he could *not* travel on account of being inside a Spellbinding?

And then, into my mind flashed the words of Prattle back at the Spellbinding conference. *"The Whispering King has been boasting of a Whisper he heard long ago from the future. That this very year, his own grandchild would step forward and help* release *the Whisperers from the Spellbinding!"*

If my grandfather was the Whispering King, I was not the royal child who would cause difficulties for the Whispering grandchild, I *was* the Whispering grandchild!

Well, that part was ridiculous.

I would never help to release the Whispering people.

"Razdazzle Moonlight Circus in Nina Bay!" shouted a newsboy. "First show sold out! Read all about it!"

Razdazzle Moonlight Circus, I thought. *That's the circus Taylor planned to join!*

There was a clattering and shouting in the square. A horse was weaving between stalls and drinkers, and people were cursing it loudly.

It was the midnight-blue horse I'd seen galloping alongside my coach. The rider leaned forward as she trotted closer to me. Her dark hair was tied into a very high ponytail, like a fountain streaming in the wind.

"Taylor!" I shouted.

"Junior Captain Bronte!" she shouted back. "I'm here to fetch you! Climb aboard! Something *terrible* has happened!"

78

Thundering hooves and rushing wind made it impossible to talk as we rode through the streets of Nina Bay on Taylor's horse, my suitcase jammed between us.

We wheeled into the front yard of a big, old, ramshackle house.

Two constables stood at attention on either side of the front door.

Taylor talked fast as we dismounted.

"You're probably wondering how it is that I know your Aunt Franny," she said.

"I suppose," I agreed. "But I'm wondering more what terrible thing has happened."

"I joined the circus," Taylor said, deciding to answer her own question instead. "And we've been touring, as circuses do. Got here to Nina Bay a few days back, and we open tomorrow. Turned out your Aunt Franny had bought out opening night for a party. Came by to see us the other day and told us the party was in memory of Patrick and Lida Mettlestone. So I recognize the name and I figure she's your aunt. Introduced myself. She invited me over to be here when you arrived. Which is why I was here earlier when... Well, go knock on the door while I see to Midnight." She scratched the horse's ear. "Just ignore the constables."

"Taylor," I said. "What's happened?"

"Go knock," she repeated. "Franny will tell you."

I ran to the front door, tried to smile politely at the two constables, and knocked.

The door opened. Aunt Franny flipped the carrot from her mouth and scratched at her wild grey hair. "Bronte," she said. "Thatta girl. Come on in. We've got a situation here. It's your cousin Prince William. The pirates have got him." She swung around before I'd finished gasping. "Dump your bag there," she said, pointing to the floor just inside.

"Pirates?" I asked, or squeaked really. "When?"

"Around lunchtime today. William was on his way here to meet his mother, under care of royal guards. Pirates from the *Dagger and Serpent* attacked."

"But weren't those pirates taken by the Anti-Pirate League?"

"Escaped," Franny said. "Cut the throats of half the royal guard. Gutted the other half."

I was glad she was the kind of adult who doesn't try to hide things from children, but also wished she was that kind of adult.

"Come through." Aunt Franny led me into a huge living room, where I stopped, startled. People, large and small, sat on couches or on the worn carpet, and I knew them all.

There was Aunt Sue, Uncle Josh, and their boys; Aunt Nancy, Uncle Nigel (perfectly bald, as Aunt Nancy had promised), and their girls; Aunt Emma from Lantern Island; Aunt Claire from her conferences; Aunt Sophy from her dragons; Aunts Maya and Lisbeth from the cruise ship; and – huddled between the arms of Maya and Lisbeth – a tear-streaked Aunt Alys.

Everyone, even the children – even Uncle Josh, who was always funny – looked either serious or frightened.

"Most of the family arrived today," Aunt Franny explained, "ready for the party tomorrow. Take a seat, Bronte."

"At least we're here," Aunt Emma put in. She was kneeling on the floor by Alys's feet, hugging Alys's ankles. "For darling Alys. The water sprites came along with me too, for a lark, and they're swimming in the bay. They've promised to help in any way they can."

"I can't think what help they could be," Aunt Nancy muttered, "in the water."

"And the rest are due tomorrow morning," Aunt Sue put in quickly. "Aren't they due tomorrow? *All* the sisters will be here, Alys—"

"Even Carrie?" Aunt Nancy interrupted. "I thought she never left her cottage!"

"She telegrammed this morning to say she'd take the overnight coach," Aunt Franny said firmly. "Plenty of Patrick and Lida's old friends are coming too. Between us, we'll figure what to do."

Aunt Alys nodded slowly.

"There's not much we can do, is there?" Aunt Nancy asked. "Except wait to hear what they want. No doubt they'll demand a ransom, and we can decide whether to pay it."

"Decide?" cried Aunt Alys.

Other aunts made soothing sounds and hissed at Aunt Nancy, then Aunt Franny spoke in a big, strident voice. "A prince has been abducted by pirates," she said. "That is a *serious* matter to authorities. The K&E Security Force has been called. The *chief* is taking personal charge of the case. He says he's contacted Gustav Spectaculo and The Scorpion, urging them to return to the

Anti-Pirate League on temporary assignment. If anybody can rescue the prince, they can. They have unique experience with the most brutal and cutthroat pirates."

"Oh," murmured Aunt Alys, and everybody winced.

"That was stupid of me," Franny said. "I only meant we have the very *best*. Alys, I am *certain* they will bring your boy home."

"What about that boy we rescued?" I remembered suddenly, turning to Aunts Maya and Lisbeth. "Alejandro? Is he still on your ship? He was from the *Dagger and Serpent* pirate ship, so he might know something about the pirates? Like where they hide or something?"

But both cruise captains shook their heads. "He's vanished," Aunt Lisbeth said. "We were bringing him here to meet Alys. She wanted to thank him for sending her the telegram to warn her."

"Turned out to be a useless warning, didn't it?" Aunt Nancy put in. We ignored her.

"But now we can't find him anywhere," Lisbeth finished.

"Joined up with the pirates again, no doubt," Aunt Nancy said darkly. "He was probably part of the plot all along."

The aunts began to quarrel, and my cousins and I looked at each other without speaking. Taylor slipped into the room, having finished dealing with her horse, and perched on the back of a couch.

If Prince William was really a handful, I thought, *maybe the pirates would get tired of him? Or maybe he could be enough of a handful to escape himself?*

371

"Is the prince big for his age?" I asked the room. "Or small?"

The aunts stopped arguing and turned to me.

"Bronte," Aunt Maya said gently. "When Alys told us all that pirates planned to capture Prince William, we knew they'd be looking for him on land. We decided the best hiding place would be at sea."

"We had him on our cruise ship," Aunt Lisbeth said, "until the pirates attacked. Alys collected him then, and placed him in a safe house in Hertfordshire until this morning."

Now Taylor spoke up. "You already know how big he is, Bronte," she said. "It's Billy. The pirates have gone and taken Billy."

19

I felt as if somebody had thrown a basketball, very hard, at my stomach. I even arched backwards. *Billy! Taken by pirates!*

I honestly don't know what happened for the rest of the afternoon. I think the aunts talked in circles, and somebody made sandwiches. But all I could think of was Billy.

His tidy hair and starched collars. His friendly smile and patient billiard lessons. The way he threw himself on his head when he tried to do somersaults.

Word arrived that the authorities wanted Aunt Alys to come to town to talk with them. More constables would be sent over to accompany her. Aunts Maya and Lisbeth offered to go along, but the other aunts stayed behind.

It was lucky they stayed, because when the clock began to strike nine, Aunt Emma said, "So late! We must get these children to bed!" – and suddenly I remembered the instructions.

I was supposed to give Aunt Franny her gift at 9:00 p.m. on the night I arrived. I tore to the front door where my suitcase was still standing, threw it open, got the gift, and skidded back to Aunt Franny.

"I know this is not a good time," I said. "But the instructions..."

Franny squeezed my shoulder. "I know," she said, and opened the gift. It was a packet of dried mushrooms.

"Oh!" said Aunt Franny. "Now, I wonder why dried mushrooms... Well, I'm glad you gave it to me, Bronte. My sisters brought along their gifts so we could share stories. Will you run and put these in the kitchen with the others?"

The kitchen seemed a strange place for gifts, but there they were, little boxes and jars, lined up on the counter. Not so strange, I decided. Mostly my parents' gifts seemed to be food. Maybe they were only meant as a contribution to a feast?

When I got back to the living room, Aunt Sue and Aunt Nancy had organized blankets and cushions for the children. My boy cousins, girl cousins, and Taylor were already under their covers, and Aunt Emma was handing around glasses of milk. Nobody was saying much. Even little Benjamin had curled himself up and was sucking his thumb.

I returned to the foyer to fetch my suitcase so I could change into pyjamas.

The front door was ajar.

There were hushed voices, just outside in the darkness. I could hear Aunt Alys crying, and Aunt Franny was saying, "Tell me. Just tell me what they said."

The others must have come back from town, and Franny had gone outside to meet them. I crouched so they wouldn't catch sight of my shadow.

Aunt Maya's voice spoke up. "Gustav and The Scorpion tracked down the pirates," she said, sounding hoarse. "But they didn't have Billy anymore."

"He's escaped!" Aunt Franny cried.

"No. They'd handed him over to the Whispering King."

I heard a quick intake of breath from Franny. It was loud enough to cover my own.

"But why?"

"The Whispering King had *commissioned* the pirates to kidnap Billy," Aunt Lisbeth put in.

"They do work together often," Aunt Franny told the others grimly. "Whisperers pay the pirates in diamonds. They use the postal chute for their transactions. Authorities are always trying to put a stop to it."

"Well, it seems nobody can get into the Whispering Kingdom to rescue him," Aunt Maya said. "Not without a Whisperer to open the Whispering Gates."

"Of course," Aunt Franny murmured. "But *why* would the Whispering King want William?"

There was a moment of quiet. The only sound was Aunt Alys, still weeping.

"The Whispering King gave the pirates a message," Aunt Maya said eventually, her voice seeming to drag itself through mud. "To pass on to the authorities. Remove the Majestic Spellbinding, or Billy will be killed at dawn."

Aunt Franny's voice became urgent and angry. "Well, then, they have to do it! They *have* to remove the Spellbinding! Deal with the consequences afterwards! Have they started? Have they got in the Spellbinders to take it down?"

Again, a silence. Then Aunt Lisbeth's voice: "The authorities refuse. They've already convened an urgent meeting of the K&E Alliance and voted against it. Too dangerous, they say. They've sent a message back to the Whispering King saying they will have negotiators there by noon tomorrow, and are willing to give generous gifts in exchange for the release of the prince. But that removal of the Spellbinding is out of the question."

"Alys," Aunt Franny said quickly. "It will be all right. The king won't hurt Billy. He's bluffing. Alys, it's okay. It's all talk. He'll

375

need Billy alive for his negotiations. I swear to you, Alys, it's going to be all right."

But Alys's crying had turned into one long, violent moan, and it built and built, louder and harsher, as the other aunts tried to calm her. It was terrible to hear.

80

The other children were sleeping, but I was wide awake.

I heard the sounds of the aunts talking in the kitchen until late, telling each other, over and over, that the king would *never* kill Billy, and then doors closing around the house as they went to bed themselves.

I pushed away the scratchy blanket and sat up.

The king was an evil Dark Mage. He *would* kill Billy at dawn. There was no question.

I had to rescue Billy at once.

Only, there were two problems: the Whispering Gates and the Whispering King.

Well, I was half-Whisperer. I could get through the Whispering Gates!

Of course, I hadn't even been able to make an old woman give me a sweet, so I was not at all sure I *could* get through the Gates.

I would just have to whisper more loudly.

As for the Whispering King, it would take Carabella-the-Great to Spellbind him, and she had already said she was too weak to work. Besides, she was not arriving until morning. By then, Billy would be dead.

But *I* was a Spellbinder. My toenails had turned blue. *I* would bind the king myself. True, Aunt Carrie had told me I was too young to Spellbind, and I had no training, and—

I blinked. I did have *some* training. I'd been to the Spellbinding Conference. I had the folder of potions! "A potion to bind the Whispering King," I remembered, speaking aloud, "by Carabella-the-Great."

Some ingredients were missing, I recalled, because of water damage. Aunt Carrie had told me her tears had made ink run – that must be the water damage. But surely I could figure it out? I was good at puzzles.

I crept across the room, stepping over sleeping, snuffling cousins, until I found my suitcase.

Enough moonlight fell through the window for me to flip through the folder until I found the potion.

Oh, I thought when I found it.

I'd forgotten just how bad it was:

Combine a spoonful of —n—, it said, with a pinch of –i—a— and a sprinkling of d—e– –h—is. Add a heaped tablespoon of –u–a–, a scattering of —nk —e p–t—s, three or four c–a—r—e–, a little d—ed –a—n—, a pinch of –ut—g, 1 finely chopped –r—d —us—m and mix well. Finally, add a cup of — — — — — —.

Impossible.

Ridiculous.

Still, Billy needed me. I found a pencil in my suitcase and used a blank sheet at the back of the folder to write out the ingredients.

     —n —

     –i —a —

     d —e– –h —is

     –u–a–

     —nk —e p–t —s

     c–a—r —e–

     d —ed –a —n —

     –ut —g

-r —d -us —m

— — — — — —

Then I stared at these.

And stared.

I kept on staring.

I slammed my hand against the window. *Thwap.*

Imogen murmured in her sleep. Nicholas coughed.

There was quiet again.

This was not fair. I had taken a long and difficult journey, frightened the whole time about breaking the Faery cross-stitch. I'd given Aunt Franny the final gift. Now I should be able to celebrate!

Instead, I was sitting in the moonlight with an impossible puzzle, and Billy was going to die.

Tears slid down my cheeks.

It was all my parents' fault. They had made Aunt Franny have a party, and that's why Billy had been travelling here. My parents were nonsensical! Sending me off with silly little gifts – honey and cinnamon, lavender and mushrooms! As if they wanted us to bake some awful cake! Well, the honey and cinnamon might be delicious, of course, but—

Honey and cinnamon.

I looked back at the list of ingredients.

I picked up the pencil and filled in the first two words, speaking them aloud.

Honey

Cinnamon

I looked at the next word. My heart began to hammer. I filled it in very slowly:

Dried chillis

It was the gifts! My parents' gifts! Now I was scribbling, breathless.

Sugar

Pink rose petals

Cranberries

Dried Lavender

Nutmeg

Dried Mushroom

I was laughing, crying, and saying the words aloud at the same time (but trying to do this quietly).

I reached the final ingredient.

— — — — — —

My laughter fell away. I'd run out of gifts.

I counted on my fingers. I whispered names of aunts. But dried mushrooms was the *final* gift!

I pulled on my hair, furious, reached out to *thwap* the window again, and then I smiled.

"No gift for Aunt Isabelle," I said aloud. "She got the cloud-berry tea."

Cloudberry tea, I wrote. It fit perfectly.

81

I mixed up the Spellbinding potion in Aunt Franny's kitchen, borrowing from the aunts' gifts.

Nutmeg was in the pantry, and cloudberry tea, the other missing gift, was in a canister on the countertop (so Franny must like it too).

I tipped the potion into a jar, screwed on the lid, and put it in my coat pocket. I left a note.

But how to slip out of Aunt Franny's house with constables guarding the front door?

Easy. I slipped out the back door.

I remembered my way to Nina Bay Square and found a coach driver with hairy knuckles and an ink tattoo on his neck. I offered him twenty silver pieces to take me as close to the Whispering Kingdom as he could.

"Never tell my Aunt Isabelle I did this, will you?" I said, and he replied that he could only make that promise for another ten silver.

I laughed, but I think he was quite serious.

Now I was standing outside the Whispering Kingdom.

Spangled frost on leaves. Moonlight on waves. Black road curving between forest and sea.

And at least fifty signs. These were nailed to posts and strung in the trees and they all said something like this:

WARNING. DO NOT ENTER.
THIS SPELLBINDING IS HERE FOR YOUR PROTECTION.

Or:

ATTENTION: WHISPERING KINGDOM AHEAD
IF YOU PASS THROUGH THIS SPELLBINDING, THERE
WILL BE NOTHING TO STOP A WHISPERER FROM
CAPTURING YOU.

One sign was scribbled:

YOU'RE A FOOL IF YOU GO THROUGH. THE
WHISPERING GATES WILL KEEP YOU OUT OF
THE WHISPERING KINGDOM ANYWAY, SO YOU
WON'T SEE ANYTHING. EXCEPT MAYBE A
WHISPERER - THEY CAN COME OUT OF THE
GATES - AND THEN THEY'LL EAT YOUR BRAIN.
IF YOU WANT TO SEE THE WHISPERING
KINGDOM, HEAD BACK INTO TOWN AND BUY
AUTHENTIC PICTURE POSTCARDS FROM
LARRY'S EMPORIUM, ONLY 15 SILVER
PIECES EACH.

Hmm.

I didn't think Whisperers did eat people's brains. And fifteen silver pieces was a *lot* for a picture postcard.

I stared at the Spellbinding. It was perfectly transparent and you could only see it when it caught the light. A strange thing, it was like a hazy curtain with a tightly woven diamond pattern. To my right, it disappeared into the forest, strung over trees like ice; to my left, it curved around the coastline, shimmering in the moonlight. Above, it extended up and over, as far as I could see.

A red mailbox stood by the side of the road, seemingly jammed right through the Spellbinding. That must be the postal chute.

Well, I thought with a deep breath, *I'd better go in and rescue Billy.*

My eyes landed on yet another sign:

NONE WHO ENTER
THIS SPELLBINDING
WILL
EVER
RETURN

"Oh nonsense," I said, and walked through.

The Whispering King

82

It felt damp, like walking through soap bubbles.

The road carried on between forest and sea, curved once, and crashed into an iron gate.

The first of the Whispering Gates.

I am half-Whisperer, I told myself. *I will Whisper this gate open.*

"Open," I whispered.

Nothing happened.

I shout-whispered, "Open! Open!"

Again, nothing.

I pressed an ear against the bars, hoping to hear some kind of Whispering magic, but jumped back from the ice-cold.

I rattled it. The padlock jangled. Shoved at it with both hands. Next, I hefted up the padlock, its cold weight in my palm, and let it fall again. It clanged.

I scrambled up the gate, trying to climb it, and slid back down.

Maybe I could go around the gate? On one side, the road plunged into the wild water of the sea. Well, the other way. The

Impenetrable Forest might be famous for being impenetrable, but maybe people just fell for the name?

I pushed into the trees and was instantly flung back. I tried this again. And again.

No, it was more than just a name.

Now I was panting quite hard, each puff a burst of mist in the cold air.

I made myself slow down. *Whisper. You must Whisper.* I narrowed my eyes and stared at the padlock. I locked all my ferocity into my stare. *Open,* I whispered, deep in my mind.

"Bronte!" said a voice. "It is you!"

I looked sideways and there was Alejandro, the boy with no shoes, climbing the rocks from the sea and wringing out the water from his hair.

83

"The pirates of the *Dagger and Serpent* have escaped," Alejandro told me.

"I know."

"They have taken the Prince William."

"I know."

"They have given him to the Whispering King."

"Yes. I know."

"Bronte," Alejandro said, wringing out his shirt now. "You know everything."

"Not how to open this gate," I said. "I'm going to rescue him."

"This is also my plan." Alejandro nodded. "He is the boy who rescued me from the turtle hole — along with you and the girl, Taylor. He is the nephew of Maya and Lisbeth, who took me aboard. To rescue *him* is the least that I can do."

"I heard you disappeared," I told him.

"Yes, I slipped away to go to the public houses favoured by my old pirate friends. I disguised myself and joined their conversations."

"Dangerous!" I told him. "They could have captured you again!"

He frowned. "Did you not hear me say that I disguised myself? This means that I looked different than usual."

"I know what disguised means," I said.

He shivered violently. I took off my scarf and wrapped it around his neck.

"I asked the pirates what they knew of the Whispering Gates," he said, nodding his thanks for the scarf. "I told them they knew *nothing*, which is the best way to get someone to tell you what they know." His teeth still chattered.

"I can't *think* why you went into the ocean on such a cold night," I scolded.

"They told me that there are hidden keys for each of the Whispering Gates," said Alejandro. "The first is in the ocean—"

"Oh," I said. "That's why."

"The second in the sky, the third on the earth."

"Hm," I said.

"Hm," he said, "is correct. Their information is useless. I have been diving in those wild waves some time, and found no key."

I peered out at the black water. It was rippled with moonlight, patterned with crashing white waves.

"I could try," I said doubtfully.

But the ocean is vast and a key is small. We needed a team of swimmers. Swimmers who could *see* in the night ocean. We needed fish, really, but I could not speak fish. If only there were fish who could speak—

"Alejandro!" I said. "Help me find a stick!"

"What sort of stick?" I was pleased he was not the kind of boy who demands explanations.

"I need two," I told him, scanning the forest and road. "Any kind, I think."

We found them quickly and I clambered down the rocks towards the water, dragging these with me.

Alejandro stood on the road and watched. "The water is very deep there," he called.

"Over-my-head deep?"

"Yes."

I would have to sit on a rock. I took off my shoes and dangled my feet in the water.

Trembling from cold, I raised the sticks above my head and held them there, closing my eyes tightly, trying to remember the pattern.

Thwack.

I hit the sticks together. The moment that I did, it came back to me.

Thwack-thwack-thwack

thwack ... thwack ... thwack

thwack.

I stopped.

The water sighed and rippled around me.

I tried again.

A distant splash, and I turned quickly. But it was nothing.

Again.

Over and over, I beat the sticks together. I looked up at

Alejandro. He was watching me calmly, his chin buried in my scarf.

I began to see that this was useless. Nina Bay was too far away. They'd never hear.

One more try, I thought, lifting the sticks, and then the water burst open, and burst open again, and two figures rose side by side.

"My title is Cyphus, King of the Water Sprites! May I know your title?"

"My title is Serfpio, King of the Water Sprites! Who is it calls us this fine night?"

"It's me," I said. "Bronte Mettlestone? From Lantern Island? My Aunt Emma—"

But the water sprites were spinning their arms so that water fanned and crashed. "Bronte! It is Bronte!" They embraced each other, dove down, and leapt up again, arms spinning.

"All the Kingdoms and Empires," said Cyphus.

"All the stars in the heavens," said Serfpio.

"Could not contain our delight!"

"At seeing you again, Bronte Mettlestone! What news have you of your days since we last saw you?"

"You must tell us every detail. You left Lantern Island on a ferry boat, yes? And then what? Begin there."

There was a rush of sound behind me and here was Alejandro, scrambling down to join us. "You know *water sprites*?" He stared from me to the water sprites and back. "Please," he said. "It is an honour to meet you, water sprites. All my life I have sailed the seas and *never* have I met a water sprite."

"The honour is ours," Cyphus told him.

"Any friend of Bronte's," Serfpio added. "What is your title, young man?"

Here, I interrupted and said that this was Alejandro, and that we were trying to rescue my cousin, and wondered if they might help?

They insisted that nothing would make them more joyous than to help.

"The key to the first Whispering Gate," we said, "is some-where in the ocean here."

"Speak no more!" proclaimed Cyphus, and he turned to Serfpio. They spoke to each other in low, fast mutters. Both nodded, and there was another splash as they disappeared beneath the waves.

Within minutes they were back, surging out of the water, a huge bronze key held up between them.

84

The key was the size of a wine bottle, and very heavy.

Alejandro lifted it, I guided it into the lock, and between us, slowly, we turned it. There was a low, grinding sound. A click.

The padlock fell loose.

Before our eyes, the key dissolved and disappeared. We glanced at each other, then pushed hard on the gate.

It swung open.

But we hardly had time to be delighted when an engine sounded behind us.

"I thought that was too easy," I said.

"It wasn't *that* easy," Alejandro pointed out.

We waited, halfway through the gate, as an automobile approached, its lights swinging right and left. Straight through the Spellbinding it drove, knocking over a couple of signs.

It pulled up, its doors flew open, and a crowd of children fell out onto the moonlit street.

"Bronte! You crept away without us!"

"If you wanted to attempt a rescue, why not wake us, darling?"

"We left Benjamin sleeping. He'll be so mad when he finds us gone."

"Not half so mad as the adults will be."

"Connor got up for a glass of water and found your note."

"This is Aunt Claire's automobile! Imogen drove! Sebastian wanted to, but they flipped a coin and Imogen won."

"She was quite good."

"Except for the bit when she nearly drove us into the ocean."

"I got distracted by a dragon shooting flames over the hood!"

"Anybody would have been, darling, don't blame yourself."

"Taylor – the circus girl – she's coming too. Separately."

It was my cousins: Sebastian, Nicholas, and Connor, Imogen, Esther, and Astrid. A moment later, with a thundering of hooves, Taylor rode up on Midnight.

"I suppose," Alejandro murmured doubtfully, "it is better to be many than few?"

85

My cousins left the automobile parked at the Whispering Gate, but Taylor carried on riding. Immediately beyond the gate, the road swerved away from the ocean and deep into the forest.

Midnight's ears flickered. "Nothing to worry about," Taylor soothed him.

Alejandro and I raised eyebrows at each other. We were on the road to the Whispering Kingdom. Plenty to worry about.

I was also worried that my boy cousins would argue and my girl cousins would offer hugs. However, everybody simply set off, the others introducing themselves to Alejandro as we walked.

"Settle a dispute for me, Alejandro," Taylor said, trotting along on Midnight. "Were you ever a boy-with-no-shoes who helped Bronte rescue a baby?"

"I was," Alejandro said.

"You *weren't*," said Taylor.

"I was," Alejandro repeated.

"In that case, I owe you an apology, Bronte," Taylor declared. "I'll give it to you once we've rescued Billy."

We rounded another curve and the second gate appeared, identical to the first.

The others began rattling it, climbing it, playing with the lock, and so on.

"There is no point," Alejandro told them. "The key is in the sky."

As one, we all looked up.

"Full moon," Sebastian said. "A few clouds. Plenty of dragons. No key."

Nicholas, the skinniest cousin, was trying to squeeze between the bars. "We should ask the dragons to fly us over," he huffed.

The others chuckled, but I said, "Of course! Well, not fly us over – there's some kind of mist the dragons can't get through. But of course!"

Could I remember any Dragon? I closed my eyes and visualized Dragon Great Damian lying beside me, his ankle propped onto a mattress. Snorting smoke clouds of laughter at my Dragon. I set that memory aside. It was unhelpful.

I squinted harder, running through our lessons. Then I opened my eyes.

Quickly, I gathered up a handful of dried leaves from the forest floor, crumpled these, and clapped four times. "Crch, crch, shhh, vip, crch?" I said. The others stared.

I repeated the whole procedure several times, without looking up, but then I happened to notice the other children backing themselves into the gate. Midnight's eyes were white and he was snorting and ducking his head. "Easy. Easy," Taylor was saying.

I looked up.

About twenty-five dragons were soaring directly towards us.

86

Not twenty-five.

It only looked that way. It was five or six, I think.

Anyway, they landed on the road with mighty thuds. My cousins stared, eyes huge. Connor hid behind Sebastian.

I folded my arms and bowed in the Dragon gesture of friendship. The dragons folded their wings in a great rush of warmth and rustling darkness.

Next I tried to explain things to the dragons. As I didn't know the Dragon for missing, cousin, locked, gate, key, or sky, this was tricky. The dragons, however, listened in silence then conferred, exchanging many glances and chuckles, before politely turning back to me.

Again, they bowed, there was another rush of wings, and they wheeled away into the stars.

The other children exhaled all at once.

"*What* just happened?" Esther demanded.

"They're looking for the key," I said, "I think."

Alejandro asked if he could shake my hand. "You are friends with water sprites," he told me. "And *dragons*!"

"Well," I pointed out, "you're a pirate."

He smiled wryly.

My cousins' confidence returned: Imogen and Sebastian expressed scientific interest in Dragon language while the others complained that they would have *loved* to ride a dragon, why had I not arranged that?

A few moments later, a single female dragon hovered just above our heads. (The cousins were instantly silent.) A huge silver key was clutched in her claws. She released this and it tumbled onto the road.

I think she told me that she had spied the key in the highest branches of a tree. We both bowed and I thanked her and wished her a marvellous evening under the moonlight. I think that's what I wished her anyway. She smiled.

87

By the time we reached the third gate, I was wondering which new friend I would have to call upon now.

I was interested to find out. Also a bit anxious. This next key was supposed to be in the *earth*, but I hadn't befriended any *digging* creatures, had I? Moles, say? No. I'd have remembered that.

This gate was exactly the same as the first two, except that it had three gargoyles – sculptures of ugly heads – staring down from the top bar. Each face was dark-greenish and scowling, and each wore a padlock on a chain around his neck.

"We need *three* keys here?" Taylor demanded.

"They want to make it harder now we're at the third gate," Sebastian suggested.

"Not fair." Nicholas flicked each padlock in turn. "We should be rewarded for making it this far."

"Indeed not!" boomed a voice, and we all leapt in fright, looking behind, above, into the forest, and down at our feet.

"It's me!" the voice growled impatiently. "Up here!"

"It is one of the gargoyles!" Alejandro exclaimed, and he was right. It was the one on the left.

Now the middle one spoke: "You'll never find the key," he said.

"Never," agreed the one on the right.

"And if you do," piped up the first, "you'll never know which lock to use!"

"Only one of our padlocks opens the gate!"

"If you try the wrong one, the key dissolves! The gate stays shut!"

"But you'll never find the key."

Alejandro sighed deeply. "You are very discouraging," he said.

"We only speak the truth," sang the middle gargoyle. The other two smirked.

"Irritating," Esther muttered. "Insufferable."

"We can *hear* you," the first gargoyle said, sounding affronted. "Do you imagine we have no *feelings*?"

"You are very handsome gargoyles." Connor drew himself up and spoke with great sincerity. "I've never seen such handsome, intelligent gargoyles. And your voices are so—"

"Resonant?" Imogen suggested.

"If that's a good thing," agreed Connor.

"Flattery won't work," the gargoyles chanted in unison. "We'll *never* help you find the key."

"Good try anyway, Connor," we all told him.

There was a long silence.

The gargoyles looked at us sneeringly, and we looked at each other.

"It's in the earth somewhere," Alejandro reminded us, so we began kicking at the road – it was dirt and gravel, edged with thick clumps of leaves and clustered trees. Taylor slid from Midnight's back to help.

At this point, my heart started a low, quick thudding.

Because now I *had* to make my Whispering work. No magical friends.

I must do this myself. Alone.

"*Open,*" I whispered to the gate. I looked the first gargoyle deep in his eyes. "*Open,*" I hissed at him.

He blinked. "Eh?" he said.

"*Hey!*" shouted Sebastian.

I swung around. He was pointing at the road. "Something just…"

"There!" cried Astrid.

"Over there!"

"No! There!"

I had no idea what they were shrieking about, but then I shouted too: "It's *there*!"

A golden key lay in the centre of the road. Then it didn't.

"It's over here!"

"It's here!"

The key zigged. It zagged. It moved so fast it was a blur.

"I'll get it!" Connor threw himself onto his stomach then sat up, looking at his empty hands in surprise.

"Got it!" Taylor stamped her shoe. Raised it. The key was gone.

A metallic glint. A flash of gold. The key skidded. It skated.

The gargoyles cackled. "You'll *never* catch it!" one said.

"It likes to play with you!"

"It will keep you playing for *eternity*."

"Unlikely." Imogen narrowed her eyes. "I'm not staying that long."

Sebastian was standing perfectly still. His eyes darted back and forth, following the key. Nicholas, noticing this, began springing from side to side. Connor crouched low and swayed.

There was something familiar about the way the three of them were positioned.

"Behind you," Sebastian snapped, and Nicholas spun around, got his foot behind the key, and kicked. It flew into the air. Connor slammed forward and *thwack* went the key against his forehead. It thudded onto the grass, bouncing once.

But Sebastian, leaping sideways, caught it with the side of his shoe, and began a sort of shuffle movement forward. *Glint!* went the key, glancing from shoe to shoe, always the inside of the shoe, as Sebastian twisted and turned, his knees slightly bent, one moment slow, the next rapid, and then *thwack*, he sent it flying straight to Connor.

Of course, I thought. *It's* football.

The rest of us faded back, out of the way, watching. Now Connor flicked the key into the air above his right foot, caught it with his left, did the same with his right, and then kicked it hard towards Nicholas. The key landed on the road. It swung to the right, paused, and swung back to the left.

"Come on, boys," Sebastian muttered. "We've got it rattled now."

After that, things sped up to a blur. Sparks of metal, bursts of dust, Sebastian barked instructions, Nicholas danced, Connor stampeded. More and more, the boys closed in, passing the key back and forth between them. The key seemed to wobble in panic, then it swerved one way but Sebastian was faster, skidding onto his side on the road and catching it with the toe of his shoe. It flew into the air, and Nicholas leapt up and thwacked it hard, legs to the side in a scissor kick. At which point Connor launched himself onto his stomach, hands outstretched, crashed onto the dirt – and rose up, coughing dust, both hands clutched around the key.

The rest of us cheered.

"Whoa," said the first gargoyle.

"Did that just happen?" asked the second.

"Not bad," admitted the third, raising an eyebrow. "Never seen *that* done before."

"Useless to you, of course," sang the first. "Since you don't know which lock to use."

The brothers, still getting their breath back, told the gargoyles to shut their traps.

Now Imogen stepped up to the gate.

"So if we use the key in *your* padlock," she said to the first gargoyle, "it will dissolve?"

The gargoyle grinned. "Depends," he said, "on whether I'm the right one or not."

"Well, are you?" she asked.

"That'd be telling, wouldn't it?"

Imogen sidestepped so she faced the second gargoyle. "Are you the one?"

The second gargoyle winked.

She studied his face a moment, then slid to the right again.

"And you?"

The third sighed elaborately. "You'll never figure it out this way."

Imogen turned to her sisters, who were watching this with interest. "What do you think?" she asked.

Esther and Astrid stepped closer to the gate.

"Is it you?" Esther asked the first.

"What do *you* think?" he responded.

"You?" she tried the second.

He grinned.

"You?"

The third gargoyle sniffed.

Astrid took a turn. She did not ask any questions, but stepped from face to face, nodding politely at each.

"It's the middle one," she said.

"I agree," said Imogen.

"Me too," Esther chimed in.

The girls turned to Connor. "Try the middle one," they said, and Connor took a step.

"Hold up," Sebastian said.

We all turned. He had his breath back now. "Don't *waste* the key," he said. "How do you know it's the middle one?"

"Shouldn't we have to solve riddles?" Alejandro suggested.

"We don't do those," the three gargoyles apologized in unison.

"The first one is bluster," Imogen explained. "The third is indifference. They're both double-bluffing, so that leaves the middle one."

"The middle one has a tiny crease above his right brow," Esther added. "It flickers."

"It's the middle one," Astrid repeated. We looked at her. "I didn't know until just now, when I *said* it was," she added. "Then I knew. All three faces told me I was right."

"How?" Sebastian asked.

Astrid shrugged. "Just did."

"If Astrid says it is, then it is," Imogen declared. "She can read faces. A poker champion. Connor, use the key in the middle lock."

"Connor, stay where you are," Sebastian said.

There was a long moment during which Imogen and Sebastian held each other's gaze.

"Make a decision," Taylor said. "It's almost dawn. See the sky?"

We all looked up, and as we did, Taylor swept forward, slid the key from Connor's hand, and jammed it in the middle lock.

88

It worked.

I knew it would.

Taylor hadn't known, though, and she let out a whoosh of relief. The girls' expressions said: *Told you so.* The boys' said: *Well, still. Risky.*

Taylor rode, and the rest of us jogged through the open gate. I thought maybe the gargoyles would congratulate us, but they only grumbled to each other.

"What now?" said Esther, but the road turned another corner and there it was, rising before us, bathed in moonlight: the Whispering Kingdom.

Cobblestone streets, lit by streetlamps and lined with narrow houses, wound up the hill towards a castle. We were standing on damp grass, dark clumps all around us. I looked closely at one of these clumps: a rosebush. We were in a rose garden. Silent, we gazed up at the kingdom.

"It doesn't *look* especially evil," Imogen said in a low voice.

"It's picturesque." Sebastian nodded.

"Going to find Billy," Taylor announced, clicking at Midnight and trotting away between rosebushes.

"Wait!" we all hissed, but she was already galloping, the horse's hooves echoing along the empty street.

"What's your plan, Bronte?" Nicholas inquired.

My plan was to go to the castle, find the Whispering King, drink the potion from the jar in my pocket, Spellbind him, and rescue Billy.

It had seemed sensible enough back at Aunt Franny's house. Now I saw one or two holes.

"Somebody's coming!" Alejandro barked. "Hide!"

We scattered, most of us ending up behind a rosebush. A figure moved steadily towards us, scrunching over the grass, weaving between bushes, bumping into some.

It was a small figure.

Very small.

"Ouch," it said, quietly. "Roses *must* have thorns, what?"

"It's Billy!" I said, bouncing up.

"Oh, Bronte!" Billy said. "Is that you? Perfect. Do you happen to know the way out of here? Only, the soldiers got distracted trying to figure out how to carry a sort of cage they had, and I ran off. Not sure how long I've got."

The others loomed up now, and Billy yelped.

"It's okay," I whispered. "These are all the other cousins. And that's Alejandro, you remember the boy we rescued? Everyone, this is our cousin Billy."

"Let's go!" Imogen murmured, and then she bit her lip. "Only where's the circus girl?"

We all looked towards the street, hoping to see Taylor, but what we saw was a battalion of soldiers moving steadily towards us.

"Run," said Sebastian. "Turn around and *run*."

89

We flew towards the gargoyle gate. It was still ajar, and all our hands reached out and threw it open.

Along the road, around the curves.

Behind us, the tramping of soldiers' boots.

Through the second gate.

Our feet pounded; we panted desperately.

"Help!" A whimper from behind. I turned.

Billy had fallen to his knees, his hands clamped to his ears. "Stop it!" he shrieked. "Stop! Stop the noise!"

The others also turned and stared. Billy struggled to his feet, then immediately fell again. "Keep going!" he shouted at us. "Leave me here!"

"Come on!" Sebastian called. "It's not far!"

But Alejandro was shaking his head. "It's the Whisperers. They're Whispering at him to stay."

"Then we have to carry him out!" Esther cried, and we dashed back towards Billy.

The soldiers' steady tramping was growing and quickening. There was the clanging of the gargoyle gate.

Two of the cousins reached out to Billy, and he stretched his hands towards them, but abruptly he pulled away and urged again, "Keep going! I'm staying!"

We all got ahold of him then, but his feet dragged on the dirt and he punched out wildly. *"Leave me!"* he screamed. Between us, we hoisted him into the air and stumble-ran, half falling while Billy writhed around in our arms.

Behind us, the soldiers marched closer.

We were at the first gate.

The soldiers were paces back, inky bulks in the shadows. We were pushing through the first gate.

The Spellbinding was there, right there.

Billy was screaming and slapping now. "Put me down!"

"*Almost* there," we panted, and the soft dampness of the Spellbinding was on my face and hands, and we were almost through and—

Billy twisted out of our hands and threw himself back inside.

90

Soldiers grabbed him by the scruff of his shirt and wrenched him to his feet.

Billy looked at us ruefully. But we knew it was not his fault. We'd all heard how vicious a Whisper was.

The sky was paling now, a smudge of orange on the horizon, and there was a strange moment of quiet. The ocean carried on smashing its waves, and the forest still rustled the leaves of its trees, but my cousins and I stared through the Spellbinding in silence. On the other side, five or six Whispering soldiers faced us, grouped around Billy.

The soldiers were so close that we could see the expressions on their faces, the buttons on their jackets, the tangles in their long hair. On their wrists were red-and-black armbands. *The shadow bands*, I realized.

From the direction of the Whispering Kingdom came the sound of horses' hooves and the creak and clang of gates. The sounds grew. A carriage approached, and the soldiers swivelled smartly, two keeping firm hold of Billy's shoulders.

"All bow for His Majesty, the Whispering King!" pronounced a soldier, and my cousins and I glanced at each other. The Whispering King?

An old man climbed out of the carriage. He moved very slowly – I couldn't tell whether this was because he was old or because he was trying to act kingly. His hair was long and perfectly white, and something glinted on his chest. The soldiers bowed. I noticed Esther beside me going to do the same and then stopping herself.

The king spoke in a low voice to two or three soldiers. I heard him say, "Prepare the cage," and also, "Gather the citizens." A few soldiers marched briskly back through the gate while others took Billy somewhere out of sight.

Now the king stepped close to the Spellbinding. The glinting object slung across his chest turned out to be a dagger. A tremor seemed to run right through us children as we noticed this. His eyes ran back and forth over us, and then they paused on me.

"Which of you is Bronte Mettlestone?" he asked.

I jumped. He nodded to himself and stared at me. There were creases under his eyes.

"You are the child of Patrick and Lida Mettlestone?" he inquired next. His voice seemed friendly and interested.

"Yes," I replied.

"Then, Bronte," he said, "you are my grandchild."

91

There was a lot of muttered exclamations from my cousins and Alejandro. The soldiers at attention behind the king remained perfectly still.

My heart was fluttering. I studied him, trying to see if he *could* be my grandfather. He had that regular, wrinkled-old-man appearance, but his long, white hair made him resemble a dessert. Somebody seemed to have poured cream onto his head, letting it spill down both sides to his feet.

"Pleased to meet you, Grandfather," I said, remembering my manners. He nodded, but he did not seem about to bundle me into a bear hug of welcome. The Spellbinding would have stopped that anyway, of course, and the dagger slung against his chest might have made it uncomfortable. "Could you kindly release my cousin Billy?" I asked next. "We are all tired and would like to go home. I will . . . visit you tomorrow."

"Certainly I will release Billy," the king replied, and I sighed with relief. "But I need a small favour first." He clicked his fingers, and a soldier stepped forward, handing him a small red box.

"Dear grandchild," said the king. "Long ago, I heard a Whisper from the future. It told me that *you* would play a key role in my plans today."

"It did?" I asked, but I was distracted. There was much movement and sound behind the king now. Several more soldiers had appeared, marching through the gate, and behind them came streams of men, women, and children. They wore coats over nightclothes, and had sleepy eyes and long, tousled hair. The soldiers must have woken them and brought them here. They stopped when the soldiers instructed them to, so now a crowd stretched back, through the gate and into the darkness beyond. I noticed the red and black of shadow bands on many wrists.

"Dear grandchild," the king said again, and he wiped at his eye. Was he crying? "I am so proud of you. As your mother is dead, you are now heir to the throne of the Whispering Kingdom." He half turned and shouted the next part so that the crowd could hear. "YOUR FIRST GREAT ACT AS PRINCESS BRONTE WILL BE TO *SET THE WHISPERING PEOPLE FREE*!"

The crowd clapped.

On either side of me, my cousins were shaking their heads wildly. "Don't do it," they hissed. "They're *Whisperers*!"

"Don't worry," I hissed back. "I wouldn't even know how."

The king turned back to me. "Inside this box is my Whisper," he said. "Very powerful. You will reach through the Spellbinding and take it from me. Once it is through, open the clasp and release the Whisper. And then WE WILL BE FREE!" (He was shouting again. The crowd applauded.)

"But Whispers can't come through the Spellbinding," I said, confused.

"They can if *you* take them." He grinned. "You are half-Whisperer and half-Spellbinder, dear grandchild. In all the Kingdoms and Empires, you are the one person who can defeat the Spellbinding."

Again, my cousins shook their heads at me. I was annoyed at them because of *course* I wasn't going to do it. But it was also difficult. All those people waiting for me to be a hero. And it seemed I had a special talent. I was the *one person* who could do this.

"Er, Your Majesty?" Sebastian spoke up bravely. "How is your Whisper going to set your kingdom free?"

The king turned his smile on Sebastian. "This Whisper will clamp down so hard on the minds of every Spellbinder," he explained, "in all the Kingdoms and Empires, that their Spellbinding powers will be crushed. Not only will this Majestic Spellbinding dissolve, but we the Whisperers will *never* be bound again."

"So you'll all be able to go around making people do what you want, like you did during the Whispering Wars?" Imogen frowned.

"Precisely," the king said. "WITH THE HELP OF PRINCESS BRONTE, WE WILL ONCE AGAIN BE THE MOST POWERFUL KINGDOM IN ALL THE KINGDOMS AND EMPIRES!"

Another burst of applause.

"But if Bronte is really a Spellbinder," Esther piped up, "you'll be clamping down on *her* brain too."

"I put in an exception for her," the king promised. "Come along, Bronte. Take the box." He held it out to me.

I stared down at his hands. He wore a ring with a skull insignia that reminded me of pirates. "I'm very sorry, Grandfather," I said. "But I can't do that. So if you'd just let us take Billy home . . ."

"You won't do it?" the king checked.

"No," I said firmly. "I will not. But we . . . we wish you well with your . . . endeavours."

"PIRATES!" shouted the king. "SOLDIERS!"

From the forest behind us came a swarm of pirates who surrounded us children. Meanwhile, right before us, soldiers were hoisting a cage high into the air. Billy was crouching inside.

92

"Oh, well," Imogen said. "Nice try anyway, Bronte."

We were crammed together now, trussed up with chains, the pirates swaggering beside us as if they deserved praise. But honestly, we were just a bunch of children.

The king clicked his finger again and pointed, and the pirates unwound me from the rest and pushed me back towards the Spellbinding.

"Not long ago," the king told me, smiling again, "I heard a second Whisper from the future. It said that another royal child of ten years old would cause you difficulties today." He pointed up to the wooden cage, suspended high above us. "So I had my pirate friends capture the only other royal ten-year-old in all the Kingdoms and Empires! This way I get to *choose* the difficulties he causes you!" He laughed proudly.

Billy sat cross-legged on the cage's floor, peering down at us. A thick rope was looped around the top of the cage and strung over the branch of a tree. The rope then ran all the way down to the road, ending at a metal tube with a handle. It was a sort of pulley system, I realized. Someone on the ground could raise or lower the cage, using the handle.

"PRINCESS BRONTE!" the king bellowed, facing the crowd. "REACH YOUR HAND THROUGH THE SPELLBINDING AND TAKE THIS WHISPER!"

I stared at him.

"No," I said.

"Princess Bronte," the king repeated. "Do you see this rope?" He pointed to the rope running diagonal through the air. Obviously, I could see it. "And do you see this dagger?"

I looked at the dagger, lying flat against his chest. Polished silver with an ornamental hilt.

"Do you understand what will happen if I cut the rope with this dagger?"

My eyes ran along the rope, up to the tree and to the cage that shivered in the air. If the king cut the rope, the cage would crash to the ground. Billy would be killed.

I looked back at the king.

"If you do not reach through and take this Whisper," said the king, "I will cut the rope."

With his other hand, he placed the edge of his dagger against the rope. "You have sixty seconds," he added, almost chattily.

93

I don't know if you have ever had to choose between allowing your cousin Billy to crash to his death, and releasing a Whisper that will crush the powers of every Spellbinder in the Kingdoms and Empires.

It's tricky.

"Forty-five seconds," sang the king. "Or your cousin gets taken out."

"You're counting too fast!" I protested.

In fact, I had no idea how many seconds had passed. My head seemed to swarm with insects. I would not let him kill Billy! But I could not release this Whisper!

I looked around at my cousins and Alejandro, pressed together in chains. They stared back at me, eyes wide in helpless panic. Beside them, the pirates appeared interested, as if they were watching a penalty shoot-out in a football game.

I looked up at Billy, his cage swinging alarmingly. At the dagger touching the rope. At the small red box poised before me.

Now my heart clattered like a steam locomotive.

This is impossible! I thought.

And then I slapped my hand against my chest.

The Elvish Medal for Bravery.

I still wore it.

You remember the Matron at the boarding school had told me its secret?

Here is what she said:

"If you hold the medal in your hand and you speak these words aloud, the medal itself will become the very thing you need."

"Twenty seconds!" the king cried.

I clutched the medal and spoke the words: "I have never been so afraid."

94

The medal jumbled about in my hand, pushing so hard against my fingers that I had to let go. It rattled, then clunked against my chest.

I lowered my chin to look. It now looked much like the case where the Butler keeps his spectacles.

I reached my fingertips into the case and touched something cold and metallic. Was it a *dagger* of my own? Was I supposed to *fight* the king?

I drew out the object.

"Ten seconds!" shouted the king.

"Hush!" I told him, annoyed.

I was busy staring. My medal had become a pair of scissors.

95

Again, I don't know if you've ever been in a situation where you expect to receive *the very thing you need*, and instead you get a pair of scissors.

It's annoying.

"Five seconds," the king said languidly. He had slowed his countdown, but he was staring at me intently, the edge of the blade firm against the rope. He meant what he said. He would kill Billy. And then, I guessed, he would threaten the other cousins and Alejandro, having the pirates kill them one by one until I finally took the red box.

I could see all this in his eyes.

I was going to have to take it. I reached out my hand.

Then I dropped my hand. If the Whispering King was all-powerful, thousands could die.

I was going to have to let Billy die.

"Come on," said the king.

Helpless, I glanced at the scissors – and saw a glint of movement in them.

They were polished and reflective, I realized, mirroring the pirates and the chain-bound children behind me. That must be the movement I had seen.

But there was something else. Behind the pirates, behind the children, darting shapes. Two figures dressed in black with masks. Exploding skull and crossbones on each.

Gustav and The Scorpion.

They slipped back into the shadows, and my heart sped up like something tumbling down a hill.

"Time's up," said the king, and he raised the dagger high.

"Wait!" I said.

"You've had at *least* sixty seconds," the king replied testily.

I looked at the scissors.

Even if Gustav and The Scorpion dealt with the pirates, how could they save Billy?

Billy, tiny in his cage. Soldiers lined up neatly, the crowd of Whisperers behind them.

The coats and nightwear of the Whisperers seemed shabby to me. One or two, I noticed, were playing with the shadow bands on their wrists, sliding them up and down or twisting them.

Unexpectedly, I heard Aunt Sophy's voice in my head: *"You know how certain things are famous throughout Kingdoms and Empires for being dangerous and wicked?"*

I shook my head and looked down at the scissors again.

Back at the crowd of Whisperers.

To the king with his dagger.

To the Whisperers again—

Quite suddenly, I knew what I must do.

"Just a moment, Grandfather," I said. "I'm thirsty."

I took the jar from my pocket, unscrewed the lid, and swallowed it whole. Then I lifted the scissors and, in one great swoop, I cut through the Spellbinding.

Many things happened all at once.

Behind me, Gustav and The Scorpion rushed the pirates. There was a flurry of flashing swords.

The king stared at the tear in the binding. A slow smile formed. He dropped the dagger to the ground and stepped forward, raising the red box. Desperate, I looked behind him at the crowd of civilians. For a terrible moment, they simply stood, their faces blank. And then, all at once, they gave a mighty roar and the whole crowd surged forward. They crashed into the soldiers, shoving and shouting as they came. Soldiers stumbled and fell. The king was jostled hard – the red box slipped from his hand and was kicked away and trampled.

I lost sight of him for a moment as the Whispering soldiers and civilians flew at each other. Fists hammered, nails scratched. Guns were kicked from soldiers' hands or wrenched from their arms. Rolling, wrestling bodies crashed towards the binding.

The other children had pressed themselves into the forest as far as they could and were watching as Gustav and The Scorpion fought the pirates. They worked together beautifully. As I watched, The Scorpion leapt through the air, knocking out a pirate who was lunging at Gustav. Next moment, The Scorpion herself had been disarmed, and Gustav, who was facing the other way, flicked a pirate's sword high, so that it somersaulted through the air and landed in her hand.

I looked back through the Spellbinding at the Whisperers. There was the king, crawling between the fighters – his long hair got caught under a boot for a moment and he winced. Steadily, he made his way towards the rip in the binding. He reached it. He pushed himself onto his knees, and closed his eyes.

His mouth began to move.

He was Whispering.

He was going to make the same Whisper again, and send it through the tear.

My whole body shook. I clutched my arms to stop the trembling. I knew what I had to do.

I took a deep breath and pictured a table set with twine and tools, just as I had learned at the Spellbinding Convention. My hands began to move.

But the king was Whispering fast, and my arms looked wrong. Flimsy, ridiculous.

Panic built in my chest.

I took another breath and closed my eyes.

And there it was. The King's Whisper. I could *see* it forming. It was like a small black worm, curled in the air. Red-and-black cross-stitch was spreading across its surface, and this seemed to harden the Whisper, making it stronger and sturdier. The Shadow Magic, I realized.

I moved my hands and arms, back and forth, up and down, as I had practised with Prattle, and nothing was happening, nothing was happening. The Whisper was stretching and growing, billowing even, and *nothing.*

Then something.

Faintly, the green-gold of Spellbinding twine. A little to the right of the Whisper – I was making my net in the wrong place.

I shifted slightly and worked my hands more rapidly.

The net began to form around the Whisper. The Whisper sagged a little.

I was doing it!

I opened my eyes. The king had also opened his eyes, and he was staring at me in astonishment.

He scowled. His eyes snapped closed and suddenly his voice was in my head. It was a voice like flames and poison.

I stumbled backwards.

Vaguely, I could see the Whisper expanding again, snapping the twine of my net, reaching up and out, but the king's voice was crawling through my head like stinging nettles, wasps, fire ants.

He was going to win. There was nothing I could do.

I was sinking to the road. The Whisper was growing.

My hands clutched my head, and I heard myself screaming.

"Bronte," said a voice. It was a firm voice, kind. I swung around. The pirates had been defeated, I saw, and Gustav Spectaculo was shackling them with their own chains. But The Scorpion was standing apart, staring at me. "Bronte," she repeated. But how did she know my name?

"Bronte," said another voice. Faintly, I made out a single Spellbinder, approaching along the road. Her cape dipped so I glimpsed her face, and it was Aunt Carrie – Carabella-the-Great – hurrying towards me. "Bronte," she said again. Strange that I could hear her at such a distance.

I forced my hands away from my head and wove them through the air again. Reached for the twine, wound it around an imaginary loom, twisted, and knotted.

A drop of honey, a puff of cinnamon.

A whirl of chilli peppers, a dusting of sugar.

Each gift was a taste in the back of my throat.

The king's voice loosened its grip. The net began to form again.

Rose petals, cranberries, lavender.

My fingers twisted through the air.

The net wound its way around the Whisper, like pirates winding their chain around children, like me winding my scarf around Alejandro, little Benji winding paper chains around the legs of chairs.

Nutmeg, dried mushrooms.

I tightened the net, pressed it more closely.

The Whisper shrivelled.

It crumbled into pieces. Cloudberry tea washed it away.

I opened my eyes.

I had Spellbound the Whispering King.

98

He was openmouthed, astounded.

I saw his eyes flicker to somewhere behind me and I turned.

Gustav and The Scorpion were striding towards us, along with the authorities: the local constabulary had arrived, the K&E Security Force, the Anti-Pirate League, and, led by Carabella-the-Great, a team of Spellbinders dressed in the usual Spellbinding capes with hoods.

Behind *them* came the aunts.

It was going to be all right. The grown-ups were here. At last, it was truly all right.

*

But when I turned back to the king, a flash of rage crossed his face. He leapt up and shoved through the crowd. He was reaching for something – a glint on the road.

The dagger.

Now he was heading for the rope that held Billy's cage.

99

There was the sound of galloping hooves and a dog barking.

Midnight tore along the side of the road, Taylor kneeling on his back. She pushed herself to standing position, holding her balance, arms outstretched. Right as the horse passed beneath the tree, she sprang from his back.

Her hands grasped at a branch. She swung her feet against the trunk and began to climb.

At the same moment, the door to Billy's cage opened. He clambered out onto the cage's roof, where he crouched, clinging to the bars.

The king lunged towards the rope. He raised the dagger high.

"Billy, grab my hands!" Taylor screamed. She had curled her legs around a branch and now swung forward like a trapeze artist, her arms outstretched.

Billy hesitated, then launched himself from the roof of the cage. His palms hit hers. Their hands clasped.

Taylor swung back again.

The blade sliced through the rope.

The cage smashed to the ground below and broke into a hundred pieces.

100

Billy and Taylor climbed down from the tree, and the grown-ups took charge of everything.

Spellbinders sorted out the Whispering crowd, binding the soldiers so that the citizens could stop kicking them in the face.

Carabella-the-Great twirled her hands at the king, and he stood up and followed her, head bowed. (The other Spellbinders gawped at her the way people do at cinema stars.)

The Anti-Pirate League led the pirates away in carts.

Meanwhile, the aunts rushed to the children. They had woken early, it turned out, and found us gone and my note, so they had alerted the authorities. Aunt Sue hugged her boys, Aunt Nancy scolded her girls, Aunt Alys cried into Billy's hair, and Aunt Franny gave Taylor a high five.

"It was the dream!" Billy said. "A dog barked, and it was the dog from my genie dream! Now, the dream dog had told me there was a loose bar at the top of the cage, which I could use to reach the latch, and there was! That's how I got out! Look! There's the dog that barked! It's a stray, I think. Can we take it home?"

"You're allergic to dogs, Billy," Aunt Alys reminded him.

Taylor said the tree she had climbed was the tree from *her* dream too. Without the warning from the dream, she would have climbed onto the branch carrying the cage, and it would have cracked. "Billy would have crashed to the ground! Dead!" she said.

"Oh," whispered Aunt Alys.

"As it was, Billy only *just* got himself out, and I only *just* swung him away before the cage crashed anyway!"

"Oh," breathed Aunt Alys.

"Seconds! Less than that! A *millisecond*! A *breath* of a second later, and he'd have been smashed to pieces! Like a watermelon trampled by oxen!"

Aunt Alys looked as if she might faint, and some other aunts hurried over to change the subject.

Of course, many aunts checked to see that I was all right, and to ask what I'd been thinking, sneaking out like that, or to say, "Well done for sneaking out!" – but they were mostly distracted by their own children, or by Whisperers in pyjamas.

Aunt Isabelle and the Butler were not expected in Nina Bay until later that morning, so there was nobody there who especially belonged to me.

The road was crowded, people busy in every direction, and I climbed a little way down onto the rocks. My head was aching. Each time a wave crashed, I felt tiredness from the top of my head all the way to my toes. It was true that I'd been awake all night, but it seemed deeper than that.

"You were binding the king," said a voice behind me. "This is why you feel so weary."

It was Alejandro. Standing on a rock, just above me.

"You cut through the Majestic Spellbinding," he added. "The Whisperers could have poured out."

"Yes," I agreed.

"They could have spread across Kingdoms and Empires, controlling everyone and everything."

"Mm."

"It could have meant doom for all."

"Yes, yes," I said. "All right. But they didn't."

"No, it worked perfectly. How did you know the Whispering people would turn on the king's soldiers in that way?"

I considered. "People laugh in different ways," I began slowly, "and they're sad in different ways. But they also cheer variously. I was thinking of how the crowd cheered at the elves playing football in Livingston. And the passengers cheered my aunts on the cruise ship. But every time the Whisperers clapped for the king, it was different. Something was missing."

Alejandro picked up a pebble and tossed it out to sea.

"I saw one of them touch his shadow band," I continued. "And I thought, what if they could be good even *with* Shadow Magic? And they want to stop the Whispering King?"

"Your grandfather," Alejandro said. "Did you know you were half-Whisperer, Bronte?"

"I only found out yesterday," I admitted. "When a trumpeter told me."

Alejandro nodded, as if it was the usual thing to find out you're a Whisperer from a trumpeter.

"And you are the heir to the Whispering Kingdom," he said next. "Now that the king has been arrested, I think you must be its queen."

That gave me a fright. I didn't want to be a queen! I wanted to go home to Gainsleigh!

"Shall we take a look at your kingdom?" Alejandro pointed up at the open gate on the road, people still streaming in and out of it.

I took a deep breath. I supposed I had better.

101

As we walked through the streets of the Whispering Kingdom, we saw some Whisperers running along, singing, some sitting on benches and staring into space, and many gathered together on street corners, talking. We heard bits of what they were saying as we passed. Everyone seemed to have a different opinion.

"Me?" said a fierce-looking man with a beard. "I'm heading home to pack right away. Get out of here, I say, before they throw up another Spellbinding and trap us again."

"No, no, they won't do that now they know it was really the king," a woman scoffed. "We just need to hand over the shadow thread. It's all in the treaty."

"Not going anywhere until we see the king properly tried," a younger woman declared.

"You can't trust them," the bearded man argued. "Get out while you can, I tell you."

"I think we should hold a town meeting," another declared. "And have cake."

Being queen of this place was going to be *extremely* complicated. And the people looked so worn-out and faded, even the children. They kept tiredly pushing their hair behind their shoulders. As well as sorting out the political issues, I was going to have to cheer them up.

We found ourselves climbing up the cobblestone street towards the castle. It was a grand castle, white with bright red flags, each flag decorated with a thistle. In the grounds, there were hedges and flower beds, and two cats slept in the shade of an apple tree.

Well, that was something. At least my castle would be pleasant.

Another gathering of people stood talking in the castle gardens. They were arguing even more urgently than the other groups. Alejandro and I stopped to watch.

"At least twenty," a man was saying. He was wearing striped pyjamas, and he had pushed the sleeves up over his bony elbows. "In the castle dungeon."

"The king's prisoners," a woman said. "We need to get them out."

I thought maybe that was my job now. "Is it safe to let prisoners out?" I inquired politely.

The adults turned and looked down at me.

"It's her," one of them said. "The granddaughter. What was her name again?"

"Bronte," I said.

"Well, good job, Bronte, you're a hero around here. We owe you. But you know nothing. These are political prisoners. They stood up to the king and he threw them in his dungeon, so they're even bigger heroes than you. No offence."

"Do you need a key?" Alejandro asked. "Is that the problem?" He was maybe thinking that we'd found three keys for the Whispering Gates and so we were experts in key-finding.

"Not a key," the man with the bony elbows replied. "It's a code. The king has Whispered the entry to the dungeon closed. Only if we Whisper the right code, will it open."

"They say he always uses the same numbers," someone called. "Every time he has to choose numbers, he uses the day he met his wife, the day he proposed, and her favourite number."

"Very romantic," somebody said drily. "I suppose nobody knows what those days are?"

"Nobody. He kept it secret." There was a silence, and then people began talking again.

But I had stopped listening. I was so weary. I looked across at Alejandro, who was frowning along with the conversation.

He was the boy with no shoes running along the river, the boy in the turtle hole, almost dead, and the boy in the cruise ship infirmary telling me a story. Now he was a boy who, like me, did not have a family.

Only, he had never known what happened to his parents, whereas I'd received a telegram.

Sleepily, I wondered who had sent the telegram telling us my parents had been killed. *Taken out by cannon fire from the decks of the pirate ship* Thistleskull – a ship that Alejandro didn't know.

The strangest sensation fell through me. You know when you take a bottle of water from the refrigerator on a hot day, and you see drops of water running down the outside of the glass? Those same ice-cold drops seemed to run through my blood.

"I think I know the code," I said.

102

The group turned to me, doubtfully.

"It's 208," I said, "103, and 24."

"You mean the dates are 20th of August, and 10th of March? And her favourite number was 24?"

"I don't know."

They furrowed their brows at me.

"But you're sure that's the code?"

"No."

They shrugged. "We'll give it a try," they said. "She did bind the king."

We all tramped down a ramp until we reached the castle dungeon. It was damp down here, and the stone walls were rotting and mildewy. There was a sort of wheel clamped around the gate's padlock.

"It's 208?" the man with the elbows asked me.

I nodded. "Then 103 and 24."

Click-click-click went the wheel as the man turned it. Around to the left, to the right, to the left. *Click-click-click.* Pause. *Click-click-click.*

Clunk.

The gate swung open.

103

You remember the telegram that Aunt Isabelle received?

WE REGRET TO INFORM YOU THAT PATRICK AND LIDA METTLE-STONE HAVE BEEN TAKEN OUT BY CANNON FIRE FROM THE DECKS OF THE PIRATE SHIP *THISTLESKULL* (208 TON, 103 FT LONG, 24 FT AT THE BEAM).

Thistles on the flags. A skull on the king's ring.

Thistleskull: a ship that Alejandro did not know.

It was the king who had sent the telegram.

I did not know why he had done this; I only knew, quite suddenly, that there was no such ship as the *Thistleskull*, and that the name, along with the numbers in the telegram, had been invented by the king.

I suppose you might find it strange that I remembered the exact words and numbers in the telegram. But that is because you have never received a telegram telling you that your parents have been killed by cannon fire from the decks of the pirate ship *Thistleskull*.

104

Alejandro and I stood back.

The Whisperers rushed in and, after some time, prisoners began to file out through the gates. They moved slowly, blinking in the sunlight. Some held tightly to each other, some wept quietly. The prisoners were thin, weak, and pale. Some stumbled or limped. They stared around in confusion.

Near the end of the line came a man and woman, dirty and bedraggled, leaning into each other. They paused at the gate, and then both at once turned towards me. Their faces crumpled.

Even with crumpled faces, I recognized them. The whirling pair of dancers from the photograph.

My parents.

Patrick and Lida

105

As I wasn't used to having parents, it took me a while to think of them that way. To me, they were Patrick and Lida.

We brought them back to Aunt Franny's house.

Every single aunt screamed and then burst into tears. I suppose that made sense, but it did become a bit boring. "Oh, Patrick! Oh, Lida! You're alive! You're alive!" That sort of thing. And a lot of hugging.

We children stared at the red-eyed, hugging grown-ups. Some of us even started imitating the adults to each other: "Oh, you're alive! You're alive! Boo-hoo! Oh, me!"

"But whatever happened?" Aunt Nancy demanded eventually. "Are you truly the daughter of the Whispering King, Lida? And where have you *been* all this time! And why did we think you were dead?! Explain yourselves!"

At this point, we were all crammed into the foyer of Franny's place and it was getting stuffy. Patrick cleared his throat, and Lida said, "Well," and then they both turned to each other.

"Not now!" Aunt Franny boomed. "We *all* need baths, food,

and rest. *Especially* Patrick and Lida. We can hear their story later. For now, let's have three cheers for the safe and happy return of Billy, and of Patrick and Lida, and for the children who have brought them home to us. Hip hip!"

We all shouted, "Hooray!"

Later that afternoon, I woke up on the living room floor. The other children were still napping on mats around me, and the house was quiet. But I could hear some gentle conversation somewhere.

I crept out of the room, following the sound, and found it in the kitchen. A teapot and cups sat on the table, along with a plate of biscuits. Patrick and Lida were sitting facing me. They had washed and combed their hair, and they wore fresh clothes, but they still looked skinny and bewildered. Walter the trumpeter was also at the table, gazing at my parents, his chin propped on his hands. And so was Aunt Carrie. Opposite these four sat a man and a woman. Their backs were to me, but I knew them anyway.

"Aunt Isabelle!" I said. "And the Butler!"

It was lovely, their reaction. Bursts of elation came from both of them, and happy sighs. Then they remembered to be their proper selves again.

"Well, Bronte," Aunt Isabelle said, reaching out to brush something from the shoulder of my nightdress. "Have you enjoyed your adventures?"

"Oh yes," I said. "Very much."

"And did you encounter any witches? Or Sterling Silver Foxes?"

I shook my head.

"But I hear you've had a run-in with the Whispering King?" Aunt Isabelle arched an eyebrow, but a dimple appeared in her cheek, and everyone laughed.

"Look, Bronte!" Walter said. "It's your parents! Alive!" He rubbed his fists on the top of both their heads, and they ducked away from him, smiling.

"She is the one who rescued us," Patrick said, speaking softly. "We were about to tell our story, Bronte. If you'd like to hear it?"

"Should we wait for everyone else?" I suggested. I felt shy suddenly, and wanted all my aunts and cousins.

"Let them sleep," Aunt Carrie said. "Lida, do you want to start?"

Lida took a deep breath.

"I was the first and only child of the Whispering King," she began. "And my mother died not long after I was born. My father did terrible things then, as you know, and started the Whispering Wars. I grew up in the castle, not knowing much of politics or battles, but when I turned twelve, I began to see my father as he truly was. I was supposed to begin wearing the shadow band on my fifteenth birthday." She held up her bare wrist and studied it. "It was the law. None could refuse. So I ran away from home."

"There was Spellbinding around the Whispering Kingdom then," Aunt Carrie put in. "But it was weak enough to find fragile parts and break through."

Patrick sipped from his tea. "Lida came to Gainsleigh," he said. "And we fell in love. But when she turned seventeen—"

"I got a letter from my father," Lida put in. "He had discovered where I was. His letter said he would send for my firstborn child to take my place as heir to the throne."

Everyone looked over at me: firstborn child.

"We had never told anybody that Lida was a Whisperer," Patrick put in. "Not even my sisters. It was too soon after the Whispering Wars."

"Except for me," Walter added. "I knew there was something special about Patrick's new girlfriend. I've got Faery in me, so I sense things, and I cajoled Patrick into confiding in me. But he never confided that she was the daughter of the *king*."

Patrick pushed the plate of biscuits towards his friend. "Here, have one of these to make up for it," he offered.

Lida smiled. "We decided my father was bluffing," she said. "We got married, and you were born, Bronte."

"And then there was the telegram," Patrick said grimly. "Instructing us to bring our new baby to the Whispering Kingdom within forty-eight hours, or else—"

"Or else pirates would be sent to take her."

Around the table, people shook their heads grimly.

"We rushed to the wharf to take the first ship out to the Whispering Kingdom," Patrick said. "Lida could get through the Whispering Gates, of course. We left Bronte in the lobby of Isabelle's building with a note."

"And some cloudberry tea," Aunt Isabelle prompted. "Because you knew I liked it so?"

"Because *all* of Patrick's sisters love cloudberry tea." Lida smiled. "We threw it in the pram at the last minute, as an apology for asking you to babysit. We thought it would only be for a few days."

"We *all* like it?" Isabelle cried. "I thought it was just me!" She seemed miffed.

"Franny has some on the countertop right there," Patrick pointed out.

"You're the eldest sister," Carrie consoled Isabelle. "So you probably started it."

Lida carried on with the story. "I thought I could persuade my father to leave my daughter be," she said. "I was going to make up with him and offer to return as queen myself when the time came. But right away, we realized that wasn't going to work."

"It turned out the king wanted Bronte because of the Whisper he'd heard from the future," Patrick said. "He wanted to raise her himself, make sure she'd be on his side."

The Butler nodded slowly. "That explains why he kept inviting her to stay with him."

"I did the right thing," Aunt Isabelle declared, "in refusing."

Everybody nodded and patted Isabelle's arms or shoulders.

"There were people in the Whispering Kingdom who hated the king," Lida continued, "and wanted to end his reign. We thought the best way to save Bronte would be to join them."

"We were arrested and put in the dungeons," Patrick said.

"There were other resistance fighters in there," Lida continued. "We tried to escape."

"Nothing worked," Patrick sighed. "I'm a Spellbinder myself, but I hadn't started training yet and had no idea what to do. I mean, I *tried*—"

"Without instruction," Aunt Carrie said, "you would have been useless. Don't blame yourself."

Patrick offered her a sort of frowning smile, as if he *did* blame himself.

"And then we heard that the king had come up with a new plan to get Bronte to visit," Lida said. "Pretend we were dead. Send a telegram informing our family, and then insist Bronte visit."

"The fact is, Bronte *was* going to come to the Whispering Kingdom," Patrick added. "The king had heard the Whisper, so we knew this was fate. We had to figure out how to keep her safe when she arrived."

"And how to help her play the *right* role," Lida put in.

"You didn't trust me?" I said. "To do the right thing?"

Lida's face fell. "Of course we did," she said. "Only, we knew you would have to believe in yourself."

"And understand the true history of the Whisperers," Patrick added. "That's why we had you on the cruise ship with Maya and Lisbeth for four weeks. They have a historian doing talks, and he loves to discuss the Whispering Kingdom. In four weeks, we thought, you must surely hear his talk at least *once*."

I shook my head. "Not once. Taylor told me he was deathly dull and I should give him a miss."

Patrick and Lida both spat out their tea.

"It's all right," I said. "I read one of Uncle Nigel's books."

"Anyway," Lida said, chuckling, "we drew up plans for your journey, using the will as a disguise."

"We were trying to figure out how to let my sisters know what was happening, so they could protect you, Bronte."

"And that's when *I* heard the Whisper from the future," Lida said. "I dreamed that a child's voice was speaking to me." She looked at me shyly. "I think it was *your* voice, Bronte. *A Potion to Bind the Whispering King*, you said, soft and clear, *by Carabella-the-Great. Honey*, you said next, *cinnamon, dried chillis* – and so on."

I blinked. "But that was just last night."

"It was like you were reading aloud to me," Lida said. "You *gave* me the potion."

"So," Patrick said, "we would tell the lawyers to gather the ingredients, have Bronte deliver them, and then get the aunts together to *talk* about their 'gifts'. We figured Carrie would surely recognize the ingredients and get the message."

"Why's that, then?" Walter wondered.

There was an awkward pause, but Aunt Carrie smiled. "It's all right," she said. "I trust everyone here."

"She's Carabella-the-Great," Lida explained. "I knew it the first time I met you, Carrie. Whisperers can sense the strongest Spellbinders. That's why we asked you to go see her, Walter. And why we had Bronte stay with her awhile."

"I'm so sorry," Carrie murmured. "I wasn't there for you."

"Well, but you were," Patrick argued. "You wrote the potion to bind the Whispering King, didn't you? And the remarkable thing was that almost all the ingredients matched up with my sisters somehow."

"Not so remarkable." Aunt Carrie shook her head. "The best Spellbinding potions are created out of love and sadness. I developed that potion not long after I lost Bear. I poured all my love for my sisters into it – Sue's fondness for honey; Emma and how she liked to paint with cinnamon; Nancy and her pink rose petals."

"She prefers red," I pointed out.

"Oh, that's the thing with Nancy," Carrie sighed. "She's the middle sister. We're always forgetting about her. That's probably why she's the way she is. Anyway, cloudberry tea was for *all* the sisters." She gave Isabelle an apologetic nod. "And dried mushrooms for Bear. He loved them so."

We glanced at her and then turned away to drink tea or play with teaspoons.

Aunt Isabelle was drumming her nails on the table. "It was almost a good plan," she said. "But something went awry."

Lida nodded. "My father heard the Whisper about another royal child being important," she said. "And had the pirates kidnap Prince William."

"So Bronte went to the Whispering Kingdom before we'd had a chance to talk about the gifts," Aunt Carrie said slowly.

"The whole plan was terribly risky," Patrick said, "which might make you wonder why we included silly things, like recommendations for cafés and restaurants, and so on?"

He glanced at me, almost shyly. Lida reached out and placed her hand on his. "There was every chance, Bronte," he continued, "that things would...not work out for us. That this would be the only chance we ever had to be *parents* to you. To share things with you like our favourite hot chocolates and cheesecakes. To us, they were not silly...in the slightest."

There was a long pause. I felt a strange pounding in my head that seemed like it might explode into tears.

"Well, somehow things *did* work out," Aunt Isabella said briskly, drumming her nails on the table. "And here you are. What a story!" she added, shaking her head.

"A story?" said a voice. "What story?" Aunt Franny had just shuffled into the kitchen, hair still ruffled from sleep. "Don't tell me Patrick and Lida have told their story without *me* here! Begin again!"

But then she looked at the clock. "Hold that thought. We need to be at the circus in less than an hour. Better start waking everybody up to get ready."

"Skip the circus," Aunt Carrie suggested.

Aunt Franny had found a carrot. She took a noisy bite. "Can't skip it," she said. "It's the party to celebrate Patrick and Lida. Final thing on the will. And the will is Faery cross-stitched, remember?"

At this, we all spun around and looked hard at Patrick and Lida.

"Why," I asked, "did you have to use Faery cross-stitch?"

"Yes," said several other voices, as more people shuffled into the kitchen. "Why the Faery cross-stitch? Didn't you trust Bronte to do as you asked?"

Patrick and Lida stared.

"Faery cross-stitch?" they murmured.

Walter cleared his throat. "Oh," he said. "That was me. You told me to be *sure* the will got to the lawyers? So I found some bright thread in my grandmother's old sewing box, and added the border myself."

"You what?" Lida cried.

"Faery cross-stitch!" Patrick exclaimed.

"But how frightening for Bronte!"

"Gainsleigh could have been torn to pieces!"

"Walter!" they both wailed in unison.

Walter clicked his tongue. "Oops," he said. "That's what cross-stitch does?"

106

Everybody went to the circus that night, even the water sprites. (They sat in barrels.)

I'm sure that the circus was good, but mostly we all just looked sideways at Patrick and Lida. Also Uncle Josh and Uncle Nigel competed to see which could make the children giggle. They were both very funny.

We did concentrate on Taylor's part of the show. Handstands, cartwheels, tumble turns in the air, and all while Midnight cantered around the ring. She was a real spitfire, as Aunt Claire declared. We gave her a standing ovation until the people in the seats behind shouted for us to sit down.

As everyone packed to go home the next day, there was a knock on the front door. My cousins and I were playing in the foyer at the time, so we opened it.

A very thin man stared down at us, his face pale. He reminded me of the prisoners from the Whispering dungeon, except that his hair was cut very short.

"Would Bronte Mettlestone be here?" he asked, and I stepped forward.

"My name is Ronaldo C. Torrington," he said. "You sent me a postcard about a painting of mine?"

"Oh, yes! The children in the playground!"

He nodded. "I was away, so only received it yesterday, and I travelled directly to Stantonville the moment I got it."

I was shocked. "You didn't need to do that," I murmured. "I only wondered if you knew anything about people acting out your paintings."

"Well, no," he said. "That was interesting, and a little flattering, I admit — but I'm afraid I can't explain it. The reason I came…"

He paused and scratched his head.

"Bronte, your postcard mentioned you were staying with Carrie Mettlestone," he said at last. "I once knew her, you see. And I lost touch. So I was excited to learn of her address. But the man at the Stantonville post office told me she'd gone to Nina Bay. So. Here I am."

He looked about him nervously and suddenly I saw the truth. He was in love with Aunt Carrie.

Oh dear, I thought. *She likes* big *men with* wild *hair. And you have* neither.

Still, maybe Aunt Carrie could be encouraged to consider a wider range of men?

There was a noise behind me then, and I turned to see Aunt Carrie standing on the staircase. Suddenly, she was leaping across the foyer, shouting, "Bear! Bear! It's you! It's you!" and knocking him back through the open front door.

He had become skinny too, it turned out. It's one of the things I learned on my journey: a broken heart can make you cut your hair and become slender.

He'd only stayed married to the other woman a few months, as he'd missed Carrie too much. Since then, he'd been painting pictures madly to express his sadness.

(Much later, my mother told me that she'd instructed the family lawyers to send the letter to the children, asking them to recreate the painting. After Walter informed my parents about Aunt Carrie's illness and loneliness, my mother had decided to set out clues for me that might lead me to the artist. "It was a long shot," she admitted. "But I knew we needed Carrie well again, and I hoped that you and I might have enough of a Whispering connection for the plan to work. And we do, Bronte," she added, and kissed my forehead. I remember I touched my forehead, thinking that this must be the spot where our Whispering connection dwelt. I felt pleased with that spot.)

So that is my story.

I am now, as I mentioned, writing this in a hammock while my dog, Will, sleeps in the grass at my feet. Will is the stray dog from Billy's dream. I brought him home and named him after Billy.

I'm in the garden of Aunt Isabelle's apartment: my parents have moved into the guest wing, and Alejandro lives in the blue room in the east wing.

Aunt Isabelle and the Butler travel often these days and are rarely home, so it's lucky my parents are here.

My mother, as heir to the throne of the Whispering Kingdom, should actually be running the place, but she suggested they try out democracy. They've already voted to hand over the shadow thread and destroy all their wristbands, and the darkness is fading out of most of them.

While writing this, I have taken breaks, of course. I haven't just been lying in the hammock this whole time.

I've even been away on short trips. I've visited Aunt Sue, Uncle Josh, and the boys. We caught up with the elves and ate oranges from the family's orchard: not quite as delicious now that I've tasted a Ricochet orange, but don't tell Aunt Sue I said that.

I've also been to see Aunt Emma on Lantern Island (where we had a party on the beach, along with Sugar Rixel, Barnabas, the librarian, and even Detective Riley, while the water sprites splashed in the waves), Aunt Sophy in her dragon hospital (where I practised my Dragon and my Dragon-flight), and Queen Alys and Prince William in the Mellifluous Kingdom (where Walter is now official trumpeter). While I was in the Mellifluous Kingdom, the Razdazzle Moonlight Circus came to town, so I also caught up with Taylor, and this time I watched the circus properly.

Billy, Taylor, and I had a midnight feast, ate Maywish Chocolate, and reminisced about our days on the *Riddle and Popcorn* cruise ship. Billy's favourite day to reminisce about was the one where I told them that my cousin Prince William was a real handful and that I planned to tame him. He laughed about that memory until he cried.

Meanwhile, here in Gainsleigh, I've been getting to know my parents. They are quieter than I had expected, based on the whirling in the photograph, but they can be very funny, and, on occasion, they dance on the table.

I've also begun going to school. Alejandro is in my class, and the two of us are known as the Pirate and the Whisperer. Other children seem a bit frightened of us, which we quite enjoy.

I've also been out for lemonade and cakes at the Arlington Tea Rooms, once with Aunts Maya and Lisbeth (when their ship docked at Gainsleigh for an afternoon), three times with Aunt Carrie and her husband, Bear (both of whom are growing happily sturdy), and most often with my governess, Dee, for old time's sake.

During my girl cousins' most recent school holiday, Aunt Nancy brought them to stay with us for a few days. A curious thing happened one night while we were taking tea in the drawing room and chatting about my adventures.

"What I can't figure out," Esther said, "is how the pirates knew that Billy was on board the cruise ship."

Aunt Isabelle sighed. "Who can tell?" she said. "*Nobody* knew he was hidden there except us sisters. And we certainly would not have told a soul."

At that moment, I happened to glance at Aunt Nancy. Her face had turned as white as paper. I suddenly knew that *she* had mentioned Billy's hiding place to somebody. Probably she had been gossiping with her subcommittees, laughing at the foolishness of her sister, Alys, for being a queen.

I also knew that she had done this thoughtlessly, not callously, never realizing that the story would be passed on and would somehow make its way to the pirates.

And I knew that Aunt Nancy herself knew that her mistake could have ended in the deaths of her sisters – the captains – her nephew, her niece, and of every other person on board.

I don't know if all this knowing was my being wise, or if it was the Whisperer in me.

Either way, I decided not to speak up. It was enough that Aunt

Nancy realized exactly what she had done, and who she was, for just that moment.

108

There are only a couple more things to tell you, and one is this.

Not long after we all came back to Gainsleigh, I was having breakfast with Aunt Isabelle, the Butler, and my parents one day.

My parents were telling more of their story, and it suddenly occurred to me that I'd been in danger my whole life. If the Whispering King wanted me, he didn't need to send an invitation. He could have sent pirates to kidnap me the same way he sent pirates to capture Billy.

My mother seemed to guess my thoughts — she often does that; I think it's a Whispering thing — because she suddenly leaned forward. "Whisperers sometimes know things," she said. "Secret things. And I knew you'd be safe with Isabelle and the Butler."

I blinked. As much as I loved Aunt Isabelle and the Butler, I could not imagine them grappling with pirates.

But all four adults were exchanging quick smiles.

"They got close once or twice," the Butler said. "Remember when they broke my nose?"

"And I broke my ankle," laughed Isabelle, "when it connected with a pirate's elbow."

"Oh, and that day when they managed to get in through the drawing room windows! Remember that stormy day? We dispatched them, though, like lightning."

They both made *ket-sham!* noises, imitating lightning.

I had no idea what they were on about.

And then the Butler reached for a sugar cube and flicked it high, so that it somersaulted through the air and landed with a faint splash in Aunt Isabelle's coffee cup. Suddenly, *ket-sham!* I saw the truth.

Anyway, that is why they are travelling so much these days. I can't say any more here, except that the incident with Billy had reminded them how much they'd liked their work. So, to the great joy of all the Kingdoms and Empires, and especially the Anti-Pirate League, they've come out of retirement.

109

You might have been wondering what I said to my parents when I first met them.

I did not say a word.

For some time, actually, I hardly spoke except to be polite. I had no idea *what* you are supposed to say when you haven't seen your parents since you were a baby and you think they've been killed by pirates, and then they turn up, dusty but alive.

Neither Aunt Isabelle nor my governess had taught me.

So I only stared. They looked at me with eyes that seemed filled with sadness and love, but they were careful to give me space.

Once, not long after we'd returned to Gainsleigh, my father said, "When you are ready, Bronte, we would like to hug you and never stop."

I nodded politely and turned away. Partly, I wanted to tell him that this would be pretty inconvenient. Partly, I wanted to thank them both for trying to protect me and ending up in prison, or to apologize for having felt crankily towards them. But none of those things seemed quite right.

And then a thought occurred to me.

"Excuse me," I said, and I ran to my room and found it.

Remember the book that Sugar Rixel gave me on Lantern Island? *If you are ever at a loss for words,* she had told me, *you give it a good shake and the words you need will fall out.*

I carried it back to the drawing room.

My parents, Aunt Isabelle, and the Butler looked at me with interest.

I shook the book hard. Words fell out.

They lay in the palm of my hand. Only three words. Not much of a book, I thought.

But not all books can have 109 chapters.

I read the three words to myself and I realized that they were actually not true. So, instead of speaking them, I spoke the truth: "Mother? Father? I've been perfectly all right without you, all this time, because I've had Aunt Isabelle and the Butler."

My parents' smiles were beautiful.

This was a shock. I had expected them to look disappointed.

However, something about their smiles made me realize that, in some ways, the three words *were* true. "But," I said, and I spoke the words: "I missed you."

My parents took this as permission to gather me into their arms and weep. Both the Butler and Aunt Isabelle reached over and ruffled my hair at the same time.

All of this, I allowed.

The End

Acknowledgements

Everything about the publication of this book has been preposterously pleasurable and fantastically fun and that is because my publishers are magnificent, publishing rock stars. I am honoured to be published by Guppy Books, and working with Bella Pearson has been a delight: thank you so much to Bella and her team. Thank you also to Arthur Levine and his team at Scholastic in the US, and to Anna McFarlane, Radhiah Chowdhury and their people at Allen and Unwin Australia.

The illustrations by Karl James Mountford in this book are an absolute joy and delight to me. Every one made me smile, and I thank him for the gift of his art. (And thank you to Kelly Canby, for her equally delightful yet completely different illustrations for the Australian edition.)

Thank you to my US agent, Jill Grinberg, whose reaction to the opening chapter of this book was the reason I carried on writing it, and who made some excellent suggestions on the first draft. Both Jill and my Australian agent, Tara Wynne, are smart, funny, determined, and beautiful friends to me.

Thank you also to: my parents, Diane and Bernie, easily the best parents imaginable; my aunts, Maureen, Rae, Julie, Pauline, Elizabeth, and Julie (again) for being complete yet mysterious people; my sisters, Liane, Kati, Fiona, and Nicola, for reading, proofreading, tea, cake, chocolate, conversation, and for being very fine aunts themselves; Steve Menasse, for online genius, art consultation, and for being one of the first & best readers of this book (and a fine uncle); my niece, Maddie, the first child reader of this book, for her lovely enthusiasm and for asking if she could change her name to Bronte and go on an "unsupervised adventure" please; Rachel Cohn, for reading and being delightful; Michael McCabe for sailing and pirate advice & general wisdom; to Laura, Corrie, Jo, Elizabeth, Suzy, Hannah, and Jane, for friendship and inspiration.

A very special mention to Deborah, Maria, and Rebecca, my dear friends at Coco Chocolate Kirribilli, where much of this book was written. I'm pretty sure that if you melted down the pages you'd end up with a mug of hot chocolate.

And finally, an extremely special mention to my boys, the (sort of) grown-up one, Nigel, and the (technically) young one, Charlie, for listening, reading, suggestions, inspiration, bike rides, ski trips, being hilarious, and making life a proper adventure.

Jaclyn Moriarty is the prize-winning author of novels for readers of all ages. They include the Ashbury High books: *Feeling Sorry for Celia, Finding Cassie Crazy, Becoming Bindy Mackenzie* and *Dreaming of Amelia*.

Jaclyn grew up in Sydney, Australia with four sisters (including authors Liane and Nicola Moriarty), one brother, two dogs and twelve chickens.

She has lived in the US, UK and Canada, but now lives in Sydney again, along with her son, Charlie. She is very fond of chocolate, blueberries and sleep.

GUPPY BOOKS

Guppy Books is an independent children's publisher based in Oxford in the UK, publishing exceptional fiction for children of all ages. Small and responsive, inclusive and communicative, Guppy Books was set up in 2019 and publishes only the very best authors and illustrators from around the world.

From brilliantly funny illustrated tales for five-year-olds to inspiring and thought-provoking novels for young adults, Guppy Books promises to publish something for everyone. If you'd like to know more about our authors and books, go to the Guppy Aquarium on YouTube where you'll find interviews, drawalongs and all sorts of fun.

We hope that our books bring pleasure to young people of all ages, and also to the adults sharing these books with them. Children's literature plays a part in giving both young and old the resources and reflection needed to grow up in today's ever-changing world, and we hope that you enjoy this small piece of magic!

Bella Pearson
Publisher

www.guppybooks.co.uk